Undone

SHANNON RICHARD

A Country Roads Novel

FOREVER

NEW YORK   BOSTON

Copyright © 2013 by Shannon Richard
Excerpt from *Undeniable* copyright © 2013 by Shannon Richard
All rights reserved. In accordance with the U.S. Copyright Act of 1976, the scanning, uploading, and electronic sharing of any part of this book without the permission of the publisher is unlawful piracy and theft of the author's intellectual property. If you would like to use material from the book (other than for review purposes), prior written permission must be obtained by contacting the publisher at permissions@hbgusa.com. Thank you for your support of the author's rights.

Forever
Hachette Book Group
237 Park Avenue, New York, NY 10017
www.hachettebookgroup.com
www.twitter.com/foreverromance

Printed in the United States of America
OPM

Originally published as an ebook
First mass market edition: February 2014

10 9 8 7 6 5 4 3 2 1

Forever is an imprint of Grand Central Publishing.
The Forever name and logo are trademarks of Hachette Book Group, Inc.

The publisher is not responsible for websites (or their content) that are not owned by the publisher.

The Hachette Speakers Bureau provides a wide range of authors for speaking events. To find out more, go to www.hachettespeakersbureau.com or call (866) 376-6591.

ATTENTION CORPORATIONS AND ORGANIZATIONS:

Most Hachette Book Group books are available at quantity discounts with bulk purchase for educational, business, or sales promotional use. For information, please call or write:

Special Markets Department, Hachette Book Group
237 Park Avenue, New York, NY 10017
Telephone: 1-800-222-6747 Fax: 1-800-477-5925

To my parents,
for believing in me
and supporting my dreams.
I couldn't have done this
without you.

Acknowledgments

There are a number of people who helped me write this book. Words cannot even begin to express how grateful I am for all of you.

To Sarah E. Younger, my amazing agent and friend. Thank you for taking a chance on me and appreciating all of my many, many quirks. Our music mind-melds prove that we were meant to work together, and I'm so blessed to get to work with you and everyone at the Nancy Yost Literary Agency.

To Selina McLemore, my ingenious editor who uncovered a path that I didn't even know existed. Thank you for helping me turn *Undone* into something so much more than I ever imagined it could be.

To Gloria Berry, for putting up with me and my crazy on a daily basis. Thank you for reading every day, listening to my ramblings, and helping me figure things out.

To Sarah Purcell, thank you for reading along the way and listening to more rants than I can count.

To Amy Smith and Chris Pennell, for being the most supportive bosses a girl could ask for. I owe you both many, many thanks.

To Kaitie Hotard, Katie Crandall, Catie Humphreys, Jenna Robinson, Jennifer Pezzuto, Jennifer Ewing, Diana Oliveira, Kelly Filippini, Marina Coleman, Amanda Blanchard, Michelle Blanchard, and Ronald Richard, thank you all for reading the manuscript and giving me invaluable feedback.

And to my mom and dad, thank you for all of your love and support. I owe you everything.

Chapter One

Short Fuses and a Whole Lot of Sparks

Bethelda Grimshaw was a snot-nosed wench. She was an evil, mean-spirited, vindictive, horrible human being.

Paige should've known. She should've known the instant she'd walked into that office and sat down. Bethelda Grimshaw had a malevolent stench radiating off her, kind of like roadkill in ninety-degree weather. The interview, if it could even be called that, had been a complete waste of time.

"She didn't even read my résumé," Paige said, slamming her hand against the steering wheel as she pulled out of the parking lot of the Mirabelle Information Center.

No, Bethelda had barely even looked at said résumé before she'd set it down on the desk and leaned back in her chair, appraising Paige over her cat's-eye glasses.

"So you're the *infamous* Paige Morrison," Bethelda had said, raising a perfectly plucked, bright red eyebrow. "You've caused *quite* a stir since you came to town."

Quite a stir?

2 *Shannon Richard*

Okay, so there had been that incident down at the Piggly Wiggly, but that hadn't been Paige's fault. Betty Whitehurst might seem like a sweet, little old lady but in reality she was as blind as a bat and as vicious as a shrew. Betty drove her shopping cart like she was racing in the Indy 500, which was an accomplishment, as she barely cleared the handle. She'd slammed her cart into Paige, who in turn fell into a display of cans. Paige had been calm for all of about five seconds before Betty had started screeching at her about watching where she was going.

Paige wasn't one to take things lying down covered in cans of creamed corn, so she'd calmly explained to Betty that she *had* been watching where she was going. "Calmly" being that Paige had started yelling and the store manager had to get involved to quiet everyone down.

Yeah, Paige didn't deal very well with certain types of people. Certain types being evil, mean-spirited, vindictive, horrible human beings. And Bethelda Grimshaw was quickly climbing to the top of that list.

"As it turns out," Bethelda had said, pursing her lips in a patronizing pout, "we already filled the position. I'm afraid there was a mistake in having you come down here today."

"When?"

"Excuse me?" Bethelda had asked, her eyes sparkling with glee.

"When did you fill the position?" Paige had repeated, trying to stay calm.

"Last week."

Really? So the phone call Paige had gotten that morning to confirm the time of the interview had been a mistake?

This was the eleventh job interview she'd gone on in the last two months. And it had most definitely been the worst. It hadn't even been an interview. She'd been set up; she just didn't understand why. But she hadn't been about to ask that question out loud. So instead of flying off the handle and losing the last bit of restraint she had, Paige had calmly gotten up from the chair and left without making a scene. The whole thing was a freaking joke, which fit perfectly for the current theme of Paige's life.

Six months ago, Paige had been living in Philadelphia. She'd had a good job in the art department of an advertising agency. She'd shared a tiny two-bedroom apartment above a coffee shop with her best friend, Abby Fields. And she'd had Dylan, a man who she'd been very much in love with.

And then the rug got pulled out from under her and she'd fallen flat on her ass.

First off, Abby got a job at an up-and-coming PR firm. Which was good news, and Paige had been very excited for her, except the job was in Washington, DC, which Paige was not excited about. Then, before Paige could find a new roommate, she'd lost her job. The advertising agency was bought out and she was in the first round of cuts. Without a job, she couldn't renew her lease, and was therefore homeless. So she'd moved in with Dylan. It was always supposed to be a temporary thing, just until Paige could find another job and get on her feet again.

But it never happened.

Paige had tried for two months and found nothing, and

then the real bomb hit. She was either blind or just distracted by everything else that was going on, but either way, she never saw it coming.

Paige had been with Dylan for about a year and she'd really thought he'd been the one. Okay, he tended to be a bit of a snob when it came to certain things. For example, wine. Oh was he ever a wine snob, rather obnoxious about it, really. He would always swirl it around in his glass, take a sip, sniff, and then take another loud sip, smacking his lips together.

He was also a snob about books. Paige enjoyed reading the classics, but she also liked reading romance, mystery, and fantasy. Whenever she would curl up with one of her books, Dylan tended to give her a rather patronizing look and shake his head.

"Reading fluff again, I see," he would always say.

Yeah, she didn't miss *that* at all. Or the way he would roll his eyes when she and Abby would quote movies and TV shows to each other. Or how he'd never liked her music and flat-out refused to dance with her. Which had always been frustrating because Paige loved to dance. But despite all of that, she'd loved him. Loved the way he would run his fingers through his hair when he was distracted, loved his big goofy grin, and loved the way his glasses would slide down his nose.

But the thing was, he hadn't loved her.

One night, he'd come back to his apartment and sat Paige down on the couch. Looking back on it, she'd been an idiot, because there was a small part of her that thought he was actually about to propose.

"Paige," he'd said, sitting down on the coffee table and grabbing her hands. "I know that this was supposed to be a temporary thing, but weeks have turned into months. Living with you has brought a lot of things to light."

It was wrong, everything about that moment was *all wrong*. She could tell by the look in his eyes, by the tone of his voice, by the way he said *Paige* and *light*. In that moment she'd known exactly where he was going, and it wasn't anywhere with her. He wasn't proposing. He was breaking up with her.

She'd pulled her hands out of his and shrank back into the couch.

"This," he'd said, gesturing between the two of them, "was never going to go further than where we are right now."

And that was the part where her ears had started ringing.

"At one point I thought I might love you, but I've realized I'm not *in* love with you." He shook his head. "I feel like you've thought this was going to go further, but the truth is I'm never going to marry you. Paige, you're not the one. I'm tired of pretending. I'm tired of putting in the effort for a relationship that isn't going anywhere else. It's not worth it to me."

"You mean I'm not worth it," she'd said, shocked.

"Paige, you deserve to be with someone who wants to make the effort, and I deserve to be with someone who I'm willing to make the effort for. It's better that we end this now, instead of delaying the inevitable."

He'd made it sound like he was doing her a favor, like he had her best interests at heart.

But all she'd heard was *You're not worth it* and *I'm not in love with you*. And those were the words that kept repeating in her head, over and over and over again.

Dylan had told her he was going to go stay with one of his friends for the week. She'd told him she'd be out before the end of the next day. She'd spent the entire night packing up her stuff. Well, packing and crying and drinking two entire bottles of the prick's wine.

Paige didn't have a lot of stuff. Most of the furniture from her and Abby's apartment had been Abby's. Everything that Paige owned had fit into the back of her Jeep and the U-Haul trailer that she'd rented the first thing the following morning. She'd loaded up and gotten out of there before four o'clock in the afternoon.

She'd stayed the night in a hotel room just outside of Philadelphia, where she'd promptly passed out. She'd been exhausted after her marathon packing, which was good because it was harder for a person to feel beyond pathetic in her sleep. No, that was what the following eighteen-hour drive had been reserved for.

Jobless, homeless, and brokenhearted, Paige had nowhere else to go but home to her parents. The problem was, there was no *home* anymore. The house in Philadelphia that Paige had grown up in was no longer her parents'. They'd sold it and retired to a little town in the South.

Mirabelle, Florida: population five thousand.

There was roughly the same amount of people in the six hundred square miles of Mirabelle as there were in half a square mile of Philadelphia. Well, unless the mosquitoes were counted as residents.

People who thought that Florida was all sunshine and sand were sorely mistaken. It did have its fair share of beautiful beaches. The entire southeast side of Mirabelle was the Gulf of Mexico. But about half of the town was made up of water. And all of that water, combined with the humidity that plagued the area, created the perfect breeding ground for mosquitoes. Otherwise known as tiny, blood-sucking villains that loved to bite the crap out of Paige's legs.

Paige had visited her parents a handful of times over the last couple of years, but she'd never been in love with Mirabelle like her parents were. And she still wasn't. She'd spent a month moping around her parents' house. Again, she was pathetic enough to believe that maybe, just maybe, Dylan would call her and tell her that he'd been wrong. That he missed her. That he loved her.

He never called, and Paige realized he was never going to. That was when Paige resigned herself to the fact that she had to move on with her life. So she'd started looking for a job.

Which had proved to be highly unsuccessful.

Paige had been living in Mirabelle for three months now. Three long, miserable months where nothing had gone right. Not one single thing.

And as that delightful thought crossed her mind, she noticed that her engine was smoking. Great white plumes of steam escaped from the hood of her Jeep Cherokee.

"You've got to be kidding me," she said as she pulled off to the side of the road and turned the engine off. "Fan-freaking-tastic."

Paige grabbed her purse and started digging around in the infinite abyss, searching for her cell phone. She sifted through old receipts, a paperback book, her wallet, lip gloss, a nail file, gum...*ah*, cell phone. She pressed speed dial for her father. She held the phone against her ear while she leaned over and searched for her shoes that she'd thrown on the floor of the passenger side. As her hand closed over one of her black wedges, the phone beeped in her ear and disconnected. She sat up and held her phone out, staring at the display screen in disbelief.

No service.

"This has to be some sick, twisted joke," she said, banging her head down on the steering wheel. No service on her cell phone shouldn't have been that surprising; there were plenty of dead zones around Mirabelle. Apparently there was a lack of cell phone towers in this little piece of purgatory.

Paige resigned herself to the fact that she was going to have to walk to find civilization, or at least a bar of service on her cell phone. She went in search of her other wedge, locating it under the passenger seat.

The air conditioner had been off for less than two minutes, and it was already starting to warm up inside the Jeep. It was going to be a long, hot walk. Paige grabbed a hair tie from the gearshift, put her long brown hair up into a messy bun, and opened the door to the sweltering heat.

I hate *this godforsaken place.*

Paige missed Philadelphia. She missed her friends, her apartment with its rafters and squeaky floors. She missed having a job, missed having a paycheck, missed buying shoes. And even though she hated it, she still missed Dylan. Missed his dark shaggy hair, and the way he would nibble on her lower lip when they kissed. She even missed his humming when he cooked.

She shook her head and snapped back to the present. She might as well focus on the task at hand and stop thinking about what was no longer her life.

Paige walked for twenty minutes down the road to

nowhere, not a single car passing her. By the time she got to Skeeter's Bait, Tackle, Guns, and Gas, she was sweating like nobody's business, her dress was sticking to her everywhere, and her feet were killing her. She had a nice blister on the back of her left heel.

She pushed the door open and was greeted with the smell of fish mixed with bleach, making her stomach turn. At least the air conditioner was cranked to full blast. There was a huge stuffed turkey sitting on the counter. The fleshy red thing on its neck looked like the stuff nightmares were made of, and the wall behind the register was covered in mounted fish. She really didn't get the whole "dead animal as a trophy" motif that the South had going on.

There was a display on the counter that had tiny little bottles that looked like energy drinks.

New and improved scent. Great for attracting the perfect game.

She picked up one of the tiny bottles and looked at it. It was doe urine.

She took a closer look at the display. They apparently also had the buck urine variety. She looked at the bottle in her hand, trying to grasp why people would cover themselves in this stuff. Was hunting really worth smelling like an animal's pee?

"Can I help you?"

The voice startled Paige and she looked up into the face of a very large balding man, his apron covered in God only knew what. She dropped the tiny bottle she had in her hand. It fell to the ground. The cap smashed on the tile floor and liquid poured out everywhere.

It took a total of three seconds for the smell to punch

her in the nose. It had to be the most foul scent she'd ever inhaled.

Oh crap. Oh crap, oh crap, oh crap.

She was just stellar at first impressions these days.

"I'm so sorry," she said, trying not to gag. She took a step back from the offending puddle and looked up at the man.

His arms were folded across his chest and he frowned at her, saying nothing.

"Do you, uh, have something I can clean this up with?" she asked nervously.

"You're not from around here," he said, looking at her with his deadpan stare. It wasn't a question. It was a statement, one that she got whenever she met someone new. One that she was so sick and tired of she could scream. Yeah, all of the remorse she'd felt over spilling that bottle drained from her.

In Philadelphia, Paige's bohemian style was normal, but in Mirabelle her big earrings, multiple rings, and loud clothing tended to get her noticed. Her parents' neighbor, Mrs. Forns, thought that Paige was trouble, which she complained about on an almost daily basis.

"You know that marijuana is still illegal," Mrs. Forns had said the other night, standing on her parents' porch, and lecturing Paige's mother. "And I won't hesitate to call the authorities if I see your hippie daughter growing anything suspicious or doing any other illegal activities."

Denise Morrison, ever the queen of politeness, had just smiled. "You have nothing to be concerned about."

"But she's doing *something* in that shed of yours in the backyard."

The *something* that Paige did in the shed was paint.

She'd converted it into her art studio, complete with ceiling fan.

"Don't worry, Mrs. Forns," Paige had said, sticking her head over her mother's shoulder. "I'll wait to have my orgies on your bingo nights. Is that on Tuesdays or Wednesdays?"

"Paige!" Denise shoved Paige back into the house and closed the door in her face.

Five minutes later, Denise had come into the kitchen shaking her head.

"Really, Paige? You had to tell her that you're having *orgies* in the backyard?"

Paige's father, Trevor Morrison, chuckled as he went through the mail at his desk.

"You need to control your temper and that smart mouth of yours," Denise had said.

"You know what you should start doing?" Trevor looked up with a big grin. "You should grow oregano in pots on the windowsill and then throw little dime bags into her yard."

"Trevor, don't encourage her harassing that woman. Paige, she's a little bit older, very set in her ways, and a tad bit nosey."

"She needs to learn to keep her nose on her side of the fence," Paige had said.

"Don't let her bother you."

"That's easier said than done."

"Well then, maybe you should practice holding your tongue."

"Yes, mother, I'll get right on that."

So, as Paige stared at the massive man in front of her, whom she assumed to be Skeeter, she pursed her lips and held back the smart-ass retort that was on the tip of her tongue.

Be polite. She heard her mother's voice in her head. *You just spilled animal pee all over his store. And you need to use his phone.*

"No." Paige pushed her big sunglasses up her nose and into her hair. "My car broke down and I don't have any cell phone service. I was wondering if I could use your phone to call a tow truck."

"I'd call King's if I were you. They're the best," he said as he ripped a piece of receipt paper off the cash register and grabbed a pen with a broken plastic spoon taped to the top. He wrote something down and pushed the paper across the counter.

"Thank you. I can clean that up first." She pointed to the floor.

"I got it. I'd hate for you to get those hands of yours dirty," he said, moving the phone to her side of the counter.

She just couldn't win.

* * *

Brendan King leaned against the front bumper of Mr. Thame's minivan. He was switching out the old belt and replacing it with a new one when his grandfather stuck his head out of the office.

"Brendan," Oliver King said. "A car broke down on Buckland Road. It's Paige Morrison, Trevor and Denise Morrison's daughter. She said the engine was smoking. She had to walk to Skeeter's to use the phone. I told her you'd pick her up so she didn't have to walk back."

Oliver King didn't look his seventy years. His salt-and-pepper hair was still thick and growing only on the top of his head, and not out of his ears. He had a bit of a belly, but he'd had that for the last twenty years and it wasn't going anywhere. He'd opened King's Auto forty-three years ago, when he was twenty-seven. Now, he mainly worked behind the front counter, due to the arthritis in his hands and back. But it was a good thing because King's Auto was one of only a handful of auto shops in the county. They were always busy, so they needed a constant presence running things out of the shop.

Including Brendan and his grandfather, there were four full-time mechanics and two part-time kids who were still in high school and who worked in the garage. Part of the service that King's provided was towing, and Brendan was the man on duty on Mondays. And oh was he ever so happy he was on duty today.

Paige Morrison was the new girl in town. Her parents had moved down from Pennsylvania when they'd retired about two years ago, and Paige had moved in with them three months ago. Brendan had yet to meet her but he'd most definitely seen her. You couldn't really miss her as she jogged around town, with her very long legs, in a wide variety of the brightest and shortest shorts he'd ever seen in his life. His favorite pair had by far been the hot-pink pair, but the zebra-print ones came in a very close second.

He'd also heard about her. People had a lot to say about her more-than-*interesting* style. It was rumored that she had a bit of a temper and a pretty mouth that said whatever it wanted. Not that Brendan took a lot of stock in gossip. He'd wait to reserve his own judgment.

"Got it," Brendan said, pulling his gloves off and sticking them in his back pocket. "Tell Randall this still needs new spark plugs." He pointed to the minivan before walking into the office.

"I will." Oliver nodded and handed Brendan the keys to the tow truck.

Brendan grabbed two waters from the mini-fridge and his sunglasses from the desk and headed off into the scorching heat. It was a hot one, ninety-eight degrees, but the humidity made it feel like one hundred and three. He flipped his baseball cap so that the bill would actually give him some cover from the August sun and when he got into the tow truck he cranked the air as high as it would go.

It took him about fifteen minutes to get to Skeeter's and when he pulled up into the gravel parking lot, the door to the little shop opened and Brendan couldn't help but smile.

Paige Morrison's mile-long legs were shooting out of the sexiest shoes he'd ever seen. She was also wearing a flowing yellow dress that didn't really cover her amazing legs but did hug her chest and waist, and besides the two skinny straps at her shoulders, her arms were completely bare. Massive sunglasses covered her eyes and her dark brown hair was piled on top of her head.

There was no doubt about it; she was beautiful all right.

Brendan put the truck in park and hopped out.

"Ms. Morrison?" he asked even though he already knew who she was.

"Paige," she corrected, stopping in front of him. She

was probably five foot ten or so, but her shoes added about three inches, making her just as tall as him. If he weren't wearing his work boots she would've been taller than him.

"I'm Brendan King." He stuck his hand out to shake hers. Her hand was soft and warm. He liked how it felt in his. He also liked the freckles that were sprinkled across her high cheekbones and straight, pert nose.

"I'm about a mile up the road," she said, letting go of his hand and pointing in the opposite direction that he'd come.

"Not the most sensible walking shoes." He eyed her feet. The toes that peeked out of her shoes were bright red, and a thin band of silver wrapped around the second toe on her right foot. He looked back up to see her arched eyebrows come together for a second before she took a deep breath.

"Thanks for the observation," she said, walking past him and heading for the passenger door.

Well, this was going to be fun.

* * *

Stupid jerk.

Not the most sensible walking shoes, Paige repeated in her head.

Well, no shit, Sherlock.

Paige sat in the cab of Brendan's tow truck, trying to keep her temper in check. Her feet were killing her, and she really wanted to kick off her shoes. But she couldn't do that in front of him because then he would *know* that her feet were killing her.

"I'm guessing the orange Jeep is yours?" Brendan asked as it came into view.

"Another outstanding observation," she mumbled under her breath.

"I'm sorry?"

"Yes, it's mine," she said, trying to hide her sarcasm.

"Well, at least the engine isn't smoking anymore." He pulled in behind it and jumped out of the truck. Paige grabbed her keys from her purse and followed, closing the door behind her.

He stopped behind the back of her Jeep for a moment, studying the half a dozen stickers that covered her bumper and part of her back window.

She had one that said MAKE ART NOT WAR in big blue letters, another said LOVE with a peace sign in the *O*. There was also a sea turtle, an owl with reading glasses, the Cat in the Hat, and her favorite, which said I LOVE BIG BOOKS AND I CANNOT LIE.

He shook his head and laughed, walking to the front of the Jeep.

"What's so funny?" she asked, catching up to his long stride and standing next to him.

"Keys?" he asked, holding out his hand.

She put them in his palm but didn't let go.

"What's so funny?" she repeated.

"Just that you're clearly not from around here." He smiled, closing his hand over hers.

Brendan had a southern accent, not nearly as thick as some of the other people's in town, and a wide cocky smile that she really hated, but only because she kind of liked it. She also kind of liked the five o'clock shadow that covered his square jaw. She couldn't see anything above his chiseled nose, as half of his face was covered by his sunglasses and the shadow from his grease-stained baseball cap, but she could tell his smile reached all the way up to his eyes.

He was most definitely physically fit, filling out his shirt and pants with wide biceps and thighs. His navy blue button-up shirt had short sleeves, showing off his tanned arms that were covered in tiny blond hairs.

God, he was attractive. But he was also pissing her off.

"I am so sick of everyone saying that," she said, ripping her hand out of his. "Is it such a bad thing to not be from around here?"

"No." His mouth quirked. "It's just very obvious that you're not."

"Would I fit in more if I had a bumper sticker that said MY OTHER CAR IS A TRACTOR or one that said IF YOU'RE NOT CONSERVATIVE YOU JUST AREN'T WORTH IT, or what about WHO NEEDS LITERACY WHEN YOU CAN SHOOT THINGS? What if I had a gun rack mounted on the back window or if I used buck piss as perfume to attract a husband? Would those things make me fit in?" she finished, folding her arms across her chest.

"No, I'd say you could start with not being so judgmental though," he said with a sarcastic smirk.

"Excuse me?"

"Ma'am, you just called everyone around here gun-toting, illiterate rednecks who like to participate in bestiality. Insulting people really isn't a way to fit in." He shook his head. "I would also refrain from spreading your liberal views to the masses, as politics are a bit of a hot-button topic around here. And if you want to attract a husband, you should stick with wearing doe urine, because that attracts only males. The buck urine attracts both males and females." He stopped and looked her up and down with a slow smile. "But maybe you're into that sort of thing."

"Yeah, well, everyone in this town thinks that I'm an amoral, promiscuous pothead. And you," she said, shoving her finger into his chest, "aren't any better. People make snap judgments about me before I even open my mouth. And just so you know, *I'm not even a liberal*," she screamed as she jabbed her finger into his chest a couple of times. She took a deep breath and stepped back, composing herself. "So maybe I would be *nice* if people would be just a little bit *nice* to me."

"I'm quite capable of being nice to people who deserve it. Can I look at your car now, or would you like to yell at me some more?"

"Be my guest," she said, glaring at him as she moved out of his way.

He unlocked the Jeep and popped the hood. As he moved to the front he pulled off his baseball cap and wiped the top of his head with his hand. Paige glimpsed his short, dirty-blond hair before he put the hat on backward. As moved around in her engine his shirt pulled tight across his back and shoulders. He twisted off the cap to something and stuck it in his pocket. Then he walked back to his truck and grabbed a jug from a metal box on the side. He came back and poured the liquid into something in the engine and after a few seconds it gushed out of the bottom.

"Your radiator is cracked," he said, grabbing the cap out of his pocket and screwing it back on. "I'm going to have to tow this back to the shop to replace it."

"How much?"

"For everything? We're looking at four maybe five hundred."

"Just perfect," she mumbled.

"Would you like a ride? Or were you planning on showing those shoes more of the countryside?"

"I'll take the ride."

* * *

Paige was quiet the whole time Brendan loaded her Jeep onto the truck. Her arms were folded under her perfect breasts and she stared at him with her full lips bunched in a scowl. Even pissed off she was stunning, and God, that mouth of hers. He really wanted to see it with an actual smile on it. He was pretty sure it would knock him on his ass.

Speaking of asses, seeing her smile probably wasn't likely at the moment. True, he had purposefully egged her on, but he couldn't resist going off on her when she'd let loose her colorful interpretations of the people from the area. A lot of them were true, but there was a difference between making fun of your own people and having an outsider make fun of them. But still, according to her, the people around here hadn't exactly been nice to her.

Twenty minutes later, with Paige's Jeep on the back of the tow truck, they were on their way to the shop. Brendan glanced over at her as he drove. She was looking out the window with her back to him. Her shoulders were stiff and she looked like she'd probably had enough stress before her car had decided to die on her.

Brendan looked back at the road and cleared his throat.

"I'm sorry about what I said back there."

Out of the corner of his eye he saw her shift in her seat and he could feel her eyes on him.

"Thank you. I should have kept my mouth shut, too. I just haven't had the best day."

"Why?" he asked, glancing over at her again.

Her body was angled toward him, but her arms were still folded across her chest like a shield. He couldn't help but glance down and see that her dress was slowly riding up her thighs. She had nice thighs, soft but strong. They would be good for... well, a lot of things.

He quickly looked back at the road, thankful he was wearing sunglasses.

"I've been trying to get a job. Today I had an interview, except it wasn't much of an interview."

"What was it?" he asked.

"A setup."

"A setup for what?"

"That *is* the question," she said bitterly.

"Huh?" he asked, looking at her again.

"I'm assuming you know who Bethelda Grimshaw is?"

Brendan's blood pressure had a tendency to rise at the mere mention of that name. Knowing that Bethelda had a part in Paige's current mood had Brendan's temper flaring instantly.

"What did she do?" he asked darkly.

Paige's eyebrows raised a fraction at his tone. She stared at him for a second before she answered. "There was a job opening at the Mirabelle Information Center to take pictures for the brochures and the local businesses for their Web site. They filled the position last week, something that Mrs. Grimshaw failed to mention when she called this morning to confirm my interview."

"She's looking for her next story."

"What?"

"Bethelda Grimshaw is Mirabelle's resident gossip," Brendan said harshly as he looked back to the road. "She got fired from the newspaper a couple of years ago because of the trash she wrote. Now she has a blog to spread her crap around."

"And she wants to write about me? Why?"

"I can think of a few reasons."

"What's that supposed to mean?" she asked, her voice going up an octave or two.

"Your ability to fly off the handle. Did you give her something to write about?" He raised an eyebrow as he spared a glance at her.

"No," she said, bunching her full lips together. "I saved my freak-out for you."

"I deserved it. I wasn't exactly nice to you," Brendan said, shifting his hands down the steering wheel.

"You were a jerk."

Brendan came to a stop at a stop sign and turned completely in his seat to face Paige. Her eyebrows rose high over her sunglasses and she held her breath.

"I was, and I'm sorry." He put every ounce of sincerity into his words.

"It's...I forgive you," she said softly and nodded her head.

Brendan turned back to the intersection and made a right. Paige was silent for a few moments, but he could feel her gaze on him as if she wanted to say something.

"What?"

"Why does buck urine attract males and females?"

Brendan couldn't help but smile.

"Bucks like to fight each other," he said, looking at her.

"Oh." She nodded and leaned back in her seat staring out the front window.

"You thirsty?" Brendan asked as he grabbed one of the waters in the cup holder and held it out to her.

"Yes, thank you," she said, grabbing it and downing half of the bottle.

"Who were the other interviews with?" Brendan grabbed the other bottle for himself. He twisted the cap off and threw it into the cup holder.

"Landingham Printing and Design. Mrs. Landingham said I wouldn't be a good fit. Which is completely false because the program they use is one that I've used before."

Now he couldn't help but laugh.

"Uh, Paige, I can tell you right now why you didn't get that job. Mrs. Landingham didn't want you around Mr. Landingham."

"What?" she said, sitting up in her seat again. "What did she think I was going to do, steal her husband? I don't make plays on married men. Or men in their forties for that matter."

"Did you wear something like what you're wearing now to the interview?" He looked at her and took another eyeful of those long legs.

"I wore a black blazer with this. It's just so hot outside that I took it off."

"Maybe you should try wearing pants next time, and flats," he said before he took a sip of water.

"What's wrong with this dress?" she asked, looking down at herself. "It isn't that short."

"Sweetheart, with those legs, anything looks short."

"Don't call me sweetheart. And it isn't my fault I'm tall."

"No, it isn't, but people think the way they think."

"So southern hospitality only goes so far when people think you're a whore."

"Hey, I didn't say that. I was just saying that your legs are long without those shoes that you're currently wearing. With them, you're pretty damn intimidating."

"Let's stop talking about my legs."

"Fine." He shrugged, looking back to the road. "But it is a rather visually stimulating conversation."

"Oh no. You are *not* allowed to flirt with me."

"Why not?"

"You were mean to me. I do *not* flirt with mean men."

"I can be nice," he said, turning to her and giving her a big smile.

"Stop it," she said, raising her eyebrows above her glasses in warning. "I mean it."

"So what about some of the other interviews? Who were they with?"

"Lindy's Frame Shop, that art gallery over on the beach—"

"Avenue Ocean?"

"Yeah, that one. And I also went to Picture Perfect. They all said I wasn't a good fit for one reason or another," she said dejected.

"Look, I'm really not one to get involved in town gossip. I've been on the receiving end my fair share of times and it isn't fun. But this is a small town, and everybody knows one another's business. Since you're new, you have no idea. Cynthia Bowers at Picture Perfect would've never hired you. Her husband has monogamy issues. The owner of Avenue Ocean, Mindy Trist, doesn't like anyone that's competition."

"Competition?"

Mindy Trist was a man-eater. Brendan knew this to be a fact because Mindy had been trying to get into his bed for years. He wasn't even remotely interested.

"You're prettier than she is."

Understatement of the year.

Paige was suddenly silent on her side of the truck.

"And as for Hurst and Marlene Lindy," Brendan continued, "they, uh, tend to be a little more conservative."

"Look," she said, snapping out of her silence.

Brendan couldn't help himself; her sudden burst of vehemence made him look at her again. If he kept this up he was going to drive into a ditch.

"I know I might appear to be some free-spirited hippie, but I'm really not. I'm moderate when it comes to politics," she said, holding up one finger. "I eat meat like it's nobody's business." Two fingers. "And I've never done drugs in my life." Three fingers.

"You don't have to convince me," he said, shaking his head. "So I'm sensing a pattern here with all of these jobs. Are you a photographer?"

"Yes, but I do graphic design and I paint."

"So a woman of many talents."

"I don't know about that."

"Oh, I'm sure you have a lot of talent. It's probably proportional to the length of your legs."

"What did I tell you about flirting?" she asked seriously, but betrayed herself when the corner of her mouth quirked up.

"Look, Paige, don't let it get to you. Not everyone is all bad."

"So I've just been fortunate enough to meet everyone who's mean."

"You've met me."

"Yeah, well, the jury's still out on you."

"Then I guess I'll have to prove myself."

"I guess so," she said, leaning back in her seat. Her arms now rested in her lap, her shield coming down a little.

"I have a question," Brendan said, slowing down at another stop sign. "If you eat meat, why do you have such a problem with hunting?"

"It just seems a little barbaric. Hiding out in the woods to shoot Bambi and then mounting his head on a wall."

"Let me give you two scenarios."

"Okay."

"In scenario one, we have Bessie the cow. Bessie was born in a stall, taken away from her mother shortly after birth where she was moved to a pasture for a couple of years, all the while being injected with hormones and then shoved into a semitruck, where she was shipped off to be slaughtered. And I don't think that you even want me to get started on that process.

"In scenario two, we have Bambi. Bambi was born in the wilderness and wasn't taken away from his mother. He then found a mate, had babies, and one day was killed. He never saw it coming. Not only is Bambi's meat hormone free, but he also lived a happy life in the wild, with no fences.

"Now you tell me, which scenario sounds better: Being raised to be slaughtered, or living free where you might or might not be killed."

She was silent for a few moments before she sighed.

"Fine, you win. The second sounds better."

"Yeah, that's what I thought," Brendan said as he pulled into the parking lot of King's Auto. "How are you getting home?" He put the truck into park.

"I called my dad after I called you. He's here actually," she said, pointing to a black Chevy Impala.

They both got out of the truck and headed toward the auto shop. Brendan held the door open for Paige, shoving his sunglasses into his shirt pocket. His grandfather and a man who Brendan recognized as Paige's father stood up from their chairs as Brendan and Paige walked in.

Trevor Morrison was a tall man, maybe six foot four or six foot five. He had light reddish-brown wispy hair on his head and large glasses perched on his nose. And like his daughter, his face and arms were covered in freckles.

"Hi, Daddy," Paige said, pushing her glasses up her nose and into her hair.

Brendan immediately noticed the change in her voice. Her cautious demeanor vanished and her shoulders relaxed. He'd caught a glimpse of this in the truck, but not to this extent.

"Mr. Morrison." Brendan took a step forward and stuck his hand out.

Trevor grabbed Brendan's hand firmly. "Brendan," he said, giving him a warm smile and nodding his head. Trevor let go of Brendan's hand and turned to his daughter. "Paige, this is Oliver King." He gestured to Brendan's grandfather, who was standing behind his desk. "Oliver, this is my daughter, Paige."

"I haven't had the pleasure," Oliver said, moving out from behind his desk and sticking out his hand.

Paige moved forward past Brendan, her arm brushing his as she passed.

"It's nice to meet you, sir," she said, grabbing Oliver's hand.

Oliver nodded as he let go of Paige's hand and looked up at Brendan. "So what happened?"

Paige turned to look at Brendan too. It was the first time he'd gotten a full look at her face without her sunglasses on. She had long dark eyelashes that framed her large gray irises. It took him a second to remember how to speak. He cleared his throat and looked past her to the other two men.

"It's the radiator. I'm going to have to order a new one, so it's going to take a few days."

"That's fine," she said, shrugging her shoulders. "It's not like I have anywhere to go."

Trevor's face fell. "The interview didn't go well?"

"Nope." Paige shook her head. The tension in her shoulders came back but she tried to mask it by pasting a smile on her face. He desperately wanted to see a genuine, full-on smile from her.

"Things haven't exactly gone Paige's way since she moved here," Trevor said.

"Oh, I think my bad luck started long before I moved here." She folded her arms across her chest. Every time she did that, it pushed her breasts up and it took everything in Brendan not to stare.

"I don't think it was Paige's fault," Brendan said and everyone turned to look at him. "It was with Bethelda Grimshaw," he said to Oliver.

"Oh." Oliver shook his head ruefully. "Don't let anything she says get to you. She's a horrible hag."

Paige laughed and the sound of it did funny things to Brendan's stomach.

"Told you," Brendan said, looking at her. Paige turned to him, a small smile lingering on her lips and in her eyes.

God, she was beautiful.

"Things will turn around," Oliver said. "We'll call you with an estimate before we do anything to your car."

They said their good-byes and as Paige walked out with her father she gave Brendan one last look, her lips quirking up slightly before she shook her head and walked out the door.

"I don't believe any of that nonsense people are saying about her," Oliver said as they both watched Paige and her dad walk out. "She's lovely."

Lovely? Yeah, that wasn't exactly the word Brendan would have used to describe her.

Hot? Yes. *Fiery?* Absolutely.

"Yeah, she's something all right."

"Oh, don't tell me you aren't a fan of hers. Son, you barely took your eyes off her."

"I'm not denying she's beautiful." How could he? "I bet she's a handful though and she's got a temper on her, along with a smart mouth." But he sure did like that smart mouth.

"That's a bit of the pot calling the kettle black," Oliver said, raising one bushy eyebrow. "If all of her experiences in this town have been similar to what Bethelda dishes out, I'm not surprised she's turned on the defense. You know what it's like to be the center of less than unsavory gossip in this town. To have a lot of the people turn their backs on you and turn you into a pariah," Oliver said, giving Brendan a knowing look.

"I know," Brendan conceded. "She deserves a break."

"You should help her find a job."

"With who?"

"You'll think of something," Oliver said, patting Brendan on the shoulder before going back to his desk. "You always do."

Chapter Two

Find the Beat Again

I want to hear more about your hot mechanic."

"Abby, I already told you, he's not *my* hot mechanic. He's just *a* hot mechanic," Paige said as she fidgeted with the pillow in her lap.

Paige had called Abby pretty much the second she'd gotten back to her parents' house. She needed to get some perspective, and who better to help her get it than her best friend? They'd met on the first day of kindergarten almost twenty years ago, bonding over a love for puffy Cheetos and their *Little Mermaid* lunch boxes.

"Hmm, but I think you want him to be *your* hot mechanic."

"Can we stop calling him that?" Paige asked, flopping back onto her bed. "His name is Brendan."

Brendan the beautiful.

That was an apt description of him. Paige had known he was hot, but when she'd gotten a full-on look at his face without his sunglasses, she'd about melted to the floor. He had the clearest, brightest blue eyes she'd ever seen on a man. And damn, when they'd been intently focused on her she'd about lost all reason, like the fact that she couldn't possibly like him already.

It was a problem. He was a problem. She couldn't have feelings for him. She'd just met him, and he'd been an ass. But he'd also been really nice. And God, that smile. She'd been right—it did reach all the way up to his eyes.

"So you're not denying it?" Paige could hear the smile in Abby's voice. "You do want him to be yours."

"I don't even know him. I spent a total of an hour with the man and he drove me crazy for half of it."

"What about the other half?"

For the other half he'd still driven her crazy. Just in a completely different way. There'd been that moment in his truck when he'd turned to her and apologized. It had taken Paige so off guard she'd forgotten how to speak...and how to breathe. He was lethal when he was sincere. Who was she kidding? He was lethal just existing.

"For the other half I tolerated him."

"Liar," Abby said, laughing through the phone. "Just admit it, you want him."

"Can we talk about something else?" Paige pleaded.

"Fine. If you want to delude yourself you go ahead and do that. But I'm going to say one last thing."

"Fine. Go."

"This is the first time that I've talked to you in the past three months when you've actually sounded like you again."

"I..." Paige trailed off, staring at the ceiling fan as it spun in a slow, lazy circle. She got dizzy and she closed her eyes. Too bad her spinning head had nothing to do with the fan.

"So anyways," Abby continued, saving Paige from examining the feelings, or whatever they were, that she might or might not have for the hot mechanic.

* * *

The morning after Paige's car had broken down, she sat in the kitchen in front of the computer, still wearing her pajamas and sipping on a strong cup of cinnamon-vanilla coffee. Her legs were arranged on the chair in a way that she was able to rest her chin on her left knee while her right was tucked underneath her.

She was back on the job hunt, and since she flat-out refused to use the Mirabelle Information Center Web site, she was currently scrolling through the classifieds on the town newspaper site.

"Anything?" Denise asked from the stove where she was frying bacon and scrambling eggs.

"Nope," Paige said. "Well, they need a pizza delivery person for Papa Pan's, but as my car isn't running I don't think that's an option."

"Hmm, maybe not. Soooo," Denise said, dragging out the word, "has *anybody* called about your car?"

And by *anybody*, Denise meant Brendan. As soon as Trevor had mentioned Brendan's name the night before, Denise's face had lit up and she'd asked about a hundred questions. She was just as bad as Abby. Though Denise hadn't called him the *hot mechanic*. No, she'd referred to him as *that nice young man*.

Oh, that *nice young man* towed your car?

Doesn't that *nice young man* just have the most gorgeous smile?

I'm sure that *nice young man* would be quite the catch.

Don't you think that *nice young man* would be more than capable of making love to you for hours on end and so thoroughly that you'd forget your own name?

Okay, so that last one was definitely something that Paige had thought and not something that Denise had said.

"No, Mother. Brendan hasn't called."

"Oh, I didn't mention *that nice young man's* name. So you were thinking about him? I knew there was a spark there."

"Mom," Paige said, looking over her shoulder.

"What?" she asked innocently as she glanced up from the stove.

"You know what? I don't know him at all."

"That's the funny thing about sparks. They're just these teeny, tiny little embers that come out of the simplest of things and then out of nowhere you get this giant inferno."

Paige rolled her eyes and turned back to the computer, trying to hide her smile.

"Look, I'm just happy that you're not moping over that *asshole* anymore."

"Wow," Paige said, looking back at her mom in surprise. Denise Morrison did not cuss, nor had she really said anything about Dylan in the last three months. She'd pretty much just put on a face of support and kept her opinions to herself. Apparently all bets were off now. "Tell me how you really feel."

"I do *not* like that horrible man. He wasn't worthy

of you in any capacity. Not in any way, shape, or form. And as far as I'm concerned you're better off without that smarmy, little prick in your life."

"What's with the sudden honesty?"

"You were different yesterday. Different than you've been since you got here. I wasn't lying when I said there was a spark, and I saw it in your eyes."

Well, if she wasn't the second person to say that Paige had changed since meeting Brendan.

Dylan hadn't really been on her mind at all in the last twenty or so hours. Not since this *hot mechanic/nice young man* had crossed her path. She was still upset about the job-interview joke that had happened, and she was really bummed about her Jeep, but things were definitely different today. Good different. Hopeful different.

The phone started ringing. Paige turned back to the desk and grabbed the phone next to the computer.

"Hello?" she said, running her finger down the handle of her coffee cup.

"May I speak with Paige Morrison?" Except the thickly accented male voice said *Pie-ge* instead of *Paige*.

"Speaking." Her hand stilled.

"This is Burley Adams over at Adams and Family. I was calling about a job opening."

Paige's head shot up. She hadn't applied to any place called Adams and Family. She wasn't even sure what they did.

"I'd like to set up an interview. For today if possible."

"That's possible. What time should I come in?"

"Would one o'clock work?"

"Yes."

"Just come into the office. We're over on the corner of

Apple Orchard and Fifth Street. Just ask for me when you come in."

"Mr. Adams, how did you hear about me?"

"Brendan King gave me your name."

Brendan?

"Oh." Her mind went blank. "Well, thank you. I'll see you at one," she said before she hung up.

She stared at the phone for a second in shock, unsure of what to do from here. She turned around slowly to look at her mother. Denise was beaming.

"Will you look at that? Where's the interview?"

"Adams and Family."

"What's that?" Denise asked, furrowing her brow.

"I'm not sure." Paige shook her head. She'd been so thrown by Brendan's recommendation that she'd forgotten to ask.

"How did they hear about you?"

"Brendan."

"Huh." Denise grinned, looking more than a little satisfied with herself. "What did I tell you. *Sparks.*"

Yeah, Paige was just concerned she was going to go up in flames again, and this time there would be nothing left.

* * *

Adams and Family was a funeral home.

Da-na-na, snap, snap.

Paige stood outside of the old Victorian house staring up at the two floors. It was yellow with white trim and green shutters. There was a large black sign on the lawn that read ADAMS AND FAMILY FUNERAL HOME in big white letters. Two shiny gray hearses were parked on the side of the building.

It's a job, she told herself over and over again.

Yeah, but it's a job at a funeral home ... with dead bodies.

That's true, but you need a new radiator, which requires money, which you don't have.

Dead bodies.

No car.

Dead bodies.

NO CAR.

Paige looked down at her bright blue silk blouse, the sleeves coming down to just above her elbows, and made sure that she was all in order. She'd gone with black pants instead of a skirt, and flat sandals instead of heels. Nothing too flashy.

"It's now or never," she said, walking up the steps to the porch and opening the door.

Tacky green-and-gold wallpaper covered the walls of the hallway. The carpet was a deep crimson, which really freaked her out. They could have picked any color carpet and they picked blood red?

So creepy.

A staircase stood directly in front of the door, and there was an open room to the right where a woman with short hair sat behind a desk talking on the phone.

"Yes, Mr. Landell," she said, typing into her computer. "We have an available service on the twelfth. You can come in tomorrow at two to meet with Mr. Adams."

She looked up at Paige and smiled, holding up a finger, and then looked back to her computer as she continued to type.

Paige took a closer look around the room as the woman wrapped up the phone call. The awful wallpaper had spilled into this room as well, the green and gold swirls not getting any better on closer inspection.

"How can I help you?" asked the woman as she stood up and walked around the desk.

She looked like she might be in her late thirties. She had a rather striking appearance. Her face screamed angles, with her sharp cheekbones and chin and the slanted cut of her short reddish-brown hair. She wore a lot of makeup, but she wore it in a flattering way, highlighting her features. She had massive perky breasts that defied gravity and she was taller than Paige.

Paige glanced down to the woman's feet and saw four-inch black stilettos.

Now, why is she allowed to wear heels and I'm not?

"I'm here for an interview with Mr. Adams."

"Oh, he'll be back any minute. I'm Tara, Tara Montgomery," she said with her southern belle accent, sticking out her hand.

"Paige Morrison," she said, shaking Tara's hand.

"Oh, I've heard about you," Tara said, giving her a big smile.

Something in Paige's face must have dropped because Tara squeezed her hand before she let go.

"And I don't believe any of it." Tara shook her head. "Some of these town people tend to be small-minded, but don't you let it worry you. They weren't that welcoming of me either when I moved down."

"How long ago did you move here?"

"About three years."

"And how long did it take them to warm up to you?"

Tara gave her a self-deprecating smile. "Any day now."

The front door behind Paige opened and she turned to see the largest man she'd ever seen in her life. He was probably a foot taller than her and completely bald. There was a bright red tie around his big beefy neck, and his black suit jacket fit snuggly across his wide shoulders.

"Mr. Adams, this is Paige Morrison. She's here for her interview," Tara said.

He pulled out a handkerchief from the inside pocket of his jacket and rubbed it across his enormous forehead, up to the top of his head, and down to the back of his neck. He shoved it back into the inside of his jacket as he walked into the office.

"Ms. Morrison," he said, sticking out his hand.

Paige grabbed it, thankful it wasn't the same hand he'd just wiped his sweaty head with.

"If you'll just come with me." He walked to the closed doors next to Tara's desk and slid them open.

Paige followed him into a room that was just slightly bigger than Tara's, but really not much better when it came to decorating. The wallpaper hadn't followed them in here, but the god-awful carpet had.

"Please sit," Mr. Adams said, gesturing to a chair while he walked around his desk and sat down. "So, Ms. Morrison, I hear you're looking for a job."

"Paige," she said, crossing her legs.

"Paige," he amended. "Brendan King said you might be able to help me with my new technological issue."

"And what issue is that?"

"There is this thing that funeral homes are doing for services. It involves taking pictures and videos of the deceased and putting them to music."

"A slideshow?"

"Yes," he said, leaning back in his chair. "But maybe just a little bit more fancy. I would also like to update our prayer cards and booklets. Brendan said you're a photographer."

"Yes, sir," she said, suddenly getting nervous.

If he wanted her to take pictures of dead bodies there was no way in hell she was going to take this job. What if they wanted to dress the deceased up in weird costumes? Like a picture album from beyond the dead?

"What did you have in mind?" she asked cautiously.

"I wanted to incorporate local scenery into the background of the pictures instead of the generic stuff that comes with the program. The people from around here are used to a more southern atmosphere. Eagles soaring over a mountain pass don't really fit into that. I want to give them something in death that they had in life. For many of these people this area was their life," he said, turning slightly in his chair.

"What else would the job entail?"

Please don't say dead bodies. Please don't say dead bodies.

"Updating the Web site and writing obituaries."

Paige and her mother had looked up Adams and Family on the Internet to figure out what it was, and neither of them had been impressed with the Web site. It was outdated and boring.

"I could do that."

"Then it's settled. Tara will help you fill out the paperwork today and you can start tomorrow if you're available."

"I'm available," Paige said, more than a little overwhelmed.

This had been the shortest interview of her life, and Mr. Adams hadn't looked at her résumé or even her work portfolio. He had no idea if she was any good or not. He was basing it all on a reference from one person.

Brendan King.

* * *

Brendan had been working on cars since he was six. Back then, it had always been under the supervision of his grandfather. Oliver would put a chair next to the car he was working on and point out every single part for Brendan. Oliver let him attempt to loosen the bolts, which he wasn't able to do alone until he was ten. Oliver had been the only father figure Brendan had ever known, his real father having walked out on his mother before he'd been born.

Brendan's mother, Claire King, had been a beautiful woman and the light of her parents' world. She'd had a brilliant smile and an infectious laugh. When Brendan was six, Claire gave him a baby sister. That father was never talked about either. Well, at least not in the King household. As for the people of Mirabelle, they'd talked about that juicy bit of gossip for years, and it sometimes still came up in conversations. Some said he was one of the many tourists who came to the beach in the summer. Others said he was a married man from the area.

In school, Brendan had gotten into more fights than he could count. He had a temper and would snap when kids made fun of him and his sister. But the harsh gossip had stopped when Brendan was sixteen, because that was when Claire had died. By the time the doctors had found it, it had been too late. She'd only been diagnosed with breast cancer for seven months before it had killed her.

At his mother's funeral, holding his little sister's hand in his, Brendan had become an adult. He'd never turned back. Twelve years later, at the age of twenty-eight, he owned half of King's Auto and his own house.

But at the moment he felt like he was fifteen again and in no control of his hormones, because he couldn't get Paige Morrison out of his head. He kept seeing her in those sexy as hell shoes. Kept seeing her eyebrows bunch together before she went off on a rant. Kept seeing that pretty mouth of hers. And it was all messing with his head.

"B.K.!" Greg called from the front. "Someone's here to see you."

Brendan turned around to the front of the garage to see Paige standing in the doorway wearing a frown. If only it were as easy as thinking about her to always make her appear.

He pulled his gloves off, sticking them in his back pocket as he walked toward her. He couldn't help but smile as he took in her clothing. A pair of black pants covered her long legs and her red toes peeked out of a pair of flat sandals. She wore a bright blue shirt made of some satiny material that he wanted to reach out and rub between his fingers.

"I need to talk to you." She shifted from one foot to the other, her frown still firmly in place.

"All right," Brendan said, gesturing to the empty office with his hand. He held the door open as she walked past him and he couldn't help but stare at her hair. He hadn't seen it down before, and today it flowed past the middle of her long, graceful back. It was chestnut brown, thick, and full of curls. He wanted to reach out and touch that too.

She turned to him as he shut the door behind them, her arms folded across her chest.

"How can I help you?" Brendan asked, leaning back against the wall.

"I don't understand you," she said, shaking her head, her mouth twitching.

"What is it you don't understand?"

"You got me a job interview."

"Yes." He nodded.

"Why? Why did you get me a job interview?"

"Because you needed a job." She was clearly agitated, and it was most definitely directed at him. "Are you angry with me?"

"Yes. No. I don't know," she said, throwing her hands up in the air.

"I don't understand *you*," he said, pushing off the wall and walking toward her. "You say that no one in this town will give you a chance, that no one in this town has been nice to you. Yet when someone does give you a chance," he said, stopping in front of her, "when someone is nice to you, you get all uptight and agitated." He reached out and grabbed a piece of her hair, rubbing the soft curl between his fingers.

"W-what are you doing?" she asked, looking up at him, alarmed.

"I noticed you didn't wear those shoes of yours today." He let go of her hair.

"Yeah, well," she said and shrugged, not finishing her sentence.

"And you wore pants." He eyed her legs.

"Stop that," she said, putting her hand on his chest to push him away, but when she touched him, they both stopped and just stared at each other.

Her hand was pressed right above his heart, and warmth spread from her palm and long thin fingers, settling in his chest. He reached up and covered her hand with his, not letting her move it from his chest. She swallowed hard and continued to stare at his face.

"Did you get the job?" he asked, tilting his head to the side.

She nodded, breathing unevenly.

"You know, here in the South, we say 'thank you' for something like that." He gave her a slow smile.

"Thank you," she said softly.

"Paige," he said, leaning in closer, his eyes focused on her lips.

The door opened behind them, the blinds on the window hitting the glass as the door bounced against the wall. Paige and Brendan jumped apart as Oliver walked into the office.

Brendan would've kissed her; he'd only had to move in a few more inches and he would've done it. She would've let him too. He'd seen the desire in her eyes. It was the same desire he'd felt pounding through his entire body.

His grandfather had impeccable timing.

Oliver had a cell phone to his ear and an invoice in front of his face. He didn't even notice Brendan and Paige until he looked up.

"See you then." He ended the call. "Paige," he said, putting his cell phone in his pocket. "To what do we owe the pleasure?"

"I, uh, I came by to thank Brendan?" She said it like a question.

Brendan couldn't help but smile at her inability to think properly.

"Thank him for what?" Oliver asked, raising an eyebrow.

"The, uh, job," she said, still trying to find her bearings.

"You got a job? That's great news," Oliver said, giving Paige a genuine smile. "Did Brendan tell you about your car yet?"

"We didn't get that far," Brendan said.

"My car?" Paige said, coming back to herself.

"Yeah, we ordered the part. It'll be in tomorrow morning and you should have your Jeep back by closing."

"How much?" she asked, biting her lip.

"We're looking at about five hundred for everything."

Brendan watched as Paige's whole face fell.

Oliver opened his mouth to say something but Brendan cut him off. "We can set up a payment plan." He took a step toward her.

Oliver glanced at Brendan, a dumbfounded look on his face.

"When do you start your job?" Brendan asked.

"Tomorrow," she said, looking back and forth between the men. "I can't ask you to do that."

"It isn't a problem," Brendan said, shaking his head. "We'll discuss terms when you pick up your car tomorrow."

"Brendan, I—"

"It's done, Paige. Don't worry about it."

"Thank you," she said softly.

"No problem."

"I have to go." She backed up toward the door. "My dad needs his car back. I'll, uh, hear from you tomorrow?" she asked, looking at Brendan.

"Tomorrow." He nodded.

"What was that?" Oliver asked as the door shut behind Paige. "Payment plan?"

"She's going to pay us back."

"Oh, I have no doubt about that. But if this is one of your new ideas for the garage I'm going to have to veto it immediately." Oliver frowned.

"We aren't going to offer it to everyone," Brendan said, shaking his head. "Just her."

"Just *her*," Oliver repeated, his frown slowly turning into a smile. "You know I wasn't that engrossed in that invoice when I walked into the office. I saw you two spring apart like the other was on fire."

Brendan had no doubt about that.

* * *

"You almost kissed him?"

"I didn't almost kiss him," Paige said as she paced the floor in her bedroom. "*He* almost kissed *me*."

"Are you kidding me? You're going to try to discuss semantics with me?" Even though Abby was almost one thousand miles away, Paige could see her as if she was standing in the same room, waving her arm in the air in exasperation.

"It's not *semantics*. It's what happened."

"Did you attempt to move away?"

"Well no, but—"

"No. No buts. You would've let him kiss you. You wanted him to kiss you."

"You're like a dog with a bone."

"And you're completely delusional. Just admit it. You wanted your hot mechanic to kiss you."

"Brendan. His name is Brendan. And as I've told you a dozen times, he is *not* mine."

"But he will be. Just give it time."

Chapter Three

A Harlot at the Funeral Home

On Wednesday, Tara dragged Paige into the kitchen for a cup of coffee before she gave Paige the full tour of the Adams and Family funeral home.

The kitchen had black-and-white tile on the floors and counter. The cabinets were old fashioned but the white paint on them was fresh. An industrial refrigerator stood in one corner and an old stove in the other.

"We make punch and coffee for the funerals, but all of the food is catered." Tara handed Paige a green coffee cup. "So mainly staff uses the kitchen," she said as she poured both cups full of the steaming liquid. "Coffee, milk, and sugar are communal." She opened the fridge and pulled out a gallon of milk.

As they fixed their coffee, a small bony woman with streaky gray hair came into the kitchen. She put a bag in the refrigerator and turned around.

"Hi, Verna," Tara said brightly. "This is Paige Morrison. She's going to be making those new tributes."

Verna looked at them, a scowl on her face. She looked
Paige up and down, her eyes focusing on Paige's feet.
Paige was wearing her bright red peep-toed heels, which
she'd paired with a conservative stretchy black dress that
hit her just below the knee. The only reason she'd worn
flats the day before was because her feet had still been
killing her from her trek along the highway, and she
might have been a little self-conscious after Brendan's
comment. But when she'd seen Tara's four-inch heels the
day before, she'd decided she wasn't going to let anyone mess with her shoes. Some things were sacred, and
Paige's shoe choice was one of them.

"Only harlots wear red shoes," Verna said, pointing to
Paige's feet before she walked out of the kitchen.

Paige wasn't sure whether to laugh or scream. And
who said "harlot" anymore?

"Verna Wisenbacker is a real joy to work with," Tara
said. "She's terrible to everyone except Missy."

"Who's Missy?" Paige asked, taking a sip of her coffee.

"The assistant funeral director."

"And what does Verna do?"

"She's in charge of the finances. If you ever need a new
stapler, be prepared for a five-week waiting period, because she'll make you fill out enough paperwork to keep
you busy for that long. And I'm just giving you fair warning," she said, pointing to the fridge. "Never, and I mean
never, touch anything in there that's Verna's."

"Noted."

"Now on to happier things. These are from Café Lula,"
she said, opening a box on the counter. "These are orange
and these are strawberry." She pointed to the different
scones. "Both will be heaven in your mouth."

Yeah, Paige and Tara were going to be friends. Not only did Tara have a bit of a smart mouth, but she'd also provided Paige with caffeine and showed her where the sweets were.

"Oh my gosh," Paige moaned as she took a bite of the orange scone. "This is incredible."

"Just wait until you try their rhubarb and strawberry cobbler with fresh ice cream," Tara said as she bit into her own scone, an extreme look of pleasure on her face.

After finishing their treats, Paige followed Tara around the first floor, all the while clutching her cup of coffee. The viewing parlor was a large room directly to the left of the front door. About fifteen pews on either side of the aisle ran up to the front of the room. Each pew was covered in one long crimson seat cushion, flattened from decades of use. Heavy gold curtains hung from the floor-to-ceiling windows.

The more Paige saw of the funeral home, the more she knew just how outdated it was. It could really be a beautiful building if they did a couple of things, like tear down that retched green-and-gold wallpaper, which had also made an appearance in the viewing room.

"Down there is another hallway," Tara said, pointing to a closed door. "There's a room where the bodies are stored and then a cremation and embalming room where Juris works. The storage closets are down there too."

Embalming. Gross, gross, gross.

"Juris?" Paige asked.

"Juris is my husband." Tara's face lit up. "He does the embalming but he's also a taxidermist. If you see a stuffed animal anywhere in this county, my Juris did that," she said proudly.

Paige's mind immediately traveled back to the scary turkey at Skeeter's Bait, Tackle, Guns, and Gas.

"Wow," Paige said, trying her hardest to sound enthusiastic, but it was difficult because for some reason she was imagining a corpse with its arms lovingly wrapped around a dead stuffed cat.

"We met online." Tara lowered her voice. "I'm from South Carolina originally, but I moved down here to be with Juris. I just knew that he was the one. You know, my soul mate," she said with that same overjoyed expression.

Paige had never had that look on her face when she'd been talking about Dylan. She'd never gotten that giddy little catch in her throat either. He'd never made her weak in the knees or made speaking difficult. And then suddenly Paige's brain flashed to Brendan, who *had* done those things. He'd almost kissed her yesterday; she'd wanted him to kiss her. She couldn't get it out of her mind. His fingers curling around hers, the spicy scent of his skin as he'd stepped in close to her, the way he looked at her with his bright blue eyes.

What was wrong with her? She didn't know anything about the man. She didn't need to be thinking about him, and yet... she was.

"That's wonderful," Paige said, pushing Brendan to the back of her mind and refocusing on Tara.

"It is." Tara nodded. "There's another smaller parlor in the back of the building," she said, switching back to tour guide, "but we don't really use that one very much. If we have multiple funerals we might, but for the most part we use the main one. You can grab your purse," Tara said as they walked back to the front of the funeral home. "From here it's onward and upward."

Paige followed Tara up the staircase to a long landing with doors scattered along both sides. Light streamed into the hallway from the opened doors and floor-to-ceiling windows.

"Verna and Missy's offices are down there," Tara said, pointing to the left. "Missy is at a conference, but she'll be back next week," she told Paige as they walked into the room next to the stairwell. "This is the showroom for the coffins." She gestured to over a dozen different coffins varying in color and size that were displayed on stands all over the room.

"This used to be two rooms way back when, but they tore the wall down to make it bigger." They walked through the room and back into the hallway through another door in the room. "This room has all of the urns for when a person is cremated," Tara said, leading Paige into the next room. "We also display the jewelry in here."

"Jewelry?" Paige asked, following her in.

"Yeah, some people like to carry a piece of their loved ones with them."

A piece? What did she mean by a piece?

"I'm sorry?" Paige asked, walking over to a display of necklaces.

"You see," Tara said, opening the clasp on a pendant covered in amethyst. "You can put your loved one's ashes in here." She indicated a part inside the necklace.

"Please tell me you're joking," Paige said, feeling queasy.

"Oh, I wish I was," Tara said, closing the necklace. "Other options are getting a thumbprint and wearing that."

"I'm sorry, but this is bizarre."

"Oh, believe you me, sweetie, I completely agree."

Paige turned from the morbid, and more than a little disgusting, jewelry to a display of about thirty urns lined up on three tables. After a quick scan they left that room and continued the tour. Paige's suspicions were confirmed as they walked down the hallway. Besides the kitchen and bathrooms, every inch of the building was covered in the horrendous crimson carpet.

"Those rooms are empty," Tara said, indicating the very last two rooms down the hall. "But you'll be in here." She pushed a door open.

There were five big boxes stacked on the two desks that were in the middle of the room and an empty bookshelf in the corner. An old leather office chair and two wooden armchairs were pushed against one wall. The seats of the armchairs were covered in puce velvet. The walls were painted a seafoam green that wasn't bad at all, but up against that obnoxious carpet it really had no hope.

"The offices on this side of the building have access to the second-floor balcony," Tara said, pointing to the French doors in the corner that opened up onto the landing outside. "They also have a better view of the trees."

"Thank you," Paige said, giving Tara a genuine smile. She'd obviously tried to give Paige what she thought was the best office available.

"It's no problem." Tara waved away Paige's thanks with her hand. "The computer is all yours. Mr. Adams got the best one for the new program that he wants you to start using. Verna had a fit when she ordered it last week," she added, lowering her voice. "You can set up your office anyway you want. I put some office supplies in that box," she said, pointing to one that was stacked on the desk. "If there's something you need that isn't in there, the closet is down the hall. Unfortunately it's right next to Verna's office, so if you need to go in there, prepare to be ambushed."

"Thank you," Paige repeated. "I really am grateful."

"If you need anything I'll be downstairs," Tara said, leaving Paige to her own devices.

Paige walked to the desks and ran her hand over the smooth brown wood. They were antiques, carved and stained to emphasize the natural rings and spots. They were beautiful.

She grabbed the big leather chair and rolled it behind the desk. She sat down and slowly spun around to get a full view of her new office, taking an inventory of everything. Her eye caught on the corner of the room where the carpet met the floorboards. She got down on her hands and knees and pulled the corner of the carpet back. Underneath were hardwood floors. She stood up and took another long look around the room.

"Ms. Morrison," a booming voice said from behind her. "How is everything?"

Paige turned to see Mr. Adams taking up the entire width of the doorway.

"Mr. Adams, please call me Paige," she said, smoothing out her dress.

"All right, how is everything going, Paige?" He still said *Pie-ge* instead of *Paige*.

"Very good. Tara showed me around."

"Good, good. Well, you make yourself comfortable here."

"Thank you."

He nodded and began to turn away.

"Mr. Adams?" she called after him.

"Yes?"

"How attached are you to this carpet?"

* * *

Brendan stared down into the engine of Paige's Jeep. He'd just finished installing the new radiator and was checking to make sure that everything else was in working order. He pulled the support bar out from under the hood and let it slam shut. He got in behind the driver's seat and started the engine, which purred to life.

The inside of Paige's Jeep was just as loud as the outside. She had a big sunflower wrapped around the bar that attached her visor to the roof. Both visors had CD holders on them. He pulled out a couple of disks to see who she listened to but he hadn't heard of most of the artists. There was a pink-and-orange glass heart hanging from her rearview mirror and a blue-and-black robot bobblehead attached to her dashboard. Multiple hair ties were stacked on her gearshift and a zebra-print cover was around her steering wheel.

Brendan turned the car off and checked his watch. It was three thirty. He'd come into work early and was free to go by four since Wallace was closing. He made his way into the office and sat down behind the computer. He pulled up Paige's customer information and looked for her phone number.

"Hello?"

"Mr. Morrison? This is Brendan King."

"Oh. Hey, Brendan. What's going on?"

"Paige's Jeep is ready."

"Well, she started her new job today. I'm going to have to go pick her up at five. Can we swing by afterward?"

"I can pick her up," Brendan said before he even realized what he was saying.

"Really?"

"Yeah. She's just up the road from here. That way you don't have to drive all the way down here."

"Are you sure?"

"Yeah," Brendan repeated. "It's no trouble at all. You said she'd be done at five?" he asked, looking at his watch.

It made sense for Brendan to go pick Paige up. She was just up the road, whereas if her father picked her up, he would have to drive all the way into town. Which would take him at least twenty minutes. It made more sense this way. He just wasn't going to get off at four now, and he really didn't mind at all.

* * *

Paige had been going nonstop since she'd started that morning. She'd pulled Tara away from her desk and down the scary, dead-body hallway to help her find tools in the storage room. Even though there weren't any dead bodies in there at the moment, Paige was still completely creeped out going in there.

With her newly pilfered tools, Paige pulled up the carpet on one side of the room, rolling it as she went. When she'd reached the furniture, she'd dragged Tara upstairs to help her move the heavy desks to the other side of the room, sans carpet.

"These floors are beautiful," Tara said, sitting down in Paige's chair. "We should rip out all of the carpet."

After the carpet was rolled up and dragged into the hallway, Paige went around the room and pried out the tiny nails around the edge. It was at this point that Verna stuck her head into the room.

"What in God's name are you doing?" she screamed, outraged. "Mr. Adams is not going to approve of this."

"He already said it was fine," Paige said, giving her a sweet smile.

"Nothing is good enough for you, is it? You just have to come in here and wreak havoc," she said as she stormed out of the office.

Yeah, Paige and Verna were going to get along real well.

By four o'clock she'd set up her desk and computer. She decided to start reading through the instructions on the program she was supposed to use. About an hour later, there was a knock on the door and Paige looked up to see Brendan leaning against the doorjamb. He was wearing his navy blue pants and shirt and his five o'clock shadow.

Dear God he doesn't play fair.

"You've been busy," he said, looking around. "I ran into Mrs. Wisenbacker downstairs, who yelled at me for helping the havoc-inducing harlot get a job. I see you're making friends."

"She didn't like my shoes."

"What?"

"My shoes," Paige said, turning in her chair so she could show Brendan her feet. "Apparently only harlots wear red shoes."

He pushed off the doorjamb and walked into the room, stopping next to her desk. He looked down at her feet and his gaze slowly traveled up her legs. Heat rushed into her cheeks and she was thankful she was still sitting down.

"She's crazy," he said, finally meeting her eyes and grinning. "I'm a pretty big fan of those shoes."

"What are you doing here?" Paige asked, trying to focus on something besides the way he was looking at her.

"I came to pick you up. Your car's ready."

"Why did *you* come to pick me up?" she asked, panicked. She wasn't prepared to be in a close, confined environment with him.

"Because I told your dad I would. I can't believe you ripped the carpet out of here," he said, looking down at the floor. "It looks a lot better without it."

"Thanks. Can you help me carry the carpet downstairs?" she asked, pointing to the hallway where the rug still sat.

"Are you serious?"

"I can't carry it by myself," she said, standing up. If he was here she might as well get him to do something useful besides scrambling her brain.

"What's in it for me?"

"What do you want?" she asked, before she could stop herself.

She was flirting with him. Why was she flirting with him? Stupid thing to do, really.

"I have a couple of ideas," he said as his gaze flickered to her mouth.

There was another knock and they both turned to see Mr. Adams walk into the room.

"Brendan," he said in his big booming voice.

"Mr. Adams," Brendan said, holding out his hand.

"You come here to check up on your girl?" he asked, shaking Brendan's hand and clapping Brendan on the back with his other large hand.

His girl? Brendan's girl?

Paige's stomach flipped. She opened her mouth to correct him but Brendan cut her off.

"Yeah." He winked at Paige. "She's done a good job with this office."

"She sure has," Mr. Adams said, looking around. He looked down at the floor, a thoughtful expression on his face. "You know, I've been wanting to get rid of that red carpet for a while now. And these wooden floors are looking mighty fine. Maybe you've got something going here, Paige. Just leave that carpet in the hallway," he said as he continued to study the floor. "I might not want to store it after all."

"Really?" she asked, shocked.

"Yeah." Mr. Adams looked at her. "Maybe we should change things up here a little. Did you get a chance to look at the tribute program?"

"A little. I'm going to really get into it tomorrow."

"All right, you two have a nice night together," Mr. Adams said, backing toward the door.

"We will," Brendan said, waving.

Paige was too confused to say anything besides "bye."

"Your girl?" she whispered, turning to him when she heard Mr. Adams's loud steps descending the stairs. "Why didn't you correct him?"

"Because I didn't want to." He turned back to her. "But I can tell you I'm disappointed I can't get the 'whatever I want' for helping you move your carpet now."

"I didn't say you could get *whatever* you wanted. I asked *what* you wanted."

"I guess you did," he said, letting his eyes dip to her mouth again.

"So, uh, what did you want?"

"Is the offer still on the table?"

"I don't need you to move the rug anymore, so no."

"Then I'm not telling." He grinned.

She didn't want to know what he wanted anyways...all right, fine, she really, really did.

"You ready to go?"

"Whenever you are," he said, taking a step back toward the door.

Paige shut her computer down, grabbed her purse, and followed Brendan down the stairs.

"You done for the day, sweetie?" Tara asked as they stopped in front of her desk.

"Yes. I'll see you bright and early tomorrow."

"Yes, ma'am. I'll be waiting to hear all about your evening," she said, giving the two of them a sly smile. "Have fun."

"Oh, no—"

"We will," Brendan said, cutting Paige off. "Night, Tara." He put his hand on Paige's arm and guided her out of the office.

Once they got outside, Paige pulled her arm out of his hand and elbowed him in the ribs.

"Ouch," he said, rubbing his side. "What was that for?"

"You know exactly what that was for. You're having fun with this, aren't you?"

"Having fun with what?" he asked as they made their way to his car.

"Letting people think we're together."

"Would that be so bad?" he asked as he smiled over his shoulder.

She stopped in her tracks as he continued to walk.

"You coming?" he called out. "Or are you going to walk?"

She caught up to him as he opened the passenger-side door of a black pickup truck. She eyed the high step carefully, trying to figure out how to get in. She reached up with one hand and, before she knew it, her other was in Brendan's and he had a hand on her back helping her up.

"Thank you," she said, turning to him when her butt was firmly in the seat.

The brief physical contact had shocked her, and she wanted to "accidentally" fall out of his truck so that he would have to help her in again.

"No problem," he said, taking a step up onto the ledge of the truck and leaning in the cab toward her. His face was just a couple of inches from hers, his eyes focused intently on hers. "And Paige, it's just a matter of time."

"W-what is?"

He just grinned as he stepped down and shut the door.

Paige sat there with her mouth hanging open as Brendan rounded the truck. He opened the door and got in easily. He buckled his seat belt and started the engine, putting his hand on the back of her headrest as he looked behind himself and backed out.

Paige looked around, trying to focus on anything besides how close he was to her, or on what he'd just said. His truck was clean, no wrappers or sticky candy attached to the floor. There was a stack of papers stuck in the front right corner of the dashboard and a gym bag in the backseat. A black baseball hat with a stingray hung from the rearview mirror. There was a picture next to his speedometer of him in his teens. He was wearing a baseball uniform, which he easily filled out. Apparently he'd had muscles from an early age; they were just bigger now. His arms were stretched across the shoulders of a woman and a little girl. All three of them were wearing matching baseball hats and laughing as they looked at the camera.

"So," Paige said as he made a right. "Are you really not going to tell me what you wanted in exchange?"

"Not a chance," he said, glancing over at her.

"Why not?"

"Because, if I show you the cards in my hand, I've got nothing left to bargain with. And with the way you need favors, I'm sure I'll be able to get that offer back on the table."

"When did we start playing poker?"

He just looked at her and grinned.

"Fine," she said, folding her arms across her chest. "But I'm not much of a gambling girl. So don't hold your breath."

"We'll see."

They pulled into King's Auto and Paige jumped out of Brendan's truck before he made it around to help her. She didn't need him touching her again, because every time he did, all rational thought went out the window. She followed him into the office, where he pulled a folder off his desk and opened it.

"I just need you to sign here," he said, putting the paper on the desk. "It just says you agree to pay the full amount for the work that was done."

"What about the payment plan?" she asked, looking at him.

"What are you going to be able to do?"

"I can pay half with my first pay check, and half with the second."

"That's fine."

"Really?"

"Yeah." He nodded and grabbed a pen from one of many in a coffee cup.

"Why?"

"What?"

"Why are you doing this for me?" she asked. "I know this isn't part of your normal billing options."

"And how do you know that?"

"Because when you offered it, Oliver looked at you like you were crazy."

"He often looks at me like that," he said, handing her the pen.

"Brendan?"

"I know what it's like to have everything fall apart. Sometimes you just need a little time to get back on your feet," he said, not elaborating.

There was a glimpse of pain in his eyes and she really wanted to ask him about it but refrained because she had no desire to discuss what had happened to her, or the credit card and student loan payments that she hadn't been able to pay for months.

"Half with the first paycheck, the other half with the second," he repeated.

"Thank you," she said, genuinely grateful.

Chapter Four

One of the Gals

On Thursday, Paige walked into Adams and Family to loud hammering. The viewing room was in complete disorder as the pews had been shoved to one side of the room and the carpet was being ripped out.

Paige turned to see Tara leaning back against her desk, a cup of coffee in her hand, as she watched two men carry out a piece of rolled-up carpet.

"What's going on?" Paige asked.

"Mr. Adams has been here since six this morning and so have all of these men. Apparently, the little renovation in your office has inspired him," Tara said, handing Paige a steaming cup of coffee that had been sitting on her desk.

"Thank you." Paige dropped her purse onto a chair and grabbed the cup. She leaned against the desk next to Tara and watched the chaos ensue.

"I'm hoping the wallpaper is next," Tara said, pointing to the walls.

"You don't like that either?" Paige asked, taking a sip of her coffee that Tara had fixed perfectly the way she liked it. Paige had to give her credit, the woman was observant.

"God no." She shook her head dramatically. "This place has needed a makeover for decades. And you were just the thing to put a bug up Mr. Adams's butt."

Paige inhaled her coffee and started choking.

Bad visual. Bad, bad visual.

"You okay?" Tara asked, slapping her on the back.

"I will be." Paige coughed, eyes streaming.

"So what's going on with you and Brendan?" Tara asked, raising her perfectly plucked eyebrows.

"Nothing," Paige said a little too quickly, her voice going up an octave. She was lucky she hadn't taken another sip; otherwise she would have started choking again.

"Right," Tara said slowly.

"There isn't. He's just helped me out with my car a couple of times."

"Mmm-hmm."

Paige looked down to her coffee cup, tracing the purple rim with her fingertip. She was trying not to debate the mystery that was Brendan King, but it was useless. He'd told her that it was just a matter of time. *What* was just a matter of time was still uncertain, but Paige had a feeling that she knew exactly what that *what* was, and it scared the crap out of her.

"Oh no," Tara whispered.

"What?" Paige asked, looking up to see a clearly infuriated Verna advancing on them.

"You did this," Verna screamed above the banging, pointing a gnarled, bony finger at Paige. "You come in here and disrupt *everything* with your radical ideas. I've got my eye on you," she said, squinting at Paige before she stormed out of the room.

"What was that?" Paige looked over at Tara, who was laughing so hard she was snorting.

"I've never seen her get so worked up," Tara said, wiping the tears from under her eyes.

"What's so radical about getting rid of carpet?" Paige asked, confused.

Tara snorted again and Paige couldn't help but start laughing too.

"I should get to work." Paige stood up and grabbed her purse. "Thanks again," she said, holding up her coffee cup and walking toward the door.

"Hold up," Tara said before she had left. "We're going to go to lunch today. The other girls are dying to meet you."

"What other girls?"

"The other girls who do the side jobs around here. We'll leave at one."

"All right." Paige nodded and headed up the stairs.

* * *

Four hours later, Paige was taking pictures that she'd found on the Internet and placing them into the tribute program. She wanted to see how easy it was to replace the stock pictures. She set up a memorial slide with pictures from *The Flintstones*. Fred had died in a tragic hang-gliding accident involving a pterodactyl.

"You ready?" Tara asked from the doorway.

"Yeah," Paige said, standing up and stretching. "I'm

starving." Apparently killing off beloved cartoon characters worked up an appetite in a person.

"Good." Tara grinned. "It's always best to go to Lula Mae's when you're hungry."

"Isn't that who made those scones?" Paige asked as she followed Tara down the stairs.

"Yes. But you ain't seen nothin' yet."

* * *

Café Lula was on the beach. It was a renovated cottage painted in bright colors. The door was turquoise, the shutters yellow, the eaves and roof lilac, and the building itself salmon. A large green sign that read CAFÉ LULA in big, black letters hung from the overhang above the door.

Paige followed Tara up the green steps and through the front door. A bell rang as they entered. The inside of the shop had the same bright colors as the outside. The hardwood floors were blond, the walls were turquoise, and the doors and windows were yellow. The tables and chairs that were scattered around the café were all painted in a variety of colors. And the entire shop smelled like apples baked with vanilla and cinnamon.

"Wow," Paige said, closing her eyes and taking a deep breath. "That smells incredible."

"Why, thank you."

Paige opened her eyes to see a woman coming from around the corner. She had white hair cut in choppy layers all around her head and framing her face. She was ample everywhere, but it worked with her kind face and bright blue eyes.

"Lula Mae, this is Paige. Paige, Lula Mae."

"A pleasure," Lula Mae said, sticking out her hand.

"I had some of your scones." Paige shook her hand. "They were amazing."

"I'd like to take credit for those, but my granddaughter Gracie makes most of the pastries," she said, indicating a petite blonde in a pink T-shirt who was behind the register and taking care of some customers.

"Where are the twins?" Tara asked, making her way to one of the display cases.

"On the way." Lula Mae went behind the counter. "Paige, what would you like to drink?"

"Try the mango sweet tea," Tara said. "It's divine."

"Sounds good." Paige nodded at Lula Mae.

"Just pick whatever you want in there," Lula Mae said, pointing to the display case that Tara was hovering over.

"It's all made fresh," Tara said when Paige came up next to her.

They had chicken salad made with fruit and nuts on croissants, tomato and mozzarella on focaccia, and roast beef on French bread.

The bell rang again and Paige turned to see two short, thin women walking through the door. They were both in their midfifties with strawberry-blonde hair, big green eyes, and large chests, but that was where their similarities stopped.

One of them wore her hair very short and had gelled the strands to stick up all over her head like a stylish porcupine. Her eyebrows had been waxed within an inch of their lives, and she wore so much green eye shadow that it was ridiculous. She had on a tie-dye T-shirt, a black leather biker vest, and jeans. The other wore her hair longer, her big, thick curls brushing the top of her shoulders. Her eyebrows were still intact and her lips were as red as a cherry. She wore a green dress circa 1950 that made her look like Lucille Ball.

"I don't know," Porcupine said. "He just can't be *that* oblivious."

"Oh, I think he can be," the Lucy look-a-like said, sounding a little agitated.

They both looked over to the display and spotted Tara and then they zeroed in on Paige.

"Paige," Tara said, grabbing her arm and pulling her along to the duo. "These are the twins. Pinky," she said, indicating Porcupine with her hand. "And Panky Player," she said, moving her hand in the direction of the Lucy look-a-like.

"And this is Paige," Tara continued with her introductions.

"Nice to meet you," Paige said, shaking their hands in turn.

"They both work part time at the funeral home. Pinky does the hair and makeup for the deceased, but she also owns a hair salon. And Panky does all of the flowers for the funeral home but she also has her own shop. They're Lula Mae's cousins."

"How are you liking the funeral home?" Panky asked.

"I'm still settling in," Paige said.

"Wait until I tell you guys about Verna," Tara said excitedly.

"You better wait for us before you talk about anything," Lula Mae said from behind the counter. "Gracie and I want to hear all about this too."

Someone else took over Grace's position at the register. She came around the counter, wiping her hands on her apron. She had bright blue eyes and light blonde hair. A few pieces of her hair had fallen out of her low ponytail and framed her heart-shaped face. She had a light tan, like she was used to spending lots of time in the sun with sunscreen.

"So you're Paige," Grace said, her eyes lighting up as she stuck out her hand. "I'm Grace."

"Your scones were delicious," Paige said, unable to think of anything else. She wasn't sure why she was so nervous about meeting a bunch of new people. She'd made friends easily enough before moving down here. Maybe it was her bad luck with first impressions these days.

"Thanks." Grace laughed and pointed to the display case. "What do you want for lunch?"

"The chicken salad," Paige said.

"Make that two," Panky said.

"I'll have the roast beef," Pinky said, walking over to a large round table tucked into the corner of the shop. She hung her purse on the back of one of the chairs and sat down.

"Tomato and mozzarella," Tara said, following Pinky.

"Coming right up." Grace headed behind the counter to get their lunches ready.

* * *

Thirty minutes later, all six women sat around the table laughing loudly. Paige was finishing her incredible sandwich while Tara told everyone about Verna and her rather loud objections to Paige. She'd just done a spot-on imitation of Verna's outburst that morning.

"You've got to be kidding me," Pinky said, slapping the table.

Panky and Grace were laughing so hard they couldn't speak.

"She's nuts." Lula Mae took another bite of her chicken salad sandwich.

"You've got her all in a twist," Tara said, leaning back in her chair. "I even saw her screaming at Brendan yesterday."

"Why was she screaming at Brendan?" Panky asked, taking a sip of her drink.

"Because he got me the job," Paige said, before she even realized she was speaking.

Everyone stopped talking and turned to look at Paige.

"Brendan?" Grace asked, breaking the silence. "Brendan King?"

"Yeah," Paige said, shifting in her chair. "He, uh, did me a favor."

"Well, that was nice of him," Lula Mae said.

"Where did you see her screaming at him?" Pinky asked Tara.

"At the funeral home, when he came to pick up Paige," Tara said, letting the corner of her mouth quirk up.

Paige had the urge to kick Tara under the table.

"Why was he picking you up from work?" Panky asked, her eyes going wide as she leaned over the table.

"My Jeep's been in the shop," Paige said, trying to affect a nonchalant tone, which she was horribly unsuccessful at pulling off because her cheeks were flaming.

"Right," Grace said skeptically.

"Who wants dessert?" Lula Mae asked, taking pity on Paige and changing the subject. "Grace made apple pie."

"Yes, please," came the chorus from everyone around the table.

"Sit down, Grams." Grace stood up. "I'll get it."

"I'll help." Paige stood up, too, and followed Grace through a swinging door.

The small kitchen was tame, with yellow and blue tiles on the floor and climbing up two-thirds of the wall where they stopped and a light blue paint continued and reached up to the ceiling. Pale yellow shelves were in one corner, organizing all of the dishes. Stainless-steel countertops and appliances took up the rest of the space.

"Here," Grace said, going to the freezer and pulling out a container. "You can put the ice cream on the pie." Grace opened a drawer and handed Paige an ice cream scoop and then went to grab a stack of plates. "So," Grace said, pulling out a knife from a wooden block, "how are you liking it down here?"

"The last couple of days have been way more pleasant than the last couple of months," Paige said honestly.

"Even with Verna?" Grace asked, cutting the pie.

"Even with Verna."

"So you haven't made a lot of friends around here?" Grace handed Paige a plate with pie on it.

"Not exactly."

"Well, I can tell you that all of those women in that room are glad you're here. And so am I. We meet up for lunch every Thursday. You should come with Tara from now on."

"Thank you," Paige said, taken aback, a smile quickly growing on her face. So maybe she was still capable of making good first impressions. That was a relief.

"What are you doing on Sunday?" Grace asked, handing Paige another plate.

"No plans."

"I'm going to the beach with a couple of friends around eleven. And if you come over to my grandparents' early, you can have some of Grams' amazing breakfast."

"Really? What time?"

"I'll pick you up around nine thirty."

"All right." Paige nodded. "I'm in. It sounds like fun."

"Oh, I'm counting on it."

Chapter Five

Turning Up the Heat

Friday went by uneventfully, except for the banging that traveled upstairs. The entire downstairs had been stripped of the carpet and they were now working on the rooms next to Paige. She'd shoved a pair of earbuds into her ears and turned up her iPod to drown out the noise.

She'd figured out most of the nuances of the tribute program. Then she'd moved over to the Web site, trying to figure out ways to make it better, which she worked on until she'd left work that evening.

On Saturday, Paige got up early to run and then spent the afternoon in her art studio/shed while her parents worked in the yard. Her parents owned a three-bedroom house on the river. They'd bought it for the hardwood floors, big bay windows, and the massive backyard. Denise and Trevor had always dreamed of having a big yard when they retired, and now they did.

Half a dozen large oak trees were scattered in the yard, and rose bushes and wisteria surrounded them. Jasmine climbed up the lattice over the back porch, and honey-suckle grew all along the fence. Paige's parents had put in pavers to create a path through the grass, and built a deck right on the water. It was their little oasis.

When Paige had moved in, her father had moved all of the stuff out of the shed and into the garage so that Paige could have an art studio. It was a small building with a window on the back wall. Shelves covered one wall, while another housed a sink and a tiny counter.

She'd quickly made it her own space, painting the inside walls a lime green, filling the shelves with her painting supplies, hanging white lace curtains over the window, and putting up that blessed fan. The outside of the shed matched her parents' house, white with blue trim, and one side of it was covered in lattice wound with jasmine. Her parents had been kind enough to give her a little oasis of her own.

* * *

On Sunday morning, Paige woke up to a clear blue sky. She pulled on her bathing suit, a tank top, and a pair of running shorts. She threw a big beach towel, sunscreen, some lip gloss, and a book into her beach bag and headed into the kitchen.

"You leaving soon?" Trevor asked over his newspaper.

"Yeah, in about five minutes," Paige said, grabbing a plastic bottle from the cupboard and filling it with ice water.

The doorbell rang and Paige heard her mother answer

the door. Grace laughed as she walked into the kitchen with Denise.

"You tell your grandmother that I'm going to go down and get some of that chicken pot pie of hers. I've never had anything that amazing in my life."

"I'll tell her. Hi, Mr. Morrison." Grace waved from the doorway.

"Hello. Have you and your grandmother been busy?" he asked over his coffee cup.

"Lately we have been. What about you? How's everything going here?"

"Pretty good. Retirement is mighty fine."

"You girls have fun," Denise said, sitting down at the table next to Trevor.

"We will," Paige said, walking over to her parents and kissing them on the cheeks. "I'll see you guys later."

"Love you, Little Miss," Trevor called after her as they walked out of the kitchen.

"Little Miss?" Grace asked, looking at her.

"Nickname that I've had all my life," Paige said while slipping on her leather flip-flops.

Five minutes later, they pulled into Lula Mae's driveway. The sound of a lawn mower greeted them as they got out of Grace's vintage yellow Volkswagen Bug. Paige followed Grace up the steps to a whitewashed beach house with a red roof and a screened-in front porch.

"Grams," Grace called out as they walked in the front door. "We're here."

The house was simple with beige tile running through the hallway and walls that were painted a soft peach. Before they rounded the corner, a loud tapping noise made Paige look to her right where a large but beautiful black and gray dog came skidding across the tile.

"Sydney, sit," Grace said, putting her hand out.

The dog sat at Grace's feet, her feathery tail sweeping the floor as it wagged back and forth.

"Good girl," Grace said, scratching her head. "This is my brother's dog, Sydney. He comes over on Sundays to mow the lawn."

"Can I pet her?" Paige asked, holding out her hand.

"Yeah. She isn't mean or anything. She just tends to ignore people who she doesn't know or like, so don't be offended if she walks away."

Paige held her hand in front of Sydney's nose to sniff. Sydney stuck her nose into Paige's palm and her tongue shot out, wrapping around the back of her hand.

"Hi, pretty girl," Paige said, running her fingers through the fur on the dog's head and down to the side of her neck. "What is she?"

"Part Siberian husky and part something else. My brother thinks she might be part black Lab and that there's a little German shepherd in there somewhere. Come on," Grace said, rounding the corner.

Paige followed her into the kitchen, where Lula Mae stood in front of the stove, a sunshine-yellow apron tied around her waist.

"Morning, Grams," Grace said, kissing her on the cheek.

"Morning." Lula Mae turned around. "Paige, I'm so glad you came."

"Thanks for having me," Paige said, leaning against the counter. Sydney came up to her, butting Paige's leg with her head. Paige leaned down and started scratching her neck again.

"That's weird," Grace said.

"What?" Paige asked, looking up as she continued to pet Sydney.

"She doesn't normally respond well to women who she doesn't know, or to any girl who my brother has dated."

Sydney pawed at Paige's legs so Paige sat down on the tile floor. Sydney sat down in between Paige's bent knees and Paige scratched her chest. She closed her blue eyes as her back leg started to hit the tile with a loud *thump, thump, thump*.

"It's true." Lula Mae looked at Paige and the dog, her eyebrows raised in surprise.

"The last girl my brother dated, Sydney ate her shoes."

"Oh, and she hated Marty," Lula Mae added, pointing to Sydney. "Whenever she would come over, Sydney would whine the entire time."

"Yeah, well, I felt like crying whenever Marty was around too."

"I'm so glad she isn't in the picture anymore."

"She wasn't good enough for Brendan anyway," Grace said.

"Brendan?" Paige asked, looking up, panicked. "Your brother is Brendan?" She looked at Grace. "He's your grandson?" She turned to Lula Mae.

Grace and Lula Mae looked at Paige with matching expressions of amusement and guilt.

"Did we forget to mention that?" Grace asked innocently.

"Well, isn't this an interesting picture?" a deep voice said to Paige's right.

Paige turned and nearly swallowed her tongue. Brendan was standing there wearing a pair of green athletic shorts and sneakers. Sweat dripped down his face and bare chest. He had a light dusting of blond hair across his tanned chest; the trail narrowed as it traveled down his flat stomach and disappeared into shorts that hung low on his hips.

He had a tattoo on his left bicep. It was on the inside of his arm and all that Paige could see was what looked like a tree trunk extending down to just above the crook of his arm.

It was then that Sydney started swatting Paige in the face. Paige had stopped scratching her chest, being too distracted ogling everything that was Brendan King.

* * *

Brendan was jealous of his dog. There was no other explanation for it. Sydney was sitting in between Paige's thighs getting her chest scratched and looking like she was in heaven. He was pretty sure that if he could've traded places with Sydney, he would've had a dazed look on his face too.

The last thing that Brendan had expected when he'd walked into his grandmother's kitchen was to find Paige sitting on the floor playing with his dog, a dog he was now extremely jealous of. Then it hit him; Paige was playing with Sydney, Sydney who hated every girl he'd ever brought home. And at the moment, Sydney was swatting a stunned Paige in the face, trying to get her to resume her scratching.

Brendan had noticed the way that Paige was looking at him, her gray eyes going wide with wonder as they'd skimmed his body and her mouth falling open. He'd known that she was attracted to him; he'd figured that out when he'd almost kissed her in his office. But the look he saw on her face went much deeper than just attraction.

He'd been thinking about her all week. Ever since he'd met her, he couldn't get her off his mind. She was driving him crazy when she wasn't around him and she was most definitely driving him crazy now with that heated look on her face.

"Paige is going to the beach with us," Grace said brightly.

"Is she now?" he asked, walking over to the refrigerator and pulling out a pitcher of orange juice.

"Who else is going?" his grandmother asked as she stirred the batter.

"Mel, Harper, Jax, and Shep," Grace said.

"Jax and Shep should be here soon." Brendan grabbed a glass from the cupboard. "When I told them you were making your butter pecan pancakes they couldn't resist," he said as he poured himself a tall glass of juice and drank half of it in one gulp.

He sighed in relief as he pulled the glass from his mouth and looked down at Paige again. She was staring at him, her lovely chest rising and falling a little fast, and a light blush creeping up her freckled chest and neck. And with that Brendan walked out of the kitchen to go take a cold shower.

* * *

"You set me up," Paige said, looking at the satisfied smiles on Grace and Lula Mae's faces.

"I have no idea what you're talking about." Lula Mae turned and started fiddling with the griddle.

"Yeah, absolutely no idea," Grace said as she hopped up onto the countertop.

Paige raised her eyebrows at their lies.

"All right, fine. We set you up. But the element of surprise always reveals so much," Grace conceded.

"Oh, I'm sure it does," Paige grumbled.

Paige had probably revealed too much about herself in the couple of minutes that Brendan had been in the kitchen. She was surprised she hadn't started panting. She tried not to be obvious, but that was difficult whenever he was breathing the same air as her. And really, he'd just been standing in the kitchen half naked and sweaty and looking hot as hell. It wasn't her fault. It was his fault.

Stupid hot mechanic.

"Well, isn't that something," Oliver said as he walked into the kitchen and stared down at Paige. "That dog is putty in your hands."

"She isn't the only one," Grace muttered under her breath.

Paige looked at Grace, trying to give her the evil eye but failing miserably when Grace started cracking up.

The front door opened and closed and deep voices traveled down the hallway. Two tall and very attractive men walked into the kitchen. Sydney sure was some guard dog. She didn't even look up, just scooted closer and rested her head against Paige's shoulder.

"Paige, this is Jaxson Anderson," Grace said, not moving from her perch and indicating the tall redheaded man with freckly, tanned skin and deep green eyes. "And Nathanial Shepherd," she said, pointing to the guy with thick, wavy black hair, dark blue eyes, and arm tattoos. "Jax is a deputy sheriff, and Shep helps his family run the Sleepy Sheep, which is a bar out on the beach. They've been friends with Brendan since preschool."

Paige couldn't even imagine the trouble that those three had probably gotten into growing up. They had mischief written all over them. Paige could read it on all of their muscles.

"This is Paige," Grace continued. "She just got a job at the funeral home. Brendan helped her get it," she added, covering her smirk with her mug as she took a sip of coffee.

Jax and Shep gave each other significant looks and grinned at each other. Jax had dimples and Shep's blue eyes seemed to glow. Yup, these boys were just as lethal as Brendan, especially when they smiled.

"Nice to meet you," Jax said, holding out his hand. Paige stopped scratching Sydney and shook Jax's hand before Shep stepped in and grabbed her hand.

"It's good to put a face to the name," Shep said. "Brendan's talked about you."

He what?

"Now, if you boys don't come over here and give me some sugar I won't be serving you any pancakes," Lula Mae said, crossing her arms.

"Sorry, Grams." Jax walked over to her and gave her a kiss on the cheek.

"Won't happen again," Shep said, giving her a loud smacking kiss on her other cheek.

"It better not." Lula Mae gave them a stern look.

"How you boys doing?" Oliver asked, patting each of them on the back.

"Pretty good; the bar has been busy the last couple of nights," Shep said, leaning back against the counter.

"Did Grace say it was called the Sleepy Sheep?" Paige asked.

"It goes with the whole Shepherd thing."

"Right." Paige nodded.

"I see you haven't moved," Brendan said, coming back into the room. Much to Paige's relief, he was wearing a white T-shirt with red swimming trunks. She didn't need to get all hot and bothered again with all of these men in the room.

"I think Sydney might have switched allegiances," Jax said.

"Me too," Brendan said, smiling at Paige, his eyes lighting up as they traveled up her legs. "Not that I blame her."

Apparently it didn't matter that he was wearing a shirt. There was no skin-to-temperature ratio where he was concerned. He made her hot and bothered anyways. He shouldn't be allowed to look at her like that; it wasn't fair.

"I'm going to start making the pancakes," Lula Mae said, scooping dollops of batter onto the sizzling griddle. "You boys go set the table," she said and made a shooing gesture.

"Yes, ma'am." Shep pushed off the counter and all three of them left the kitchen.

* * *

"So that's her." Jax leaned back to look at Paige through the kitchen doorway.

"Yeah," Brendan said, going over to his grandmother's china cabinet and pulling out a stack of dishes.

"Damn those legs are long," Shep whispered, leaning over Jax's shoulder to get another look at her too.

"I will kill the both of you," Brendan said, putting the dishes down on the table and folding his arms across his chest.

Both men turned back to him, grinning.

"Grace wasn't kidding." Shep raised his eyebrows. "The new girl's got your panties all in a twist."

"Shut up."

"Yes, sir," Jax said, giving Brendan a mocking salute and grabbing the juice glasses.

* * *

Breakfast turned out to be an interesting event with all seven of them crowded around the dining room table. Brendan was conveniently seated next to Paige. He was pretty sure everyone had conspired to make sure they sat next to each other. And she'd been so incredibly flustered it was ridiculous. It probably didn't help her any that he kept deliberately letting his arms and legs brush up against hers. He'd pushed his thigh into hers as he'd passed her the sausage and she'd almost dropped the entire plate into his lap.

"Stop it," she whispered after she passed the plate along.

"Stop what?" he whispered back innocently.

"You know what." She grabbed her napkin and put it in her lap. "You're doing it on purpose."

And he'd continued to do it for the rest of the meal.

When they'd loaded up into Jax's truck, Brendan and Paige magically wound up sitting next to each other in the backseat. Brendan kept up his shenanigans on the drive down to the beach. He really couldn't be held responsible for his actions. Paige was literally pushed up against him and he desperately wanted to turn his face into her neck and just breathe her in. But since it wasn't the right time for that, he made due with letting his arm brush up against hers.

When they pulled into the parking lot of the beach, Brendan jumped out and turned to help Paige get out on his side. She hesitated for a second but then scooted closer to the door. He put his hands on her hips and guided her down in front of him.

"Thank you." She looked up at him.

"No problem," he said, reaching up and pushing a strand of hair behind her ear.

Paige inhaled sharply as his finger grazed her skin. Brendan dropped his hand and stepped back, giving Paige the space to step by him. Grace sidled up to Paige as they all unloaded the stuff from the back. Paige muttered something under her breath that made Grace crack up. Brendan grabbed his bag and a cooler and followed as everyone made their way down to the beach. They stopped where two girls were already spread out on the sand.

Melanie O'Bryan and Harper Laurence were Grace's closest friends. After high school, Mel had gone to Florida State University in Tallahassee. She'd gotten her bachelor's in education and had just moved back to town a couple of months ago. She was now teaching math at the high school. Harper was a massage therapist. She split her time working at a resort on the beach and a spa that was in downtown Mirabelle.

Grace introduced the girls to Paige and then they set up their towels next to them. Brendan watched Paige out of the corner of his sunglasses, trying desperately not to be obvious. She pulled off her tank top and then did a little shimmy getting out of her shorts that nearly killed him. She was wearing a modest green one-piece that did amazing things to her curves.

She lifted her arms to tie her hair up and her bathing suit pulled, showing the side of her left breast where she had a quarter-size birthmark in the shape of a strawberry.

"Did you just groan?" Shep asked, coming up next to him.

"No," Brendan said, taking the beer that Shep handed him.

"Damn, you've got it bad," he said, shaking his head.

"Shut up."

* * *

Three months of being in this stupid town and nothing had gone right. No job, no friends, no social life. And then a week ago Paige had met Brendan, and poof, all of that changed.

She didn't want to like him—she really, *really* didn't. The ache in her chest was just beginning to grow smaller and she knew that Brendan had the potential to crack that wide open. She didn't want to be cracked open. She wanted to be safe and whole but every time he looked at her she just wanted to let herself fall.

Paige put her book down and propped herself up on her

elbows, looking out at the water. Brendan was out there with Jax, Shep, and Mel. All of them had beers in their hands and were talking as the waves rolled in, splashing around them.

Mel and Harper were more than friendly and easy to talk to. They were average height, shorter than Paige, but then again most girls were. Both women were beautiful but in different ways. Mel was slim, with long thin legs and a tiny waist. She had corkscrew honey-blonde curls, amber eyes, and a warm, welcoming face that inspired confidence and trust. Harper was more exotic looking, with long, thick black hair, violet almond eyes, and killer curves.

"You going out there?" Grace asked, rolling over onto her side.

"I was thinking about it."

"Come on." Grace stood up and grabbed her beer. "You coming, Harper?"

"Yeah," Harper said.

Paige grabbed her beer and followed them out toward the water. She hesitated on the hard-packed wet sand and let a wave wash up around her feet. The water was warm but it felt cool against her sun-baked skin. They waded out where everyone else was and joined the circle.

"So, Paige," Mel said, shoving a strand of her curly blonde hair behind her ear. "What did you do in Philadelphia?"

"I worked in the art department of an advertising agency," she answered, taking a sip of beer. "But when they were bought out I lost my job."

"Oh. I'm sorry."

"Don't be." Paige shrugged. "It happens."

"So you moved here after that?" Harper asked.

"No. I moved down here after my boyfriend and I broke up." Paige glanced over at Brendan.

She wasn't sure why she'd just told them that. It wasn't to make sure that Brendan knew she was single or anything. No, she would need him to know that only if she was interested in dating him. Which she wasn't. Not at all. But Brendan didn't say a word and she couldn't read his expression because his sunglasses covered his eyes.

"It seems you haven't had the best of months," Shep said as they all jumped to dodge a wave that would have slapped them in the face.

"No." She shook her head. "But it's getting better," she said, unable to stop herself from looking at Brendan again.

* * *

Brendan's mouth quirked. He couldn't seem to help it when Paige was around. Something about her always made him want to smile. He was also ridiculously happy to hear that she was single. He'd been pretty sure she was, but now that she'd just confirmed it he was ecstatic.

"So what kind of art do you do?" Jax asked.

"Everything really. Painting is my passion, but for the advertising agency I did graphic art, but I didn't enjoy that as much. And I also take pictures."

"I wish I was artistic," Mel said. "But I was only ever good at math. That's why I teach it now."

"What grade?" Paige asked

"Ninth through twelfth. Mirabelle High School is pretty small."

"Go Pirates," Shep said.

"The boys all played baseball together. They won state their senior year and they still bask in the glory of it," Grace said.

"Hey," Brendan said, pointing at Grace. "We're still pretty good."

"Shmeh. You're okay," Grace said, shrugging her shoulders.

"You better watch yourself, Princess," Jax said to Grace. There was something about the way Jax said *princess* that caught Paige's attention. It wasn't a taunt at all. It was a term of endearment.

"So do you guys still play?" Paige asked.

"Yeah. There's a county league," Jax said. "Eighteen and older. I pitch, Shep is shortstop, and Brendan is the catcher."

"So you're still good at catching things?" Paige asked Brendan.

His mouth quirked again. *Was that a challenge?*

"Things I want to catch." And boy, did she fit firmly into that category.

"They have a game this Saturday," Mel said. "You should come."

"I just might."

"Are you a baseball fan?" Jax asked.

"Every once in a while I'd go to some of the Phillies games with my friends."

"The Phillies are okay." Jax nodded.

"But not the best?" Paige asked.

"Nope." He grinned. "That would be the Yankees."

"No, that would be the Red Sox," Grace said.

"Oh great," Mel mumbled. "They've started."

"Listen up, Princess. I don't know how many times I have to tell you, the Yankees are the best," Jax started in on Grace.

Harper rolled her eyes and turned to Paige. "We've heard this argument enough times to last a lifetime. We're going to head in. I'll take those for you." She reached for Paige and Brendan's empty beer cans.

Shep took Jax and Grace's cans, neither of them even acknowledging him as they continued to argue with each other.

"Look at who's won more World Series," Jax said.

"Past winning doesn't prove anything against current talent," Grace snapped back.

Brendan moved in closer to Paige as the others wadded to the shore.

"Do they always do that?" Paige asked, glancing over at Jax and Grace, who were about three yards away and at full volume.

"All the time." He laughed. "Shep, Jax, and I have been fans since we were little. When Grace was six, she started rooting for the Red Sox just to spite us all. She and Jax tend to debate it. A lot."

"I can see." Paige glanced over at them.

"So what happened with you and your boyfriend?"

"We broke up," Paige said, turning back to Brendan. Her mouth turned down into a frown and he wanted to reach out and soothe her lips.

"Yeah." His eyebrows raised. "Why?"

"It didn't work out."

"That's all you're going to tell me?"

"He didn't love me." She shrugged and looked out to the horizon.

"Did you love him?"

"I thought I did," Paige said, looking back to Brendan. He couldn't see her eyes past the dark lenses of her glasses, but there was something about the rest of her face that said pain.

"Yeah," he said, nodding and taking a step closer to her. "I know a little about that."

"Would that be Marty?"

"How do you know about Marty?" he asked, confused. His lips formed a frown that mirrored hers. Thinking about Marty tended to make him scowl.

"Grace and Lula Mae mentioned her and how Sydney hated her."

Brendan laughed. "Yeah, well they had a mutual dislike of each other."

"Did you love her?"

"No." He shook his head. He'd never been in love before.

"What happened?"

"She sailed off with some guy who promised to take her around the world in his boat. She came back six months later. Alone and broke."

"Wow."

"Yeah, it was pretty bad at the time, but I'm grateful it happened. She wasn't the one," he said simply.

"I wish I was that levelheaded."

"Time heals all wounds," he said sagely. Well, maybe not all wounds, but it had healed the whole thing with Marty.

Paige laughed, and he felt it everywhere from his head down to his toes. He could listen to that laugh for a lifetime and never get tired of it. A wave came up and both of them jumped with it. Water splashed up around Paige and hit her in the face. Brendan moved in closer to her and pushed a strand of hair that clung to her cheek behind her ear.

"Thank you," she whispered. There was a moment where they just stared at each other before she dipped her chin. "What's your tattoo of?" she asked, reaching for his left arm. She grabbed his elbow and he let her roll his arm to get a better look.

"It's an oak tree." He tried to focus on anything besides her hands on his skin.

He was unsuccessful.

"It's beautiful," she said, tracing the intricate branches with her fingertips.

If he turned his head just a couple of inches, he'd be able to press his nose into her hair.

Next thing Brendan knew he was underwater, Paige's body firmly pressed against his. They had both lost their balance as a wave crashed down around them. Instinctively, Brendan wrapped his arms around her and pulled them up. She started coughing when they surfaced, her hands gripping his hips for balance.

"You okay?" he asked, on the verge of losing his mind. He could feel every single one of her curves pressed up against his body. He blinked the salt out of his eyes and let go of her.

She took a step back, pulling her sunglasses off her face and wiping her eyes.

"Yeah." She nodded, still coughing. When she caught her breath she looked up at him, her gray eyes wide with shock. "Sorry, I, uh..." She shook her head, still staring at him. "Thanks for pulling me up," she said, putting her glasses back on.

"No problem."

"I, uh, I'm going back up to the beach," she said, backing away from him.

"Okay." He nodded.

She turned around and practically ran out of the water. Brendan turned to see Grace and Jax staring at him— Grace with an excited smile, Jax with an exasperated shake of the head.

Yup, Brendan was sinking fast and he didn't even want to search for an escape hatch.

Chapter Six

Free Falling

Paige woke up early on Monday morning to go running. She'd had to do something or she was going to go crazy. She'd barely slept the night before, tossing and turning and remembering what it felt like to be plastered up against Brendan's body. After the wave incident, Paige had tried her hardest to act like a normal human being, but that was pretty much impossible. She couldn't think clearly around him, couldn't focus on anything but him when he was around. Every time he talked to her she had the urge to pounce on him and kiss him.

Abby had been almost impossible on the phone.

"You were plastered up against his wet, shirtless body? I want exact details, leave nothing out," Abby had begged.

"What's with you? You need to get a boyfriend."

"I can't. No time. Work has been crazy so I choose to live vicariously through you. So start with this tattooed bicep..."

Yup, exactly what Paige needed, to think about Brendan in detail.

At nine that morning, Paige stopped by the funeral home because she needed to tell Mr. Adams she was going to be driving around for the day and looking for pictures to take of the local scenery.

"Good," he said, going through a stack of papers. "We're going to have services on Thursday, Friday, and Saturday, so you'll need to be able to put those tributes together."

Paige stopped by Tara's desk on her way out for a short chat to go along with her morning cup of coffee.

"You have a good weekend?" Tara asked.

"Yeah, painted a little on Saturday and then I went to the beach with Grace and a few people on Sunday."

"One of them being Brendan?" Tara grinned.

"Yes," Paige said, trying to effect an air of nonchalance.

"And?"

"It was uneventful really. Very relaxing."

"Hmm," Tara said, studying Paige's face. "You're really bad at lying. Just admit it already; you have the hots for him."

"Am I that obvious?" Paige asked, pained.

"I've seen you two together only the one time, but I could tell there was something there. And based on what Grace told me, it's mutual. Apparently Brendan's just as obvious. Grace said he couldn't take his eyes off you the entire time you guys were at the beach."

It was suddenly very warm in the office. It must be the coffee. Yeah, the coffee was too warm.

Just as Paige was contemplating grabbing a folder off

Tara's desk and fanning herself with it, the front door opened and she turned to see a yeti in flannel standing in the doorway. He had a long light brown beard growing past his chin and stretching down his chest. His bushy beard and mustache covered the entire lower half of his face. His hair was the same color as his beard and almost just as long. His ponytail reached down to the middle of his back.

"Juris!" Tara stood up. "I'm so glad you got here in time," she said excitedly. "Juris, this is Paige. Paige, this is my husband, Juris."

"It's nice to meet you," Paige said, sticking out her hand.

"You too." He nodded. He let go of her hand, gave Tara a quick kiss on the lips, and walked down the hallway.

"He isn't much of a talker," Tara said with that dreamy look still in her eyes. "At least not with anyone but me."

"Some people are just shy," Paige said, trying to be polite.

"Yes, well, you have fun running around town today."

"I will," Paige said, grabbing her purse and walking outside.

* * *

Paige decided to start with the beach. She'd spotted some shots the day before that she knew would be perfect. There was a large pile of beach wood that had been stacked in front of a patch of grass, the tall feathery stalks swaying in the wind. She took a couple of pictures of the lighthouse, and then climbed the stairs to the top to take some more pictures. She switched filters and angles with every couple of shots. She caught a flock of seagulls as they landed on the beach and stayed around long enough to watch them take off again.

After about two hours on the beach, she drove to a park that sat on the water. There were oak trees covered in moss everywhere. The biggest one was isolated off to the side. The branches formed an odd pattern, making a crisscrossed heart on one side where they grew out of the trunk. The greenish-blue water of the ocean stretched out behind it.

It was stunning.

Paige got out of her Jeep and put the thick strap of her camera around her neck. She stared at the tree for a couple of minutes and tried to figure out how she wanted to capture it. She held the camera up to her eye, focusing in on the tree, and started snapping picture after picture. She stayed at it for almost thirty minutes, moving around the tree slowly. When she finished, she headed back to her car and noticed that the front right tire was flat.

* * *

"B.K., phone's for you."

Brendan turned his head to see a pair of dirty work boots appear next to the car.

"Can't you see that I'm underneath a car?" Brendan asked, scooting out and looking up into Wallace's face.

"Yes, I can. But she specifically asked for you."

"She?" he asked, getting up so fast he almost banged his head on the bumper.

"She didn't give me a name," Wallace called out as Brendan practically sprinted into the office.

"This is Brendan," he said, picking up the receiver.

The other end of the line was silent before he heard a shaky intake of breath.

"It's Paige."

"What's up?" he asked, unable to control the smile that quickly spread across his face.

"I, uh, I have a flat tire."

"Where are you?"

"Ocean Oak Park."

"And you don't know how to change a flat?" he asked, trying not to sound amused.

There was another moment of hesitation.

"No. And even if I did, it wouldn't be of any good to me."

"Why's that?"

"Because I don't have a spare."

"I'll be there in five," he said and hung up the phone. He grabbed some sodas and a bag from the fridge. "Wallace, I'll be back in an hour," he said, walking out to his truck and throwing his stuff into the passenger seat. He jogged back to the shop and found a tire big enough to work as a spare for her Jeep and threw it into the bed of his truck.

Things had a funny way of working out sometimes. All morning Brendan had been going over reasons that he could stop by the funeral home and see Paige, each excuse lamer than the last. But he was at the point where he didn't care how lame he was. He liked her and he wanted to see her.

* * *

When Brendan pulled into the shade of the park he saw Paige sitting on top of a picnic table. She was staring down at the screen of her camera, biting the corner of her lip. She looked up at the tree and then back down to her camera, shaking her head. Brendan pushed his sunglasses to the top of his head, grabbed his loot, and got out of his truck. When he slammed the door shut she looked over at him. She turned her camera off and shoved it into a bag that was on the table.

"Hey," she said, standing up and brushing the back of her orange dress down before she started walking toward him.

"Hi." He walked past her and sat down on top of the picnic table.

"What are you doing?" she asked, spinning around and looking at him. "My Jeep's over there."

"Yes," he said, grabbing a Coke and popping the top. "But lunch is over here."

"I thought you were going to change my flat," she said, frowning.

"I am, after I eat lunch. Care to join me?" He patted the empty space next to him.

"You're serious?"

"Paige, it's almost one o'clock, so I'm going to eat. You can either stand there and watch me, or you can split this Cajun turkey sandwich that my grandmother made," he said, taking the sandwich out of the bag.

She shook her head and smiled.

"You, Brendan King, are a whole mess of trouble," she said, walking over to the bench and sitting down next to him.

"Good choice," he said, handing her half. "What are

you doing out here?" He took a bite of his half of the sandwich.

"Taking pictures."

"For?"

"The tribute program that Mr. Adams wants to start using during the memorial services. He wants to use local pictures instead of the stock pictures that are already in the program."

"That sounds like it's right up your alley."

"It is actually," she said, reaching for the other can of soda and popping the top.

"Don't sound so surprised."

"Why? That I could actually fit in around here? It does surprise me."

"Why?"

"I'm not used to this whole small-town thing, where everybody knows everybody and their business."

"Yeah, that's one of the things about small towns that sucks," he said, opening a bag of chips and holding it out for her.

"You can say that again." She reached for a chip. "Why don't you have oil stains on your hands? I thought all mechanics had oil stains."

"I wear gloves," he said, grabbing a few chips for himself and popping them into his mouth.

"Right." She glanced down and frowned, reaching out for his arm.

"The tree," she whispered, grabbing his elbow and pushing up the sleeve of his shirt.

Her soft, delicate fingers lightly traced the lines of his tattoo. It took only one simple touch from her for him to completely lose his mind again.

"I knew I'd seen it somewhere." She looked up to the oak tree in front of them and then back down to his arm. "Why do you have that tree tattooed on your arm?" she asked, looking up at him.

She must have seen the heated look in his eyes because she let go of him and started blushing.

"Sorry, I just...yesterday when I'd been looking at your tattoo, it just sort of fascinated me, and...and it's that tree," she said, pointing to the tree in front of them.

"It is." He cleared his throat and finished his sandwich. He grabbed an orange from the bag on the table and started peeling it. "My mom loved that tree," he said, looking up at it for a second. "She would bring me and Grace here all the time."

"Loved?" Paige asked.

"She died." He turned to look at her. "Twelve years ago from breast cancer."

"Oh God, Brendan. I'm so sorry."

"I am too. She was a great woman. Grams still can't talk about her without losing it."

"Wait, your mom was Lula Mae and Oliver's daughter?" she asked, confused.

"Yeah." He looked over at her. "I know a little bit about being the center of town talk too. My dad walked out on us before I was born, and Grace's dad, well, no one knows who Grace's dad is. My mom wouldn't tell anybody. That was a source of gossip for years," he said, handing her half of the peeled orange.

The orange was still cold from being in the refrigerator. Brendan stuck a slice in his mouth, the juice bursting across his tongue. Paige sat next to him in silence, eating her half.

"How do you do it?" she asked, looking at him.

"Do what?"

"Accept stuff like that? Move on? I lost my job, my apartment, and my boyfriend all within a span of a few months and I thought that everything was falling down around me. But you? God, Brendan, you had a girlfriend run off with another man, your dad abandoned you, and your mom, she..." Paige trailed off. She looked down at her empty hands shaking her head. "You make my problems look trivial."

"Paige," he said, edging closer to her and pressing his thigh against hers.

She looked at him, her hair falling in her eyes. He reached out and pushed it behind her ear, letting his fingers trail down to her chin.

"That stuff happened over a long span of time, and I've had years to deal with it. You had to deal with a lot over a very *short* amount of time, and it didn't happen so long ago. It isn't trivial," he said, rubbing his thumb across her jaw. "One day, you'll wake up and it won't hurt as bad. You'll be able to move on."

"I think I had that breakthrough a week ago," she whispered, her eyes dipping to his mouth before they came back up to his eyes.

"Really?" He smiled, moving in closer. "And what was the catalyst for that development?" he asked, moving his hand to the back of her head, his fingers tunneling in her hair.

"A cracked radiator," she said, putting her palms on his chest.

He brought her mouth to his. She parted her lips and when his tongue touched hers he lost himself. She tasted like oranges, like the sweetest freaking oranges that he'd ever eaten. He wrapped his free arm around her back, pulling her into his chest as he slanted his mouth over hers, deepening the kiss. One of her hands was in his hair, her nails racking the back of his head.

Brendan pulled back and looked at her, both of them breathing hard. He was still holding her face in one of his hands as he ran his thumb across her lower lip.

"That was..." He couldn't even find the words to describe exactly what it was.

"Yeah." She looked at him, dazed as she fisted her hand tighter in his shirt and pulled him back to her. And then they were off again and neither of them had any desire to come back up for air for a long time.

* * *

Sometime later, Brendan was searching through the back of Paige's Jeep. She was lightheaded from all of the kissing, and the skin around her mouth felt a little raw from Brendan's scruff. But that was a small price to pay because, dear God, she'd never been kissed like that.

"You don't even have the right stuff to change a tire," he said, exasperated. "What happened to all of the tools it came with?" He turned around.

Paige bit her lip. "Um, they're probably in the same place as the spare."

"Which is?" he asked

"I have no idea."

He just smiled and shook his head at her.

"What?" she asked, folding her arms across her chest.

"You're helpless," he said, walking over to his truck.

"Or maybe this is all part of the plan," she said, following him.

"What plan?" he asked, releasing the hitch and pulling it down. He climbed into the back of his truck and unlocked the big metal box that ran along the back of the cab.

"If I knew how to change a tire, and had all of the things to do it, you wouldn't be *here* right *now*."

He looked up as he pulled a bag out of the box. "You make a valid point," he conceded.

"That's what I thought."

"But that's an awful lot of effort just to get me to kiss you," Brendan said, pulling out a jack. He walked to the back and put both items down by the edge before he hopped down in front of her. "I was going to kiss you anyways," he said, stepping into her and kissing the corner of her mouth.

"You were taking an awfully long time to get there." She lightly bit down on his lower lip.

He groaned. "What did you want me to do? Tackle you in front of a beach full of people?"

"That sounds promising," she said against his mouth before she kissed him.

"Mmm-hmm," he hummed in her mouth as his hands came up and gripped her waist. "I think you should stand far, far away from me while I change your flat," he said, pulling his mouth away from hers. "Otherwise I might lose a limb."

"You mean you aren't going to show me how to change it myself?"

"No, then you won't have any reason to call me."

"Oh, I'm sure I'll be able to come up with a few reasons."

"You're dangerous." He let go of her and stepped back. He grabbed the stuff from the hitch and walked to the front of her car. He went back for the spare tire, and after he put it down on the ground he turned to Paige. "You have to stand at least five feet away from me," he said, pointing to a spot behind him.

"I'm staying back," she said, holding her hands up in surrender.

Paige watched from a safe distance away as he put the jack under her Jeep and turned a metal bar. The Jeep slowly raised and when it was far enough off the ground he pulled some tool out of his bag and unscrewed the hubcap. He moved so efficiently, doing something in minutes that would have taken her forever to do. He made it all look so effortless. She wondered if he did everything like that.

"Done," he said, standing up and pulling his gloves off. "I'm hoping that it just needs a plug," he said, picking up the deflated tire. "But I won't know until I get it back to the shop."

Her stomach dropped. She hadn't really thought about replacing the tire. It was one more thing for her to pay for with her nonexistent money.

"I bought those tires last year." She frowned at the tire in his hands.

He put all of his stuff away and hopped down, slamming the hitch shut.

"Follow me back and we'll get it all fixed up."

"Okay," she said, still thinking about the stupid tire. She went to turn away but he snagged her wrist and pulled her into him.

"Hey, what's wrong?"

"How do you know something's wrong?"

He didn't say anything, just raised his eyebrows over his sunglasses and waited for her to answer.

"It's just one more thing that I can't really afford at the moment," she said, waving her hand in the direction of her car. "It stresses me out."

"How about you not worry about it yet." He came in closer, his lips brushing across hers before he kissed her. And any concern for the tire magically disappeared from her otherwise thoroughly occupied brain.

* * *

"We can plug it," Brendan said, coming into the office. He'd told her to wait in there while he checked out her tire. "It's a tiny hole. You probably ran over a nail. We'll get it fixed up."

"Thanks. Just add it to my bill."

"Will do." He nodded. "So you want any company for the rest of the day?"

"What?"

"I can show you around. Take you to all of the best places to get pictures."

"Really?"

"Yeah, I can drive and you can observe. I'd hate for you to miss anything," he said, reaching out and running his hands up her arms.

"So you're going to play hooky from work?" She stepped into him and put her hands on his chest.

"It's one of the perks of being one of the bosses. You can do what you want sometimes."

"And what do you want to do?" she asked, tilting her head to the side.

"Oh, there's a list of things. But none of them would be appropriate at the moment."

"If you go with me, will you tell me about that list?"

"Only if you behave yourself."

"There isn't a chance in hell that will happen." She laughed.

"That's what I was hoping for." He grinned.

* * *

Getting a flat tire was a blessing in disguise. Brendan took Paige all around Mirabelle, showing her places she'd never been before. Apparently there was a lot to see around the little town.

He took her all downtown, showing her the old brick buildings where the WWII troops had stayed. The US Air Force had used Mirabelle's beach to practice water-invasion tactics. He also took her to all six of the light-houses that were scattered around the town, half of which were on Whiskey River.

"So Whiskey River cuts Mirabelle in half," Brendan told her. "It runs all the way from the Gulf of Mexico up into Georgia where it branches off into three other rivers. During Prohibition, it was used to transport alcohol illegally."

"Of course it was," she said, grinning.

"Mirabelle's own Melvin Buffkin was the main supplier. But there were plenty of bootleggers down here who made their own stuff to sell. Well, one day Melvin decided to drive his boat up the river during a really bad storm. He crashed it into a fallen tree and the boat sank, filled with barrels of his famous whiskey. Random barrels washed up for the next couple of years. And that's where you get Whiskey River," he finished.

Brendan took her to a field full of wildflowers that housed about fifteen antique cars. They were mostly rusted out, the doors hanging off the hinges and the springs sticking out of the seats, but they were beyond fascinating and flat-out amazing to capture with a camera.

Brendan told her about growing up in Mirabelle and about all of the trouble he used to get into with Jax and Shep.

"You must have driven your parents crazy."

"Yeah, we did. I remember this one time when Shep's mom caught us playing with fire. We were seven and we went out onto his parents' property and built a bonfire. We thought we were good as gold because we were so far in the woods, but she saw the smoke rising over the trees. I've never seen her angrier in my life, still haven't. All of us were grounded for months. Then when we were thirteen, we stole a bottle of vodka from the Sleepy Sheep. The three of us split it, adding it to the grape soda we found at my house. God, I've never been that sick in my life. I still can't drink vodka or anything grape-flavored."

Paige laughed.

"We were all hell on wheels."

"Sounds like it."

"What about you? What were you like?" he asked, looking at her.

"Trouble." She grinned at him over her shoulder.

"So not much different than now?"

"I have no idea what you're talking about," she said, shaking her head as she peered at him from over the top of her sunglasses that had slid down her nose.

"No, seriously. What were you like? Did you drive all the boys crazy?"

"No, the opposite in fact. I was the tallest in my class from kindergarten until about the eighth grade." She sighed, remembering how tough it really had been growing up. How many times she'd come home crying to her parents because she'd just wanted to fit in. Looked like things hadn't changed much over the years.

"Boys were cruel for the most part until high school. Then they started to like my height. But the girls weren't as accepting. I tended to stand out, and kids who don't fit in usually make good targets. It was really just my best friend, Abby, and me. We were quite the duo."

"Why's that?"

"I was the tallest girl in my class. And Abby, well, Abby was the shortest. She's about five foot two. Her height tends to throw a lot of people off. They aren't expecting what she dishes out."

"Is she intimidating?" he asked.

"Oh yeah. She has been since we were about ten."

Brendan glanced over at her, waiting for her to continue.

"Her dad decided he didn't want to be married with a child, so he left. Very few people get to see her vulnerable side."

"Yeah, that'll do it." Brendan nodded, turning back to the road. "That'll make you tough real fast. What does she do now?"

"PR for a firm up in DC. She really likes it; she's just been crazy busy."

"So are you two still close?"

"Yeah, she was my roommate for the last seven years.

It's crazy not seeing her every day. I think that was part of what made it so hard being here, not having any close friends. I mean, I love my parents, but it's different, you know?"

"Yeah, I know." He looked at her again. "But what about now? Are things still difficult?"

"They're turning up," Paige said. "As it turns out, not everyone around here has a problem with my *alternative ways*."

"Paige, if it means anything to you, I'm glad you're not like anybody from around here."

"That does mean something, Brendan. It means a whole hell of a lot," she said as a large smile spread across her face.

The next couple of hours passed in the same easy conversation. The more they talked, the more it confirmed just how much she liked him. She lost all track of time listening to him. And by seven o'clock, Paige had more pictures than she knew what to do with.

"Where are we going?" she asked as Brendan turned right and started driving toward the beach instead of going straight toward the auto shop. "I already went to the beach."

"Yeah," he said, glancing over at her. "But not at sunset."

When they pulled into the parking lot, Brendan pulled off his socks and shoes and rolled up the hem of his pants. Paige threw her sandals on the floor of his truck and they walked out through the sand. There was a group of teenage girls out by the water, laughing as they kicked at the waves.

"Did you always want to stay here?" Paige asked, looking out at the water.

"Yeah," Brendan answered, playing with a piece of her hair. It was such a simple thing, his hand going around in a slow lazy circle, wrapping her curls around his finger. Every time his hand brushed her shoulder, tingles spread out across her skin. "I mean, don't get me wrong, I get it when people don't want to stay in one place their entire lives, but I never had that bug. This has always been home, where I've belonged even when I really didn't belong. And it's where I want to stay."

"I felt that way about Philadelphia," Paige said. "I thought it was where I was supposed to be. That's why I got so freaked out when everything changed. It wasn't part of my plan."

"And now?"

"Now I'm trying to adapt. Get used to the changes. Stop freaking out."

"How's that working out for you?"

"I'll let you know when I figure it out."

"You do that." He laughed as he stopped walking. He pulled Paige to him, pressing his hand to her lower back. He kept his other hand in her hair, running his fingers through it and down her back. "What about me? Do I freak you out?"

"Yes."

"Why?"

"Because I like you," she whispered, looking him directly in the eyes. The way he was looking at her...God, it made her...she didn't even know.

"Good, because I like you, Paige. I like you a lot."

"You know that after a week?"

"I knew that after a day."

She took a deep breath and let it out on a smile. She

was terrified; there was no doubt about it, but it was a good terrified, a thrilled terrified. Like that feeling she'd gotten the one and only time she'd gone bungee jumping. The first step had scared her beyond words, but the free fall had put her heart in her throat.

* * *

"Finally," Abby just about screamed into the phone.

"What are you talking about *finally*? We met exactly a week ago. That is not a long time to wait to kiss a guy that you just met."

"In this case it is. You and your hot mechanic saga have been driving me insane."

"He is *not* my hot mechanic."

"Right." Abby laughed into the phone. "How long are you going to keep saying that before you realize it isn't true? Did he or did he not say that he likes you?"

"He did, but liking somebody doesn't mean that they're yours."

"Oh boy. You really are clueless."

"Okay, fine. It's true, I like him..." Paige paused, chewing on her bottom lip. "I like him a lot. I just don't want to make this into something before it really is something, you know. I'm...I'm scared."

"Oh, sweetie," Abby said, suddenly getting serious. "I know. But you can't let what that ass-wipe Dylan did ruin this."

"I know. I'm trying."

"Good. Because I've got a good feeling about this guy. Plus I don't want the saga to end."

Chapter Seven

Staking a Claim

Over the next two days, Paige and Brendan exchanged some flirty phone calls and some more-than-flirty texts. Every time Paige's phone beeped she pounced on it, eager to see what he had to say. Apparently he wanted to see her just as badly as she wanted to see him, but after taking off half of the day on Monday he was playing catch-up all day Tuesday and later that night he had baseball practice.

Paige didn't have time to spare either. She'd spent all of Tuesday going through the pictures she'd taken and finding the best ones for the tribute. She edited them for hours, highlighting some colors and fading others, while changing some pictures to black and white. She stayed late that night to finish because the next day she had to do her first tribute.

On Wednesday, Paige spent the day going through the pictures of a man named Talbert Ingrid and creating the tribute for his funeral on Thursday. He'd been eighty-four when he'd died, and his wife, RuthAnne, sat in Paige's office for hours talking about her husband and going through the pictures one by one. It was obvious that the couple had loved each other dearly, and it broke Paige's heart.

She was going to have to get a tougher skin if she was going to survive this job. Otherwise, she was going to be depressed all the time. But even though it was sad, it was amazing to see Talbert's journey through life. RuthAnne came back before they'd closed to see what Paige had done, and even though she'd stayed fairly composed that morning, she'd lost it when she saw the final product. But even through her tears, RuthAnne was incredibly grateful for what Paige had done for her husband.

* * *

Brendan hadn't seen Paige for about forty-eight hours. It was too long. Twenty-four hours had been bad. It was now unbearable. He'd gone home as soon as he'd gotten off work to take a shower and put on a clean pair of jeans and a T-shirt. Now, interestingly enough, he was driving over to her parents' house. He might have *wanted* to see her the day before, but he *had* to see her now. The few conversations they'd had over the phone weren't nearly enough.

He pulled in behind her orange Jeep and practically ran up the stairs to ring the doorbell.

"Brendan." Trevor opened the door. "Come in, come in," he said, moving aside.

"I came by to talk to Paige. Is she busy?" Brendan asked as Trevor shut the door.

"She's out in the back painting," Trevor said, leading

Brendan through a hallway and into the kitchen. Paige's mom was sitting at the kitchen table chopping vegetables and listening to the news on a small TV in the corner.

"Denise," Trevor said as they walked into the room. "You remember Brendan King, that nice young man who's been helping Paige out?" There was something about the way he said *nice young man* that clued Brendan in on the fact that the Morrisons might not be naïve to what was going on between Paige and Brendan.

"Brendan." Denise stood up and wiped her hands on her apron. "Of course I remember you," she said, pulling him into a hug. "How are you?"

"I'm doing good. I just stopped by to talk to Paige, if that's all right."

"Oh, of course it is." Her eyes lit up before she turned and walked over to the fridge. "Would you like some lemonade?" she asked. "It's freshly squeezed."

"I'd love some," he said as she poured two glasses.

"Be a dear and bring some out to Paige. When she gets in her zone she tends to forget about things like drinking and eating," she said, opening the French doors and practically shoving him outside.

Brendan looked around the stunning backyard as he followed the sound of music to a small shed off to the side. When he stepped into the open door, the sight that greeted him almost made him lose his mind.

Paige was wearing a long white button-up shirt that was covered in paint. It reached down to the middle of her thighs where she wasn't wearing anything else. The sleeves were rolled up to her elbows, her hair was thrown up into that messy bun thing that she did, and her feet were completely bare. She was dancing to the blaring music, her hips moving to the beat and her head bobbing. She reached over and dipped her paintbrush into a jar of red paint that was on the table next to her.

Brendan stepped into the shed and put the glasses down on the counter. He turned to lean against the counter and take in the show. It was fascinating watching Paige paint, the way she controlled each stroke. She went to dip her brush into the jar again but stepped back and shook her head. She turned slightly and jumped when she saw Brendan.

"You scared me," she said, reaching up to the stereo and turning down the volume.

"Sorry. You're very entertaining to watch."

"How long have you been watching me?" she asked, a horrified expression on her face.

"Long enough. Are you wearing anything under that?" He gestured to her paint-covered shirt.

"Of course I am," she said, shocked. "Do you think I'd walk around my parents' house in just my underwear?"

"Paige, it doesn't matter the circumstances, a man can dream," he said, grabbing his lemonade from the table and taking a sip. "Your mom gave me that to bring out to you," he said, gesturing toward the other glass. "Right before she pushed me out the back door."

"She did not." Paige grabbed her own glass.

"Oh, she did. She seemed a little anxious for me to come out here and talk to you."

"Yeah, well," she said and brought the glass to her lips so that she didn't have to finish her sentence.

"What's that of?" He walked up to the painting. "Is that the funeral home?"

"Yeah," she said, coming up next to him. "There's this

program where you scan a painting and you can mix the images with a photograph. I'm going to do something for the Web site mixing this painting with a picture I took."

"I'd like to see the final product. This is pretty incredible," he said, pointing to her painting. Her detailing was impeccable. She'd captured the moss hanging on the oaks with skilled perfection. He'd suspected she was good, but he hadn't been prepared for just how talented she actually was. "I'd like to see some of your other stuff sometime."

"Really?" She looked up at him.

"Why do you sound so surprised?"

"I don't know." She shrugged. "I just am."

"Brendan King," a loud voice shouted from over the fence next to them. "What are you doing over there with that girl? Is she trying to get you involved in her Wednesday-night orgies?"

It was very unfortunate that Brendan had decided to take a sip of his lemonade at that moment because he inhaled it and started choking.

"Wednesday-night orgies?" he asked when he could breathe again.

"I might have told Mrs. Forns that that's what takes place here sometimes," she said, putting her glass down on the counter.

"She's trouble, Brendan," Mrs. Forns called out. "I suggest you stay away from her."

"Not going to happen," he called back as he put his glass down and grabbed Paige's arms, pulling her into him. "And I suggest you mind your own business."

Mrs. Forns made an exasperated sound before a door slammed shut.

"I'm covered in paint," Paige whispered as Brendan lowered his face to hers.

"I don't care," he said right before he kissed her.

She wrapped her arms around his shoulders while he gripped her hips and worked his hands down to her thighs. He trailed them under the hem of her shirt and felt material just a little bit farther up.

"I told you I was wearing shorts," she said against his mouth.

"Yes, but I had to investigate. It was necessary."

"Hmm," she hummed against his mouth before she opened hers.

She tasted like the lemonade that they'd been drinking. At the rate they were going, he wasn't going to be able to look at citrus the same way.

"So tell me about these orgies." He brought his hands back to her hips.

"It was just something I said to piss her off," she said, breathless.

"Oh." He laughed. "So it was just you being your usual charming self?" He put his mouth against her jaw.

"Pretty much." She sucked in a shallow breath as he pressed his open mouth against her skin.

"So there's no truth to them?"

She shook her head and let it roll back as he continued his journey down her neck and to her collarbone. "You've got nothing to worry about."

"Good, 'cause I would've gotten territorial," he said, bringing his mouth back to hers.

Paige moved her hands up and grabbed onto the front of Brendan's shirt. She pulled her mouth back from his and looked him in the eyes.

"Is this you staking a claim?" she asked like it was a joke. But she couldn't hide the vulnerability in her soft gray eyes.

He reached up, tracing the shell of her ear with his fingers. She closed her eyes and leaned into his touch. She had a green smear of paint along her freckled cheek. A few short strands of her soft brown hair were too short to pull back into her bun and they curled around her temples. Her full lips were slightly parted, her breath washing out of her mouth as her chest fell and rose.

Paige Morrison was without a doubt the most beautiful woman he'd ever seen in his life. And here she was in his arms, asking him what he wanted.

"Paige."

She opened her eyes and looked at him.

"I want to be with you. I want to date you, and touch you, and kiss you. And I want to be the only one who gets to do those things," he said, bringing his hand back down to her chin. "Do you want that? Do you want to be with me?"

"Yes," she whispered.

"Can I take you to dinner on Friday?"

"Yes." She nodded.

"Seven?"

"Yes."

"Can I kiss you again?"

"Yes," she said, and the smile that spread across her face was so contagious that he couldn't help but mirror it.

* * *

Brendan stayed for dinner. He sat next to Paige, eating chicken stir-fry and laughing at the stories her dad told him about being a high school history teacher. And he listened to her mom talk about being a nurse practitioner for thirty-five years. They continued to talk for a good amount of time after dinner; all the while, Brendan rested his arm on the back of Paige's chair and twirled a strand of her hair around his finger.

After dinner, Brendan asked Paige if he could see some of her work.

She showed him a painting of a field of pink and yellow tulips, one of two swans floating in the middle of a pond, one of a forest with a stream running under a bridge, another of a woman dancing in a red dress in the middle of a crowd of black-and-white people, and one of a field of pine trees covered in snow.

There were some from when she'd gone crazy with a peacock color scheme. Using the colors of submerged purple flowers over green rocks, making the petals look like the eyes in the feathers. Another was of a brilliant blue sky over a field of violets, the flowers stretching up to the skies and swaying in the breeze like feathers. And then some of the paintings were of actual peacocks.

She had a book filled with her photography. There were multiple pictures of sunsets, parks, and birds in flight. Close-ups of different flowers in bloom, and others of vast fields. There was one of people running through a giant puddle on what Paige remembered to be a particularly cold and rainy day in Philadelphia.

She also had quite a few other creations. She'd found two old windowpanes at an antique store. On one, she'd stained the wood a dark brown and painted the glass with varying shades of oranges, yellows, and reds, making it look like there were autumn leaves embedded in the glass. The other window was bright blue and green, with daisies printed on the glass. There were pieces of aluminum siding on which she'd painted the words *love*, *hope*, *peace*, and *dream*. Each piece was only one word but she'd repeated it in dozens of different colors, sizes, and print, all of them overlapping but still clearly visible.

"You're really talented," he said, looking up at her with a gleam in his eyes.

His words affected her more than they should have. She really didn't want to examine the overwhelming pleasure that his approval brought her. He wanted to know where she got her inspirations from, how long it took her to finish a painting, which one was her favorite. He asked her question after question and she could tell that the interest in his eyes was genuine.

Dylan had never really been interested in Paige's work. For the most part, he'd just look at it and say, "Well, that's nice," before he returned to whatever he was doing. He never asked questions, and whenever she tried to talk something out with him, he would give her a few perfunctory responses before he would change the subject. He hadn't cared about her work. He hadn't cared about her.

Brendan was different from Dylan in so many ways. The more she learned about Brendan, the more she liked him, and the more she wanted to learn about him. She was surprised at how much she'd opened up to him in such a short period of time, and it was still more than just a little bit scary for her.

When Paige walked Brendan out to his truck that night, he pushed her up against the door and kissed her until she forgot her own name.

"I want to see you tomorrow," he told her.

"When?"

"Lunch?"

"I can't. I'm going to your grandmother's for lunch."

"Oh yeah." He grinned. "You're part of their Thursday-afternoon gossip fest."

"Tomorrow night?"

"Can't. I have baseball practice."

"So Friday then," she said, disappointed that she had to wait that long to see him.

"I don't know if I can handle that. I'll have to think of something," he said before he leaned in for another kiss.

* * *

Paige was still giddy on Thursday when she walked into work. She kept biting the corner of her lip in an attempt to hide her smile, but there really wasn't anything for it. Short of wearing a mask, there was nothing she could do to hide how she felt.

"What's with you?" Tara asked as they sipped their coffee in the kitchen.

"Nothing." Paige shook her head.

"I don't believe you," Tara said. "You're practically glowing."

"Must be the sun," Paige said, looking at her coffee. "I'm just tan."

"Right," Tara said slowly. "Oh great," she muttered under her breath a second later. "The witch is back."

Paige looked up as a petite blonde woman with overly teased hair, a pointy nose, and equally pointy heels walked down the hallway. The *witch's* eyes narrowed on Paige as she walked into the kitchen and came up to them.

"Missy," Tara said, switching into southern belle mode. "This is Paige Morrison. Mr. Adams hired her last week. Paige, this is Missy Lee. She's the assistant funeral director."

"And the great, great, great-niece of one Robert E. Lee," Missy said, letting her southern twang loose on every single syllable.

"It's nice to meet you," Paige said, sticking out her hand.

"Likewise," Missy said through a saccharine smile. "A real *pleasure.* I've heard that you're to *thank* for our new *renovations.*" She gestured to the hardwood floor out in the hallway. "How *creative* of you."

Every word she emphasized felt like an insult.

"Thank you?" Paige asked.

"How was the conference?" Tara asked, changing the subject.

"Very informative," Missy said, but didn't elaborate on anything that she'd been "informed" about. "You come to me if you have any *questions* or *ideas* about *anything,*" she said to Paige. "I'd be more than *happy* to help you. You two have a *great* day," she said and then walked out of the kitchen.

"Is she a pod person?" Paige whispered.

"Probably."

"That was the weirdest freaking conversation I've ever had."

"Get used to it. And I'm not joking when I say watch your back when it comes to her."

"Why?"

"I'll tell you at lunch," Tara said, getting more coffee. "Too many ears around here, even the dead ones."

* * *

"From what we've gathered, Missy Lee has been married four times and engaged seven," Pinky said over her Caesar salad.

"You're joking," Paige said.

"Nope," Tara said. "And two of them died."

"You're serious?"

"The second and fourth," Panky said, holding up her fingers.

"To be fair," Grace added, "the second one was very old."

"How old?" Paige asked.

"Seventy?" Lula Mae shrugged and looked around the table for affirmation.

"About that." Grace nodded.

"How old was she?" Paige asked, both disgusted and perversely fascinated.

"Oh, she was twenty-seven when she was married to Rubel Ruffin," Lula Mae said.

"Rubel?" Paige asked bewildered.

"Yes." Panky nodded.

"Ruffin?" she asked, saying it slowly.

"Yes," Pinky said.

"And he was forty-three years older than her?"

"Yup," Grace said.

"That's disgusting." Paige pushed her empty plate away and took a sip of her tea.

"Just imagine all that loose skin," Pinky said. "And his old balls."

Paige choked, spitting tea all over the table. Tara and Grace snorted.

"Pinky," Panky said, scandalized. "I can't believe you just said that."

"I'm just speaking the truth," she said with absolutely no repentance. "The sex was probably horrible."

"Pinky." Panky shook her head, her soft red curls bouncing around her shoulders. "Do you filter anything that comes out of your mouth?"

"Now, where would the fun be in that?" Pinky said. "Anyways, the fourth one died in some sort of freak hunting accident."

"Freak?"

"Yeah, he shot himself in the foot or something."

"Or something?" Paige asked.

"Well, it was a little fishy. But Missy was never implicated," Grace said.

"What happened to the first husband?"

"Divorced, and the third one as well," Lula Mae said.

"And she made a killing on both of them," Panky added.

"That's one of the most bizarre things I've ever heard." Paige leaned back in her chair. No wonder she needed to watch her back. The woman was a gold-digging, bad-luck charm. "What about all of the engagements?"

"She only married locals the first and second time," Grace explained. "The others she tends to find online. She sets her hooks in them—"

"Fangs more like it," Panky said. "That woman is a black widow."

"Yeah," Grace said. "She is a black widow. So anyways, she gets her fangs in them, gets them to propose, and then keeps the ring. I don't know who her next victim is though."

"Geez." Paige shook her head.

"Yeah, so be careful around her," Tara said. "She's very manipulative."

"Enough about Missy," Pinky said. "What's going on with you, Paige? Delta Forns came in to get her roots touched up. She told me that Brendan came over to your parents' last night."

Paige's eyes nearly bugged out of her head.

"So that's why you were glowing," Tara said, slapping the table.

"You were with Brendan last night?" Lula Mae asked. The bell rang and her eyes flickered to the door behind Paige.

"Glowing?" Grace smiled. "Why would Brendan make you glow, Paige?"

"Yeah," a deep voice said in her ear. "Why would I make you glow?"

Paige jumped out of her seat as Brendan pressed his lips to her neck.

"Hi, ladies," he said as he walked over to Lula Mae and kissed her on the cheek.

"What are you doing here?" Paige looked over at him, her mouth hanging open.

"I'm going to drive you back to work. You guys done?"

"We haven't had dessert yet," Grace said, standing up. "Sit down." She gestured to the now vacant seat next to Paige. "I'll go get it."

"I'll help you," Pinky said, standing up too. "Tara, why don't you help us?"

"Panky," Lula Mae said, pushing her chair back. "Let me show you that thing I was telling you about."

"Oh, yeah." Panky nodded, following her. "That *thing*."

"Well..." Brendan laughed as he pulled a chair close to Paige and sat down. "I've never seen them scatter faster in my life."

"You know that they're all watching us."

"Then let's give them something to watch," he said before he leaned in to kiss her.

"Stop it." She smiled and pushed him away.

"Why?" he asked lightly, pressing his mouth to her jaw before he sat back in his chair.

"Because there are people everywhere." She looked around the small café. But no one was even paying attention to them.

"Do you not want people to know that we're together?" he asked, raising an eyebrow.

"No, it's not that." She shook her head. "I just don't want to be the center of more town gossip."

"Oh, sweetie," Pinky said, coming back to the table with Grace and Tara, their hands full of bowls of banana pudding. "If Delta Forns knows about the two of you, then everyone knows about the two of you." She sat down in a chair.

"Yeah," Grace said as Lula Mae and Panky sat down. "I heard about the two of you making out all over town on Monday."

"Oh my God." Paige put her hands to her flaming cheeks. This couldn't be happening; this just could *not* be happening. "How?" she asked, looking around the table. "How does everyone know?"

"Paige, if you're going to live in a small town, you need to understand that if one person sees something interesting, it's pretty much going to be news," Panky said, shoving a spoonful of pudding into her mouth.

"Hell, if you get a speeding ticket around here they put it in the paper," Pinky said.

"Please tell me we aren't in the paper." Paige gave Brendan a pleading look.

"You all are freaking Paige out," Brendan said, putting his hand underneath her elbow and pulling her to her feet as he stood up. "We're going to take these to go," he said, picking up Paige's bowl and handing it to her. He grabbed his own and put his free hand on her back. "You ladies have a nice rest of the day. Come on, Paige." He guided her out the door.

He kept his hand on her back as they walked to his truck. He let go of her as he opened the door, grabbed the pudding from her, and put both bowls down on the seat. He grabbed her waist and pulled her into him, his hands on her back and his lips coming down hard on hers.

"I've wanted to do that since I walked in there," he said against the hollow of her ear. "God, you smell good." His mouth trailed down and he pressed his nose into her neck. "How do you smell this good? Like oranges and vanilla only so much better. Mmm," he hummed against her skin.

"You work with men and cars all day. You haven't got much to compare me to."

He pulled back so he could look at her. "No, Paige," he said and shook his head. "There's nothing that compares to *you*."

Chapter Eight

The Ugly-Underwear Theory

P aige was wrapped in just a towel as she searched for something to wear. She had exactly twenty minutes before Brendan was supposed to pick her up. There was a knock on her door as her hands closed over a pair of jeans.

"Come in," she called over her shoulder.

The door opened and Paige turned, throwing her jeans onto her bed.

"What time is he picking you up?" Denise asked as she stuck her head inside the doorway.

Paige had a sudden flashback to high school when her mother would help her get ready before a date. She immediately thought of Brendan and Grace and how their mother had died when they were both so young. They'd missed out on so much, especially Grace. Paige couldn't imagine not having all of those years with her mother and she felt intensely grateful for every single one of them.

"At seven. You busy?"

"No." Denise shook her head.

"Will you sit and talk with me while I get ready?" Paige asked.

"Yeah," Denise said, her mouth breaking into a smile. She opened the door farther and walked into the room, a glass of wine in hand. She shut the door behind her and sat down on the edge of Paige's bed, just like old times. "What are you going to wear?" she asked, grabbing a pillow and playing with the frilly lace edging.

"Jeans." Paige pointed to the pair on her bed. "I haven't decided on a shirt though," she said and turned back to her closet.

"Shoes?"

"My black wedges." She thought it was appropriate, as she'd been wearing them the first time she'd met Brendan.

"What about your red peasant top. The one that hangs off your shoulders and hugs your waist."

Paige grabbed the shirt and turned around, holding it up to show her mom.

"Red on a first date?"

"You look good in red," Denise said.

"You don't think it's too much?"

Her mother gave the blouse a critical eye. "Just wear ugly underwear. If you wear stuff that you don't want him to see, you'll be less likely to sleep with him."

"Mom!" Paige said, shocked. "I'm not going to sleep with him on the first date."

"I know. Just wear something to keep you grounded, and then you won't slip."

"I have some self-control."

"Yes, well, I've seen that boy. Slipping would be completely justifiable considering the circumstances."

"What circumstances would those be?" Paige asked as she walked over to her dresser and opened her underwear drawer.

"That gleam in his eyes."

"What gleam?" Paige asked, turning to her mom.

"The one he gets when he's looking at you. It's something that goes way beyond sex."

"Well, he *is* a nice young man," Paige said mockingly.

"Yes, he is." Denise nodded, taking a sip of her wine.

Paige turned back around to her dresser. She riffled through her drawer, looking for this supposed ugly underwear that would keep her grounded, but she didn't own any. Along with shoes, another one of her vices was fun panties. What was the point in buying anything ugly?

She grabbed a fairly tame pair with yellow and white stripes. Stripes didn't scream "I'm going to have sex tonight," at least not like black or red lace would have. She could've sworn she'd read that stripes were unflattering on most people.

She dug around in the drawer and found her strapless bra. She grabbed her clothes from the bed and went into the bathroom.

"So where is he taking you?" her mother asked through the door.

"To Caliente's, and then we're going to Shep's bar." Paige hung her towel on the back of the door and started to get dressed. "Are you and dad still going to go to the baseball game tomorrow?"

"Yes."

"I'm going to go with you guys and then leave with Brendan. They're doing a cookout at Shep's house," Paige said as she struggled into her skinny jeans.

"Oh, that'll be fun. His friends are nice?" Denise asked.

"Yeah."

"So the whole town doesn't have it out against you?"

"It would seem that isn't the case," Paige said as she pulled her shirt over her head.

"So you don't hate it as much down here anymore?"

"No. It's a lot better now," Paige said, opening the door.

"You look beautiful." Denise smiled.

"Are you sure it isn't too much?" Paige asked, fidgeting with the sleeves on her shirt.

"No, not at all. What are you doing with your hair?"

"I was just going to wear it down," Paige said, pulling the clip out of her hair and flipping her head over. She fluffed her messy curls with her fingertips and flipped her head back.

"I wish I had your hair," Denise said ruefully as she ran her fingers through her own straight bob. "Those curls of yours are just so beautiful."

"So is your hair, Mom." Paige walked over to her mother and kissed her on the forehead. "Thanks for helping me get ready."

"Paige," Denise said, grabbing her hand before she moved away. "I know the circumstances that got you here weren't the best. And I know you've had a rough couple of months, but I'm glad you're here. I've missed you, Little Miss."

"Thanks, Mom." Paige tightened her hand around her mother's.

"I'm also happy you're smiling again."

The doorbell rang and Denise squeezed Paige's hand

twice before she let go. A fresh wave of nerves ran through Paige's stomach and she took a deep breath, trying to steady herself. She shouldn't be nervous. She'd dated before. This was nothing new or different. Except with Brendan everything was new and different.

"Wear those dangly black earrings," Denise said, standing up. "No necklace."

Paige heard her father answer the door and a second later his and Brendan's voices echoed down the hallway.

Paige went to her dresser and found the black earrings, sticking them into her ears. She put on a couple of rings and then slipped her shoes on. She stood in front of her mother and waited for the final verdict.

"Perfect," her mother said, scooping Paige's purse off the bed and handing it to her.

Paige followed her mom out the door and down the hallway. As they rounded the corner, she saw Brendan and her father laughing. When Brendan saw her, his laugh died and he took a deep breath as he stared at her. His eyes traveled down the length of her body and then back up again to her eyes.

He didn't look half bad himself in a light gray polo and faded jeans that hugged his thighs and, she suspected, his very nice butt.

"Well, you two have fun," Denise said and stood up on her tiptoes to kiss Paige on the cheek. "And no sex," she whispered to Paige.

"Oh God." Paige's cheeks immediately started flaming. Her mother was talking about sex with Brendan while he was less than four feet away. Paige just couldn't handle it. "You ready?" she asked, looking at Brendan with pleading eyes.

"Yeah. It was nice talking to you, Mr. Morrison. You two have a good night."

"You too, but just not *too* good of a night," Trevor said.

"Oh jeez. Bye, Daddy." Paige kissed her father on the cheek before she shoved Brendan out the front door.

* * *

Paige was incredibly flustered as Brendan walked her out to his truck. Truth be told, so was he. She was wearing the tightest pair of jeans he'd ever seen, a red shirt that exposed her freckled shoulders and hugged her very nice curves, and those black wedges that drove him out of his mind. When he'd seen her, all of the blood had drained from his head and gone south.

"What did your mom say to you?" he asked, helping her into his truck.

"Don't worry about it," she said as her cheeks flamed again.

"Oh come on," he said, holding onto the door as she settled in the seat. "She said something to get you all flustered."

"I'm not flustered," she said, her voice going up an octave.

"You're a bad liar." He shut door.

When he got into his side of the truck, he shut the door and slid to the middle, pressing Paige up against the back of her seat. She gasped right before he covered her mouth with his. Her hands fisted in his shirt. God, he loved it when she did that.

"You look beautiful," he said against her lips.

"So do you," she said, dazed.

"I look beautiful?" he asked, pulling back to look at her face.

"Yes. You, Brendan King, look beautiful."

"Aw, Paige, you're going to make me blush." He grinned.

"I don't think I could make you blush if I tried."

"Oh, I disagree with you there." He shook his head as he came in for another kiss.

After a couple more minutes, he retreated to his side of the car.

"You're dangerous," he said, shaking his head as he put his truck into gear.

"I'm dangerous?" she asked. "You started it."

"I suppose I did." Brendan smiled. "So how was your first entire week of work? Any more interesting encounters?"

"No. Verna's pretty much ignored me since she yelled at me last week."

"What about Missy?"

"Every time I go downstairs, she heads me off in the hallway. She wants me to run everything by her before I run it by Mr. Adams. *It's a way to be more efficient*," she said, imitating Missy's thick southern drawl.

"You do that pretty well." He laughed.

"Why, thank you," she said, still sounding like Missy.

"But seriously, watch out for her," Brendan said. "My mother grew up with her and she can be nasty."

"Aww, are you worried about me, Mr. King?" she asked playfully.

"Yes." He looked over at her.

Something in her eyes flickered as he held her gaze but she didn't break eye contact.

"Well, thank you," she said softly and smiled.

Instinctively, he let go of the steering wheel with his right hand and grabbed hers, lacing his fingers through hers.

* * *

Almost every single guy stared at Paige as they walked through Caliente's. Brendan had his hand at the small of her back to make sure that all of those wondering eyes understood that she was off the market. He let go only when he went to help her into her chair.

"What would you like to drink?" the waiter asked as he handed them menus.

"I'd like a margarita," Paige said. "Frozen with extra salt."

"Make that two." Brendan held up two fingers.

"So what's good?" Paige asked as she opened her menu and stared down.

"Everything. What are you in the mood for?" he asked, watching her.

"I haven't had enchiladas in forever, but the steak fajitas sound amazing."

"Let's get both and share."

"Really?" she asked, looking up at him, genuine shock on her face.

"I don't mind sharing with you." He'd had his tongue down her throat on multiple occasions. Sharing food wasn't that big of a deal.

The waiter came over a second later and gave them their margaritas, a bowl of golden-yellow tortilla chips, and salsa. Brendan handed him the menus and gave him their order.

"So," he said, looking at Paige, "you going to tell me what your mom said to you?"

"Nope." She grabbed her margarita. Her tongue darted out onto the rim of the glass, grabbing some of the salt before she took a sip of the lime green slush.

"Aww, come on," he said, still watching her mouth in fascination.

"Uh-uh," she said, shaking her head. "I'm not going to tell you."

"You know, Paige, starting off a relationship with secrets is never a good thing."

"If I told you everything," she said, grabbing a chip and breaking it in half, "there would be no mystery." She dipped her chip into the salsa and scooped some up, bringing it to her mouth. "And where would the fun be in that?" she asked after she swallowed.

She was going to torture him throughout the entire dinner. There was no way he was going to survive it. He reached out and grabbed his drink, desperately needing something to cool himself down with. It would've been more effective if he just poured the drink directly onto his lap.

* * *

Dylan had never shared food with Paige. He would hoard his plate on his side of the table and if she asked for a bite he would get annoyed with her.

"If you wanted this, why didn't you just order it?" he would always ask.

But Brendan had no problem with it.

They ate their way through both plates and a second

margarita each. All the while, Brendan told her about playing baseball in high school and about the team he played on now.

"So you've always played with Jax and Shep?" she asked, chasing some enchilada sauce around her plate with a chip.

"Yup, since we were five."

"Wow. That's crazy."

"What about you? Did you ever play any sports?"

"Cross-country. But that isn't really a team sport."

"Oh yeah. You and those long legs of yours," he said, grinning at her. "You must have left everyone else in your dust."

"Sometimes."

"You'd leave me in the dust."

"How do you know?"

"I've seen you running around town before. You and those crazy shorts of yours," he said, finishing his drink.

"What's so crazy about my shorts?" she asked.

"Would you like to discuss length or color? Because both are fascinating topics."

"They aren't *that* short."

"Right."

"They aren't," she said, indignant. "They just look short because I have long legs."

"Hmm." He leaned back in his chair so he could see her legs under the table. "I might need to see said shorts on you again. I observed you from a distance. Maybe upon closer inspection I'd come to a different conclusion."

The waiter came back with Brendan's credit card. He signed the receipt and stood up, shoving his wallet into his back pocket.

"You ready?" he asked, holding out his hand.

"Yes," she said, putting her hand in his and letting him pull her up next to him.

He laced his fingers with hers again, and just like it had in the car, it sent a thrill of excitement through her.

* * *

The Sleepy Sheep was a landmark in Mirabelle. Shep's grandparents had built it when they'd moved down about sixty-five years ago. It looked like a Scottish pub and the locals and tourists loved it. There were large, paned windows on either side of the front door and a hanging sign above the door that swayed in the warm beach breeze. It read THE SLEEPY SHEEP in big green letters, and two sheep slept in the corner, Zs trailing above their heads.

"This looks like fun," Paige said as they walked inside.

The same dark wood that was outside also covered the walls, floors, and ceiling on the inside. There were framed cartoon pictures of drunken sheep everywhere, and all of the other wall space was covered in signed dollar bills. The bar took up the entire back wall, while booths were lined up on the walls to the left. There were dozens of tables surrounded by chairs scattered all over the floor. To the right, there were two pool tables and a dartboard. There was a stage in the far corner where a live band played sometimes. But tonight, music blared from the jukebox.

Brendan placed his hand firmly on Paige's lower back as he guided her through the bar. Again, men's heads turned as they walked past their tables. Shep looked up as he passed a beer to a man across the counter. He grinned when he spotted the two of them.

"You two are going to have an audience tonight," he said as he walked over to them.

"Who?" Brendan asked.

Shep pointed behind them, and Brendan turned around to see Grace and Mel at one of the pool tables. Grace waved and took a sip of her drink.

"Why does that not surprise me?" Brendan asked, turning back to the bar.

"What do you guys want?" Shep asked, wiping a towel across the counter.

"Just a beer for me," Brendan said.

"Same," Paige said.

"Got it." Shep grabbed two frosted mugs and brought them to the tap.

"I like your place," Paige said as Shep filled one glass and put it down in front of her. "It reminds me of this bar that I used to go to in Philly."

"But mine's better, right?" he asked as he started to fill the other glass.

"Oh, undoubtedly," she said, grabbing her beer and taking a sip.

"Good answer," Shep said, putting the other glass down in front of Brendan. "I'll have a beer with you in a little while," he said, moving back down the bar to a waiting customer.

"Let's go say hey, and then we'll find a seat," Brendan said, moving his hand to the side of her waist and lightly squeezing.

"All right." She nodded.

Brendan led her across the bar to the pool table where Grace and Mel were playing.

"Fancy seeing you here," Brendan said as they stopped in front of Grace.

"It's Friday night. I like to hang out here too." Grace leaned back against the table. "I have no need to spy anyways. I've already seen the two of you in action."

"Thanks, Grace," he said, shaking his head.

"You two want to play?" Mel asked, coming up to them. "You any good?" she asked Paige.

"I'm okay." Paige shrugged her shoulders. "Nothing spectacular, but I'd like to play."

False. She was in fact incredibly spectacular. Proof in point, the fact that half of the men in the bar were still staring at her. Hell, he was staring at her. He hadn't been able to take his eyes off her all night.

"We can play teams." Brendan put his beer down at the high-top that was next to the pool table. "Me and Paige against you two."

"You're about to get your ass kicked," Grace said, putting on what Brendan knew to be her game face.

"Not before I kick yours," Brendan countered.

"And the trash talk begins," Mel said as she went to rack up the balls.

Brendan let go of Paige, something he really didn't want to do, and walked over to the pool cues. He grabbed two and walked back to the table. Paige was laughing at something that Grace had said, her head tilted back and her smile wide. Brendan came up behind her, his hand sliding around her waist as he pressed his lips against her throat.

Paige's hand came to a rest on his, holding his arm

around her waist. She turned her head to look at him and he leaned in closer, pressing a soft kiss to her mouth.

"You ready to play?" Grace asked, sounding exasperated.

"Yup," Brendan said, looking at his little sister. "You break."

He didn't let go of Paige as Grace made the first shot, the two going in the corner pocket.

"We're solids," Grace called as she moved around the table to line up another shot. She hit the four into the side pocket, but missed the seven.

"You go." Brendan let go of Paige.

"All right," she said, stepping around the table.

Grace had set Paige up for an easy shot in the corner pocket. Paige made the shot and moved around to line up her next shot right in front of Brendan. As she bent over, the hem of her shirt pulled up, exposing the small of her back. She had a tattoo of a dove on the right side of her back, the tail wrapping around her hip while one of the wings dipped down beneath her jeans.

"Well, isn't that pretty," someone said in Brendan's ear.

Brendan looked over at Shep, who was sipping on a beer and staring at Paige, who was currently still bent over.

"You better look at something else; otherwise I might be forced to punch you in the face."

"I was merely referring to the art on your girlfriend's back," Shep said, turning to Brendan. "And judging by that stunned look on your face, I'm guessing you appreciate it too."

"Appreciate what?" Paige asked, coming up to them.

"The beer," Shep said, holding up his glass. "It's a new brew."

"I like it," Paige said, grabbing her glass and taking a sip.

"So does Brendan." Shep smiled.

Oh yeah, he liked it all right. And he really wanted to see the whole thing with a private, up close and personal view. But that wasn't going to happen anytime soon, so for the present he had to distract himself with playing pool.

They lost the first game. Most likely due to the fact that Paige's tattoo kept playing peekaboo and Brendan couldn't concentrate for shit.

"You okay?" Paige asked him as Grace racked up the balls for the next game. "You seem tense."

Oh, he was tense all right.

He focused more during the second game, wrapping it up quickly as he shot the last of their three balls and finished with the eight ball in the side pocket.

"You ready to call it a night?" Brendan asked, walking up to Paige.

Disappointment flickered on her face for a second before she nodded.

"I just meant call it a night here," he whispered, leaning into her ear and pressing an open-mouthed kiss to her neck.

"We're going to go," Paige said quickly, pulling away from Brendan and grabbing her purse. "I'll see you guys tomorrow?" she asked Grace and Mel.

"We'll be there." Mel nodded.

"Have a good night," Grace said, waggling her eyebrows at the two of them.

Brendan shook his head at Grace and guided Paige to the bar. They said good night to Shep and walked out to Brendan's truck.

"So," Brendan said when they were back on the road. "You didn't tell me you have a tattoo."

"Who said I have only one?"

He turned to her so quickly that he almost drove off the road.

"Where are the other ones?" he asked quickly.

"That's for me to know," she said coyly.

"And for me to find out?"

"Maybe."

"You don't play fair." He turned back to the road.

"You're a fine one to talk about playing fair, Mr. King."

"What do you mean?"

"Back there," she said, "if you'd kissed my neck one more time I was going to spontaneously combust."

"Good to know I have that effect on you."

"Oh shut up, you know you have that effect on me."

"Maybe I've noticed something," he said. "So you going to tell me what your mom said to you before we left?"

"She told me not to have sex with you tonight."

This time Brendan did swerve off the road.

"Are you trying to kill us?"

"You asked," she said.

"Yeah, but you've been refusing to tell me all night, and then you finally decide to tell me when I'm driving?"

"I was just checking to see how big of an effect I have on you."

"Maybe you shouldn't test that when I'm driving a vehicle," he told her.

"I'll keep that in mind."

"So is that why you practically ran out of the house when I picked you up? Because your mother was telling you not to sleep with me?"

"Yeah, that and I felt like my dad was about to pull out his old go-to lecture that he told every boy I dated in high school."

Brendan laughed. "It did feel a bit like I was picking you up for a high school date."

"What did you do for dates when you were in high school? *Go wrastle gators?*" she asked, putting on a thick southern accent.

Brendan really, really needed to not think about wrestling at the moment.

"No." He shook his head. "We dressed up in camo and covered ourselves in buck urine."

"Disgusting." She laughed.

"So what was your dad's lecture?" he asked.

"Oh, you know. 'Break my daughter's heart and I'll break you.' That or he promised to fail them whenever they took his class."

"Sounds tame compared to what my grandfather and I used to do to Grace's dates."

"Oh dear, what did you two do?" she asked eagerly.

"We would sit on the front porch with shotguns. Neither of us saying a word."

"How did she not kill you?"

"Oh, she threatened to more times than I can count."

"I'm surprised she didn't follow through," she said.

"Me too." He laughed.

He pulled up in front of her parents' house and turned off his truck.

"So you know how I said that when I picked you up I felt like we were in high school again?" He unbuckled his seat belt and then hers.

"Yeah." She smiled as he pulled her toward him.

"Well, I was thinking," he whispered against her mouth, "that we could make out in my truck and blow your curfew."

"I should warn you," Paige said, pressing herself up against him. "I might be just a little bit tipsy." She held her hand up, a small gap between her thumb and index finger.

"I can handle that," he said right before she opened her mouth on his and sucked his bottom lip into her mouth.

They began to attack each other's mouths. Her hands were in his hair, her fingers kneading the back of his head. Brendan had no idea where he wanted to put his hands because he wanted to put them *everywhere*. They were in her hair one second and then on her thighs the next. Before he knew what he was doing, his hands wrapped around her waist and he pulled her out of her seat, dragging her onto his lap so she straddled him.

She pulled her mouth from his and let it trail down his chin to his throat. His hands traveled up under her shirt, his palms on her bare back, pushing her against him.

"You feel incredible," he said, letting his head fall back against the headrest.

She pulled her mouth from his neck and looked at him, her chest rising and falling rapidly. He stared up at her, the glow from the moon lighting up her face. Her lips were puffy and wet, and her hair was everywhere, probably from his wandering hands.

"God, Paige, you're beautiful," he said, pulling one

of his hands from her back and reaching up to her face.

He brushed her hair behind her ear and let it trail down her neck to her bare shoulder. Something flashed across her face before she inhaled sharply, and then she dived back into his mouth. Brendan's hand was still working its way up her back, his fingers somehow at her bra, undoing the hooks. It loosened and he reached around and pulled it off, throwing it somewhere in the cab of his truck. And then his hands were on her naked breasts. She groaned into his mouth and her fingers dug into his shoulders.

It was a testament to how distracted he was that he never saw the blue and red flashing lights. But he did hear the *tap, tap, tap* on his window and someone saying his name.

"Shit." Brendan pulled back from Paige.

"Oh my God," she said, scrambling out of his lap, almost kicking him in a very unfortunate place.

Brendan turned his car on and rolled down the window. Jax was frowning at them, shaking his head.

"Your neighbor Mrs. Forns called," Jax said, ducking his head and looking at Paige. "She thought someone was having sex in a parked car in front of her house."

Brendan looked at Paige. She was still breathing hard, her hair was everywhere, and the front of her shirt was molded to her naked breasts, showing absolutely everything. Yeah, he would have had sex with her in his truck and not even thought twice about it.

"That stupid, nosey old hag needs to learn to mind her own damn business." She was pissed off now, and that turned him on even more. What the *hell* was wrong with him?

"We weren't having sex," Brendan said, turning back

to Jax, because if he kept looking at Paige he wasn't going to be held responsible for his actions.

Jax only raised his eyebrows, that disapproving look of his still written all over his face.

"I have to go," Paige said as the light over the Morrisons' front door flickered on and Trevor stuck his head outside. "I'll see you guys tomorrow," she said as she opened the door and practically ran up the steps to her father. They both walked in and he shut the door behind them.

"You just couldn't let me say good night to her," Brendan said, turning back to Jax.

"Oh, I think you said good night all right." Jax's frown didn't even waiver. Ever since he'd gotten that badge he'd become too freaking serious. "If I'd walked away she probably would've been back in your lap again in less than two seconds."

"I doubt that. Your flashing lights kind of killed the mood."

"Not that much," Jax said, glancing down to Brendan's crotch, where it was pretty obvious that his mood had in no way been killed.

"You're an asshole." Brendan put his truck in gear. "I'm going home now. Happy?"

"Extremely," Jax said before he turned around and walked back to his truck.

* * *

When Paige walked into the house and told her parents why there was a county sheriff truck in front of their house, they both thought it was hilarious.

"Mrs. Forns called the cops on you for making out?" her father asked, trying not to laugh. Paige didn't feel the need to describe to her parents in graphic detail what she'd been doing with Brendan.

Abby on the other hand was a completely different story.

"You almost had sex with him in his truck?"

"I didn't almost have sex with him," Paige whispered into the phone. "We were just, you know, making out a little aggressively."

"Sweetie, straddling a boy is just a little bit more than *aggressive*."

"I don't know how it happened. One second I was sitting next to him, and the next I was on his lap."

Paige hadn't been lying when she'd told Brendan she was tipsy, but she'd been fully in control of her actions...in a way that she wasn't in control of them at all when he was around.

"So he just picked you up like it was nothing?" Abby said a little dreamily.

"Pretty much."

"And then what happened."

"Well after he got my bra off—"

"After he what?" Abby interrupted.

"I didn't even notice it was gone."

"So the hot mechanic has magic hands? Nice."

"I know," Paige said unable to stop her own grin.

"What happened after that?"

"After that, a deputy sheriff, who is thankfully Brendan's friend, pulled up and put a stop to his *magic hands*."

"Wait, what?"

"My parents' neighbor called the cops on us."

Abby was gone, laughing so hard that she was snorting through the phone.

"It isn't funny, Abby."

"No," she said, trying to talk. "It really, really is. Oh God, Paige, I'm crying. This is . . . there are just no words for what this is."

"I'm so glad that I can be a constant source of entertainment for you."

"Believe me, so am I."

Chapter Nine

The Case of the Disappearing Bra

The school's baseball teams didn't use the field during the summer months, so the county league got to use it for their games. Brendan had spent more hours on this field with Jax and Shep than he could count. From sixth to twelfth grade they'd practically lived on this field during baseball season, and for all of them, it was another home.

Brendan pulled into the parking lot and parked next to Shep's black '67 Mustang. Brendan and Jax had helped him restore it ten years ago and it was Shep's pride and joy.

Brendan got out of his truck and opened the back door. Sydney jumped down next to him as he grabbed his baseball bag from the backseat. She followed him as he walked to the dugout. Out of the ten guys who were on the team, five were already there. Brendan walked down to the end of the dugout and dropped his bag onto the bench next to Shep.

"Hey, Syd," Shep said, rubbing her head.

"Do you need me to pick anything up for this afternoon?" Brendan asked, leaning over his bag and digging through it.

"Nope. Everything's good to go. The steaks are already marinating. Is Paige still coming?"

"Yeah." Brendan's head snapped up. "Why wouldn't she be?"

Brendan had been a little nervous about the events of the night before. He hadn't been embarrassed that Jax had caught them, but he was concerned that Paige might've been. He hadn't seen her today, and there was only so much a person could infer from text messages. So there was a part of him that was just a bit anxious.

"I was just asking," Shep said, his eyes narrowing on Brendan. "You guys have an interesting night?" he asked as he bent over to tie his cleats. Except he didn't really ask the question; there was an implied undertone in his voice.

"Damn it. I thought Jax was supposed to keep his mouth shut when it came to sheriff business."

"I do keep my mouth shut."

Brendan turned to see Jax's customary frown. Jax dropped his own bag onto the bench and sat down.

"You and Paige got busted by Jax when he was on patrol?" Shep looked up and grinned.

"I thought that was what you were talking about."

"No, I was talking about that huge hickey on your neck," Shep said, pointing to a spot on his own neck, just below his jaw.

"Doesn't surprise me with the way you two were going at it," Jax said.

"So you did catch them?" Shep excitedly asked, slapping his thigh with his hand. "That's just too good. Where were they?"

"In his truck out front of her parents' house. Mrs. Forns called it in."

Shep howled with laughter.

"Thanks," Brendan said, looking at Jax.

"What?" Jax shrugged his shoulders. "It's going to be in the paper. You know they report everything they find in the police reports. Doesn't matter how uninteresting it is. And with the way Paige was riding you, that's going to be interesting news."

"You put that in the report?" Brendan asked, outraged as Shep continued to laugh.

"No. I just said you two were kissing," Jax said, finding his own cleats and putting them on. "You're lucky I didn't fine you two for indecent exposure."

"Nothing was exposed," Brendan said a little too loudly. The other guys in the dugout looked over at them. "We were still fully dressed." Brendan lowered his voice.

"Yeah, ten more seconds and that would've been a completely different story."

"If anything, Jax saved your ass last night," Shep said, standing up.

"Yeah, you should be thanking me," Jax said as the corner of his mouth twitched.

"I hate both of you." Brendan sat down on the bench. "You both suck at being friends."

"Aw, we love you too, man," Shep said, grabbing his glove and going out onto the field to warm up.

"Why did you have to file a report?" Brendan asked, pulling off his sneakers.

Jax looked at him like he'd just said that the Red Sox were the greatest team in baseball.

"Because Delta Forns called it in, and you know that woman always follows up. You want me to get in trouble?"

"No, I don't," Brendan said, running his hands across his face. "Paige is going to kill me."

"Why?"

"Because making out in my truck was my idea."

"The way I see it, she's just as guilty as you. Just make sure that next time you're in the privacy of your own home."

"Thanks for the advice," Brendan said, not hiding his sarcasm.

"Anytime. And here's another piece, don't let her near your neck anymore," Jax said, pointing at him. "That hickey's huge."

* * *

Paige, alongside her parents, made her way down to the field. The breeze making the gauzy, black fabric of her skirt wrap around her knees.

"Which team is Brendan's?" Denise asked.

"The Stingrays. They're wearing black and white," Paige said, scanning the field.

She spotted Brendan crouched near the dugout. Jax pitched a ball to him and it sailed into his glove. All of the guys on his team were wearing black baseball hats with a white stingray over the bill, tight black baseball pants, and white jerseys that said STINGRAYS on the front and their last names over a number on the back. Brendan was number four.

"Paige," Grace shouted from the bleachers behind home plate. She was sitting on the bottom row in front of Lula Mae and Oliver, Sydney lying at her feet.

After saying hello to Lula Mae and Oliver, Paige slid into the seat next to Grace. Denise and Trevor sat on the row above and started talking to Oliver and Lula Mae.

"Where are Mel and Harper?" Paige asked as Sydney sat up and put her head in Paige's lap.

"Mel has to supervise the concession stand. The high school students run it and it switches off which teacher has to help. And Harper booked a client at the spa, so she's going to join us at Shep's house."

"Oh." Paige nodded and looked out to the field again.

Brendan was jogging over to them with a big grin on his face. Paige's stomach flipped.

"Hello, Mr. and Mrs. Morrison." Brendan stopped in front of them and nodded to her parents. "Can I talk to you real quick, Paige?" he asked, holding out his hand.

"Yeah," she said, reaching up and putting her hand in his. He pulled her up alongside him, his fingers lacing with hers.

"We'll be right back," he said to them. "Stay, Sydney," he said when she went to follow. Sydney whined as they walked away but she lay back down at Grace's feet.

"What's up?" she asked as Brendan pulled her through the grass.

He turned to her when they were a good fifty feet from the bleachers. "This." He pulled her into his chest. His hand came up and cupped the back of her head as he brought her mouth to his.

She relaxed against him, putting her hands at his waist.

"Did you get in trouble last night?" he asked, pulling

back only a fraction of an inch from her mouth. She couldn't see his eyes because of his sunglasses, but his mouth said mischief.

"No." She laughed. "Did you get in trouble?"

"With Jax? No. But I was worried about you being upset with me."

"Why?"

"Because you ran into the house without your bra on." His mouth quirked.

"You have sneaky fingers," she said, pinching his side.

"Ow." He flinched but didn't let go of her. "You didn't have any complaints last night when you were sucking on my neck," he said, raising an eyebrow.

"Yeah, well." Her gaze traveled down. "Oh my gosh," she said, seeing the purple bruise on his skin. "I gave you a hickey?" She reached up and lightly ran her fingers over the small mark.

"Yeah. I haven't had one of those since I was eighteen. Apparently last night was full of high school flashbacks."

"You going to give me my bra back?"

"To the victors go the spoils." He grinned.

"Do you make a habit of collecting bras, Brendan King?"

"No," he whispered against her lips. "Just yours."

"Brendan," Shep shouted from behind the fence. "Hurry it up, we're about to start."

"You should go," Paige said, lightly pressing her lips against the hickey and pulling back.

"Not yet," he said, suddenly frowning. "Paige, I need to tell you something."

Her stomach dropped. Those words accompanied with a frown never boded well.

"What?" she said, trying to take a step back.

Brendan's hands dropped to her waist and he squeezed lightly. "Jax has to report all of the calls that he goes on."

The blood drained from her face. "What did his report say?" she asked, trying to remain calm. If Jax put everything that he saw into his report, she was going to kill him.

"Just that he found us kissing. He left out the, uh, other details."

"Oh thank God," Paige said as the blood returned to her face.

"Paige, it's still going to say that Mrs. Forns thought we were having sex. And it's going to be in the paper."

"I know." She sighed. "But—"

"Brendan," Jax was shouting at him now. "We have to start."

"Go," Paige said, letting go of him.

"You're not mad?" he asked, taking a step back.

"Not at you."

Relief washed over his face. He stepped back into her and kissed her before he turned and ran off to the field.

It shouldn't have surprised her that the whole town was about to find out about their little indiscretion. Nothing stayed a secret around here, and she was going to have to get used to it; otherwise she was going to go crazy.

Paige made her way back to the bleachers and sat down next to Grace. The announcer came on over the P.A. system, introducing the teams, and then everyone stood up as three girls from the high school choir sang the national anthem.

"So, are they named after the fish or the hairstyle?"

Paige asked Grace about the opposing team, which was unfortunately named the Mullets.

"Both," Grace answered as the Stingrays fanned out onto the field.

Brendan grinned at Paige as he walked behind home plate, now wearing all of his pads. He flipped his baseball cap backward, and put on his catcher's mask. Shep and Jax walked out onto the field together. They split as Jax took his place at the mound and Shep went to his spot between second and third.

"So do their numbers have significance?" Paige asked Grace.

"Brendan is number four because my mom's birthday was August fourth. Jax is seven because his favorite Yankee has always been Mickey Mantle and that was his number, and Shep is thirteen because it's his lucky number."

"Shep likes to go against the grain, doesn't he?" Paige asked.

"Always has."

Paige watched as Jax stretched his shoulders, a grim look on his mouth.

"Jax always looks so serious," Paige said. "Has he always been that way?"

"Yup," Grace said. "He's serious about everything, and I do mean *everything*," she said, drawing out the last word.

Paige looked at Grace, whose attention was solely focused on Jax. Paige was pretty sure that Grace wanted Jax to be *serious* about her.

When the first batter came up to the plate, Brendan crouched down and Paige had an awesome view of his very nice butt in those very tight pants.

Jax wound the pitch and it sailed into Brendan's mitt.

"Holy shit," Paige whispered.

"I know, right?" Grace said in an equally awed voice.

The first batter struck out, but the next got a hit on the third pitch. There was a runner on first and second base when Jax struck the last batter out and the Stingrays ran into the dugout.

Shep was the first up to bat. Landing a hit on the second pitch, he made it to second base and some other guy on the team named Banners walked out to bat. Banners struck out, but McCoy hit a ball just over the first baseman. McCoy was tagged out at first but at least Shep made it to third base.

Brendan walked out onto the plate, minus all of his pads, and his baseball cap flipped forward. He tapped the bat against the inside of his cleat twice before he brought it up, his fists wrapped around the neck. The pitcher wound his arm and the loud *thwack* of the wood against the ball echoed through the field.

Brendan threw the bat down and ran as the ball sailed into the middle of the outfield, hitting the ground and rolling through the grass. Brendan ran to first base as Shep sailed past home plate, scoring the first run in the game. The next batter got Brendan to second but the third struck out and the teams switched places again. By the end of the fifth inning, the Stingrays were ahead four to three.

* * *

The Mullets tied it up in the seventh inning. In the eighth, Brendan went up to bat with only one out left. He hit the ball far into the outfield and when the center fielder threw the ball to the shortstop, he missed, the ball rolling in the red clay. Brendan tore off to second base and made it there just before the ball did.

Jax came up to bat next, and Brendan could hear Grace shouting for him to knock it out of the park. Brendan looked past Jax to where Paige was sitting. Her hair was piled on top of her head now, a few curls trailing down around her forehead. She had one long leg crossed over the other. Sydney's head was in her lap, Paige's slender fingers scratching behind Sydney's ears.

Jax missed the first pitch but his bat connected with the second. Brendan went out a couple of paces, waiting to see where the ball went but there was no need. It sailed over the left corner of the fence. He rounded third and ran to home plate. He turned to find Paige screaming his name. She put her fingers to her lips and whistled loudly as he walked by.

The next batter struck out and Brendan put his gear back on for the last inning. In the top of the ninth, the Mullets were only one run behind. Jax struck out the fourth batter, Brendan catching the last ball in his mitt. He stood and stretched, walking over to the fence. Paige stood up from the bleachers and walked over to him.

"Nice game, King," she said, putting her hand against the fence.

"Glad you liked it. Let me just grab my stuff and I'll be right back." He put his hand against hers with the chain link between them.

"I'll wait here with Grace and Syd."

He walked over to the dugout, where the team was already taking off their cleats.

"Paige and I will be at your place before two. I'm just going to go home and take a quick shower."

Shep raised his eyebrows.

"Don't even," Brendan said, holding up his hand.

"Fine. But if you show up with another one of those," Shep said, pointing to Brendan's neck, "I'm going to assume the worst. Or should I say the best?" He smirked.

Brendan just shook his head. Sometimes with Shep it was best to just not engage him.

Chapter Ten

Coming Up for Air

Brendan lived on the outskirts of Mirabelle. Paige could see the Gulf of Mexico from the big bay windows that looked out from the back of the house. The water was probably a hundred yards away from his back door, and all of the land was his. The house had been built on stilts above the open garage, and the back porch had a staircase that led out onto the grass. There was a hammock just off to the side, tied between two sturdy trees.

Paige clutched her sweating glass of sweet tea and looked around Brendan's living room. He'd told her that she was free to snoop while he took a shower, and that's exactly what she was going to do. She had to do something to take her mind off the fact that he was in the other room, naked and soaking wet...it was very distracting.

Brendan had a flat-screen TV mounted above the stone fireplace and white bookshelves lined the wall on either side. A massive brown leather sofa sat in the middle of the room and the coffee table looked like it was made of pieces of driftwood. The blond hardwood floors stretched out from the living room and into the hallway, and so did the light-green walls.

Paige wandered over to one of the bookshelves, studying the scattered picture frames. There was a fairly recent picture of Brendan, Shep, and Jax, all wearing camo and holding hunting bows. There was another of the three of them in high school wearing their baseball uniforms. There was a picture of a little boy with blond hair holding a baby wrapped in a yellow blanket. His face was turned down to look at what was in his arms. Even though she couldn't see his face, Paige knew that it was of Brendan holding Grace. There was a picture of Brendan and Oliver up to their elbows in grease as they worked on a truck, and another of a teenage Grace and Lula Mae cooking in the kitchen of Café Lula.

Paige's gaze wandered to an antique picture frame in the corner. She reached for it before she even knew what she was doing. It was of a blonde woman with Brendan's eyes and smile. She was looking at the camera, her hands resting on her protruding belly. She was wearing a light blue dress that reached down to her ankles, the gauzy material blowing in the breeze.

"That's my mom."

Paige turned with the picture still in her hands. Brendan was standing in the doorway to the hall wearing faded jeans and a maroon T-shirt. His dark blond hair was still wet from his shower and his bright blue eyes were on her.

"What was her name?"

"Claire. Claire Elizabeth King," he said, walking over to her.

"She was beautiful." Paige looked down at the picture and traced the hem of her flowing dress

"She looked like Grace."

"She looked like you," Paige said, looking up at him. "You have her smile."

"Grams tells me that all the time."

"Was she pregnant with you or Grace in this picture?"

"Grace," he said, reaching out and touching the frame.

"How old was she?"

"Twenty-three."

God, that was two years younger than Paige was now. She couldn't even imagine having one kid by herself, let alone two.

"How old was she when she had you?" she asked, putting the frame back and looking at Brendan.

He was still staring at the picture. After a second, he cleared his throat and looked at Paige. There was a deep sadness etched all over his face. She just wanted to reach up and brush his pain away, but that was impossible.

"She was eighteen."

Eighteen. It made her heart hurt.

"How old was she when she died?" Paige asked, reaching out for him and wrapping her arms around his waist.

"Thirty-four." He brought his hands up to her back and started moving them up and down.

"I—I can't even imagine," she said, shaking her head. "I'm so sorry, Brendan," she whispered, pressing her lips to his jaw before she settled her head on his shoulder.

"Thank you," he said softly. His arms tightened around

her and he buried his nose in her hair, pressing his lips
against her temple.

* * *

Shep lived in his grandparents' old house, which was just
a couple of miles from Brendan's place. When his grandfather had died, his grandmother had moved in with his
parents and Shep had gotten the house.

The grill was going and everyone was out on the deck,
beers in hand. Brendan was leaning back against the rail-
ing and Paige was leaning back against his chest. He
rested his free hand on her hip, his fingers tracing the
lace hem of her white tank top. Paige was laughing about
something with Grace, but Brendan wasn't paying attention. He was too distracted finding shapes in the freckles
on her shoulders.

Talking about his mother had always been a difficult
thing for him. Her death had never gotten easier. When
she'd died he'd felt like he was drowning, and then with
time, he'd figured out how to breathe underwater. But
when he'd talked to Paige about Claire, he'd felt like he
was coming up for air again. She'd asked him questions
and he'd wanted to talk, he'd wanted to tell her about the
woman who had raised him. He'd wanted her to comfort him, to wrap her arms around him, and she had. He
wanted her to know him in every way.

Brendan pressed his nose into Paige's hair, breathing
in the citrus scent of her shampoo. She felt so right
pushed up against him, like she fit here, in his arms and
in his life.

* * *

Paige got up early on Sunday and drove over to Brendan's. When he'd dropped her off the night before, he'd asked her if she'd go out on his boat with him for the day.

"Just you and me? Out in the middle of the ocean? Fishing?" she'd asked as they stood on her parents' porch.

"Among other things. You scared?" he challenged.

"Do I have a reason to be?"

"No." He grinned.

"Why don't I believe you?"

"Because you're a smart girl."

Yet she'd said yes anyways.

She parked in his driveway and headed up the stairs to his front door. She knocked and he opened the door a minute later, Sydney at his side, her tail whipping him in the leg.

"Morning."

"Morning," he said, pulling her inside. As soon as the door was shut he pushed her up against it and kissed her. When he pulled back sometime later he looked at her with a dazed expression that she was sure mirrored her own.

"You hungry?"

"Uh-huh," she said as her eyes dipped back down to his mouth.

"I meant for breakfast." He laughed. "Glad to know your mind is in the gutter."

"And where's yours?"

"Right next to yours," he said, grabbing her hand and pulling her into the kitchen. "Sit. I'm going to make you breakfast." He deposited her on one of the bar stools at the counter.

"I thought we had to get an early start."

"The fish will still be there in an hour. Coffee?"

"Yes, please," she said, leaning back in her chair.

For the next thirty minutes she sipped her coffee while he made breakfast. He moved around the kitchen with ease, dicing vegetables and whipping up eggs.

"Did Lula Mae teach you to cook?" Paige asked while he sprinkled cheese over the cooking omelet.

"Yes, but so did my mom."

"She was a cook too?"

"Yeah." He nodded, slipping a piece of cheese to Sydney. "She worked at Café Lula too."

"How long has it been there?"

"My grandmother opened it twenty-six years ago. She had a job at a diner and she saved up for over twenty years. When she had enough money she bought that old cottage."

"That's amazing," Paige said, twirling her spoon around her coffee. "To be able to do that. Follow your dreams and start out on your own. And your grandfather did it too."

"What are your dreams?" Brendan asked, looking over at her.

"My dreams?" she asked, touching her chest with her hand. "To sell my art in a gallery."

"Have you sold any of your work before?"

"No. After I got out of school I got a job at the advertising agency. I didn't really have a lot of free time to paint or take pictures."

"So the advertising agency, not your dream job?" he asked as he turned back to the stove and ran the spatula around the edge of the pan.

"No," Paige said, shaking her head. It really hadn't been. She'd been too confined in her work. She'd never been able to do what she'd really wanted. Whenever she'd "colored outside of the lines," as her supervisor had liked to say, she'd been reprimanded. She'd often come home with blinding headaches from being frustrated all day. There hadn't been reprieve either because on most days she'd had to bring her work home with her.

"I hated it," she said before she realized she was speaking out loud.

Brendan looked at her again, surprise in his eyes.

"I never realized it before. But I really hated that job."

"Well, maybe now's your chance to do what you love."

"Maybe." She nodded.

Brendan finished cooking and they shared the omelet and fried potatoes; everything was delicious. They both cleaned up the kitchen, since Paige refused to let Brendan clean up by himself, and then they loaded up his boat.

"Have you ever been fishing before?" Brendan asked as he pulled the boat away from the dock.

"Yes," she said, leaning back against the seat. "I used to go with my dad all the time."

"Really?" he asked, looking genuinely shocked.

"Why does that shock you?"

"I don't know. I just can't picture you fishing."

"If you didn't think I liked it, why did you ask me to come?"

"It isn't that I didn't think you liked it; it's that I can't picture you doing it. And I asked you because I wanted to spend the day with you."

And that's what they did. They fished for a couple of hours, both of them catching flounder and redfish. Multiple times during the day he'd put his pole down and come up behind her, pressing his mouth into her neck.

When they got back to Brendan's house it was just past four. He cleaned the fish while she cut up a fresh watermelon and made corn on the cob. He froze what they weren't going to eat and covered a piece of the flounder in spices and lemon juice, then wrapped it in aluminum foil and shoved it in the oven. He poured them each a glass of wine and they sat out on his deck, Paige curled up in his lap. After dinner, and two more glasses of wine each, they snuggled up on his couch to watch a movie.

Chapter Eleven

Trials and Tribulations

Paige slowly came to consciousness before she opened her eyes. She was so comfortable and every time she breathed, she inhaled a subtle spicy sent. She pressed her face deeper into her pillow and that's when she realized it was moving and not as squishy as she was used to. She opened her eyes to find herself firmly wrapped in Brendan's arms, her head on his chest and her legs tangled with his. She slowly reached for his left hand, pulling it off her hip and bringing it to her face. It was almost seven o'clock in the morning.

"Shit," she said, scrambling up.

"What?" Brendan sat up so quickly that they almost banged heads. It would have been comical except it really, really wasn't.

"Oh crap, oh crap, oh crap. We fell asleep," Paige said, shooting up from the couch and tripping over Sydney.

"Be careful." Brendan's hands shot out for her waist, steadying her before she fell into the coffee table.

"I'm going to be late. I'm supposed to be at work at eight. Shit, shit, shit," she said, grabbing her sandals from the floor and jamming them onto her feet. She ran into the kitchen to grab her bag and when she got to the front door, Brendan was already standing there, looking a little bit tousled and more than a little sexy. She stopped in front of him to give him a quick kiss but she lingered for a second before she forced herself to pull away. "I'll see you later," she said, pulling back from him with a smile before she sprinted down the stairs.

It took her five minutes to get home. She threw her car in park and ran up the steps to her parents' front door, fumbling with the keys and dropping them.

"You've got to be kidding me," she said, bending down to pick them up.

The front door opened and her mom stuck her head out.

"Paige?"

"Oh thank God. Sorry, Mom," Paige said, running past her and dashing down the hallway to her bedroom.

She threw her bag down on the bed and started stripping before she even made it to the bathroom. She jumped into the shower and turned it on, the cold water sending a shock into her system.

"Shit," she screamed, jumping back.

"Paige, what's going on?" Denise asked behind the shower curtain.

"I fell asleep at Brendan's." Paige tentatively stuck her hand in the water to check if it had warmed up.

"Did you sleep with him?"

"No, Mother." Paige groaned. "We were on his boat all day and then we drank some wine with dinner and the combination of the sun and alcohol must have made us fall asleep." She grabbed her shampoo and started scrubbing her hair.

"Good, because it's too soon to sleep with him."

"I know that, Mother," Paige shouted over the stream of water. "Right now is *not* the moment to give me a lecture. I'm going to be late for work."

"I'm not lecturing you. Just giving you some advice. Now, do you need me to do anything to help you get ready?"

"Can you iron my pencil skirt?"

"The hot-pink one?"

"Yes please," Paige said washing the soap out of her eyes. "And coffee. I *need* coffee."

"You always need coffee."

"Thanks, Mom," Paige called out as the bathroom door snapped shut.

Twenty minutes later Paige was running out of her parents' front door, her wet hair soaking into the back of her blouse. Her heels were in one hand and a cup of coffee was in the other.

"Have a nice sleepover?"

Paige looked up to see Mrs. Forns standing on her porch, pink rollers in her hair, wearing a floral-print bathrobe. Paige just kept walking toward her Jeep.

"You know, only smutty girls sleep with boys before they're married."

Breathe in and out. She's just a bitter old hag.

"I'm talking to you, young lady," Mrs. Forns screamed at her.

And I'm ignoring you.

It normally took Paige thirty-five minutes to get to

work, and when she got into her Jeep it was already past
seven thirty. She was going to be late.

Awesome, just fan-freaking-tastic.

This was all she needed. She had an appointment with
a client and she was going to be late for it. It was ten after
eight when she pulled into the parking lot of Adams and
Family Funeral Home.

Paige grabbed her purse and her shoes. She slammed
the door of her Jeep shut and ran up the steps. When she
got to the front door she slipped on her shoes, hopping on
each foot as she used the doorway to keep her balance,
and then opened the door and walked inside.

"Are the Limonites already here?" she asked as she
stopped in front of Tara's desk.

"No." Tara shook her head. "They're running late."

"Oh, thank you, God," Paige said in relief.

"You look like a drowned rat."

Paige turned to see Verna standing in the hallway.

"Is this what's professional these days? A wet head of
hair and a flashy skirt?" she asked, narrowing her eyes at
Paige. "You look ridiculous."

This was one of those times that it took everything in
Paige to keep her mouth shut. But somehow she did.

"Verna, did you forget to eat your prunes today?" Tara
asked. "I know how cranky you get when you're consti-
pated."

Verna didn't say anything; she just stomped off up the
stairs.

"Late night?" Tara whispered.

"Yes, but it wasn't what you think. I'll tell you about it
later. I have to go prepare for the Limonites," Paige said,
heading for the stairs.

"All right, but I'm anxiously waiting," Tara called out after her.

Paige only made it out onto the landing before she ran right into Missy.

"So punctuality is apparently just a suggestion to you? You have absolutely no regard for other people's time, do you? This is completely unacceptable," she said, standing in front of Paige and tapping her high-heeled shoe on the wooden floor.

"I'm sorry I'm late. That's on me."

"Yes, it is. And it better not happen again. This is getting taken out of your paycheck."

"I get paid by the hour." Paige frowned.

"Exactly, when you're not here, you're not getting paid."

"I understand how hourly works, Missy. Would you like to continue to explain it to me, or can I go get ready for this meeting?"

"Go, but we're not done with this." Missy glared at her. "We'll talk later."

"I can't wait." Paige stepped around Missy and walked down the hall.

She dropped her stuff off behind her desk and sat down, booting up her computer. The Limonites still weren't there five minutes later so she pulled up her e-mail.

When Paige had worked on the Web site, she'd added her work e-mail address. She also put it into the obituaries that she wrote, telling people from the community that if they had any pictures of the deceased that they wanted to share, they could e-mail them to her. She scrolled through her e-mails looking for anything that might be of interest to the Limonite family.

Wendell Limonite had been fifty-six when he died of a massive coronary heart attack. He'd left behind a wife and two kids and a town that had loved him. She'd gotten multiple e-mails over the last couple of days filled with pictures.

When she got to the second to last e-mail, her heart stopped as she read through it. It had nothing to do with Mr. Limonite. It was a blog article written by Bethelda Grimshaw, sent from an anonymous e-mail address, and it was about Paige.

THE GRIM TRUTH

NEW GIRL STARTS TROUBLE

Brazen Interloper has lived in Mirabelle for almost four months now. She moved down to live with her parents, and since stepping foot into our quiet little town, trouble has followed her everywhere. Coincidence? I think not. Brazen's parents moved to the area a couple of years ago, and they've managed to adapt to small-town life fairly quickly, but their daughter is an entirely different story. And she does not belong here.

Sweetie Pie has lived in Mirabelle all her life, and as Brazen's parents' next-door neighbor she's had the opportunity to observe Brazen for the last four months. "That girl is up to something," Mrs. Pie said while serving me a glass of sweet tea. "She's always in and out of that shed in her parents' backyard, doing Lord knows what. I think Deputy Ginger needs to start keeping an eye on her."

The problem is Deputy Ginger is none other than

Rogue Whoreson's best friend. And *what*, might my readers ask, is the connection there? Well, Mr. Whoreson has been seen in quite a few compromising situations with Brazen in the past couple of weeks. Just last Monday, they were seen running around town to all sorts of different locations. Multiple eyewitnesses say that they saw the couple kissing everywhere that they went.

The most interesting part of this: Brazen was supposed to be working at her new job. I'm not exactly sure how things go on in Philadelphia, but here in Mirabelle we value hard work and don't look kindly on outsiders taking advantage of the good people who give them opportunities, opportunities that they apparently do not deserve.

"I had to call the authorities on Friday night," Mrs. Pie told us. "That troublesome girl and Rogue Whoreson were outside in that truck of his for a long time, the windows going all foggy. She's a right little temptress, she is, and if he knows what's good for him, he'll stay far, far away from her, otherwise she's going to corrupt him even more with her immoral ways and those hippie drugs that she does.

"I've heard her say that she was participating in group sex acts out in that shed of hers," Mrs. Pie continued. "She has a trashy mouth and a trashy personality. I just don't know why her parents let her get away with it. And now she's moved on to public indecency right on our very streets. She has to be stopped."

As my readers will remember, Rogue Whoreson has a colorful past of his own. His father, Dick Splits, abandoned Rogue before his mother, Jeze Belle, even started showing. And let's not forget Little CoQuette, Jeze Belle's daughter, whose father is still unknown. Apparently, Rogue is going after a woman who is just like his mother was, God rest her soul.

A source, who wishes to remain anonymous, says that "Brazen has caused nothing but havoc ever since she's come down here. She's full of liberal ideas on changing our small conservative town. But we don't need her scandalous ideas and outrageous morals here."

What brought Brazen Interloper down here? What sordid past is she hiding from? Why did she leave the big city that she'd lived in her entire life? And what is she going to do to our town?

"Oh my God," Paige whispered, staring at the screen. Bethelda Grimshaw, along with Mrs. Pie, otherwise known as Mrs. Forns, and her anonymous source, most likely Verna, had just called Paige an immoral corrupter. They'd said she wasn't wanted here.

If he knows what's good for him, he'll stay far, far away from her.

She'd known this might happen. Brendan had warned her that it wasn't going to be pretty, but this was beyond anything she'd imagined. Her eyes burned and she blinked a few times trying to get past it. But she couldn't. The words kept repeating in her head. Words that she'd heard for so long now, since before she'd even come down to Mirabelle.

She didn't belong.

* * *

Brendan was still in a daze that afternoon. He'd slept the entire night with Paige in his arms and every time he thought about it he couldn't help but smile. Yeah, she'd run out of his house like a bat out of hell that morning, but that wasn't because she'd wanted to get away from him. No, she'd even kissed him before she'd sprinted out the door.

Two weeks. He'd met Paige exactly two weeks ago to the day and it blew his mind how quickly things had changed for him. It was incredible. *She* was incredible. He'd pretty much been hooked the moment she'd opened that pretty little mouth of hers, and when he'd kissed that same pretty little mouth, there'd been no way he was going to walk away.

When Brendan came into the office, Oliver was firmly located behind his newspaper. Brendan had been under a car all morning, so they hadn't talked yet.

"Hey," Oliver said as he flipped a page and peeked over at Brendan. "Have a good weekend?"

"Yup," Brendan said, throwing his baseball cap on his desk. "I spent all day yesterday with Paige out on the water."

"You guys fish?" Oliver asked, putting his paper down on the desk.

"Yeah, caught some flounder and redfish," Brendan said, sitting down in his chair and switching on his computer.

"And she liked it?" Oliver asked, surprised. "I wouldn't have pegged her as much of a fisher."

"I didn't either, but you know what, Pops?" Brendan put his hands behind his head and grinned. "When it comes to Paige, you can't peg her for anything. She shocks the hell out of me half the time."

"So she keeps you on your toes?"

"Yeah." He nodded. "She does."

"Good, you need to be with someone like that. Your grandmother has kept me on my toes for over fifty years," Oliver said, folding up his newspaper and switching over to his computer to check his e-mail.

Despite everything, Brendan considered himself lucky. He might not have had his father in his life, and he'd had his mom for only sixteen years, but he'd had his grandparents. Oliver had been Brendan and Grace's father in every sense of the word, and they'd had two mothers with Claire and Lula Mae. He'd seen what a loving relationship was through his grandparents. It would have been nice to see that with his real parents, but if his parents had stayed together, Grace wouldn't be here now, and nothing would ever make him want to give up Grace.

"Son of a bitch," Oliver said from behind his computer.

"What?" Brendan asked, coming back to the present.

Unlike Brendan, Oliver rarely lost his temper, and the fact that he was looking at the screen and cursing made Brendan worried. Oliver looked up, his brow furrowed and a frown firmly in place.

"Now, Brendan, don't fly off the handle."

"What is it?" he asked.

"Nothing good," Oliver said, shaking his head. "Phil Launders sent me an e-mail to warn me. Bethelda has a new article up today."

Brendan pulled up Bethelda's Web site and his blood started to boil immediately. It was about Paige.

Outrageous. Scandalous. Immoral. Temptress. Trashy... and the list went on and on. None of those things were true. Those words didn't describe Paige in any way.

Brendan slammed down his fist and stood up, his chair rolling back so hard that it bounced against the wall.

"Brendan," Oliver said, standing up. "Calm down."

"Calm down? Calm down? I can't *calm down*," he yelled. "Everything in there is bullshit." He pointed to the computer. "I'm so sick and tired of all of these lies that that *woman* comes up with."

"And what are you going to do? Go down there and set the place on fire?"

"She shouldn't be allowed to do this," Brendan raged. "She talked about Mom and Grace too. Doesn't that piss you off?"

"Of course it does," Oliver said, losing some of his calm. "You think it's easy for me to see my family slandered? You think it's easy for me to have *anyone* speak ill of your mother? I know what this does to you and Grace and your grandmother. It has *never* been easy for me, not for twenty-eight years. She got fired from the newspaper because of this garbage, but she just found another outlet. She does it to get a reaction; she used to get one out of me every time and she thrived on it. Do you have any idea how many times I've stormed down there? I would rant and rave and she would just smile in my face like the damn Cheshire cat."

"So that's your answer? Do nothing?"

"What do you think is going to happen if you go down there? You think Bethelda's going to feel bad? Suddenly grow a conscience and post a retraction? She isn't."

Brendan didn't say anything. He just grabbed his keys and walked out of the office.

He'd never been able to stop people from talking about his mother. He'd never been able to protect Grace from all of the gossip that had followed her around. And he apparently couldn't protect Paige either. He was completely useless.

When Brendan pulled into Adams and Family he was fuming. He remembered the first day he'd met Paige and the dejected look on her face that she'd tried to cover up. If she'd been upset before about the people in this town not accepting her, there was no telling how she was going to feel when she found out about this. When she read those words.

He bolted up the steps to the funeral home and walked inside. Tara was behind her desk, tapping on her keyboard. He must have looked as angry as he felt, because Tara's smile faltered when she saw him.

"Brendan," she said as her fingers stilled. "You okay?"

"No. Is Paige in her office?"

"Yeah." Tara nodded.

"She with a client?"

"No."

Brendan turned and ran up the stairs two at a time trying to calm himself before he talked to Paige. He paused in her doorway and watched her for a second. She was sitting at her desk, staring at her computer screen. Her shoulders were slumped, her mouth pulled down, and sadness surrounded her eyes. She was so preoccupied that she didn't even notice him standing in the doorway.

She knew. She'd seen it. She'd seen those horrible words.

"Paige," Brendan said, walking toward her.

She looked up at him and gave him a sad smile.

"Hey." She stood up. "What are you doing here?" she asked as he pulled her into his arms.

"I needed to see you," he said, burying his face in her neck and pressing his lips to her throat. "Make sure you were okay."

"You saw the article," she said softly, her hands gripping his sides.

"Yeah," he said, running his hands up and down her back. "I'm sorry, baby. What she said, it's not true. People don't think that. *I* don't think that. Neither do Grace or Grams or Pops, or any of the people who actually matter."

"I know. I'm fine."

"Hmm." He moved his hands to her arms and pulled her back so that he could look into her face. "Paige, I grew up with enough women to know that *fine* is never a good thing. Talk to me."

"They said you should stay away from me," she said, sadly.

At this point, it would be easier to stop breathing than to live in the same town as Paige and never see her. "Not going to happen," he said, leaning in and kissing her forehead. "I'm not going anywhere."

* * *

Brendan watched Paige through his grandparents' kitchen window. She and Grace were sitting on the back porch playing fetch with Sydney.

"Your grandfather told me you yelled at him today," Lula Mae said as she chopped carrots for dinner.

Brendan leaned back against the counter and looked over at his grandmother. "Did he tell you why?" Brendan asked, taking a sip of his beer.

"Oh, he didn't need to tell me why. I know what that woman wrote."

"Everyone in this whole freaking town knows what that woman wrote. It's complete bullshit," Brendan said, feeling his temper start to flare up again. Every time he thought about that damn column he wanted to punch something.

"Brendan Oliver King." Lula Mae looked up as she put down her knife and pointed a finger at him. "Don't you use that language in front of me and especially in that tone." When Lula Mae got upset, her southern accent tended to get real thick, and right now it was about as thick as her homemade vanilla custard.

"Sorry, Grams," Brendan said, bowing his head and rubbing the peeling label on the beer bottle with his thumb. It didn't matter that he was twenty-eight years old, because when his grandmother got that tone with him he still got sheepish. And she'd used his full name, which was an immediate sign of danger. "I just can't have a clear head at all when it comes to this."

"Bethelda or Paige?"

Brendan looked up to find Lula Mae watching him with a frown and raised eyebrows.

"Both," Brendan said honestly. He'd never done well with his family being trash-talked, and he hadn't been prepared for the reaction he'd had when it had been Paige. "And there's nothing I can do to fix this, or stop it from happening again. I just wish she didn't have to go through this. Didn't have yet another thing to make her life difficult. I wish I could stop people from hurting her. Stop her from hurting."

"Brendan, you can't protect her from everything. You're not Superman."

"Yeah, but for her, I want to be. And I feel useless, like there's nothing I can do to fix this. Nothing I can do to stop Bethelda from doing this."

"So you didn't go down and give her what for?" Lula Mae asked as she went over to the fridge and grabbed a stick of butter.

"No," Brendan mumbled and took another swig of beer.

"I'm sorry. I didn't hear that. You did what your grand-father told you to do?" Lula Mae asked, grabbing a frying pan from a cabinet.

"No, I didn't go," Brendan said clearly. There was no way that he would've been able to go down to where Bethelda worked and not destroy something, especially after he'd seen Paige so sad.

"Good boy." Lula Mae dropped the butter into the fry-ing pan. "You know," she said as she stirred the butter around with her spatula as it began to melt, "I've never seen you like this before, not this quickly at least. You're very protective of her, as protective as you are of Grace."

"Yeah." Brendan nodded. "I can't really explain it," he said, pretty baffled himself.

"I can. You're falling for her, Brendan."

Brendan just stared at his grandmother, dumbfounded, because she was one hundred percent right. He was abso-lutely falling for Paige.

How the hell had that happened so fast?

* * *

"Are you kidding me?" Abby asked, incredulous as she read the blog post.

"I know," Paige said miserably.

"This is bullshit. What did your hot mechanic do?"

"Brendan." Paige emphasized his name. Abby refused to call him Brendan. Paige wondered what would happen if Abby ever met him face-to-face. Would she call him *hot mechanic* the whole time? Not that Paige focused on a lot of possible future scenarios. She didn't like to think about a future with Brendan too much in case it didn't happen. "He came down to the funeral home to make sure I was okay. He just held me for a little while. Until I felt better."

"Okay, I'm calling it now."

"Calling what now?"

"This guy is going to marry you."

"What?" Paige laughed into the phone. "You can't know that. He can't even know that; how can you know that?"

"Look, I'm calling it anyway. If I'm wrong, I'll pay you a hundred dollars. If I'm right, you owe me a hundred dollars."

"I'm not betting on that."

"Why, because you know you're wrong?"

"No," Paige said quietly.

"Then why?"

"Because I'm not betting against us."

"Us? Yeah, I give it less than a year before you two are walking down the aisle."

* * *

The rest of Paige's week went by fairly uneventfully until Friday when she got her first paycheck. It was one day short of pay.

"Verna?" Paige said, lightly knocking on Verna's door frame. Verna looked up from her desk, her spectacles perched on the edge of her nose and her scowl firmly in place. "There's a problem with my paycheck."

"Problem? What *problem*?"

"It's a day short," Paige said, taking a step into the room. "This should be for eight days worth of work, but it's only seven."

"That's correct. You worked three days your first week and four last week. That's seven," Verna said, her scowl not moving an inch.

"I worked five last week," Paige corrected.

"Really, so fraternizing with your boyfriend is working? I talked to five different people who saw you being *indecent* with that man."

"Verna," Paige said calmly. "I worked that day. I got a flat and then Brendan drove me around to show me the town and the best places for the pictures that I needed."

"The pictures you *needed*? I don't believe you."

"Well," Paige said matter-of-factly, "it doesn't matter what you believe but what Mr. Adams believes. So would you like to talk to him or would you like me to?"

"Talk to Mr. Adams about what?" Paige turned to see Missy coming up behind her. "I told you, Paige. Whatever you need to discuss with Mr. Adams, you can discuss with me. That way you won't trifle him with unimportant things."

"All right." Paige tried oh-so-very hard not to roll her eyes. "My check is wrong. It was shorted a day."

"Which day?" Missy asked.

"Last Monday."

"The day you spent with Brendan?" Missy asked, raising her eyebrows. "We don't pay our employees for running around town and making out with their boyfriends."

"As I've told Verna, I got a flat and then Brendan drove me around to help me get my pictures *for work*."

"Did you get a flat this Monday? Is that why you were late for work?"

"No," Verna said, adding her two cents. "That was because they were fornicating. She stayed the night at his house."

"Oh my God," Paige said, losing her temper. "That is none of your business." She turned to Verna. "And I'm not going to have this conversation with either of you. Are you going to fix my paycheck or do I need to go talk to Mr. Adams?"

"Just fix it," Missy said to Verna. "But I have my eye on you." She turned back to Paige.

"Fantastic," Paige said, her voice dripping with sarcasm. "When you find something worth watching you let me know."

Chapter Twelve

The Power of Patience
and a Kiss Good Night

August turned into September, and before Brendan knew it, it was October. He spent every evening and every weekend with Paige. There were no more accidental sleepovers, much to Brendan's disappointment. Paige wanted to take things slowly, which Brendan understood. Considering the fact that he'd fallen for her faster than he could blink, it really was in his best interest to go slowly. It was just that slowly was torturous.

Brendan had never really slept with girls who didn't mean anything to him. One-night stands were definitely not his style. But still, it had been a while since he'd been this far into a relationship and not wound up in bed yet. Being with Paige was different. She was worth the wait; she was worth everything.

There were a few rare occasions when they ventured out into the land of the living to be with other people. They had dinner at her parents' house sometimes; other times they would go to Lula Mae and Oliver's, or they would hang out with Jax, Shep, and Grace. But on most nights they would curl up on his couch and watch TV or a movie. Well, they would start watching something, but they very rarely finished it.

Yeah, it never took Brendan long to press his face into Paige's neck and open his mouth on her throat. She'd turn to him, her mouth seeking his and then he'd lay her down on the couch. And they would proceed to spend many hours in exactly that position.

On one such night that they were fooling around, Paige flat on her back and Brendan stationed firmly between her thighs, he decided to do a little exploring. He'd had one of his hands on her breast, cupping her over her shirt and bra. But it wasn't enough. There had been some pretty heavy petting, but besides that one night in Brendan's truck, he hadn't had the pleasure of touching her naked breasts.

He let his hand travel down her body, trailing it over her rib cage and to her stomach. He slipped it underneath her shirt and slowly worked his way up. Paige didn't say anything, not that she could with the way their tongues were wrapped around each other. When he got to her bra, he traced the cup, touching the very top of her breast. He hooked his fingers in the cup and pulled it down, filling his hand. He ran his thumb over her nipple and she moaned deep into his mouth.

He needed more.

He pulled his mouth back from hers and trailed his lips down her neck as he moved down her body. He pushed her shirt up her stomach, placing a kiss below her belly before he dipped his tongue inside her navel. Her hands were on his head, her nails raking his scalp.

He pushed her shirt farther up and stopped when it was up past her ribs. There on her left side was a tattoo of a sunflower.

"So that's where the other one is," he said, looking up at her.

"You found it." She smiled.

"Hmm, I sure did," he said before he bowed his head and traced the petals with his tongue. She was writhing beneath him, her legs coming up and wrapping around his back.

"Did you draw this?"

"Yes," she said, more than somewhat breathless.

"So beautiful." He kissed the center of the tattoo.

"Thank you, I—I really like how it turned out."

"I meant you," he said, moving up her body and pushing her shirt above her breasts. "All of you, Paige," he said above her mouth.

She looked at him, breathing hard as she ran her hands up his shoulders. "You haven't seen all of me yet." She nipped at his mouth.

"Is that an invitation?" He ran his hand around to her back.

"Not quite. But the clasp is in the front," she said before she sucked his bottom lip into her mouth.

Well, that was clearly an invitation. He brought both of his hands to the spot right between her breasts and opened her bra. The cups parted and he pulled his mouth from hers, moving back down her body.

Paige had perfect breasts. Absolutely perfect. And he had to taste them.

He closed his mouth over one of her nipples, sucking it deep into his mouth. The other breast he covered with his hand. Paige gasped and her legs tightened around him, her hips picking up rhythm.

"Brendan," she said, moaning his name, long and loud.

God, she was killing him. He wanted desperately to crawl back up her body, pull her shorts and panties off, and bury himself inside of her. His body craved hers like nothing he'd ever experienced before. It was insane.

But she wasn't ready for that step; at least she hadn't informed him of any changes in her readiness. And he'd promised himself he wasn't going to push, that he would be a patient man.

But damn, patience was going to kill him.

Brendan groaned and pulled back from her. He buried his face in her neck and tried desperately to find his bearings.

"Brendan?" Paige asked, running her hands up his back. "What's wrong?"

What was wrong was that he wanted her so much it was physically painful. He'd taken more cold showers in the last two months than he'd ever taken in his life. Really, he didn't even remember what hot water felt like anymore. The thing was, the cold showers were barely putting a dent into calming his need for her. It was all-consuming, all the time.

He pulled up and looked at her worried face. "Nothing's wrong." He smiled as he brushed her hair back. "Just needed a second," he said, lowering his mouth to hers.

"A second for what?"

"To realize you aren't a dream," he said before he covered her mouth with his.

* * *

One night while snuggling on Brendan's couch and watching TV, Abby called and demanded that Paige put Brendan on the phone.

"What are you going to say to him?" Paige asked, more than a little anxious.

"Just put him on the phone," Abby practically screamed.

"Abby wants to talk to you," Paige said, handing her phone over to Brendan.

"Hello," he said with his calm, lazy drawl. He laughed and his eyes lit up as he looked at Paige. "I can promise you that will never happen." He reached out and started tracing a pattern of freckles on her knee. "Yes, I understand." He nodded. "Yes," he repeated a few more times. "It was nice talking to you too, Abby," he said before he handed the phone back to Paige.

"What was that about?" Paige asked.

"I just had to tell him that if he ever hurt you, I would fly down there and he'd be walking funny for the rest of his life."

"You're ridiculous." Paige laughed.

"I like him. He sounds sexy as hell."

"Oh, believe me, he is," Paige said as Brendan's hand trailed up the inside of her thigh. He stopped moving up when his fingers brushed just underneath the hem of her shorts. She looked at him but he just gave her that mischievous look that he got, his fingers still moving in slow, torturous circles.

"So," Brendan said when Paige hung up with Abby. "I'm your hot mechanic?" He smiled.

"Abby came up with that nickname."

"I like it." He brushed his mouth along the nape of her neck. His stubble rasped against her skin, giving her goose bumps.

"You like being known as the hot mechanic?" she asked as he moved up to nibble on her ear.

"No," he whispered. "I like being known as *yours*."

* * *

The second weekend in October, Jax and Shep dragged Brendan out to go deer hunting in north Georgia. They were leaving Friday afternoon and weren't coming back until late Sunday night. Wherever they were going, there was no cell phone reception. Paige wasn't used to not seeing Brendan every day let alone not talking to him. She wasn't prepared for how much she missed him and by Sunday afternoon she was going stir-crazy.

"You okay?" Denise asked as they made dinner.

"I'm fine. Why?" Paige asked as she dropped a potato into the sink.

"Oh, no reason," Denise said. "I'm just concerned that you might cut your finger off before the night's over. I've never seen you this fidgety."

"I'm not fidgety," Paige said as she dropped yet another potato. "These are just slippery after you peel them."

"Right," Denise said skeptically. "*That's* what's wrong. It has nothing to do with not seeing your nice young man all weekend."

"Maybe it has a little to do with that," Paige conceded. "It's just that it's only been three days, and I feel a little pathetic that I miss him so much."

"He makes you happy. You're allowed to miss him."

"I know but it's just a little bit scary."

"What's scary?" Trevor asked as he walked into the kitchen.

"Brendan." Paige grabbed another potato.

Trevor stopped and looked at her from the other side of the counter. "Care to elaborate? Because that doesn't inspire much confidence in the boy."

"I've never fallen this hard this fast before. He's . . . he's more than I imagined a man could be."

"And that's scary?" Denise asked.

"It's terrifying," Paige said.

"Why?" Trevor asked.

"Because what if I'm wrong. I thought that Dylan was this great guy. And I was so wrong about him. And I feel more for Brendan after two and a half months than I did for Dylan after a year. I don't think I could handle being wrong again. Not with him."

"I don't think you're wrong about him," Trevor said, rounding the counter. He put his arm around her shoulders and drew her into his side. "Putting yourself out there is always a scary thing and there's always that fear that someone is going to hurt you. But if you deny yourself the possibility, you're hurting only yourself. Brendan cares about you, Little Miss," he said, kissing her temple. "He's a good guy."

"Thanks, Dad," Paige whispered, turning her face up and placing a kiss on her father's jaw.

"I only want you to be happy. And you've definitely been that since he's been around."

There was no denying it; Paige was happy. And even though Brendan had been the catalyst behind that change, it definitely had more to do than just with him. She had friends in Grace, Tara, Lula Mae, Pinky, Panky, Jax, Shep, Mel, and Harper. All of them were amazing and she enjoyed being with them. And despite all of the drama with Missy and Verna at work, she really liked her job.

There was no denying that it was incredibly sad working at a funeral home, to have to talk to the families who'd had a loved one move on. But there was some comfort that Paige got to tell their stories through pictures, through art. She created timelines of their lives, watching them grow up, fall in love, and just live. It was tragic and beautiful at the same time. More often than not, she found herself tearing up whenever a family got emotional while they watched the tributes.

That wasn't to say that Paige wasn't still completely freaked out by the whole corpse thing. She'd taken to calling the dead bodies *situations* and Tara made fun of Paige's refusal to be alone in a room with one.

"It isn't funny," Paige had said the other day.

"It isn't like Mr. Abernathy is going to pop up and say hello," Tara had said, shaking her head as she'd walked into the viewing room with Paige so she could set up the projector.

"I know that. I just...They freak me out, okay? How do they not freak *you* out?"

"I'm used to it." Tara shrugged.

Paige hoped that there was never a day that she got *used* to dead bodies.

Paige had an early dinner with her parents that evening. She gave her stomach some time to digest her food before she went for a light run. The weather was starting to get cooler. The humidity was almost nonexistent on most days and a cold front had come in over the weekend, leaving the last couple of nights a little bit more than just nippy.

After her run, Paige took a hot shower to warm up, pulled on a thick pair of socks with her pajamas, and settled into bed to start a new book. At a little after ten, her phone beeped and she looked down to see a text message from Brendan.

You still up?

Yeah, you back yet?

Her phone beeped when the message sent, and then she heard a faint beep outside the French doors that led from her room into the backyard. A second later a faint knock rapped against the wood of the door.

"Paige," she heard Brendan whisper.

Her stomach flew up into her throat and she scrambled out of bed. Her sock-covered feet slid on the hardwood floors. She pulled the yellow curtains to the side and peeked out the window just to make sure that it was Brendan in her parents' backyard. He was standing there in a black hoodie with his hands shoved in the pockets of his jeans.

Paige flipped the dead bolt and opened the door. The chilly air breezed in and wrapped around her bare legs. His face split into a grin as he took her in. He pulled her into his big, warm body. His arms wrapped around her waist and his mouth landed hard on hers. She curled into him, letting her hands drift up under his sweatshirt to his bare skin.

"What are you doing?" he whispered against her mouth.

"Trying to keep warm," she said, pressing her hands into his warmth.

"Maybe if you were wearing pants you'd be warm."

Paige pulled back and looked down at herself. She was wearing an old baggy gray sweatshirt that fell about midthigh and a pair of baby-blue pajama shorts that just peeked out underneath it. She wiggled her toes, which were encased in a thick pair of rainbow-striped socks.

"It's not cold in my bed," she said, looking back up at him.

"Is that an invitation?" he asked, raising his eyebrows.

"That's not what I meant," she said, pinching his side. "It's not cold *inside* the house. So I didn't need to wear long pants."

"Oh, I'm not complaining." He grinned, letting his hands travel down to her bare thighs. "I'm pretty fond of these legs of yours."

"Hmm," she hummed. "What else are you fond of?"

"When it comes to you? Everything. God, I missed you," he said, putting his mouth on hers again.

Her fingers dug into his back as she tried to hold on to him. She was about to melt into the floor. His mouth moved down to her neck, where he pressed his nose into her skin and inhaled deeply.

"What time did you get back?" she asked as he opened his mouth on her throat.

"About an hour ago."

"What took you so long to get here?"

He pulled back and looked at her, his smile reaching all the way up to his eyes. "So you missed me too?"

"Yes." She nodded. "Very much."

"I went home to shower," he said, bringing his hands up to the back of her head and pulling her hair down from the messy bun that she'd thrown it up in earlier.

"Had to wash off all of the deer urine?" Paige asked as he pulled his fingers through her hair.

"You don't wear it. At least we don't. You spray it on rags and hang them up in trees."

"It still smells disgusting," she said, wrinkling her nose.

Brendan laughed. "Yeah, it does, and so did I after not showering all weekend."

"Well, you smell good now." She pressed her nose into his throat.

He touched her chin, lightly pushing her mouth back to his, and then let his fingers delve into her hair. Paige had no idea how long they stood there like that, kissing in the moonlight, but when he pulled back they were both breathless.

"So, did you kill anything?" she asked, brushing her lips across his neck.

"Yeah, enough deer to last me all winter."

"I've never eaten deer."

"I'm going to make you some venison burgers. Once you've eaten those, you're never going to want to eat beef again."

"Mmm, you cooking for me? I'm always game for that," she said as she moved her hands slowly up and down his back.

"I should go." Brendan pressed his lips into her temple. "If I stay much longer, this is going to turn into more than just a kiss good night."

"You're right." She sighed. "But I doubt I'm going to be able to fall asleep anytime soon. You've managed to get me all riled up," she said, pulling her hands down from underneath his sweatshirt.

"Riled up?" he asked, raising an eyebrow. "Is that just another word for horny?"

Paige punched him in the shoulder.

"You know, I don't have to take this abuse."

"You're the one who came here."

"You're right. I just can't seem to stay away. I must be a masochist. Have lunch with me tomorrow," he said, pushing her hair behind her ear.

"Pick me up at one?"

"If I can wait that long."

"I think you'll manage."

"Only if you wear those socks," he said, looking down at her feet. "Those things are awesome."

"Shut up. I get cold feet sometimes."

"Want me to warm them up?" he asked, letting his hands travel down to her butt.

"Okay, enough of that, mister." She pulled his hands away. Before she could let go, he grabbed her hands and laced his fingers with hers.

"I'll see you tomorrow," he said, kissing her softly on the lips one last time before he let go of her.

"Tomorrow," she said, watching him walk away.

* * *

Paige walked into Adams and Family on Monday to find everything in chaos. A pipe had burst in one of the bathrooms upstairs and water had run through the ceiling and down an entire wall. The wallpaper in the hallway was peeling at the top and around the edges.

There were three men in the hallway talking to Mr. Adams. One looked to be in his late fifties, with thin graying hair and a slight belly peeking over the top of his jeans. The other two were younger, no more than thirty. One had shaggy beach-blond hair. The other guy's hair was cut so close to his head that Paige couldn't tell what color it was.

"Paige," Mr. Adams said, waving her over. "This is Marlin Yance," he said, indicating the older gentleman. "He owns the best construction company here in Mirabelle."

"Nice to meet you," Paige said, sticking out her hand.

"And this is Chad Sharp," he said, indicating the blond. "And Bennett Hart," he said, patting the man with the buzz cut on the back. "Bennett just got back from his final tour in Afghanistan."

Paige shook both of their hands as well. Bennett nodded silently, but Chad gave her a sly smile, his eyes traveling slowly down her body. She felt a small prickle at the back of her neck.

"You're going to be seeing a lot of them in the next couple of weeks. That busted pipe has caused some major damage. We have to replace this whole wall."

"What about the services?" Paige asked.

"We're going to have to move them into the other parlor. We have only one service this week and it should be a small one."

"Well, I'm going to go up to my office. It was nice meeting you."

"Nice meeting you too," Chad said, still watching her.

She didn't like the way he was looking at her, especially that appreciative gleam in his eyes. It made her nervous, and just a little more than uncomfortable. She wanted to move out of his line of sight immediately. She stepped around them and headed for the kitchen, getting a cup of coffee. When she passed them on her way upstairs, she felt eyes on her again and the tiny prickle on the back of her neck got sharper.

* * *

Brendan showed up ten minutes early when he went to pick Paige up for lunch. He was surprised that he'd been able to last that long. If his impatience when it came to her was any indication, he was probably going to embarrass himself whenever they made it to bed. Hell, who was he kidding; he probably wouldn't even get that far.

It had taken everything in him to walk away from Paige the night before. He'd thought about her the whole damn time he'd been gone, missing her so much it hurt. He'd seen her every single day for over two months, and going the whole weekend had been torture. If he'd touched her for even five more seconds, he'd have backed her up into her room and stretched her out on her bed. Or the floor. The floor would have worked just fine.

When Brendan walked through the front door of the funeral home, he was greeted with loud hammering and two men taking a wall apart. Their faces were covered with masks to prevent them from inhaling the dust that was flying around them. Brendan didn't have to see their faces to know that it was Bennett Hart and Chad Sharp.

Bennett had been a year behind Brendan in high school. He'd played third base during Brendan's junior and senior years and then enlisted in the air force as soon as he'd graduated. He'd spent almost eight years in the service, most of that in Afghanistan. In his last tour, he'd been shot down in a helicopter and almost died. Only one other man on the mission survived.

Chad was four years behind Brendan in school. He'd dated Grace for a couple of months when she was a sophomore. Chad had been a senior and Brendan hadn't been a huge fan of Chad ever since. Not that Chad had ever done anything to Grace...well, not that Brendan knew of, because he would have hurt the little shit. But there was something about him that just got under Brendan's skin.

Bennett saw Brendan first. He stopped hammering and pulled his mask to the top of his head. Chad stopped too, his eyes narrowing on Brendan from above his mask.

"Long time no see," Bennett said, holding his hand out for Brendan.

"It's definitely been a while," Brendan said, grabbing Bennett's hand and slapping him on the back with the other. "How you doing?"

"Better these days."

"Good. Man, you should really come out and play on the league next year. It would be like old times."

"Maybe." Bennett nodded.

"You should come down to Shep's sometime. He'd love to see you, so would Jax."

"Maybe," Bennett repeated.

"Right." Brendan nodded. "Hey, Chad," Brendan said turning to him. "Things going good?"

"They've been going. I met your girlfriend today," he said, letting his lips curl up. "She's something."

"Yeah, she sure is," Brendan said cautiously. He really didn't like the fact that Chad had met Paige.

"Beautiful. She doesn't seem as scandalous as people say. But I guess looks can be deceiving. The only way to find out is to test it out. You tested her out yet? Which reminds me," he said, snapping his fingers together as a wide smirk spread across his face. "How's Grace doing? She been doing, I mean seeing anyone these days?"

If Brendan didn't walk away this second he was going to hurt the snot-nosed little prick.

"That's enough," Bennett said, taking a step toward both men. It was probably his years in the military that helped him sense danger, or maybe just his years knowing Brendan. "Walk away, Brendan."

"Gladly." Brendan took a step back. "Stay away from my sister and Paige."

"I'm going to be working here for the next couple of weeks." Chad shrugged. "I can't make any promises."

Brendan took another step back, shaking his head. Chad wasn't worth the energy. Brendan turned and headed up the stairs, his shoulders so tense he thought they were going to snap. Paige was going to be around that asshole and he wasn't okay with that in any way.

"Hey." She smiled, looking up from her computer.

She stood up as he walked into the room and he closed the distance, grabbing her and kissing her before she could say another word. She made a startled noise but relaxed into him after a second, her hands coming up to cup his jaw.

"You okay?" she asked, pulling back and looking at him.

"Yeah." He nodded. "Just needed to do that."

"You sure?" she asked, reaching up and tracing the space between his eyebrows.

"Let's get out of here," he said, grabbing her hand and pulling her toward the door.

"Hold on a sec." She pulled him to a stop. "Let me grab my bag."

Paige reached back and as soon as the straps of her purse were securely in her hand, Brendan pulled her out the door and as far away from Chad as he could get her.

Chapter Thirteen

A Stuffed Elephant and
a Scheming Weasel

Every year during the third weekend in October, Mirabelle hosted a fall festival. It was the biggest event of the year. The two small hotels in Mirabelle were always booked solid and every single beach house and condo was rented out. Even the very expensive resort on the beach had no vacancy. A lot of the people stayed north of Mirabelle in Tallahassee or west in Panama City and they'd make the forty-minute drive into town every day.

There was a huge crafts fair. People from all over the South came to set up booths for the weekend, selling hand-stitched quilts, baked goods, jams and preserves, jewelry, antiques, clothes, and about a hundred other things. Harper had a booth where she sold her homemade lotions and massage oils. It was the same ones that she used on her clients. She'd make the products year-round, and her supplies were completely depleted by the end of the festival.

Restaurants from all over the Panhandle came, cook-

ing their specialties and keeping everyone full of good
food. There was a cook-off each day. The main courses
changed every year. This year it was gumbo on Friday,
barbecue on Saturday, and pie on Sunday afternoon.
Grace and Lula Mae didn't set up a booth to sell their
food, because they were competing in the cook-offs. Contestants were allowed to enter only one competition. Lula
Mae was making gumbo. Grace was making pie.

The fair came into town that weekend too, complete
with a funhouse, a haunted house, a carrousel, a Ferris
wheel, a couple of small roller coasters, prize booths,
and a petting zoo. Parents lined up with their kids
to ride around on the many horses and ponies from
the area. Shep's aunt and uncle owned a horse farm
in Mirabelle, and they were the ones who provided
the four-legged entertainment. There was a pumpkin-
carving contest on Friday and a pumpkin-throwing contest on Sunday, both equally messy. And on Saturday
night, there was a dance.

Brendan picked up Paige on Friday night and they
headed over to the festival. He led her through the crowd
to the entrance, her hand in his. But the second she saw
the crafts booths, she was the one leading him, and he
happily followed. Paige wanted to see as much as possible because she was working at the festival the next
morning. Mel had roped her into doing face painting at
onc of the booths for the high school.

Paige bought some organic honey and apple butter,
wind chimes made of large antique keys, and a box of
Italian lemon mousse chocolates. She lingered at a booth
that made jewelry from spoons for a couple of minutes,
eyeing a ring that was a bit on the pricey side.

"Why don't you get it?" Brendan asked, sidling up behind her and pressing his nose to her hair. He couldn't help himself; she just smelled so damn incredible.

"No, it's too expensive." She shook her head. "I don't need a sixty-dollar ring. Come on," she said, grabbing his hand and pulling him to the next booth.

After they finished with the crafts booths, Brendan took all of their purchases to his truck before they got in line to buy tickets for the Friday cook-off. Each night the people eating the food would vote for their favorite. First place got a thousand dollars; second, seven hundred and fifty; and third, five hundred. The high school ran the cook-offs, and to keep the cooks anonymous and bias out of the voting, the students served the food. There were twenty different types of gumbo to taste, and to make sure that everyone had enough room to try everything, they served just a sample into the bowls. The contestants had to make enough for two thousand samples, and at fifteen dollars a ticket, the high school made a pretty penny.

The cook-off was held in a massive old barn that had been restored years ago. Colorful paper lanterns hung from the rafters and white Christmas lights were wrapped around the pillars and strung up along the walls and around the doors. There were over a hundred tables set up around the floor, and most of them were filled with people.

Jax was on patrol that night so that he could get Saturday night off. Shep was manning the makeshift bar that the Sleepy Sheep set up. And Harper was at her booth selling her merchandise. So it was just Brendan, Paige, Mel, and Grace for dinner. Brendan and Paige got four trays of the twenty samples, while Mel and Grace got a couple of beers. They found a table in the corner and all sat down to eat.

"So the real test here is if you can figure out which one is Lula Mae's," Grace said, handing Paige a beer.

"Under normal circumstances, I'd say that Lula Mae and Grace always win when it comes to cooking, no questions asked," Brendan said as he grabbed one of the samples. "But they've got pretty stiff competition when it comes to these cook-offs. I've not voted for them many times because I had no idea which was theirs."

"Did you help her make this?" Paige asked.

"Nope, I was busy making the pies. I had to make forty of them."

"Jeez," Paige said as she grabbed a sample and took a bite. "Oh my gosh." She moaned as she swallowed.

"Just you wait. They're all going to be amazing," Mel said.

"Mmm," Paige hummed as she took another bite.

Paige making those sounds was doing nothing to help Brendan keep up his promise of being patient. He wanted to hear her moaning like that while she was underneath him and he was inside of her.

They made their way through the gumbo, and as predicted, Brendan had no idea which one was Lula Mae's. They all voted for their favorite and then Mel and Grace went to hang out with Harper while Brendan and Paige moved on to the fair. They went to the funhouse and then the haunted house, Paige pressed up against Brendan's side the whole time. Every time something went bump in the dark, she somehow wrapped herself around him tighter.

He had absolutely no complaints.

"Come here," he said, grabbing her hand and pulling her to the prize booths. "I'm going to win you something."

"Oh are you?" She smiled.

"Yup, this is how men show their women they're cared for."

"With stuffed animals?"

"Yup, the bigger the better." He nodded.

"Well then, let's see what you're made of."

Brendan picked the booth with the water gun. He had to shoot all fifteen frogs off their lily pads to get the biggest prize. Piece of cake.

Or so he thought. The first round he hit only nine; the second, fourteen, but the third time was the charm and he knocked all of those damn frogs off their pads.

"Ooh, big manly man," Paige said as he shot the last one.

"And don't you forget it," he said, turning to her and grinning. He leaned toward her and kissed her. "Pick your prize," he said above her lips.

"Hmm," she hummed, turning to the booth and looking over her options. "The elephant." She pointed to a giant green one in the corner.

The guy behind the booth handed it over to her, and Paige hugged it close to her chest. The thing was huge, probably about the same size as Sydney.

"I can carry it," he said, holding out his hand.

"I don't think so." She shook her head. "I want to show people what my man won me."

"Is that so?"

"Yup," she said, grabbing his hand and leaning into him. She pressed her lips to his and sighed. "Thank you."

"Anytime."

Their last stop of the night was the Ferris wheel. They loaded up into the cart, green elephant in tow, and made their way slowly to the top as the other carts loaded. Paige snuggled into Brendan's side. She was wearing a jacket but she shivered slightly.

"You cold?" he asked, pulling her closer into him.

"Only a little," she said, turning as she looked out at the view. The festival was set up very close to the beach. The lighthouse could be seen in the distance. The moon and the stars reflected off the water. "It's so beautiful here," she whispered. "So quiet."

"So you're beginning to like it here in Mirabelle?"

Paige looked at him, a smile turning up her mouth. "I'm way beyond *like*, Brendan," she said softly.

She reached up, putting her hand to his face, and brought her mouth to his. Kissing him deeply. It was then that the Ferris wheel plunged them down toward the ground and Brendan wasn't sure if it was the ride or Paige that sent an exhilarating thrill through him.

His money was on Paige.

* * *

On Saturday, Paige got up early and headed over to the festival. It didn't open until nine, but there was already a crowd of people at eight thirty waiting around for the vendors to set up their booths. Paige found Mel at Harper's little booth, both of them talking while they sipped on coffee.

"Here you go," Mel said, handing Paige a to-go cup. "Grace told me you're a caffeine junkie like the rest of us.

So I thought I'd show you some appreciation for helping out."

Paige had already had two cups that morning, but she was never one to turn down coffee.

"Thanks," Paige said, taking a sip. "It's perfect."

It was a little chilly outside that morning, and the coffee was nice and hot.

"So," Harper said, "things with you and Brendan are getting serious."

Mel choked on her coffee. "Harper, stop being nosey. Just ignore her," Mel said, looking to Paige.

"No, it's okay." Paige laughed. "Things *are* getting serious."

"It's really interesting to see him fall all over himself around you." Harper grinned. "I've known him for years and I've never seen him like this. You sure do put a spark in that boy."

"Fall all over himself?" Paige asked curiously.

"Oh yeah," Mel said. "I mean he isn't nearly as stoic as, say, Jax."

"No one is as stoic as Jax. Well, except when he's around Grace. Then that boy's all over the place." Harper grinned wider. "But Brendan has very rarely been ruffled by anyone. He's always been Mr. Calm, Cool, and Collected in the relationships I've seen him in."

"That's not the case with you," Mel said.

"Well…" Paige smiled. "That's good to know. *Very* good to know."

At nine, Paige and Mel said good-bye to Harper and went to the face-painting station that was closer to the fair. Mel had already admitted to having no artistic ability whatsoever.

"If it was a paint-by-numbers thing I could so do it, but if I were to try to paint a lion or something on a kid's face it would look jaundice. No one wants to pay for that."

"I'd say that's probably true."

Mel was in charge of the money and organizing the kids between the three volunteers who were painting faces. The first kid to sit down in front of Paige was Jamie Rodgers. He was five years old, with big blue eyes and curly blond hair.

"I want a dragon. Can you do a dragon?" he asked, looking up at her.

"Jamie," his mother said sternly. "What are we forgetting?"

"Pleeeease," he begged, bouncing up and down in his seat.

Paige laughed. "I can do a dragon," she said, grabbing her paintbrush and dipping it into the green paint.

Paige worked almost nonstop. She painted unicorns and fairies, flowers, rainbows, bears, tigers, snakes, sharks, and so many other things. It was an endless line. Paige felt a great amount of satisfaction that the kids walked away beyond happy. She'd also met a lot of the people in the community, talking to the parents as she'd painted the kids faces.

At one, Paige started to clean up her stuff. She'd signed up for only four hours. Brendan was going to come down and they were going to get lunch and do a little bit more exploring.

"So is there an age limit?"

Paige looked up to see Chad Sharp standing in front of her. He might be considered attractive but his smile was smarmy and an uneasy feeling settled in Paige's stomach.

Chad was almost as big as Brendan. But he wore his T-shirt a size too small so that the muscles of his arms and chest looked bigger than they actually were. There were two other guys with him. One had brown hair and wore a sneer. The other had dark blond hair and scary eyes.

"Aren't you a little old to get your face painted?" Paige asked.

"Well, I was thinking that you could put some lipstick on and paint it with your mouth."

"I don't think so," Paige said, shaking her head. That uneasy feeling getting just a little bit worse.

"Oh, come on." He came in close so he could whisper in her ear. "If I like what I see, we can move on to you painting other places on my body."

"Excuse me?" Paige said, standing up and taking a step back from him.

"You heard me." He took a step toward her.

Paige jumped as two hands came up around her waist from behind and she was pulled back into a hard body. But she knew that body. Knew that chest and those arms. Knew the hands at her waist, how they circled her and held her.

Brendan.

"What exactly did she hear?" Brendan asked, his voice more menacing than Paige had ever heard it.

Chad just smiled wide as he took a step back, his hands in the air. "Oh, nothing," he said, shaking his head. "Just curious how talented your girlfriend here is."

"Curiosity can be a pretty dangerous thing, Chad. So how about you stop wondering."

"Yeah, problem is, once I get an idea in my head, I'm pretty damned determined to figure it out. Bye, darling," he said, waving at Paige before he walked away with his two friends.

Brendan's hands tightened on Paige's waist, not painfully, just possessively.

"What did he say to you?" he whispered low in her ear.

Paige turned in his arms and looked up at him. He was furious.

"It's okay," she said, placing her palm on his chest.

"What did he say to you?" he repeated.

Paige took a deep breath and let it out slowly. "He wanted me to kiss him," she said, simplifying it. And that was *basically* what he'd said, though Chad's proposition had been a little bit more specific.

"I really hate that guy," Brendan said. "Did he touch you?" he asked.

"No." Paige shook her head. "I'm fine, Brendan. Don't worry so much."

"Yeah, that isn't going to happen," he said, shaking his head, his eyes softening as he looked at her.

"When did you get so protective of me?" she asked, reaching up and touching his face.

"The day I met you."

Paige just looked at him, a little shocked.

"If he comes near you again, I want to know about it."

"All right." She nodded.

"Promise?"

"Promise."

Chapter Fourteen

Shake It for Me, Girl

Brendan and Paige stayed at the festival until about four and then they both headed home to get ready for the night. Paige wanted to change and shower before Brendan picked her up and they went back for the barbecue cook-off and the dance. He was on her parents' front porch by six thirty. She opened the door a moment after he knocked, smiling wide as she stepped outside.

Brendan forgot how to talk.

She was wearing that same red shirt she'd worn on their first date. Her freckled shoulders were bare and perfect. A black bohemian skirt swayed around her knees and left a good amount of her legs visible above her red cowboy boots. Her hair was pulled to the side in a low knot just above her neck.

She was stunning.

Brendan reached forward and grabbed her, pulling her into his arms and kissing her like his life depended on it.

"Wow," she said when he pulled back. "What was that for?"

"You look beautiful."

"Thank you." She smiled.

"There's just one thing missing," he said, reaching into his pocket.

"Oh?" she asked, raising her eyebrows.

Brendan pulled out that silver spoon ring that Paige had been eyeing the day before and slipped it onto her left thumb.

"Brendan," she whispered, looking down at her hand and then back up to him. There were so many emotions flittering across her face, but shock and awe were winning for the most prominent. "I can't believe you got this for me," she said, reaching up to touch his jaw. She pulled his face to hers and pressed a kiss to his mouth. "You didn't have to, you know."

"I know," he said, running his hands up and down her back. "But I wanted you to have it."

"Thank you," she said, pressing her mouth to his again. "I love it."

"Yeah?" He grinned

"Yeah."

Paige spent a few more minutes showing him her appreciation before she slipped back inside, grabbed her jacket and purse, and they headed over to the festival. When they got there, they found Grace, Mel, Harper, Jax, Shep, and, much to Brendan's surprise, Bennett.

They all ate the barbecue and voted for their favorite. The guys went and got some burgers because the samples didn't fill them up like they did the girls. They got another round of drinks and let their food settle. Some of the tables began to empty and people working the event started to put them away, clearing out a space in the middle of the barn to be used as the dance floor. Then the band filed out onto the stage and music filled the room. Brendan stood up and held out his hand for Paige.

"Come on now, let's see what you're made of."

She raised one of her eyebrows and smiled wickedly. "Is that a challenge?"

"Absolutely."

"Let's go, cowboy," she said, putting her hand in his and letting him pull her to her feet.

Brendan couldn't help but grin. He turned around and pulled her out onto the dance floor. The band was playing a fast-moving country song as he spun her around and pulled her into his arms. They moved across the floor quickly, Paige in perfect step with him. She swiveled her hips in a way that made him want to fall to his knees.

They stayed out on the floor for a few more songs before Paige leaned into him and whispered breathlessly that she needed a break. The table was empty when they got back. He scanned the room and saw that Mel was dancing with Bennett, Shep with Grace, and Harper with Greg Myers, who worked at King's. He looked around and saw Jax talking to a couple of guys in a corner, staring moodily at Shep and Grace while he drank his beer. Brendan shook his head and smiled. Some things never changed.

When the song ended, Shep and Grace came back to the table, both out of breath and a little pink in the face.

"You can dance, city girl," Grace said as she sunk down into the chair next to Paige.

"She sure can." Brendan grinned.

Jax came back to the table and sat down next to Brendan, scowl still firmly in place.

"What's wrong with you?" Grace asked, throwing a balled-up paper napkin at Jax. "Why are you brooding?"

"Princess, I don't brood," he said, narrowing his eyes at her.

"Really? You could've fooled me," Grace said, rolling her eyes.

"You want another drink?" Brendan asked Paige.

"Yeah." She nodded.

"Be right back," he said, getting up and kissing her on the head.

"I'm going to get another one too. You want anything, Grace?" Shep asked.

"Cider."

"Coming up." Shep stood, and so did Jax.

The three men made their way across the room. The bar was made from a couple of old barn doors laid out on stacked apple barrels. There was a thick crowd converging around it. Shep's family might have been running it, but he had to wait in line just like everybody else.

"So," Shep said as they joined the crowd, "you and Paige are working out."

"Yeah." Brendan nodded, taking a step forward as the crowd shifted.

"That's all you've got? Yeah?"

"What do you want me to say? That I like her a lot? I do."

"Like her a lot?" Jax asked, raising his eyebrows.

"Fine, it's a little more than like."

"How about it's *a lot* more than like. She's got you wrapped around her pretty little finger," Jax said.

"Is there a problem with that?"

"No, but I'm thinking you'd like her to be wrapped around something of yours." Shep smirked.

Brendan couldn't argue with him there.

"We're taking things slow," Brendan said.

"It's killing you, isn't it?" Shep asked.

"You have no fucking clue," Brendan admitted.

Both men laughed at him.

Brendan looked over to the table where Paige sat. She and Grace were laughing. A second later Bennett and Mel came back to the table and sat down.

"I'm glad Bennett came out tonight. He's a good guy," Brendan said, turning back.

"Yeah, he is." Jax nodded. "That war really messed with his head. He's got some demons to battle."

"It would mess with anyone's head. I couldn't imagine going through what he did," Brendan said, shaking his head.

"He seems to be having a good time tonight. He's stayed pretty active out on that dance floor," Shep said. "Unlike others, who just stand in the corner and glare. You know if you want to dance with Grace, you should just ask her, Jax."

"I don't dance," Jax mumbled.

"Maybe you should make an exception in this case," Brendan said.

Jax didn't say anything. He just turned around and stepped up to the bar.

Brendan wasn't oblivious to what was going on between one of his best friends and his baby sister. Grace and Jax had been circling each other for years. Problem was, Jax had his own demons to battle.

The guys made their way back to the table. Paige grabbed her drink from Brendan and took a long pull before she stood up. She grabbed Brendan's hand and dragged him back out onto the floor. After a couple fast songs, they played a slow one. Brendan pulled Paige in as close as he could get her and she curled around him in that way she always did. He rested one hand on her lower back while the other gripped one of her hands and held it close to his chest. He pressed his face into her hair and breathed deeply.

Brendan's life had changed so drastically since Paige had been in it. To say that it was better was an understatement. He loved having her in his arms, having her arms wrapped around him. She was becoming everything to him.

Brendan glanced up at the room for just a second and did a double take. Jax was dancing with Grace. And if Brendan didn't know any better, Jax was smiling.

Maybe those demons of his would be fought a little sooner than later.

* * *

The dance ended just before midnight, and Brendan walked Paige back to his truck, his arm around her shoulders and his nose in her hair. She'd had an amazing time but when the music had ended, she hadn't been disappointed. The plans that she had for the rest of the night would be possible only behind closed doors.

"What time is your curfew tonight?" Brendan joked as they stopped in front of the passenger door.

"Oh, didn't I tell you? I don't have one tonight," she

said, raising an eyebrow as she reached down and ran her finger along the top of his belt.

"Paige?" he asked, going still.

She stretched up, pressing into him, and put her mouth to his ear. "I want you," she whispered.

He moved so quickly she didn't even see it coming. The passenger door was opened and he'd bodily lifted her into the seat, reaching across her and buckling her seat belt. He slammed the door and ran around his truck. He climbed in and was backing out in about five seconds.

"You okay there, cowboy?" she asked, trying not to laugh.

"You aren't allowed to talk," he said as he navigated out of the parking lot.

"Why?" she asked, folding her arms across her chest.

"Because you have a tendency to say things that make me swerve off the road, and right now I need to have as much focus as possible. Otherwise I might kill us," he said, staring intently through the windshield.

"I don't have to say anything," she said, reaching across the seat and running her fingers up his forearm.

"You also have to stay on your side of the truck," he said as his hands clenched the steering wheel, his knuckles going white.

"That's no fun." Her fingers trailed up his shoulder and to his neck.

"Please, Paige, I'm begging you." He groaned.

"Hmm, I like the sound of that."

"What has gotten into you tonight?" he asked, sounding desperate.

Messing with him was fun. She shouldn't be enjoying it so much but she was. She wanted him more than she'd ever wanted any man, ever, and it was driving her crazy. So in turn she was driving him crazy. Really, it was just fair play.

"Nothing yet, but I'm hoping you'll change that."

"Okay. No more talking from you, or touching. Not until this car is parked and turned off."

"If you insist," she said, holding up her hands in surrender and placing them in her lap.

When Brendan pulled into his driveway ten minutes later, he got out of the car faster than she could blink, helped her get out, and then pulled her up the stairs to his front door.

"Shit," he said when they walked in. "I have to take Sydney out," he said as the dog in question came skidding down the hall and started circling them, her tail wagging.

"I can wait five minutes, Brendan." She reached down and scratched Sydney's nose.

"Yeah, but I don't think *I* can," he said as he walked to the back door and opened it. Sydney followed and bolted down the back stairs, disappearing into the darkness that reached past his backlights.

Paige pulled off her boots in the living room and padded out onto the porch. She came up behind Brendan, slipping her hands around his waist and gently biting him through the back of his shirt. He groaned deep in his chest as her hands dipped down to the front of his jeans.

"What are you doing?" he asked, sounding pained as she slid his belt out of the first loop of his jeans.

"You said you couldn't wait," she said in his ear. "I'm merely removing pesky barriers." She nipped at his earlobe.

He grabbed her hands and moved her around to stand

in front of him. He reached for the knot at the back of her head and pulled it out, unwinding her hair and fanning it around her shoulders.

"I've wanted to do that all night." He roped his fingers through her hair and brought her mouth to his.

Paige let her hands wander down and she started un-buttoning his shirt. Which was *not* an easy task, not at all. Because all the while, Brendan was kissing her like she was his air supply. When she finished with the buttons, she slid her hands under the two flaps of his shirt, press-ing her hands into his over-heated skin.

She walked her fingers down, tracing his flat stomach, and reached for his belt again. She unbuckled it and then undid the top button on his jeans. As she reached for the zipper, his hands covered hers and he pulled back from her mouth, his breath labored.

"Not yet. No more touching until we go inside," he said, swallowing hard. "If that zipper goes down, I'm done for."

Paige smiled but let go. "Okay," she said, taking a step back from him. She reached down and grabbed the hem of her shirt, pulling it up and over her head.

Brendan stared at her in her black strapless bra and skirt. He took a step forward and reached out, but Paige took another step back, shaking her head and smiling.

"Uh-uh, you said no more touching until we're both inside." She took another step back into the house. "I'm inside, but you seem to still be out there."

"You know what they say about payback," Brendan said, letting a smile curve his lips.

"No," she said, shaking her head innocently and drop-ping her shirt onto the floor. "What do they say?" she asked as she pushed her skirt down over her hips and let it fall into a puddle around her feet. He stared at her lace panties, his eyes going wide with wanting.

At that moment Sydney came walking into the house. Both of them were so focused on each other that they hadn't even heard her come up the stairs.

"It's a bitch," he said, coming inside.

Paige turned and ran down the hall, laughing as she bolted for his bedroom. She barely made it past his doorway when he grabbed her around the waist. He took a few steps and they fell onto his bed, landing softly with him on top, firmly between her legs. He grabbed her hands and pinned them above her head with one of his.

"So what are you going to do to me? What's my great payback?" She grinned up at him.

"Let's see . . . where to start," Brendan said, pressing his mouth to her neck while his free hand traced her knee and slowly worked up the inside of her thigh. He lightly ran his fingers over the edge of her panties before he moved up to her stomach, his fingers running around her belly button and out to her side, walking up her ribs one by one. After a moment, he let go of her hands and cradled her face in both of his.

"Paige, I want you so much it hurts," he said, looking at her like no man had ever looked at her. Like he could look at her forever and never get tired of her. It made her chest tighten.

She reached up, running her hands up his neck and into his hair. "I know the feeling," she said, pulling his face down to her and kissing him.

One of his hands trailed down her body until it was between her thighs. He pulled back her lacy panties and groaned as his fingers found a place that was warm and wet.

"Brendan," she said and moaned, her body arching up. He stroked her with two fingers and pressed his thumb against a spot that made her hips start pumping up into his hand.

Paige reached down to the front of Brendan's jeans and cupped him through the fabric. He groaned again and thrust his tongue harder into her mouth. A second later he pulled back from her, his hand disappearing from inside of her as he turned and sat on the edge of the bed. He leaned over and started unlacing his boots. Paige got up on her knees and came up behind him. She slid her hands up his back and leaned into him, kissing his neck.

When he got his boots and socks off, Paige pulled his shirt off his shoulders. The second his arms were free, he stood up and reached for the front of his pants but she grabbed his hands and pulled them away.

"Let me," she said, reaching for his zipper and pulling it down. She brought her hands up to the waistband of his jeans and pulled them, along with his boxer briefs, down his thighs. He sprang free and she wrapped her hand around him, stroking him.

He was huge and incredible, everywhere. And she wanted to put her mouth all over his body. Trace every single muscle with her tongue. But that would have to wait.

"If you continue with that, we aren't going to get very far," he said, looking like he was barely holding it together.

"We wouldn't want that," she said, letting go of him.

She sat back on the bed, reaching behind her back and un-snapping her bra before she threw it to the ground. She lay back on the bed and settled her head against the pillow, looking at him. "Well? What are you waiting for?"

"I have no freaking clue." He shook his head as he pushed his pants the rest of the way down his legs and stepped out of them. He kneeled on the bed and reached for her waist, grabbing the top of her panties and pulling them down her long legs.

"God, Paige," he said, staring at the apex of her thighs. She spread her legs and he groaned. A second later he was between her legs, his mouth on hers, and his hands on her breasts. She was writhing beneath him, absolutely unable to control her response to him.

"Brendan, please," she begged desperately. "I need you inside of me."

He reached out to his nightstand and opened a drawer, his hand returning a second later with a small packet. He ripped it open and pulled out the condom. He rolled it on and positioned himself over her. He grabbed one of her hands, stretching it up over their heads, his fingers intertwining with hers. He looked down into her eyes and entered her in one long, slow stroke.

They both stopped for a second, just staring at each other and memorizing that first moment that their bodies joined together. Brendan lowered his mouth to hers and kissed her slowly, his tongue stroking hers. Paige pulled her feet up. She planted them on the bed and lifted her hips, making Brendan slide farther into her.

Brendan's free hand slid under Paige's behind, pulling her body more firmly to his as he started to pump his hips. Brendan took his time, moving in and out of her slowly. Perfectly. She wrapped her legs around his waist, and somehow he was even deeper inside of her.

"Oh, Paige, baby," Brendan said against her mouth.

Paige's free hand gripped Brendan's back. Her nails dug into his skin as he continued to move inside of her, creating a perfect friction against every single sweet spot on her body. It was exquisite.

He pulled his mouth back from hers and looked into her eyes, and what she saw in his eyes took her breath away. The way he was looking at her made her feel like she was completely worth it, like she was completely worth everything.

And that did it.

She spiraled out of control, her body contracting around his in the most powerful orgasm of her life. Paige came completely undone in Brendan's arms, and a second later he was undone in hers.

Chapter Fifteen

Socks, Sunrises, and Sex...Lots of It

Brendan slowly opened his eyes to his dark room. He was pressed up against the back of Paige, one arm underneath her pillow. The other was wrapped around her waist, his hand on her stomach. His nose was buried in her hair, and every time he breathed in, he inhaled her citrus shampoo. He leaned up and kissed her shoulder. She sighed and shifted in her sleep, rubbing herself against a spot that was already at attention.

He didn't think he would ever get enough of her, not for as long as he lived. Everything about the night before had been amazing, more amazing than anything else. He'd thought that if they ever made it to a bed, he wouldn't be able to take things slow. He'd wanted her for so long that slow had seemed impossible. But when he'd finally gotten her stretched out beneath him, he'd wanted to take in every moment of it. He'd wanted to memorize her, to touch every inch of her and learn her by heart.

He looked over at the clock on the nightstand. It was fifteen past seven. They'd been asleep for less than five hours. After their first earth-shattering go-round, Paige had slipped out of Brendan's bed and grabbed his shirt from the floor, sliding her arms into the sleeves.

"You look good in my shirt," he'd said as he propped himself up on his arm and watched her. "But you look better out of it."

"Yes, well, it's cold," she'd said as she buttoned it up.

"Then come back to bed," he'd said, pulling the blanket back for her to join him.

"I'm going scavenging for food. You stay there and recoup. You're going to need your strength for round two."

"Round two? I like the sound of that."

"So do I." She'd smiled as she walked out of the room.

She'd returned with sliced apples and cheese, two cans of Coke, and a piece of chocolate cheesecake. He'd sat back against the headboard, Paige straddling his lap while she'd fed herself and him. When they'd moved onto the cheesecake, Brendan had started undoing the buttons on the shirt she was wearing, and by the time they were done eating they'd moved on to round two.

Brendan had thought he'd been done for when he'd seen Paige swivel her hips when she was dancing. But he'd had no freaking clue just how done for he was until she did it balanced on his lap, with him firmly inside of her.

Afterward, she'd fallen asleep quickly in his arms and he hadn't been able to bring himself to wake her up. So he'd laid there, letting his fingers trail over her hip and up her side, until he'd fallen asleep to the soft sound of her breathing.

"Paige," Brendan whispered, pressing his mouth to her ear. "Baby, wake up."

"Hmm," she hummed moving against him again. If she kept doing that he wasn't going to be able to follow through with his next plan of action.

"Paige," he said again, moving a little so that he could pull her onto her back.

Her eyes opened slowly and when she focused on him she gave him a sleepy smile.

"Mmm, morning," she said, stretching her arms above her head.

The blankets fell down around her breasts and she rolled toward him, wrapping her arms around his neck and sliding her leg up and between his. He rolled her back into the mattress, grabbing her free leg and pulling it around his waist as he covered her mouth with his. She ran her hands down his back and across his waist, and just before she reached for him, he grabbed her hands and pulled them away.

"Not yet," he said, shaking his head. "That isn't why I woke you up."

"You woke me up from a sound sleep and it wasn't to have sex?" she pouted. "You're lucky you're cute."

"Cute?" he asked, looking down at her. "I'm not cute."

"Yes, you are." She smiled. "And incredibly sexy."

"Sexy I can get used to," he said, pressing his lips to hers.

"If you don't stop doing that, I'm not going to care what your other plans are."

"Okay." He grinned, rolling off her and getting out of bed.

She eyed him appreciatively until he held out his

hand for her to grab. "We going somewhere?" She
frowned.

"Don't you trust me?"

She didn't answer, just put her hand in his and let him
pull her up and out of bed.

"It's cold out here." She rubbed her bare arms.

Brendan reached around her and pulled one of the
blankets from the bed, wrapping it around her shoulders.
Then he went over to his dresser and opened a drawer.

"So your feet don't get cold," he said, holding up a pair
of thick white socks. He kneeled down in front of her and
pulled one of her feet up from the floor, sliding the sock
over her foot. He did the same with the other one and then
stood up in front of her.

She just stared at him, her eyes going a little misty and
her mouth slightly open.

"Paige?" Brendan asked, taking a step into her. "You
okay?"

"Yeah." She nodded, leaning up and kissing him softly
on the mouth. "I'm more than okay," she said, sounding a
little stunned.

The way she was looking at him made it difficult
for him to breathe. He hadn't even thought twice about
putting the socks on her feet; he'd just wanted her to be
warm. But the look on her face said that it had meant
something to her. That he meant something to her. He
wanted to put that look on her face as many times as hu-
manly possible.

Brendan grabbed another blanket from his closet,
wrapped it around his shoulders, and grabbed Paige's
hand. He pulled her to the French doors in his bedroom
that led out onto the deck and down the stairs to the ham-

mock. Sydney followed them from the place she'd been sleeping on Brendan's bedroom floor.

Brendan let go of Paige's hand and sat down on the hammock. He lay down and opened the blanket he'd wrapped around himself so that Paige could climb in. She did, adjusting her blanket so it covered both of them. Brendan wrapped his blanket and his arms around her as she settled into his chest.

"I wanted to watch the sunrise with you," he whispered against her hair.

"Is that what we're doing?" she asked, pressing her hands into his skin. "I thought you wanted to turn me into a Popsicle."

"Are you cold?" he asked, running his hands up and down her back.

"No." She shook her head. "*Very* warm actually."

They laid in silence, the dark blue sky slowly getting lighter. Brendan ran his fingers up and down Paige's back, tracing her spine. Paige pressed her face into his neck as she reached up and ran her fingers along his collarbone.

As the sun began to rise over the water, Paige sat up, pressing her palms into Brendan's chest to keep her balance. As she stared out at the water, he stared at her. The sun slowly lit up her face, making her cheeks glow. Her unruly curls framed her face and fell down past her shoulders. Her gray eyes went wide with wonder and an amazed look framed her mouth. He'd never seen anything more beautiful in his life.

Her palm was spread over his heart, the heat from her skin seeping into his and spreading throughout his body. He'd never forget that moment for as long as he lived, because it was when he realized he was in love with someone for the first time in his life. It was the moment he *knew* he'd fallen in love with Paige.

* * *

After the sunrise, Brendan dragged Paige back to bed. They made love again and dozed in each other's arms until well after ten. She wasn't used to how much he wanted to touch her. She'd never been with a guy who was big on snuggling. Dylan had hated it. But Brendan was quite content to have her sprawled across him, using his chest as her pillow.

When they got up, Brendan pulled her into the kitchen and sat her on top of his countertop. He ran around the kitchen wearing a pair of sweatpants and a T-shirt cooking her breakfast while she sat sipping coffee wrapped in his thick blue robe. The only other thing she was wearing were the socks he'd put on her feet earlier.

Paige hadn't been prepared for what that small little action had done to her. One minute she'd been standing in the middle of Brendan's room freezing, and the next, Brendan had been kneeling in front of her, putting socks on her feet because he didn't want her to be cold. She'd fallen in love with him over a pair of socks. How crazy was that?

Brendan made eggs, hash browns, and venison sausage. He cut a piece off the first finished patty and brought the fork to her mouth.

"That's delicious," she said after she swallowed.

"So have you converted?"

"Yes, but not to animal heads as trophies."

"Damn," he said, snapping his fingers and looking

disappointed. "Now I don't know what to get you for Christmas. What if I get you a bumper sticker that says 'Shoot first, ask questions later'?"

"You think you're so cute."

"No," he said, shaking his head and grinning. "But you do. You told me so this morning."

"I was half asleep," she said, waving off his words. "Still delirious."

"No, I've seen you delirious. It involves you panting my name."

"I can't really help it when you continually make me feel like I'm having an out-of-body experience."

"Is that right?" He smiled, looking pretty proud of himself. "Well, you do the exact same thing to me."

After breakfast, Paige helped Brendan clean the kitchen. She loaded the dishwasher while he put the leftovers away. She'd spent enough time at this house to know where everything went, and they moved around the kitchen in tandem. She put the last dish away and turned to find Brendan leaning against the fridge, his arms and legs crossed as he watched her.

"See something you like?" she asked.

"I see many things I like," he said, uncrossing his limbs and pushing off the fridge. He walked across the kitchen and caged her against the counter.

"Anything in particular?"

"Oh yeah," he said, running his hand up and down her waist. "So I was thinking…"

"About?"

"I'm assuming you're going to want to stop by your parents' house and change before we head over to the festival."

"You assume correctly." She nodded.

It wouldn't be in her best interest to show up in front of half the town in the exact same clothes that she'd worn the night before.

"Well," he continued, "you should pack a bag to bring over here."

Her eyes widened in shock and she inhaled sharply.

"I want you to stay again tonight," he said, leaning in and kissing her neck. "And the night after that." He moved up to her jaw. "And the night after that," he said when he got to her cheek. "And the night after that," he said above her mouth before he kissed her. "And every night after. I'll clear out a drawer. You can hang some stuff up in the closet. We'll get that citrus shampoo of yours to leave in the shower." He pulled back as he twisted a strand of her hair around his finger.

"You're serious?" she said, searching his face.

"You're not going to find it." He shook his head.

"Find what?"

"Doubt," he said, knowing exactly what she'd been looking for. "I know what I want, and it's you. I've never been more certain of anything in my life. Paige, I loved waking up next to you this morning. I loved having you pressed up against me. And I wanted you closer. Kissing you, touching you, making love to you, it's incredible," he said, moving one of his hands up to her ribs while the other fisted in her hair. "I'm not asking you to move in with me. We can still take things slowly. I just prefer to take them slowly with you in my bed *every* night."

"That doesn't sound very slow," she said, shaking her head, trying to think over the sudden pounding in her ears.

"And?" Brendan shrugged. "It's what I want. Tell me you want it too."

Paige took a deep breath and nodded her head. "It's what I want. It's just that it scares me. *You* scare me."

"Why?"

Why? Because she'd fallen in love with him over a pair of socks.

Okay, so it was more than just the socks.

Brendan made her feel things she'd never felt before, so she couldn't even imagine what it would do to her if he broke her heart. What he wanted? God, she wanted it too. So much she could barely stand it. Maybe he wasn't asking her to move in. All of her stuff wouldn't be here at his house, but some of it would be and she'd be staying there every night. So really, what was the difference? What if being with her for that much time made him realize he didn't want it anymore? That he didn't want *her* anymore?

"Paige? Tell me, please."

"I lived with Dylan. When I lost my job and my apartment, I moved in with him. It was living with me that made him realize he didn't want to be with me. He said he was tired of putting the effort into a relationship that wasn't going anywhere. He said it wasn't worth it to him. Living with me made him realize that *I* wasn't worth it."

Brendan's jaw bunched and his hand tightened on her side. "First of all, Dylan is an idiot. But thank God he is, because if he knew just how *worth it* you are, you wouldn't be *here*, right *now*. If Dylan had any clue whatsoever, I wouldn't have you in my life." He moved his hand from the back of her head and cupped the side of her face. He ran his thumb up and down her jaw as he stared into her eyes. "I want you to have something," he said, dropping his hand and reaching into the pocket of his pajama pants.

He pulled his hand out and opened it. There on his palm was a silver key.

Paige looked back up at him and could do nothing but stare at him, speechless. No guy had ever given her a key to his place. Dylan didn't count because she'd had to move in with him. Brendan was offering this key to her freely.

God, she was so far in love with him. There was no hope for her to ever turn back.

"I want you here. I want you to be able to come and go as you please. I don't want you to have to wait at the door for me to let you in. I want to come home from work and have you already here, in the kitchen, in the shower, in bed, anywhere. I just want you here. I know you're scared. But, Paige, you're worth it. You're worth *everything* to me. Say you'll stay with me, Paige," he begged.

"I'll stay with you," she said, unable to say anything else. She couldn't deny him what he wanted. She couldn't deny *herself* what *she* wanted.

She grabbed the key from his hand and reached back to put it on the counter. He reached down to the front of the robe she was wearing and pulled at the tie. The robe parted just slightly, and Brendan reached up to push it off her shoulders. The sleeves caught at her elbows, and Brendan took a moment to just stare down at her naked body.

"It's never been like this for me before." He sounded amazed as he reached up and ran the back of his hand down the side of her breast. "I've never wanted anyone the way I want you."

"Me either," she said, shaking her head.

Brendan flipped his hand and cupped her breast, his thumb gliding across her already erect nipple. She gasped and he covered her mouth with his, his tongue thrusting in and taking charge.

Paige wound her arms around his neck at the exact same second that he reached down and grabbed her thighs, pulling her up. She wrapped her legs around him and he carried her to the dining room table. He sat her down, her bottom on the very edge of the table and her legs dangling off. Brendan pulled a condom out of the pocket of his pajama pants and put it on the table.

"You've just got everything in there, don't you?" she asked as she pulled her arms free of the robe.

"A man's got to be prepared," he said as he took off his T-shirt and shrugged out of his pants. He grabbed the condom from the table, ripped it open, and rolled it on. "Lay down," he said, pulling her legs around his waist.

She did, stretching her arms above her head and grabbing onto the edge of the table. He groaned as he looked down at her and reached up, palming her breasts. He massaged them for a minute before he let his hands wander down her body. They were both breathing hard by the time he pushed inside of her.

"Brendan," she gasped as her back bowed off the table.

This time their joining was not slow and gentle. No, it was fast and hard. One of Brendan's hands went to the apex of her thighs and he pressed his fingers into her as he moved, massaging her. The orgasm hit her and she cried out. Brendan continued to move inside of her, slowing just a little as she came back down to Earth.

His hips and fingers picked up speed again and it didn't take very long for a second and more powerful orgasm to slam into her. She was pretty sure she screamed his name this time around. Brendan let go with his own release. He reached down and pulled her up, gathering her in his arms. Paige pressed her face to his chest and kissed him.

"Is it just me, or does it keep getting better?" he asked against her temple.

"It's not just you," she said, breathless. "That was new for me." She looked up at him.

"What?" he asked, brushing her hair back from her face.

"Multiple orgasms." She grinned. "You've set a new precedent, Brendan King."

"Oh believe me, Paige," he said and smiled back at her, "there will be many repeat performances."

"Thank God."

* * *

It took Brendan and Paige a little bit longer than expected to get out of the house. They'd taken a shower together, and they'd alternated washing each other's backs and other hard-to-reach places. But Brendan got a little bit distracted from the task at hand. Who could blame the man? She had a body that drove him out of his everloving mind, and when hot water and soap were added to the equation he really couldn't be held accountable for his actions. He'd pushed her up against the wall and had indeed given her a repeat performance of what had taken place on the dining room table.

Brendan wasn't surprised he had it in him. Paige had said she would stay and the euphoria coursing through his body was enough to get him to do just about anything. She brought this light to his life that he'd never experienced before. He loved it. He loved her.

He wanted to tell her how he felt, but he needed to take some time to adjust to it himself. He'd never been in love with someone before, and he'd fallen in love with Paige fast. He also didn't want to scare her. She was hesitant about moving too fast, but she'd taken the key. And she'd gotten that same stunned look he'd seen when he'd put the socks on her feet, the stunned look that made his chest ache for wanting to see it again.

When they pulled up in front of her parents' house, he put his truck in park and turned to her. "So your parents knew that you weren't coming home last night?"

"I told my mom it was a possibility."

"So your mother knew that we were going to have sex before I did?" he asked.

"She knew it was a possibility. I knew I was ready, but I had no idea what your response was going to be."

Brendan laughed. "Paige," he said, shaking his head, "my response to sex with you will always be yes. All right." He unbuckled his seat belt. "It's now or never. How do you think your parents are going to react to your staying with me?"

"To you taking away their baby girl? You're lucky my dad doesn't own a gun."

"Did someone tell you that you were funny at some point? 'Cause you were misinformed." He frowned at her.

"Brendan," she said, unbuckling her own seat belt and moving across the cab of his truck toward him. "My parents adore you." She touched his face. "And you're a vast improvement on my last boyfriend. As long as I'm happy, they're going to be fine."

"So you're happy?"

"Very." She beamed at him. "Are you?"

"Happy? Beyond words," he said, grabbing her and pulling her against him. He kissed her hard, and she molded against him, her hands coming up to the back of his head.

She pulled back a second later, her cheeks flushed and her breath labored. "I don't know what I'm going to do with you." She shook her head. "Let's go," she said, pulling away from him and getting out of the truck.

Brendan followed her up the steps and through the front door.

"Mom, Dad," Paige called out.

Denise stepped out of the kitchen and the second she saw the two of them her face broke out into a large grin.

"Hey," she said. "You guys staying long?"

"No," Paige said, shaking her head. "I'm going to change real quick and then we're going to head over to the festival."

"Your father and I just got back," Denise said. "Those pies were to die for."

"Hey." Trevor came down the hall. "I heard you guys are heading over to the festival?"

"Yeah." Paige nodded.

"Are you going to be back for dinner?" Denise asked.

"Actually, no," Paige said, shaking her head. "I'm going back to Brendan's afterward."

Brendan had never been in this situation before. Girls hadn't stayed over at his house when he was in high school. And he'd never had to go pick any of them up at their parents' house since then. He'd also never had a relationship with his girlfriends' parents. But he ate dinner with the Morrisons regularly. He watched games with Trevor in their living room. It was a little weird for him, standing in front of her parents, when they had to know full well what had just taken place.

"Oh really?" Denise asked.

"Yeah." Paige smiled, looking up at Brendan. "I'm going to be staying there. I'm just going to pack a bag and we'll get out of your hair."

"All right," Trevor said, heading for the living room. "Just say good-bye before you leave."

"Will do," Paige said, grabbing Brendan's hand and leading him toward her bedroom.

She let go of his hand when they stepped inside and headed for her closet. She pulled out two bags and set them on the bed, opening them.

"Sit down," she said, indicating the bed.

He watched her as she ran around her room, filling both bags with clothes. It took everything in him not to say, *Pack it all up, Paige. Pack everything you have and move in with me.* But somehow he held his tongue. She needed time. Time to realize he was the real deal. Time to realize he wasn't ever going to be able to let her go.

* * *

When they got to the festival, Shep and Jax were already there, along with Grace, Mel, and Harper. Shep took one look at Brendan and his face split into a grin. Even the corners of Jax's mouth were twitching up.

Apparently, Brendan's previous tension had been a little bit more evident than he thought.

They all bought tickets and got in line for a sampling of the pies. Grace kept her mouth shut, refusing to tell anyone which one was hers. They all voted for their favorite, and then walked around. All three winners of the cook-offs would be announced at five o'clock, and then the festival would end. Everyone would pack up their stuff and head out.

The girls went off to check out some of the booths that were still up, and the guys sat around at one of the tables and enjoyed a beer.

"I don't think I've ever seen you look more relaxed in my life," Shep said to Brendan the second the girls were out of earshot.

"You guys play Scrabble or something last night?" Jax asked.

"Or something," Brendan said.

"It must have been a pretty good game. A lot of triple-word scores," Shep said.

"You two just about done with this?" Brendan asked.

"Nah," Jax said, shaking his head. "We're your best friends. If we aren't going to give you a hard time, who will?"

"You still claiming that you just 'a little more than like her'?" Shep asked before he brought his beer to his mouth.

"I gave her a key to my house."

Shep choked on his beer.

"You what?" Jax asked, raising his eyebrows.

"I gave her a key. And she's going to be staying with me."

"As in moving in?" Shep asked incredulous.

"Not yet," Brendan said.

"Yet?" Shep asked, smiling.

"You're serious?" Jax asked.

"Yeah," Brendan said, smiling widely.

"You've known Paige for less than three months," Jax said.

"You're sure about this?" Shep asked.

"You're sure about her?" Jax asked.

"I was sure the moment I met her," Brendan said simply.

"Well, all right then," Jax said and nodded.

"I think we're going to need another round of drinks to give your bachelorhood a proper send-off," Shep said.

"Yeah." Brendan nodded, taking a sip of his beer. "That ship has sailed for good."

* * *

Lula Mae got second in the seafood gumbo cook-off and Grace took third in the pie contest. After the winners were announced for all of the contests that took place over the weekend, everyone headed out. Brendan took Paige home. He made her venison burgers, which she loved, and dragged her to bed, where they spent a good portion of the night driving each other out of their minds.

* * *

The first chance Paige had to call Abby was on her way to work on Monday morning.

"Hey, what's up?"

"I had sex with Brendan."

There was silence on the other end of the phone for a few seconds before Abby started shooting off questions.

"When? Where? How many times? Was it amazing? Because he sounds like he'd be amazing."

"Saturday after the dance. The first couple of times were in his bed but we moved to the dining room table at one point, then the shower."

"Are you kidding me?" Abby screamed into the phone.

"No, I'm not. And yes, it was amazing. I still can't really believe it. He's incredible."

"I hate you."

"Why?"

"Because you had sex all weekend with your hot mechanic and I was in freaking meetings the entire weekend with difficult pain-in-the-ass clients, not having sex."

"I stayed last night too. Abby, he gave me a key to his house."

"Are you serious?"

"Yes, he said he wants me there all the time. He cleared out a drawer and space in his closet."

Silence.

"Abby, say something," Paige begged.

"I can't. I'm getting all choked up. My little girl's growing up."

"Shut up. I need perspective. I need you to tell me that this is ridiculous. That we're going too fast. That I'm crazy."

"Are you happy?" Abby asked, suddenly sounding serious.

"Yes."

"Sweetie, that's all that matters."

Chapter Sixteen

Good Enough

On Wednesday, Mr. Adams came up to Paige's office just before lunch and put a dozen paint swatches down on her desk.

"So I've been thinking about repainting and getting rid of the wallpaper."

"Really?" Paige asked, trying not to smile.

"It's outdated. My father put that wallpaper up forty years ago."

"I agree with you. I think painting everything would give this place a nice update."

"Well, what do you think of these colors?" he asked, pointing to the swatches.

She looked down at the swatches, examining the different colors. He had some bold reds and blues and a couple far tamer yellows and greens. There was a beige one that she positively hated and a dark brown that she just didn't understand.

"I think," Paige said, running her fingers over a soft

yellow, "that you should pick neutral colors. And then get your bold colors from your accents." She looked up at Mr. Adams. "If you're going to repaint, I think you should look into replacing the curtains and the upholstery too. Start everything off fresh."

"Could you help with that?" he asked, leaning back in his chair and rubbing his jaw. "You replaced the fabric in here," he said, eyeing her blue and green curtains. "Would you be able to do it for the whole funeral home?"

"I'm sure my mom would be willing to let me bring in her sewing machine."

"I'd have you do this on the clock. You could work on one room at a time until you finish. The tributes are the first priority, but whenever you aren't working on those you could be working on this."

"I can do that."

"All right," he said, leaning forward in the chair again. "Let's figure out what colors for which rooms."

* * *

On Friday, Paige finally had a chance to start measuring windows. She had to figure out how much fabric she needed between replacing the curtains and reupholstering the furniture. The last room that had to get measured was the second viewing room. It was just after five when she dropped her purse on a table and started counting the chairs in the room.

As soon as Paige was done, she was getting out of there as fast as possible. She and Brendan were staying in for the night and ordering pizza. It pretty much sounded perfect, in her opinion.

"What are you doing in here?"

Paige looked up to see Missy standing in the doorway. She managed to look down on Paige even though she was about half a foot shorter.

"Figuring out how much fabric I need to order," Paige said, looking down at the paper in her hands and writing down a number.

"Fabric for what?" Missy asked.

Paige looked up again. "Mr. Adams wants me to get rid of the old curtains and make new ones. He also wants me to reupholster all the furniture."

"Oh, he wants *you* to do this, does he? Was this another one of your brilliant ideas that's going to cost us a fortune? You're a money pit. We'll just see about this." Missy walked out of the room, her heels hitting the hardwood floor in an agitated staccato.

Paige shook her head. She really didn't care what the woman did.

The floor-to-ceiling windows were the same size as the ones in the main viewing room. But there was one window on the back wall that didn't reach down to the floor, and it had a crescent curve on the top. Paige pulled a chair over to it, slipped off her heels, and climbed up. She grabbed the measuring tape from around her neck and held it up, measuring the height of the curve.

As she stretched up on her toes the chair teetered. As she righted herself, a callused hand ran up the inside of her thigh. She jumped and almost fell off the chair but she leaned forward and grabbed onto the wall, holding onto the frame for purchase.

"What the hell?" Paige said, turning around.

Chad's hand was still moving up her skirt, the other one palming her butt.

"Get your hands off me," Paige said, trying to pull away, but the chair teetered again and she fell right into Chad's arms. He pulled her up against him, one of his arms banding around her and his hand landing on her chest. He squeezed her breast.

"Careful there," Chad said letting go of her.

"What the hell was that?" Paige asked, taking a step back from him.

"Didn't want you to fall." He smirked and took a step toward her.

"So you groped me?" she asked as her chest tightened. She took another step away from him and her back hit the wall.

"I don't know what you're talking about. I was merely making sure you didn't hurt yourself," he said, coming closer.

"Stay away from me." Paige held out her hands palms up. Her pulse was hammering in her ears and it was getting harder for her to breathe.

"Or what?" he asked, stopping in front of her. "You going to tell your boyfriend on me? You know, Paige, what he doesn't know won't hurt him. I wouldn't say no to taking you for a ride sometime." He leered at her. "Wouldn't say no to you wrapping those legs of yours around me," he said, reaching down and running his hand up her thigh again.

He was repellent. Every time he touched her she wanted to throw up.

"Get away from me," Paige said, pushing at his chest but it was pointless. He was much bigger than her.

"What's going on?" Missy asked from the doorway.

Thank God, Paige almost cried. Even though it was Missy, she'd never been more relieved in her life.

"Paige fell off the chair when she was standing on it," Chad said, taking a step back from her. "I was making sure she was okay. I'll see you later, Paige." He smiled at her as he backed up toward the door. "We can continue this *conversation* in a more private place later."

The menacing look in his eyes made Paige's stomach heave. She grabbed for the wall behind her trying to steady herself.

"What was that?" Missy asked when Chad left the room. "Are you fraternizing with more boys at work? That is completely unacceptable. Mr. Adams is going to hear about this when he comes back."

"Where is he?" Paige panicked, looking up.

"Why? You want to tell him you weren't coming onto a man while you were working?"

"That wasn't what happened. Chad came onto me. He—he touched me," she said, choking on the words. "I need to tell Mr. Adams what happened."

"Oh, I saw what happened. I'll be filing a report about this. And Mr. Adams left to go pick up a body, so whatever lies that you want to tell him will have to wait."

"You file whatever the hell you want," Paige said, slipping on her shoes. "It doesn't matter what I say to you. You won't believe it anyway." Paige walked past Missy and grabbed her purse.

Please, dear God, let him be gone. Just let him be gone, she prayed.

Paige walked past Tara's empty desk and out the front door and into the chilly evening, the cold having nothing to do with her shaking body. When she saw that the only cars that were still there were hers and Missy's, a little of the tension left her shoulders. Paige got into her Jeep and drove to Brendan's, her hands gripping the steering wheel like it was a lifeline.

She felt sick to her stomach. What the hell had happened to her? There hadn't been any fight-or-flight response. She'd pretty much just shrunk back in fear like a scared little mouse. But there was something about Chad that really freaked her out. And he'd touched her. She wanted to go home and scrub at her skin in the shower.

We can continue this conversation in a more private place later.

A chill ran through her body. She never wanted to be in a room with him again, let alone talk to him.

Brendan wasn't home when Paige pulled into the driveway. When she opened the front door Sydney came running up to her. Normally, Sydney would circle around Paige, her tail wagging in excitement. But today Sydney calmly pressed herself into Paige's thigh. Paige walked to the back door to let her out, but she wouldn't leave Paige's side. She sat down and pressed her nose into Paige's hand.

"It's okay," Paige said, scratching her head. "You can go."

Sydney whined and pawed at Paige's leg.

"Fine, I'll go down with you," Paige said, heading for the back steps. Sydney followed behind her and when they reached the grass Sydney walked a few feet away to do her business.

Paige looked out at the water, rubbing the cold out of her arms. She closed her eyes and took a deep breath of the salty air. She tried to clear her head but she kept feeling Chad's hands on her. She turned back to where she'd last seen Sydney sniffing around. The sky was starting to get dark as the sun set, and not having Sydney in sight was beginning to freak Paige out.

Two hands grabbed her elbows and Paige screamed as she jumped forward. She turned around to find a completely startled Brendan holding up his hands.

"You scared me," Paige said, clutching her heart.

"I can see that," Brendan said, studying her.

Sydney came running out from the trees barking. She circled the two of them and then walked over to Paige, bumping her head against her thigh and whining.

"Paige, what's wrong? You about came out of your skin."

She had to tell him. She had to tell him what that cretin had done. She'd promised him she would tell him if Chad ever came near her again. She just had a very bad feeling about how he was going to react. Another chill ran down her spine and she looked up at the house.

"Can we go inside?" she asked, rubbing her arms.

"Yeah." He nodded, frowning.

She walked past him, Sydney still firmly at her side, and went up the stairs. When they were inside she turned to him, her entire body shaking. Sydney sat at her feet, whining as she looked up at Paige. Brendan looked at Paige, down to Sydney, and then back up to Paige.

"Paige, what's going on?" Brendan asked, grabbing the blanket from the back of the couch and wrapping it around her. He chafed his hands against her shoulders and Paige pressed herself into his chest, seeking his warmth.

"Don't tell me nothing, because I know something's up," he said, rubbing his hands up and down her back. "Sydney won't leave your side. She only does this when she's protecting people. What's she protecting you from, Paige?"

"Something happened," she whispered into his shoulder.

Brendan's hands stilled. "Something where?"

"At work."

Brendan pulled back and grabbed her hand, leading her over to the couch.

"Start at the beginning."

* * *

Brendan watched as Paige closed her eyes and took a deep breath. Everything in his body was on high alert. It had been from the moment Paige had jumped out of his arms and screamed. And the way that Sydney was acting was putting him even more on edge.

Paige opened her eyes. "Promise me you won't freak out," she said, grabbing his hands.

"No," he said, shaking his head. "Tell me what happened, Paige."

"Before I left work tonight, I was measuring one of the windows. I—I had to stand on a chair to reach it. When I stretched up to measure, I almost fell off." She swallowed hard. "Chad was there."

"What did he do?" Brendan asked through clenched teeth.

"He touched me," Paige whispered.

Brendan let go of Paige's hands and stood up, pacing the floor.

"Where?"

She didn't answer. He stopped pacing and turned to her.

"Where did he touch you, Paige?"

"My chest, my behind, and the inside of my thigh."

He stopped breathing. "How far up?"

"Brendan, it's—"

"How far up?" he repeated loudly.

"As far up as he could go," she said, closing her eyes and turning away.

"What else? Did he say anything to you?"

"Yes," she said, still not looking at him.

"What did he say, Paige?"

When she repeated the words Chad had said to her, Brendan lost it.

"He threatened you?" Brendan asked so loudly that Sydney stood up and put herself in between Paige and Brendan.

"I don't know," Paige said, looking up at him, confused. "I was so freaked out. I—I could be wrong."

"Did you feel like he was threatening you?"

"Yes," she said softly.

Brendan walked out of the room and headed for the front door. Paige called after him but he didn't even hesitate as he ran down the steps and got into his truck. It was past five on a Friday night. Brendan knew exactly where Chad was going to be, and he was going to show the little shit what a real threat was.

* * *

The Sleepy Sheep was always busy on the weekends, and tonight was no exception. Brendan pulled his truck into the full parking lot and threw it into park. When he walked into the bar he did a quick scan and saw Chad talking to a couple of guys at one of the pool tables. Just the sight of him made Brendan want to break things. Chad's face was at the top of the list.

Chad made eye contact with Brendan about two seconds before Brendan grabbed him by the front of the shirt and shoved him up against the wall.

"If you *ever* touch her again, I will end you, you son of a bitch."

"She wanted it," Chad said, shoving at Brendan's shoulders.

"She wanted you to grope her? She wanted you to threaten her? I don't think so," Brendan said, slamming Chad into the wall again. "If I ever see you so much as looking at her again, I'll beat the shit out of you so fast you won't even see it coming."

"Come on, Brendan," someone said, coming up next to him and grabbing his shoulders, pulling him off Chad.

Brendan let go and took a step back, his entire body shaking with rage.

"That little slut asked for it," Chad said, fixing his shirt.

Brendan lunged at Chad but two sets of arms grabbed him and dragged him back. He was pulled through the bar and outside. Brendan turned to see Shep and Bennett standing in between him and the door.

"What the hell was that?" Shep said, pointing to the bar.

"That stupid little piece of trash touched Paige," Brendan yelled.

"Calm down, Brendan."

"Calm down? *Calm down?* I will not calm down. I want to *kill* him."

"Yeah, maybe screaming death threats isn't in your best interest right now," Bennett said.

"He touched her. He had his grimy little hands on her."

"I get that," Shep said calmly. "But you can't do this, Brendan. You can't threaten someone."

"He threatened her," Brendan bellowed.

Shep closed his eyes and pinched the bridge of his nose like he was talking to a five-year-old having a temper tantrum. Bennett looked over Brendan's shoulder as a car pulled into the parking lot. Out of the corner of his eye, Brendan saw Jax get out of his county sheriff's truck.

"Paige called me," Jax said, walking up to the three of them. "She said you were about to get yourself into trouble."

Brendan just looked at Jax, not talking for fear of exploding.

"Let's go, Brendan. I told her we'd meet her at her parents' house."

"At her parents'?" Brendan asked, feeling some of the anger leave him. Had he scared her? Did she not want to stay with him anymore?

"Yeah, she wanted to tell them what happened. I told her once you calmed down, we'd be over there."

Brendan took a deep breath and rubbed his face. "Fine. Let's go," he said, holding up his hands. Jax, Shep, and Bennett all visibly relaxed as Brendan took a step back toward his truck.

God, if he'd made his friends nervous he had no idea what he'd done to Paige. His stomach twisted just thinking about it.

* * *

"You can't threaten someone, Brendan," Jax said calmly from the middle of Denise and Trevor's kitchen. Paige was sitting down at the table with Denise while Trevor leaned against the counter. Brendan was pacing back and forth across the tile floor. Jax was trying to reason with him about his temper. It was making Brendan so angry he couldn't stand still.

Brendan stopped pacing and turned to Jax. "Chad touched her," he shouted, not showing an ounce of composure. "He had his hands on her and you expect me to take that sitting down? To not do something about it?"

"No, I expect you to call me and then we go about this legally."

"Legally? What are you going to do? You heard Paige," Brendan said, throwing his hand out toward the table where Paige was sitting. "No one was there, and Missy isn't going to back up Paige's story. She's going to say exactly what Chad said. That Paige came on to him. So it's Paige's word against both of theirs. Who's going to believe the truth?"

"I do," Jax said. "But now we have a bar full of people who saw you attack and threaten Chad. Do you think that helps this case? It doesn't, Brendan."

"Tell me you wouldn't have done it?" Brendan asked, taking a step toward Jax. "Tell me you wouldn't have done the exact same thing I did if someone threatened the woman you're in love with?"

The whole kitchen went silent. Jax raised his eyebrows, taking in a slow, steady breath. Brendan knew Jax was trying to hide his surprise because Brendan had never said that he'd been in love with anyone before, not ever.

"You're right. I would lose my mind," Jax said and

nodded. "But for right now, we have to do this my way. Paige." He turned to her. "I'm going to need a full statement starting from the beginning."

"I can't listen to this again," Brendan said, shaking his head and walking out the back door.

He inhaled the crisp fall air and took a seat on the steps of the porch, resting his forearms on his thighs. He sat there for a couple of minutes, staring out into the backyard and thinking about how quickly this night had turned to shit.

The entire week had been amazing. He'd woken up next to Paige for six mornings running, and every single one had been like a gift from God. He'd sat across from her every night eating dinner, and then sipped coffee with her in the mornings while they munched on toast. He'd watched her get dressed with fascination in the mornings and then he'd undressed her with eagerness at night.

When he'd gotten home that night he'd thought everything was fine. He'd thought they'd get dinner and watch TV on the couch before they'd make love in bed all night. But that wasn't a reality now. It had all been perfect and now the bubble had popped and he was sinking faster than he could think.

He was quickly learning that when it came to Paige he couldn't have a clear head. When that stupid article had come out two months ago he'd lost his mind. And today? There wasn't a word that could accurately describe how he felt today. Just thinking about that asshole's grubby hands on her made him want to punch his fist through a wall.

The other thing that he couldn't stop thinking about was the fact that he'd scared Paige. He'd seen it on her face when he'd walked into the kitchen. Her big gray eyes staring at him in a way he'd never seen before, in a way he never wanted to see again.

What if her parents thought he was a violent maniac who wasn't good enough for her? The truth was, he *wasn't* good enough for her. God, Paige deserved so much. She deserved only good things, but for some reason that wasn't working out. And the fact that he couldn't protect her made him feel useless.

The door opened behind Brendan. He turned to the side as Trevor took a seat next to him and handed him an open beer.

"I thought you might need a drink," he said, taking a swig of the bottle that was in his own hands. "I know I need one."

"Thanks," Brendan said, taking a long pull on his bottle as he looked out into the yard again.

"Not going to lie," Trevor said after a minute. "I'm a little disappointed you didn't pound that little shit into the ground."

"Me too," Brendan said, nodding his head. God, he wanted to destroy Chad.

"So you meant what you said in there?" Trevor asked.

Brendan didn't need to ask what. He knew exactly what Trevor was asking. So he turned to look Trevor in the eye, because a man needed to look another man in the eye when he said that he was in love with his daughter.

"Yes, sir," Brendan nodded. "I'm in love with Paige."

"Good," Trevor said, patting Brendan on the back. "You're a good guy, Brendan. Good enough for Paige. I thought so before, but tonight confirmed it."

"What, me losing it?" Brendan asked surprised.

"No," Trevor said, shaking his head. "You not caring what the consequences were for protecting my daughter. You didn't even think twice about it, did you?"

"No sir, I didn't."

"That's what I thought."

The back door opened again and both men turned to see Paige walk outside.

"I'll let you two talk," Trevor said, standing up. As he passed Paige he kissed her on the top of the head and then walked inside shutting the door.

Paige sat down next to Brendan and grabbed the beer out of his hands, taking a long pull. They passed the bottle back and forth in silence for a couple of minutes as they stared out into the dark night. When Paige finished the beer she set the bottle down next to her, the hollow glass clinking against the wood.

He knew what she was doing; she was giving him time. Time to sort himself out. Time to calm down. Time to just sit with her in silence so that he could figure out what to say.

"Paige, I'm sorry," Brendan said, turning to her. "I shouldn't—"

But he didn't get further than that because she grabbed his face and kissed him. He wrapped his arms around her back, holding her to him as she slanted her mouth across his. She pulled back, still holding his face in her hands, and just looked at him.

"I love you," she whispered, giving him a small smile. "I was scared to tell you before, but since you just said it in front of my parents and Jax, I figured I was okay to tell you now."

Brendan's heart pounded hard in his chest as he stared at the girl who owned it.

"You know, I've never told a girl that I was in love with her before. That's not how I wanted to tell you," he said, shaking his head. "I hadn't really planned on yelling it out and then storming out of your parents' kitchen."

"Then tell me again," she said, running her hand down the side of his neck and placing it over his heart.

"I love you, Paige."

Brendan didn't think that anything else could make him feel better after hearing Paige say that she loved him, but then she whispered, "Take me home," against his mouth.

* * *

As soon as they walked in, Paige grabbed Brendan's hand and pulled him through the bedroom and into the bathroom. She couldn't bring herself to get into Brendan's bed without showering off what had happened. She also didn't want Brendan to leave her alone at all for the rest of the night.

"Paige," Brendan said, shaking his head, "are you sure?" He searched her face as she reached for his shirt and untucked it from his pants.

"You just fought for my honor tonight and told me you love me. I'm not letting you get any farther from me than this." She began to unbutton his shirt.

They undressed each other and took a shower to wash away the cold and other things. When they were both warmed up, Brendan pulled Paige out of the shower and dried her off. He laid her out on the bed and kissed her, letting his mouth travel down her neck and over her chest to her side. He counted her ribs with his tongue and pressed his lips to her sunflower tattoo. Whispering, "I love you, I love you more, I love you more, I love you more," as he kissed every single petal.

* * *

Missy did report to Mr. Adams about what had happened on Friday between Paige and Chad, but so did Paige. And Paige had the full weight of Jax's police report behind her. Mr. Adams believed Paige's side of the story, and he promised that Chad would no longer be working on the changes at the funeral home. Missy had been livid that Mr. Adams hadn't taken any disciplinary action against Paige. Paige just ignored it. What other choice did she have? She refused to let Missy get to her. The thing was, Missy wasn't the only problem. Bethelda decided to add her own two cents to the situation.

THE GRIM TRUTH

TEMPER TANTRUMS GALORE

It should come as no shock that Brazen Interloper has caused even more chaos in our sleepy little town. "It's what happens when loose women are let out to run amuck," Sweetie Pie tells us. "Her Jeep has been missing from her parents' driveway every single night this week. They're obviously doing the wild thing. No morals, absolutely no morals, either of them." The other half to the "they're" that Mrs. Pie is referring to is none other than our very own, and notorious for his own reasons, Rogue Whoreson.

Last Friday night, there was quite a commotion over at the Den of Iniquity. Several eyewitnesses say that Rogue Whoreson burst into the bar and viciously attacked Hunky Noble with absolutely no provocation on Mr. Noble's part. Our sources tell us that Mr. Whoreson threw Mr. Noble up against the wall and threatened to "end him." Sounds like a death threat to me.

Deputy Ginger quickly responded to the scene, but Mr. Whoreson wasn't punished for his acts of violence. Why would he be when the "good" deputy is one of his best friends? It obviously pays to have friends in high places. But Deputy Ginger is no stranger to acts of violence. His own father is known for many drunken brawls, some of them even targeted toward his very own family. You'd think that Deputy Ginger would be more outspoken against the actions of Mr. Whoreson, but alas, he is not. It appears that his father's fists have made him immune.

But what caused this outburst in Mr. Whoreson? He's always been known for his short temper and his quick fists. Is he unstable? And how safe is Brazen? What if Rogue loses his temper, and Brazen is the one getting hurt?

Paige had been upset when she'd read it, but Brendan was livid. She sat across from him at the kitchen table as he read in stony silence, his jaw bunching tighter and tighter as his eyes traveled down the computer screen. She'd had no idea about Jax's past, but she had a feeling that much like Brendan's past, it had been repeated over and over again. She felt awful that Jax had been dragged into this too.

Brendan closed the laptop when he finished and put his hands down on the table as he shoved his chair back. The legs screeched across the tile. He walked over to the sink, setting his empty cup down. He grabbed the counter with both hands and leaned forward, taking a deep breath as his head hung down between his shoulders. Paige got up from her seat and came up behind him. He straightened as she wrapped her arms around him and placed her hands flat on his chest. She pressed her face against his neck as she leaned into him.

"It's okay, Brendan," she whispered.

He reached up and placed his hands over hers. "No, it isn't," he said, shaking his head. He grabbed her hands and loosened them, turning as he pulled her in front of him. "I would *never* hurt you, Paige." His eyes held so much pain that it made her chest hurt.

"I know," she said, reaching up and touching his face.

"Just the thought of it makes me sick." As he said it his voice broke and his eyes were glossy.

"Brendan," Paige said, wrapping her arms around him, "with you, I've never felt as safe, or as cared for, or as loved."

"I can't protect you from what she writes," he said, shaking his head.

"You can't protect me from everything."

"I can try," he said, leaning in and pressing his lips to her temple.

* * *

Brendan had convinced Paige to start staying at his house, thank God, but there was an ever-present fear he wouldn't be able to convince her to stay in Mirabelle. She hadn't been shy about her feelings for the tiny town the first time he'd met her. She'd never planned on relocating there, on staying there. But it wasn't like Philadelphia had been that much better for her. She hadn't been able to fulfill her dreams there, so maybe if she were able to do that in Mirabelle she'd want to stay.

And she wouldn't leave him.

For two weeks, Brendan stayed up for a little while after Paige, watching her sleep next to him, and trying to figure out a plan.

She wanted to sell her art, something that wasn't going to happen when it was tucked away in a corner. It had to be displayed so that people could see it, so that they could buy it. So he needed to find some empty walls in a high-traffic area, or in many high-traffic areas.

It was on a Thursday morning that he finally presented her with the plan. She walked into the kitchen, wearing some sort of burnt orange sweater dress that molded to her curves. He handed her a cup of coffee, thinking she might need a few sips of caffeine before he told her.

"Hmm," she hummed, taking a drink and stepping into him. "You make a damn fine cup of coffee."

"That so?" he said, leaning back against the counter and wrapping his arm around her back. He pulled her snuggly in between his thighs and let his hand drop down her waist to her bottom. "I haven't seen this dress before."

"That would be because it's only just gotten cold enough to wear it."

"I like it," he said, letting his gaze drop to her chest. "It will be fun peeling you out of it tonight."

"You think you're going to get lucky?" she asked, raising her eyebrows.

"A man can hope."

Paige got about halfway through her coffee when Brendan broached the subject. "So I was thinking," he said, putting his cup down behind him.

"About?" she asked, tilting her head to the side.

He ran both of his hands up and down her side. "You selling your art."

"What?" she asked, her eyebrows furrowing.

"You told me your dream was to sell your art. And you could do that here, Paige. There are plenty of people in town, and between the snowbirds and summer vacationers, there are a lot of people who pass through. And I think you could have a booth at the fall festival next year. People would go crazy for your work."

"I don't think so," she said, shaking her head.

"You don't think so for which part of it?"

"Any of it."

"Why not?" he asked.

"Because, I just don't think it would work." She frowned, putting her cup on the counter next to his. "I've never displayed anything before."

"That isn't true," he said, shaking his head. "You have one of your paintings hanging up in your office. You put your photographs in the tributes. The Web site for the funeral home has a lot of your designs on it. All of that is your work, and all of that is seen by people on a daily basis."

"Yes, but I'm not selling it. I don't know how that would go over."

"Well, we'll never know unless we try."

"*We?*" she asked more than just a little bit agitated. "I

didn't realize that you were out there painting with me. That it was your work too."

"I meant that I was in this with you," he said, starting to get agitated himself.

"Really?" she asked skeptically.

"You doubt me?"

"Where would we sell it?" Paige asked, ignoring his question.

"At the café, and at Pinky and Panky's shops. They were all for it."

Something blazed in her eyes as she stared at him openmouthed. It took a second for her to speak. "You already talked to people about this?" she asked, pulling herself away from him. That little gesture alone had his heart plummeting to his feet.

"I thought this was what you wanted, to display your work and sell it. You said that was your dream."

"It *is* my dream."

"Then what's the problem?"

"The *problem* is that this isn't your decision. The *problem* is that you had no right to ask other people to sell my art before you even talked to me."

"I'm talking to you about it now. I was trying to do something so you could get your dream, because *you* obviously aren't doing anything about it."

She inhaled sharply and took another step back from him.

"Paige, I didn't mean that," he said, rubbing a spot on his forehead.

"Oh, I think you did."

"Let me explain," he said, taking a step toward her. "I was just trying to help."

But she held out her hands, palms up. "I don't want to hear it. I'm done talking about this. I don't want or need your help," she said, before she turned around and walked away from him.

But all Brendan had heard was she didn't need him. And that killed him.

Chapter Seventeen

Why Don't You Stay...Forever

Focusing wasn't even an option for Paige. Every time she closed her eyes, she saw that hurt look on Brendan's face, and it made her feel awful, made her hurt.

But Brendan didn't get it. He didn't understand she was terrified. Her work was a part of her, and if people rejected her work, they were ultimately rejecting her. She didn't know if she could handle that. Selling her art *was* her dream. What if she failed? What if she couldn't sell her art in Mirabelle? What other option did she have? She couldn't leave, and that wasn't because she was stuck here, but because she didn't want to leave.

Mirabelle had become her home. Yes, it had taken a few months, but she'd finally found her place. Found a job that she actually enjoyed going to, despite Missy and Verna. She'd found a good group of friends who she'd gotten close to. And she'd found the love of her life.

Paige couldn't leave Brendan.

"What's up with you?" Grace asked as they got dessert

ready in the little kitchen at the café. "You barely talked at lunch, and you look miserable."

Paige put the spoon that she'd been scooping the cobbler with down on the dish.

"Brendan and I had a fight."

"About damn time," Grace said, picking up the spoon and resuming the scooping. "You two have just been too lovey-dovey. So what was the fight about?"

"Did he talk to you about selling my art here?" she asked, leaning back against the counter and folding her arms across her chest.

"Yes," Grace said, looking up. "He talked to me and Grams."

"When?"

"He came by on Tuesday."

"He talked to Pinky and Panky too. He said all of you were all for it."

"For doing something for you? Why wouldn't we be?" Grace asked. "And more to the point, why aren't you all for it?"

"What if no one buys it? What if no one finds my work worth it?"

"You mean what if no one finds *you* worth it?" Grace asked. "Paige, I've seen your work and it's amazing. You should hear the way Brendan talks about it, talks about you. The first time you showed him your stuff he raved about it. Went on and on and on about how incredible you are. How talented. He thinks Mirabelle has nothing to offer you and it terrifies him."

"Why is *he* scared?" Paige asked, confused.

"His father walked out on him, and though he tries to act like it doesn't affect him, it does. A lot. And our mother's death messed him up pretty good. Those two people leaving him, by choice or not, did something to him. I think that's why he's never really been in a serious relationship before. Then you slipped in and made him fall in love with you. Sweetie," Grace said, reaching over and putting her hand on Paige's arm, "he's scared he's going to lose you."

"He didn't say anything," Paige said, her heart hurting even more.

"My brother is more of a take-action kind of guy. He sees a problem and he tries to fix it. He doesn't want you to leave, so he's trying to make it so you won't."

"But, I'm not leaving," Paige said, shaking her head.

"Paige," Grace said, giving her a sad smile, "that's another thing. You can't prove yourself with words. It has to be with actions. The only way he'll know you won't leave him is if you don't leave him."

* * *

Brendan was going out of his mind. He couldn't concentrate for anything, and the shop was so slow that it was practically dead. There was nothing for Brendan to do to distract himself.

"Why don't you just go home?" Oliver finally asked around four thirty.

Why didn't he go home? Because he wasn't sure if Paige would be coming back. Wasn't sure if he was going to be sleeping alone tonight.

"You need to go and talk to her," Oliver continued. "Work things out."

Brendan merely looked at his grandfather.

"Look, if you're too chicken to deal with it, that's your own problem. But you need to get out of my hair."

"Fine," Brendan said, getting up. "And I'm not a chicken."

"Hmmm," Oliver hummed as Brendan walked out of the office.

Brendan didn't go home. He went to Shep's to get a beer. Maybe he was a bit of a chicken. So what?

Brendan walked in just after five. There were a couple of people around, but it wasn't crowded yet. Shep was behind the bar, getting everything ready for the night.

"What are you doing here?" Shep asked when he saw him.

"I need a drink," Brendan said as he sat down.

"Oh, hell, what did you do?"

"Why is it you think I did something?"

"Instinct." Shep smirked.

"You going to get me that beer?" Brendan frowned.

"Sure thing," Shep said, grabbing a mug and filling it.

A second later Jax sat down in the stool next to Brendan. "What the hell are you doing here?" he asked.

"I asked him that same question," Shep said, putting the mug down in front of Brendan. "But he won't tell me what bug is up his ass."

"What stupid thing did you do?" Jax asked.

"You know, you both royally suck as friends," Brendan said, grabbing the beer and downing a healthy portion of it.

"What's going on?" Shep asked seriously. "No more kidding around."

Brendan sighed and looked up. He told them both what he'd done. Trying to get Paige to sell her work there in Mirabelle. "I love her so damn much," Brendan told them. "And I have no fucking clue how I can get her to stay."

"She going somewhere?" Jax asked.

"Not at the moment," Brendan said.

"Then why are you worrying about it?" Shep asked.

"Because I want to spend the rest of my life with her, and I don't think that step is too far down the road."

"You're serious?" Jax asked after a beat.

"Yeah," Brendan nodded. "She's it for me."

"Wow," Shep said, looking just a little bit stunned.

"Does it surprise you that he's the first?" Jax asked.

"No," Shep said, shaking his head. "'Cause it sure as hell wasn't going to be either of us."

"Oh, you two are going to find girls who take your feet right out from under you," Brendan said. "And you aren't going to know what hit you."

"In that case, Jax's head has been spinning for years," Shep said.

Jax just frowned at Shep. And a second later Jax's phone started ringing.

"Hey, Princess," Jax said.

"Speak of the devil," Shep said and grinned.

Jax flipped him off.

* * *

Paige pulled up into Brendan's driveway at just after five. He wasn't home yet. So Paige let herself in and took Sydney outside. Then she pulled the blanket off the back of the couch and wrapped it around her shoulders. She sat down and waited for him to come home.

The uneasy feeling in her stomach had only gotten worse since she'd left the café. She just wanted to fix things with Brendan, and the longer she had to wait in this empty house, the crazier she was going. By five thirty, she needed a drink. She got up, poured herself a glass of wine, and restationed herself on the couch. By six, she was starting to feel a little bit desperate. It wasn't unusual for Brendan to be home after six. Depending on how busy they were at the shop, he'd sometimes have to stay late.

Finally at six fifteen, Sydney's head came up and she ran to the door. A minute later, Brendan's keys jangled in the lock and he pushed the door open.

"Hey," she said, pulling her legs out from under her and standing up.

She watched him walk in, studying his face. His mouth was in a firm line and his shoulders were tense.

"Hey," he said, coming into the room. "I wasn't sure if you'd be here."

"Did you not want me to be?" she asked nervously.

"Paige, I always want you here."

"About this morning—" she started.

"Don't worry about it," he said, interrupting her and holding out his hands palms up. "You made it perfectly clear you didn't want to do it. And that's fine. I won't push you, Paige. I'm done."

So Brendan was apparently still angry.

"You're done?" she asked as her stomach dropped. She thought she was going to be sick.

"Talking about it," he said, going into the kitchen.

She stood there for a second, staring at empty space, before she followed him into the kitchen. He was at the fridge, bending over and looking in the open door.

"Are you done with me?" she asked softly.

He stood up abruptly. He turned as he shut the door, a beer in his hand.

"No," he said, his eyebrows coming together.

Paige closed her eyes and took a deep breath, letting it out in a wave of relief. There was a *thunk* and Paige opened her eyes. Brendan had put his beer down on the counter and he was crossing the room to her.

He grabbed her and pulled her into him. He reached up and grabbed her face, planting his mouth firmly on hers. He worked at her mouth, nipping her bottom lip aggressively, before he pulled back.

"I'm *not* done with you Paige," he said, resting his forehead against hers. "One fight isn't going to change that."

"Did you do this because you're scared of losing me?" she asked.

He pulled back and looked into her eyes, running his thumb across her cheek. "Yes."

"I'm not going anywhere, Brendan. I'm not leaving."

"Even if you're miserable here?"

"I'm not miserable here," she said, shaking her head.

"Maybe not right now, but in ten years, when you're not doing what you dreamed of doing? What then? I don't want you to give up on anything. To make sacrifices."

"Life is about sacrifices."

"You shouldn't have to sacrifice this," he said, his mouth going back to that firm stubborn line.

"You think I can sell my work? That people will actually buy it?"

"We're talking about it?" he asked, raising his eyebrows.

"Brendan, I was wrong," she said, putting her hands on his chest. "I shouldn't have yelled at you, and I don't want you to stop pushing me. I'm so sorry."

"I'm sorry too," he said.

"You think I can do this?"

"Yes, I do. I think you've got so much to offer and people are going to fall in love with what you can do."

"And if they don't?"

"I don't see that happening. I believe in you. I believe in what you're capable of," he said, kissing her temple.

"I'm scared," she said, turning her face into his neck.

"That's how you know it's worth it. Falling in love with you was the scariest thing I've ever done. It's also the greatest."

"Me too."

They just stood there, holding each other for a moment. His hands running up and down her back.

"So are you going to do it?" he asked, pulling back so he could look at her.

"Yeah, I am," she said and nodded.

"Really?"

"Really." She smiled.

"Good. You know I would never do anything to hurt you, right?" he said, reaching up to touch her chin and gently tilting her face up so that he could place a small kiss on her lips.

"I know," she said under his mouth.

* * *

Over the next couple of weeks, Paige's stuff slowly started to accumulate at Brendan's. She'd attempted to pack a bag to take back to her parents' house to trade out for new clothes, but Brendan had told her he'd just make more room for her things. It didn't make sense to continually bring stuff back and forth.

Toward the end of November, Paige came back one day to find a dresser that hadn't been there when she'd left for work that morning. She dropped her shoes by the bedroom door and went over to it, running her fingers across the wood. It was an antique, stained a dark cherry brown with six drawers, three on each side.

"It was my great-grandmother's."

Paige turned to see Brendan standing in the doorway.

"It's beautiful. Where was it before?" she asked, turning back to the dresser and tracing a set of rings that were in the wood.

"The guest room of my grandparents' house. Bennett restores furniture, and I asked him to fix it up for you," he said as his boots echoed across the floor. A second later he was behind her, brushing the hair off her neck and kissing her throat. "Paige," he whispered, "I want you to have more than a drawer here."

"How much more?"

"Move in with me."

Paige took a deep breath and turned in his arms, leaning back against the dresser. He settled his hands on her waist as she looked up at him. "I've barely been staying here a month," she said while she traced the buttons on his shirt.

"I don't care. I wanted you to move in last month, and I still want you to move in now."

"What happened to taking things slowly?"

"Screw slowly," he said, shaking his head. "I don't

want slowly. Nothing has gone *slowly* for me since I met you. You crashed into me and set my world spinning the moment I met you. You, and those long legs of yours in those black wedges, and that smart mouth." He smiled.

"You called me judgmental the first time I met you," Paige challenged.

"Only because you called me a stupid redneck."

"Illiterate," she corrected. "I called you illiterate."

"And a jerk. Yet, you've fallen in love with me despite all of that," he said.

"I was wrong," Paige said, shaking her head. "You're none of those things."

"Then what am I, Paige?" he asked, stepping into her. He reached up and touched her jaw as he leaned into her. "What am I?" he asked above her mouth before he parted her lips with his. One of his hands settled on the nape of her neck while the other wrapped around her waist, holding her to him, which was fortunate since her knees felt weak. He held her as their tongues touched and moved against each other. She pulled back and rested her forehead against his.

"When I was little, I had training wheels on my bicycle," she said, fidgeting with his shirt. "My dad took the training wheels off, and the first time I tried to ride my bike after that I ate it. I hit the pavement hard. I scraped my elbows and knees to hell, busted open my lip. So my dad put the training wheels back on because I was too terrified to ride without them. I rode with them on for so long that it got to the point where they were useless. They weren't even touching the ground anymore they were so bent up. But every time he went to take the training wheels off I would freak out. I wasn't ready. I needed that safety net." She pulled her forehead back from his so she could look him in the eyes.

"I'm scared, Brendan. I've done this once before. I've lived with someone. Yeah, the circumstances were different, but the outcome was painful. With Dylan I fell off my bike and scraped my knees. But you?" She took a deep breath and shook her head. "You're the car crash I wouldn't be able to walk away from."

He looked at her in that way of his. The way that made her heart soar and ache at the same time.

"If you're scared about crashing, I'll be your soft landing or your safety net or whatever you want me to be."

"You promise?" she asked, blinking hard. Her eyes were prickling and she knew that she couldn't hold back the tears for much longer.

"I promise."

Paige wrapped her arms around his neck and kissed him hard. She pulled back, laughing and crying, and so happy she thought she was going to float away.

"Is that a yes?" Brendan said and smiled, pushing her hair back from her face.

"It's a yes." She nodded as more tears spilled down her cheeks.

"Why are you crying?" he asked, running his fingers under her eyes.

"Because I'm happy," she said, smiling through her tears. "If you're going to live with me, you need to get used to it."

"For you, I'll get used to anything."

* * *

They moved Paige's stuff in that weekend, and it didn't take very long because she didn't have very much. The boxes that she brought to Brendan's were filled with her clothes, shoes, books, and small knickknacks that she'd accumulated over the years. Brendan cleaned out half of the closet for her to hang up her clothes, and he built her a shoe rack. Paige firmly believed that nothing said love like a man giving her a place to organize her shoes.

While she unpacked her stuff in the bedroom, he worked on the stuff in the living room. He added her books and movies to his. There was something about the fact that he didn't keep them separated but that he mixed their things all in together.

"Can we hang this in the living room?"

Paige turned to see Brendan standing in the doorway holding one of her paintings of a giant sunflower.

"But it's of a flower," she said, looking at it and then looking up at him confused.

"Is that what this is?" he asked, attempting to sound surprised. "I had no idea."

"Shut up, smart-ass," Paige said, shaking her head. "I should have said that I'm *surprised* you want to hang that up *because* it's a flower."

"I've grown quite fond of sunflowers since I met you," he said, grinning at her. "And you painted this, so I like it even more. I'd like it to be obvious you live here, Paige. I want you in every room of this house."

"You can hang it up," she said quickly as a rush of warm affection washed through her.

And he did more than just hang up that painting. The hallway was now lined with some of her framed black-and-white photography, stuff that she didn't want to sell.

Pictures of her with her family and friends in an assortment of picture frames lined the bookcases. Her big and brightly colored coffee mugs hung from a rack in the kitchen. An old wooden clock that she'd found at an antiques store hung from the wall in the dining room. And her lamps and curtains replaced his in their bedroom.

In *their* bedroom, which was in *their* house.

Brendan also put out her candles and lit them, making the living room smell like sugar and cinnamon, and their bedroom smell like pumpkin pie.

It was crazy how all of their stuff just fit together. His was more tame and neutral, but it complemented her tendency for crazy colors. It somehow just worked, much like they somehow just worked.

* * *

People were buying Paige's pieces. In the few weeks that her stuff had been hanging up, three paintings, five photographs, one of the windowpanes, and two of the words on aluminum siding had sold. Everything put together was over a thousand dollars. It was unbelievable.

Paige tried to give the girls some of the profits, but they wouldn't take any of it. Instead they took some of her work. Well, first they'd tried to buy it from her, but Paige had refused, being just as stubborn as them. As Paige's stuff sold, she went through her plethora of pieces and replaced the blank spaces on the walls.

Mr. Adams had seen her work at Panky's flower shop. He was so impressed with it that he asked her for paintings and pictures for the funeral home.

"I'll pay you full price for all of them, of course," he

said as he sat across from her at her desk. "But I'd like you to paint some of those pictures that you took, the local ones, of the beach and the town and such, and then I'd like some of those photographs to be framed as well."

"Really?"

"Yes," he said and nodded. "We have new paint on the walls, so we should have new art on the walls."

"Wow, absolutely," she said, so overwhelmed that she could hardly stand it. She'd *never* been commissioned to paint anything before, and Mr. Adams wanted her to paint over two thousand dollars worth of art, not to mention the photography.

Paige didn't have a good space to paint at her and Brendan's place, so she still used the shed at her parents' house. She spent a lot of time there on the weekends, and she started going over after work a couple of times a week. Brendan would usually meet her over at her parents' on those days. They'd all eat dinner together, and when Paige went back out to paint, Brendan would watch some game or another with her dad.

* * *

On the first Saturday in December, Paige dragged Brendan out to get a Christmas tree. She'd snuggled up next to him that morning and asked if they could decorate. He had no problem with decorating for Christmas, and even if he had it would've been a lost cause. He had no hope of denying her anything when she was pressed up against him.

"How have you never decorated for Christmas before?" she asked as they walked onto the Christmas tree lot.

"I've never had a reason to," he said, following behind her. "Grams has always decorated, and I've always helped her with the tree and lights on the house. When I first moved out I lived with Jax, and he's not much of a decorator. Before you, it was only me at our house, so I had no need to decorate there."

Paige stopped and turned to look at him. "I guess not," she said, shaking her head. "I can't imagine not decorating for Christmas. It wouldn't be the same."

"Well, it's your house too. So you can do whatever you want."

"I like that," she said, grabbing his hand and pulling him along behind her to a large pine tree. It was at least seven feet tall and full of thick green pine needles.

"This is the one you want?" he asked.

"Yes," she said, sticking her nose close to the needles and inhaling. She looked like she was in heaven. "Mmm, smells like Christmas."

After they dropped the tree off at the house, they drove up to Tallahassee to get decorations. The few that Paige had weren't enough. So Brendan spent the next couple of hours following her around the store pushing the cart while she threw stuff in it.

"Can we get Christmas sheets?" she asked, bouncing up and down in front of one of the displays.

Christmas sheets? Was she serious? But he really couldn't say no to her, not with the excited glow that was on her face. And what did he care, as long as she was in the sheets with him? But the sheets in question were such a light blue that they were almost purple.

"What about the reindeer ones?" he asked, pointing to a green set.

"Are those more manly?" she asked, tossing them into the cart.

"Than girly snowmen? Yes, they are more manly."

"They weren't girly," she said as she started walking.

"Half of them were wearing bikinis. That's girly." He followed behind her.

"These reindeer are wearing Christmas lights on their antlers," she said, pointing to the sheets in the cart. "That says manly?"

"It's hunting meets electricity."

"That doesn't make any sense," she said, shaking her head.

"Neither do snowmen wearing bikinis."

"Hmm," she said distractedly as she started down another aisle filled with Christmas stuff. "You make a valid point."

After that, she asked him to stop at a specialty store so that she could get the ingredients to make something for dinner.

"What are you making?" he asked her as they walked in.

"It's a surprise. Go get some good wine," she said, shooing him in the direction of the alcohol.

There was Christmas music playing over the speakers and he caught himself humming along to it as he looked over the labels. Apparently Paige's holiday cheer was contagious.

He found two bottles of wine and a gourmet hot chocolate that he planned to add some peppermint schnapps to. Paige found him thirty minutes later, her loot already bought and hidden in two large brown paper bags. She added some fancy cheese to his cart and a bag of freshly baked bread before they checked out and left.

When they got home, she cranked up Christmas music on the stereo and pulled off her boots and jeans. She danced around the house while they decorated, wearing a long green sweater that didn't cover up her red underwear, and a pair of Brendan's white socks.

Yup, he was officially in the Christmas spirit.

* * *

Whatever Paige was cooking smelled incredible. It was driving Brendan crazy that she wouldn't let him in the kitchen.

"It's a surprise," she'd said, shoving a glass of wine into his hand and banishing him into the living room.

So there he sat, watching a college football game with his feet propped up on the table, slowly going insane as he sipped on a glass of wine.

Yeah, life sure was hard.

He looked around his living room and couldn't help but smile. The Christmas tree stood in the corner in front of the bay windows, the red and white lights reflecting off the glass panes. Red, green, and white balls hung from the branches and a large white snowflake sat at the top. A candy dish with a penguin wearing a scarf was on the table; it was filled with foil-wrapped chocolate Santas. There was a nativity scene on the bookcase, a Santa on the hearth, and a trio of red glittery cones sitting on the dining room table. She'd put a wreath on the front door, dish towels with snowmen in the kitchen, and the reindeer sheets on their bed.

It was below forty outside, so Brendan had lit a fire in the fireplace to add some heat. He also thoroughly enjoyed Paige walking around in no pants, so he tried to keep the house warm enough to keep that tradition alive.

"You hungry?" she called from the kitchen.

"Starving," he said, turning off the game and pulling his feet down to the floor.

He stood up, still clutching his glass of wine, and turned around to find Paige standing in the entryway to the kitchen wearing a frilly black apron with white polka dots. Her hair was stacked on the top of her head in a messy bun and the sleeves of her sweater were pushed up to her elbows. He stopped in front of her and kissed her lightly on the mouth.

"We could postpone dinner," he said against her mouth as his free hand slid down her side, "and take those reindeer sheets for a spin."

"I don't think so, cowboy," she said, grabbing his wine glass and finishing it. "Dinner first, then dessert." She pulled herself away from him and walked into the kitchen.

"Oh, you're no fun," he said, admiring the view that the open back of the apron gave him.

"I just see the bigger picture." She opened the fridge and pulled out another bottle of wine. "You should eat so you have strength for later." She uncorked the bottle and filled both of their glasses.

"Did you have something specific in mind?" he asked as he came up behind her. He untied the back of her apron and pulled it off.

"Oh, maybe one or two things."

"I like the sound of that," he said, pressing his mouth to her neck.

"You like the sound of anything that involves sex," she

said, tilting her head to the side and giving him better access.

"I like the sound of anything that involves you," he said, reaching around her. He grabbed the wineglasses and stepped back toward the table. If he didn't put some space between them pronto, there would be no hope of them eating dinner any time soon.

Paige had made chicken Thai curry. He'd never had Thai food before, but as always, Paige tended to expand his horizons. The sauce had a pretty good kick to it, which caused both of them to reach for their wineglasses more often than usual. By the time they were done eating, they'd finished a bottle of wine and were in the middle of another.

Paige slipped out of the kitchen after dinner, telling him not to peek into the living room. She was back five minutes later, and they finished cleaning up together. When Brendan went to refill their glasses, Paige shook her head, grabbing the wine bottle instead. She grabbed his hand and pulled him into the living room. There was a pallet of blankets spread out in front of the fire, pillows stacked on one end, and a string of condoms on the table.

"I thought you said one or two things," he said, eyeing the condoms. "Not six."

"What?" she asked, putting the bottle of wine down on the table before she turned to him. "You're not up for the challenge?" she asked, reaching for his belt and unbuckling it.

"Oh, I don't think *up* is going to be a problem."

"Hmm," she hummed, unsnapping his jeans and pulling down his zipper. "I'd say not," she said as she slipped her hand down and cupped him through his boxer briefs. Brendan groaned.

Paige moved her hands to his hips and pushed his jeans and underwear down his thighs. He pulled everything off his legs, and a second later his shirt was on the ground. He grabbed the hem of Paige's sweater and she stretched up her arms as he pulled it up and over her head. Her bra and panties were a matching red set. He was a pretty big fan of them, but it took him no time at all to get her completely naked.

Paige pushed him down onto the blankets and straddled him. Apparently what she'd had in mind involved Brendan looking up at her from flat on his back. She grabbed a condom and opened it. Just her rolling it down the length of him had him coming out of his skin. But it was nothing compared to the second later when she lowered herself onto him.

Brendan grabbed her hips, needing to have his hands on her body. He held onto her as she rode him, and then moved one of his hands to where their bodies joined, touching her.

"Brendan," she gasped, her hips picking up speed.

He watched her, amazed at how lucky he was to have found her. She was spectacular, and it had way more to do than just with sex. She'd changed his life. She was who he was supposed to wake up next to every day. She was who was supposed to have his kids. Share his life. She was his, and he belonged to her completely.

He sat up, wrapping his arms around her and crushing her chest to his. His mouth landed hard on hers and he found her tongue. Her hips didn't miss a beat as she adjusted to the new angle and she wound her arms around his neck. She came hard, crying out into his mouth, and Brendan followed a second later, unable to resist the sensations of her body pulsing around him.

* * *

Paige wasn't sure how long they'd been lying in front of the fire, but she did know that they'd already worked their way through two more of those condoms. She was pressed into Brendan's side, her head resting on his chest as she stared at the fire. His hand lazily traced up and down her back.

"It feels right, being here with you, living with you," she said.

"That's because it is right."

"It wasn't like this with Dylan," she said, looking up at him.

He was looking down at her, his eyes focused on her face.

"It didn't feel like home with him. I never thought of it as *our* space. It was his space, and he was just tolerating me in it. He never accepted me, for me. Whenever I didn't fit into this mold he had in mind, he put me down. I thought I belonged in Philadelphia with him, but I didn't. It wasn't until I came down here that I found where I belong."

"And where's that?" he asked.

"With you," she said, stretching up to press her mouth to his. He kissed her deeply, pulling her up onto him so that she was sprawled across him. When he pulled back she settled herself on his chest, stacking her hands on his sternum.

"Until I found you, I was missing something," he said softly. "I just didn't know it. I didn't know that my life was half full. Didn't know I was barely getting by without you."

He sat up, pulling Paige with him. Her legs fell to the outside of his thighs so that she was straddling him. He reached up and grabbed her face, cupping her jaw in both of his hands.

"Paige, you're it for me, with your kisses that taste like oranges. You're the warm sheets next to me every morning, and the bright colors in the dryer when we do laundry. You're the toothbrush next to mine on the sink. You're the first sip of coffee in the morning, and the last sip of wine at night. You're it. You're the one."

He let go of her face and reached over to the pile of his clothes on the floor. He found his jeans and pulled out a tiny black box.

"Brendan," she whispered, her breath shallow and her head spinning.

"I love you more than I've ever loved anybody. I want to spend the rest of my life with you. Paige, will you marry me?"

He opened the box and inside sat a round diamond surrounded by a circle of tiny diamonds. More tiny diamonds ran down the sides of the ring, leaving about half of the band to be solid white gold. He pulled the ring out of the box and slipped it onto her finger.

She stared down at it for a second before she looked back up at him, tears running down her face. "Yes," she said, launching herself into his arms and tackling him to the ground. "Yes, yes, yes," she said, covering his face with kisses.

Brendan brought his hands up to the back of her head and guided her mouth to his. He rolled so that she was underneath him and settled between her thighs before he pulled up and looked down at her.

"I'm the luckiest guy in the world." He swiped his thumbs under her streaming eyes. "I can't even tell you what it means to me that you said yes."

"Brendan," she said, reaching up and touching his face, "that was the only answer."

"Good," he said, pressing his mouth to hers.

"But Brendan, when we tell people how we got engaged, can we leave out the part where we were naked?" she asked.

"But that's the best part."

"I'll make it worth your while," she said as she wrapped her legs around his waist.

"I have absolutely no doubts about that."

Chapter Eighteen

Above and Beyond

Brendan had gotten Trevor and Denise's blessing before he proposed to Paige. They'd been sitting on the couch watching the Jacksonville Stampede demolish the Red Wings on the ice. Paige had been out back painting, and Denise had been curled up in a corner reading a book. Brendan had been rolling the bottom of his beer bottle back and forth on his knee, trying to figure out exactly what he was going to say.

"I was wondering if I could talk to you two about something," Brendan said.

Denise looked up from her book as Trevor muted the TV.

"What's going on?" Trevor asked.

Brendan shifted, sitting farther up on the couch and angling himself so he could see both of them better.

"I love your daughter very much," he began.

"Hold on," Denise said, putting down her book and getting up from the chair. She walked across the room and sat down between Brendan and Trevor. She reached out and put her hand on Brendan's, smiling. "Okay, go on," she said and nodded.

"Paige is a remarkable woman. She's beautiful inside and out. She's strong and smart, and so talented it blows me away. She's the love of my life. I want to ask her to marry me, and I'd like to have your blessing."

Trevor and Denise beamed. Denise looked back at Trevor and nodded, before she turned to face Brendan again.

"I've said it before, Brendan, and I'll say it again. You're a good man who is worthy of my daughter. And that's saying something because I haven't thought that about any other guy she's dated. But you? You're different. I have full faith that you'll take care of our little girl," he said as he put an arm around Denise. "You have our blessing."

He'd asked her to marry him two days later.

* * *

"Oh! My! Gosh!" Grace said, jumping up and down in front of them. "Let me see! Let me see!"

Paige held out her left hand, grinning. She hadn't stopped grinning since Brendan had proposed. He liked seeing that look on her face. Loved it.

"It's beautiful, Brendan," Lula Mae said, staring at the ring on Paige's hand.

It was beautiful, but he didn't think it was even remotely comparable to the person who was wearing it.

"So when's the big day?" Grace asked.

"We just got engaged last night," Brendan said and

laughed. "We haven't exactly had time to discuss that."
Truth be told, they hadn't done a lot of talking the night
before or that morning for that matter. They'd been too
busy doing other things, like each other.

Lula Mae had known beforehand, and she'd insisted
that Brendan bring Paige over for a dinner to celebrate. It
was more than a little difficult to share Paige at the moment. He wanted her all to himself, but really, he always
wanted her all to himself.

"Paige," Shep practically shouted as he walked into
Lula Mae's kitchen. "Come here, you beautiful creature,
you," he said, pulling her into his chest and wrapping his
arms around her. "Congratulations," he said right before
he planted a big kiss on her cheek.

"Stop monopolizing Paige." Jax pulled her away from
Shep and gave her a hug of his own.

Shep came up to Brendan and slapped him on the
back. "I can't believe you got her to say yes."

"Me either," Brendan said, shaking his head, as Paige
was now pulled into the arms of Bennett. He couldn't believe his luck. Paige had been in his life for just over four
months and he couldn't imagine living life without her.
There was no way he could go back.

"I'm proud of you," Lula Mae whispered, grabbing
Brendan by the face and bringing his head down so that
she could kiss his cheeks.

"For what?" He smiled, shaking his head.

"For falling in love. She's a good girl, one that I'm
proud you're going to spend the rest of your life with.
Your mother…" She trailed off as she patted his cheek,
giving him a watery smile. "Your mother would've been
proud of you too."

"You think so?"

"I know so. It's not an easy thing, taking the leap."

"You can't get anything extraordinary from something that's easy," Brendan said, thinking of his mother. Claire used to say that in life you got only a handful of extraordinary things. She'd always said that her extraordinary had been Brendan and Grace. Brendan had never known what that really meant until he'd met Paige.

"No, you can't," Lula Mae said, pulling him in for a hug.

As soon as Bennett was done, Grace pulled Paige away while Lula Mae shooed the boys out into the living room. Paige looked at Brendan before he left the kitchen, a huge smile turning up her perfect lips.

* * *

Brendan dropped an armful of wooden planks onto the ground just as Shep came up behind him and dropped another armful right beside his pile. Brendan had gotten Shep, along with Jax and Bennett, to help him build an art studio for Paige. He hated that she didn't have a place that she could paint at in their house. He hated that she had to go off to her parents' to find the best creative environment. He wanted her to have that space in their house, to be able to escape without having to actually escape.

The plan was to have it finished by Christmas. It was only going to take them a little over a week to build it. The hard part was keeping it a secret from Paige. He'd been able to build it while she was at work, Tara keeping an eye on her and letting him know if she left; and Oliver knew to tell Paige that Brendan was either on a towing call if she came in or with a client if she called.

The area that Brendan had picked to build the studio was a little off to the side of the property. It was behind a cluster of trees, but it still had a good view of the water. The only place that it could be seen was from the window in their bedroom. It was fairly dark when Paige got home from work in the evenings, and since Brendan had done his best to distract her when they were in their room, she still had no idea what he was doing.

Brendan and Bennett had leveled the ground and poured the concrete the weekend before. On Monday, Jax had helped him set up a water line so that Paige could have a sink and small bathroom. And on Wednesday, Shep had helped him build a good portion of the frame.

It had warmed up that week, reaching into the seventies. The warmer, dry weather had helped the concrete set easier. It also made it more enjoyable to work. Brendan had long been used to the inconsistent weather in Florida, but it still drove Paige crazy.

"It's winter," she'd said that morning, as she'd gotten dressed. "I should be wearing a scarf and a thick jacket and boots. Not a dress and sandals."

"Well, in a couple of days it will be back in the fifties and you can wear those boots of yours, and nothing else," he'd said, sidling up behind her and pressing his mouth to her neck.

"I don't know how warm I'd be in just boots." She'd sighed, leaning back into him.

"Oh, I'd make sure that you were plenty warm," he'd said, reaching around and . . .

"God, you're helpless," Shep said, bringing Brendan back to reality.

"Why do you say that?" Brendan asked, looking at him.

"Because of that shit-eating grin that you always have on your face these days."

"You're just jealous," Jax said, grabbing a plank and bringing it over for Bennett to cut.

"Oh, I absolutely am. I just don't know how he roped us into helping him out with this little project," Shep said before he took a long pull on his water bottle.

"Because one day," Bennett said, grabbing the plank from Jax, "you're going to have that same shit-eating grin on your face and you're going to need help with some project of your own."

"Yeah, we all know how helpless you are with plumbing," Brendan said.

"Because nothing says 'I love you' like outdoor plumbing," Shep mocked.

"And don't you forget it," Bennett said.

By the time the sun had set, all four walls were up, the roof was finished, and the electricity was running. The next day they painted the inside a pale yellow and then cut the wood for the shelves and countertops. Shep and Jax painted the outside the same gray the house was painted, while Brendan put in the shelves and counter and Bennett installed the sink.

"And I believe that we're done," Bennett said, turning the knob on the sink. Water gushed out of the tap, splashing against the metal bottom.

Brendan looked around the little space, very anxious for Christmas day.

* * *

On Christmas morning, Brendan woke up pressed against Paige's back. One of his arms was under her pillow, the other wrapped around her, his hand up under her T-shirt, cupping her naked breast.

Brendan reluctantly pulled his hand out from under her T-shirt. He reached up and brushed her hair back from her neck and placed a kiss on her warm skin. She stirred and one of her hands came up, reaching for the back of his head.

"Merry Christmas, baby," Brendan said into her throat.

She turned in his arms. "Merry Christmas." She smiled sleepily at him.

Brendan lowered his mouth to hers, and it didn't take long for him to settle on top of her and push inside of her warm body. He made love to her slowly, before he pulled her out of bed and into the kitchen. She made coffee while he heated up some scones that Grace had made. After they ate, they refilled their coffee and went into the living room.

Brendan sat down on the couch as Paige disappeared into one of the spare rooms. She came back a moment later holding a large, flat, square package.

"I've been working on this for months," she said nervously as she handed it to him and sat down. "I hope you like it."

"I have no doubt it's amazing," he said, ripping the paper and pulling it off.

His eyes widened as he stared at the canvas in his hands. It was a painting of the oak tree at the park. The same oak tree that had been his mother's favorite, the one that was tattooed on his arm, the one that they'd sat in front of the first time they'd kissed.

"I've never put more of myself into something, Brendan. It's the single most meaningful painting I've ever done."

"It's perfect," he said softly, unable to stop the catch in his throat. It meant more to him than he could put into words. "Absolutely beautiful, Paige." He put the painting down on the coffee table and reached for her. He kissed her, his hand coming up to the back of her head and tangling in her hair. "You're the most incredible artist," he whispered against her mouth. "You're the most incredible everything." He kissed her for another minute before he pulled back. "So your present, you can't exactly unwrap." He stood up. "Wait here a second," he said before he left the room.

* * *

Brendan came back with a pair of her fuzzy moccasins and a sweatshirt in his hands. He'd pulled on a sweatshirt of his own and a pair of sneakers.

"Another one of your adventures?" she asked before she pulled on the sweatshirt. It was one of his and it smelled like him.

"Have I ever led you wrong?" he asked, holding out his hands to pull her off the couch.

"Not yet," she said, letting him draw her to her feet. She slipped on the shoes as Brendan pulled out a scarf.

"Now, if you're going to tie me up, I feel like we should be taking off clothes, not putting them on."

Brendan froze, his mouth dropping open and his eyes going so hot she thought that her hair might've been singed.

It took him a second to find his voice. "Are you serious?"

"Well, I've never done that before. But I have a feeling it could be fun."

"You never cease to amaze me." Brendan grinned as he came up behind her and pulled the scarf over her eyes. He gently tied it at the back of her head before he brought his mouth to her ear. "And you better believe I'm going to take you up on that offer."

"Good," she said as he slipped his hand in hers and led her across the room to the back door. "I'm going to fall," Paige said as Brendan led her out onto the porch and to the steps.

"I'd never let you fall," he whispered against her mouth before he kissed her. "Now, hold onto both of my hands and listen to what I tell you to do."

"You know that I never listen well," she said and smiled.

"Oh, I'm fully aware of that." He slowly led her down, both of her hands in his. He didn't let go of her until she was safely off the stairs.

She had no idea where he was leading her. She thought he might be leading her out to the boat, but instead of going straight ahead he veered off to the right.

"All right," he said, moving behind her. He tugged at the knots on the back of her head and when the blindfold fell away from her eyes all she could do was stare.

"Oh my gosh," she said, turning around slowly. "You...you built me an art studio?"

"Well, I had some help."

"Brendan." She whispered his name as she stretched up and pressed her mouth to his. "You are an amazing, wonderful man. I don't know what I did to deserve you," she said, shaking her head as she gazed at him.

"I think you have that backward," he said as he grabbed her hand and put a key in her palm. "Go check it out."

Paige leaned up one more time and pressed her lips against his. "I can't believe you," she said and smiled, shaking her head before she took a step back from him and walked to the door of her new art studio.

It was at least twice the size of the shed she'd used at her parents'. The door had glass panes on the top, but Paige tried not to peek in as she stuck the key in the lock and turned the handle. She pushed the door open and took a deep breath as she looked around. It still smelled like paint and freshly cut wood. There were windows on the left and back wall. The back one looked out onto the water. Floor-to-ceiling shelves were on either side of the window to the left, an AC and heater unit sticking out of it, while a counter ran along the entire right wall with a deep metal sink in the center. More shelves were stacked above and under the counter. There was a door on the right wall as well and Paige stuck her head in to find a tiny bathroom.

It was perfect.

"When did you do this?" she asked, turning to Brendan, who was standing in the doorway. "How did you do this?"

"The last two weeks," he said, reaching his hand out for her. She grabbed it and he pulled her toward him, folding her into his chest. "Jax, Shep, and Bennett all helped. So you like it?" he asked, his eyes lighting up.

"Love it," Paige said, pressing her mouth against his. "And I love you."

* * *

December slipped into January. Brendan and Paige had a quiet New Year's together, spent in front of the fire, snuggled up together.

"What do you think about June?" Brendan asked as he lazily ran his fingers up Paige's arm. "Is that enough time to plan a wedding?"

Paige looked up at him. "Five months? Yeah, that's enough time."

"How about the second weekend?"

"That sounds perfect," she said and grinned.

With the date set, plans started to get underway. Before Brendan knew it, it was the beginning of April. They'd been so busy getting ready for the wedding that time had flown by. They'd started spending a lot of time over at Paige's parents' house, eating most dinners there and using it as the home base for all the wedding planning. On some nights, Lula Mae, Oliver, and Grace would come over with dinner and they'd help out too.

Whenever Brendan had been dismissed from whatever planning he'd needed to be a part of that day, he would hang out with Trevor, watching a hockey game and then baseball when the season started.

The last Saturday in April, the guys threw Brendan a bachelor party. Brendan spent the day out on the water deep-sea fishing with Oliver, Trevor, Jax, Shep, Bennett, Shep's father Nathanial Sr., Shep's little brother Finn, Shep and Finn's uncle Jacob Meadow's, all of the guys who played on the Stingrays, and all of the guys from the shop. They'd closed King's Auto for the day.

"I really don't know how fishing became the logical

substitute for a stripper," Shep said as he popped open a beer.

"I told you I didn't want that," Brendan said as he baited his hook. "I have absolutely no interest in seeing any naked woman besides Paige."

"Oh, hey there, Mr. Morrison," Shep said, looking over Brendan's shoulder.

Brendan turned quickly to find no one behind him. Trevor was on the other side of the boat talking to Oliver and Shep's dad.

"You're the least funny person I know." Brendan frowned, turning back to Shep.

"I've been telling him that for years," Finn said, shaking his head at his older brother. "But he just never shuts up."

Finn was a few years younger than Shep. They looked almost identical, same easygoing grin and deep blue eyes. There were a few differences though. Finn was slightly smaller, didn't have tattoos, and wore his thick, dark hair a little shorter than Shep. Finn had just finished his second year of veterinary school and he was home for the summer.

"So how's school going?" Bennett asked as he cast out his line.

"Long, man," Finn said, shaking his head. "This summer is my last of freedom. Clinics start next year. What about you? How's it been since you got back?"

"It's better," Bennett said and nodded. "Slowly but surely."

Bennett had been hanging out with them a lot over the last couple of months, and Brendan had definitely noticed a few changes. Bennett was quick to smile again, much like he had been in high school, and some of the haunted man had left his eyes. He'd become a good friend too, so much so that he was going to be a groomsmen along with Shep and Jax.

"We've been keeping him busy," Jax said, slapping Bennett on the shoulder. "He's helped out with a few construction projects here and there."

"What did you guys build?" Finn asked.

They told him about Paige's art studio.

"And," Jax continued, "I was looking at this property over on Whiskey River. The house was foreclosed last year. It's a complete disaster. But Bennett went out and looked at it for me. I made an offer and if all goes well, we'll start working on it in the fall."

"Looks like all of you are settling down. So which one of you is going to be the next to get married?"

No one answered. They all just looked at Jax, who frowned and returned his attention to the ocean.

* * *

All in all it was a good trip, except Trevor got seasick. He spent a good portion of the day in the bathroom belowdecks.

"I'm fine," he told Brendan as they got into his truck. "Really, don't worry about me, and don't go telling Paige and Denise. They have enough to worry about with the wedding, and there's no sense in adding this to the mix."

"All right," Brendan said.

But truth be told, he didn't really believe it. Something just felt off to Brendan.

A month before the wedding, Paige was spending the

day with Denise. They were going to the final fitting on her dress and to run a couple of other errands. Brendan went over to the Morrisons' to watch a Yankee game with Trevor. Brendan had bought a pizza, and Trevor barely even ate one slice.

Halfway through the game Trevor got up to go to the bathroom, and before he made it out of the room he grabbed onto the wall, gasping in pain.

"Trevor?" Brendan said, standing up and going over to him.

"I'm fine, I'm fine," he said, waving him off.

Trevor straightened and went to take a step but fell. Brendan lunged, catching him before he hit the ground. Brendan helped him sit on the floor and lean back against the wall. His face was pale and clammy and he was short of breath.

"It's this new medicine," Trevor said. "It's making me sick."

"Medicine?" Brendan asked.

"I need to see my doctor."

"Okay, let me call the hospital," Brendan said, pulling out his phone. "Who am I asking for?"

Trevor just looked at him for a second, something in his eyes that Brendan hadn't seen before. Pain beyond all reason. "Dr. Kendrick."

Brendan froze. He just stared at Trevor, unable to move. Dr. Kendrick was the oncologist at the county hospital. He'd been Brendan's mother's doctor.

Trevor had cancer.

Brendan leaned back against the wall and slid down, sitting next to Trevor.

He turned and looked at Trevor. "What kind?" he

asked, surprised he'd gotten a sound out of his dry throat.

Trevor blinked a couple of times, tears falling down his face.

"Pancreatic."

"Fuck," Brendan said, unable to think of anything else to say.

A small bitter laugh escaped Trevor. "My sentiments exactly."

"Does Denise know?" Brendan asked, leaning his head back against the wall.

"Not yet. I went to the doctor last month because I'd been having back pain and not feeling so great. They ran some tests. It's too advanced to do anything."

All of a sudden Brendan was back to the days when his mother had been dying. Her lucid moments had been few and far between. She'd been on a lot of painkillers and she'd go in and out of sleep throughout the day. He still remembered it all so clearly, the grayish tint to her skin, the black circles under her eyes, the croaking voice that came out of her cracked, dry lips. She hadn't looked like his mom anymore. She'd been wasting away for months to a small, frail woman. She'd always been so full of life, and then she'd just been gone.

On the day she'd died, Brendan had gone to say goodbye to her before he'd left for school and she'd grabbed his hand and held on. She'd been so weak. She'd probably thought she'd been holding on for dear life but, God, she was just so damn weak. That day, she'd held his hand and told him she loved him just like she had every day before he left. But that day? That day, she'd kept repeating herself and she'd made him promise to never forget it, made him promise to never forget her.

He'd known. That whole morning he'd waited for it, waited for the moment that someone was going to knock on his teacher's door to tell him his mom had died. It was during his fifth-period class, right after lunch. Coach Mathis and Principal Reynolds came. Brendan had never liked Principal Reynolds. He'd always been an arrogant, smarmy prick. He'd been awful to Grace and Brendan when they were in school. He never did anything about the kids that made their lives hell. But that day? That day, Brendan hated him. Grace had been hysterical. She couldn't stop crying, but some sort of strange calmness had come over Brendan. Like he'd been watching from outside his body, watching himself going through the motions.

They'd sat in Principal Reynolds's cold, empty office, Grace sniffling beside him, and he'd been staring at a cheesy picture above the secretary's desk. It was of a kitten climbing a mountain with the caption NOTHING IS IMPOSSIBLE underneath it.

Nothing is impossible?

Everything was impossible at that moment. Talking to his mom again, hearing her laugh, asking her for advice, seeing her cheering him on from the bleachers. It was all gone. She was gone and she was never coming back, because if one thing was impossible, it was coming back from the dead.

This wasn't happening again. There couldn't possibly be another person in his life who was being ripped away. Brendan didn't only love Paige. He loved her parents. They were his family too. And this was going to absolutely destroy Paige. It was just another thing that he couldn't protect her from, and that killed him.

"How long?" Brendan asked, wiping at his face. He wasn't sure when he'd started crying, but tears were streaming down his face.

"Best case? Six more months."

"When are you going to tell them?"

"After the wedding."

Brendan nodded, still looking straight ahead. He knew that he needed to get up and take Trevor to the hospital, but that involved standing up and he had no idea how to do that. The world had been ripped out from underneath him.

Again.

Chapter Nineteen

A Calling, Not a Choice

Brendan was struggling. It was hard for him to watch Paige every day. To see her so happy, when he knew that everything was about to change. It was all just an illusion. But Trevor wanted to wait to tell her and Denise, and Brendan understood that. The wedding was supposed to be this great joyous event, and that wouldn't be the case if everyone found out that Trevor was dying.

So Brendan bore the weight of it. What other choice did he have? Trevor asked him to do something, so he was going to do it. Brendan would do anything for Paige, no matter the cost. And really, Brendan's suffering was nothing, *nothing* compared to Trevor's.

As it got closer to the big day, things started to get crazier. Brendan did everything he could to lessen the burden on everyone, especially Trevor. Denise and Paige, unaware of what was going on, were asking Trevor to do the type of stuff he'd been able to do before. He was trying very hard to cover up his exhaustion and the pain he was in, only letting it show around Brendan.

Brendan took Trevor to his doctor's appointments. The new pain medicine was working better and it wasn't making him sick. It was a little difficult for Brendan to be back in the hospital. At least it didn't look the same as it had. The wing with the oncology department was being remodeled and the chaos of the construction was a nice distraction so that Brendan didn't get sucked back in. His mother hadn't died at the hospital, but she'd spent a lot of time there in her last few months, and Brendan had been with her for most of it. He'd tried to be her rock, and when she'd died he'd fractured into a thousand pieces. But he couldn't fracture this time, because Paige was going to need him.

"You're going to have to stop with all of this," Trevor told him one day when they were driving back from the doctor.

"Stop with what?"

"This funk that you're in."

"It's more than a funk," Brendan said, shaking his head.

"I'm dying, Brendan. There's nothing anybody can do to change that. It's out of our control. But you know what is in our control?"

"What's that?" Brendan asked.

"How we choose to spend the time that's left. You're about to get married to my daughter. It's a good time. Enjoy it. You can't fix everything so let it go. Do that for me."

And so Brendan did.

For now.

* * *

The weekend before the wedding, Abby flew down from DC to help with all of the last-minute wedding preparations. When Brendan and Paige had first gotten serious, Abby had told him that if he ever hurt Paige, she would hurt him. He'd seen Abby in pictures, and he'd talked to her a few times over the phone, but it was more than slightly amusing to meet the pint-size enforcer.

Abby was just over five feet tall, with auburn hair and dark blue eyes. She was ridiculously pale, but her fair skin showed off barely any freckles. It was clear that appearances could be deceiving, because as it turned out Abby was intimidating as hell.

"She scares me," Shep said the night before the wedding.

The Sleepy Sheep was closed to the public, and Shep's family was throwing the rehearsal dinner. Lula Mae and Grace, with the help of Pinky, Panky, and Tara, had spent the last three days cooking for the rehearsal dinner and the reception. Which left Brendan, Shep, Jax, and Bennett at Paige, Denise, and Abby's disposal to do whatever jobs they'd needed done.

"She's one of the most intimidating women I've ever met," Shep continued, shaking his head as they watched Abby laughing with Paige. "You'd never know she was crazy."

Abby wasn't afraid to tell someone when they didn't do something correctly, and she was more than happy to tell them when they continued to do it wrong. Well, maybe *happy* wasn't the right word. There'd been a particularly tricky moment, when Shep and Jax had been stringing the lights, where Brendan had thought that Abby's head was going to start spinning. But to be fair, neither of them had really listened to her and what she'd wanted. After that, they'd both started to pay strict attention to her details.

"She's not crazy," Brendan said, popping the last of his sandwich into his mouth. "She's just a bit of a perfectionist."

"Po*ta*to, pa*ta*to. She's so different from Paige though. It kind of blows my mind that they're so close."

It was true that Abby was a little more polished than Paige. Where Paige wore brightly colored clothes, sometimes with patterns that gravitated toward the eye-popping side, Abby tended toward black or dark, solid colors. Where Paige had no problem throwing her hair into a messy bun, Abby had hers sleeked back into some sort of twist thing. Abby was streamlined, or more simply, she colored inside the lines. Whereas Paige was not an "inside the lines" sort of person, not at all, which was one of the things that Brendan loved most about her.

At that moment, Paige looked over at Brendan, her big gray eyes smiling at him from across the room. She said something to Abby, not taking her eyes off him, and the two of them made their way across the room.

"I'm going to go check on Jax," Shep said, taking a step back.

"Chicken shit," Brendan called after him.

"Not denying it," Shep said before he turned around and headed to the bar where Jax was frowning out at the dance floor. Grace had been talking to one of Paige's cousins for most of the night, and they were currently dancing in front of the live band.

Before Paige and Abby made it over to Brendan, Denise picked off Abby and pulled her away.

"Where did Shep run off to?" Paige asked, sliding her arms around Brendan's waist. She was wearing those black wedges that still drove him out of his mind.

"You want the made-up reason or the real reason?" he asked, putting his hands on the small of her back.

"Both."

"Made up, he went to comfort Jax. Real, he's scared of Abby."

"I don't doubt that being scared of Abby is the real reason he fled. But Jax has been sulking most of the night," Paige said, glancing over at the bar.

"That's because Grace is dancing with someone who isn't him."

"Jax is a smart man, but when it comes to Grace, he's an idiot."

"Yeah, he'll figure it out one day. Do you want to dance with me?" he asked.

"Yes," she said and smiled.

He dragged her out onto the dance floor, people moving around them as the beat of the song picked up. After a couple more fast ones the band played one last slow song to wind up the night. Brendan pulled Paige in close and put his mouth to her ear.

"The next time I dance with you, we'll be married," he whispered.

"I can't wait." She pulled back and smiled at him.

"Do you have to stay at your parents' tonight?"

He hadn't spent a night away from Paige since their first night together over seven months ago. Tonight was going to be the longest night of his life for so many reasons.

"Yes," she said against his mouth, "because I want the first time you see me tomorrow to be when I'm walking down the aisle."

"That's," he said, looking down at his watch and then back up to her, "over fourteen hours from now. Too long, way too long."

"It'll be worth the wait."

"You're always worth the wait," he said, pressing his mouth to hers. Like always, the world faded away and all that there was, was Paige. And then she was pulled out of his arms.

"Say good night to your hot mechanic," Abby said.

The music had stopped and the band was starting to pack up.

How long had they been kissing for? Didn't matter, it wasn't nearly long enough. He pulled Paige back into his arms and kissed her again.

"I love you," he said, pulling back just far enough to look at her.

"I love you too," she said before Abby dragged her outside.

* * *

Brendan had made only one request when it came to the wedding, that they get married under the oak tree at Ocean Oak Park. The tree had been his mother's, but it was now Brendan and Paige's too. They'd had their first kiss in front of that tree, so it was only appropriate that they have their first kiss as man and wife in front of it too. The painting that Paige had painted for Brendan now hung above their bed, so it was yet another thing that he couldn't look at without thinking of her. But it wasn't much of a request, as Paige had wanted to get married there too.

It was just before sunset, the breeze coming off the ocean cool. It wasn't a humid day, which was good, because all of the guys were wearing suits.

"You ready?" Shep asked as he, Jax, and Bennett took their places beside him.

"Without a doubt," Brendan said as he watched Abby, Grace, and Tara make their way down the aisle, all of them wearing deep blue bridesmaid's dresses and carrying bouquets of sunflowers.

Brendan's heart kicked up hard in his chest as the music changed. Paige and her father came out from behind a cluster of trees where they'd been waiting.

She was stunning.

Her dress was simple. It was a satin material, and it flowed down her body, molding to her curves. It dipped down the front of her chest in a *V*. There were straps at her shoulders holding her dress up, and her freckled arms were exposed in all of their glory. He'd never seen anyone or anything more beautiful in his entire life.

Her eyes didn't waver from his as she made her way down the aisle with her father.

"Dearly beloved," Pastor Phillips began when Paige and Trevor stopped at the end of the aisle, "we are gathered here today in the sight of God and these witnesses to unite Brendan and Paige in holy matrimony."

Brendan just stared at Paige as the pastor continued to talk. She smiled at him and mouthed, *I love you.*

I love you, he mouthed back.

"Who gives this woman to be married to this man?" Pastor Phillips asked.

"Her mother and I do," Trevor said before turning to Paige. He pulled her into his arms, hugging her as he whispered something in her ear. Then he kissed her on the cheek and let go. He turned to Brendan and pulled him into a hug.

"You have to take care of her," Trevor said. "You have to take care of my little girl."

"Yes, sir," Brendan said as Trevor pulled back.

Trevor gave Brendan a watery smile as he grabbed Paige's hand and put it in Brendan's. He nodded at their joined hands in satisfaction before he made his way over to Denise.

When it was time for them to say their vows, Brendan was surprised that his voice came out as steady as it did.

"Paige, I didn't think it was possible to love someone as much as I love you." His voice hitched slightly but Paige squeezed his hands and he pushed through it. "I was always scared of falling in love. For years I refused to let myself fall. Then you came along out of nowhere and you undid every single one of my defenses before I even knew what was happening. I never had a choice. I promise to love you, even when it's difficult. It's the things that you have to fight for the hardest that are worth the most, and you're worth everything."

"Brendan," Paige said and took a deep breath and smiled, her eyes glistening with unshed tears. "I met you at a time in my life when I thought I was lost. As it turned out, I was following the right road the whole time because it led me to you. You've unraveled me from the beginning, pulled at the strings until you left me feeling

completely cherished, completely loved, completely undone with no chance of ever going back. I promise to love
you every single day for the rest of our lives."

Yup, he was done for.

"You're crying," she whispered as she reached up and
swiped her fingers under his eyes.

"So are you," he said, grabbing her hand and holding it to
his face. "And I thought you said happy crying was okay."

"It is."

"May I have the rings?" Pastor Phillips asked.

Brendan turned to Shep, who slipped him the rings. As
the pastor blessed the rings, Brendan couldn't focus on
anything besides the feel of Paige's soft hands in his.

"I give you this ring as a symbol of my love and with
all that I am, and all that I have, I promise to honor you.
With this ring I thee wed," he said as he slipped the ring
on her finger.

"I give you this ring as a symbol of my love and with
all that I am, and all that I have, I promise to honor you.
With this ring I thee wed," Paige repeated as she slipped
the ring onto his finger.

"Now that Brendan and Paige have pledged their love
to each other, by the power vested in me I now pronounce
them husband and wife. You may kiss the bride."

No one had to tell Brendan twice. He grabbed Paige's
face in both of his hands, brought her mouth to his, and
kissed his wife for the first time.

* * *

Paige couldn't stop smiling as Brendan slowly guided
them around the dance floor. One of his hands rested on

her lower back, his fingers brushing across her skin, while his other hand held hers. Her free hand was wrapped around the back of his head, her fingers trailing through his hair.

"Mrs. King," Brendan said as he stared at her with a big goofy grin and dazed eyes.

"Yes?"

"I just like saying it," he said, bringing his mouth to her ear. "Mrs. King, Mrs. King, Mrs. King," he whispered.

Every time he said it, a wave of euphoria ran through her body, making her want to scream and cry and laugh all at the same time. But in the interest of looking sane, and not ruining their first dance, she did none of those things. She just let Brendan lead her around the dance floor, happier than she'd ever been in her life. When the music ended, Brendan placed Paige's hand in her father's and walked off the floor.

"My Little Miss, all grown up and married," Trevor said as they began to move across the floor. "You look beautiful, beautiful and happy."

"I am happy. I love that man so much," she said, beaming.

"I'm so grateful I got to see this. Be here. Walk you down the aisle. Dance with my baby girl on her wedding day," he said, his eyes getting glassy. He blinked and a few tears ran down his face.

"Dad?" Paige asked her own eyes filling up. The day was already emotional, and the sight of her father crying really did something to her.

"I'm okay."

"Are you sure?" she asked.

"Yes," he said and nodded, smiling through his tears.

"Now, no more crying," he said as he kissed her on the temple and proceeded to lead her around the dance floor.

* * *

"Welcome home, Mrs. King," Brendan said as he carried Paige through the front door of their house. He locked the door behind them, all the while still holding Paige.

"Hmm," she hummed against his throat. "I like the sound of that."

"Close your eyes," he whispered against her temple as he carried her through the house and to their bedroom. "And keep 'em closed," he said as he set her down.

"All right." She smiled as she folded her arms across her chest. He moved around the room for a minute before music started playing and he came up behind her.

"Open your eyes," he whispered as he pressed his lips to her neck.

Paige opened her eyes to find the room glowing from a dozen or so candles. Sunflower petals were scattered across the duvet on the bed.

"Brendan," Paige said, turning in his arms, "you didn't have—"

He cut her off, covering her mouth with his. He reached up and started removing the pins from her hair as his tongue moved in perfect rhythm against hers.

"Yes, I did," he said a moment later when he came up for air.

"It's beautiful," she said as he started to unwind her hair and pull it down around her shoulders.

"No," he said, shaking his head. "It's sufficient. You

can't really say that anything is beautiful when you're in the room. Everything pales in comparison."

"Brendan—"

But that was as far as she got before he kissed her again and started unzipping the back of her dress.

* * *

Brendan and Paige went on their honeymoon the last weekend in June. Brendan had told Trevor that they could postpone the trip, but Trevor insisted. He and Denise were going to Savannah, Georgia, for the week. She'd always wanted to go, so he was going to take her.

Brendan and Paige's honeymoon was in North Carolina and they spent a week at a cabin in the mountains. Brendan was in a state of total bliss, but that bliss didn't last long. They were driving back to Mirabelle when they got the call.

Trevor had collapsed. What made matters even worse was that he had hit his head and gotten a concussion. They'd taken him to the emergency room and were running tests. But that was all they told Paige; she had no idea just how bad it really was.

They went directly to the hospital. Brendan pulled into the parking lot and turned off his truck. He turned to Paige, who was staring out of the windshield.

"I have this really bad feeling," she said. "I don't want to go in there."

He couldn't tell her it was going to be okay, because he knew damn well it wasn't going to be. So instead he grabbed her hand, brought it to his mouth, and kissed her wrist.

She turned to him, fear in her eyes.

"Whatever it is, we'll handle it," he said.

She merely nodded before she went to get out of the truck. They met at the front and he grabbed her hand, holding it as they walked inside.

Chapter Twenty

Broken Promises and Broken Hearts

P aige prayed as Brendan led her through the hallways of the hospital. She prayed that the awful feeling in her stomach wasn't true. That her father was going to be fine.

But it took one look from her mother to know that nothing was going to be fine.

Denise stepped out into the hallway, wincing at the fluorescent light. The second her mother's sad, desperate eyes focused on them, the ground dropped out from under Paige's feet.

Her father was dying.

Denise's face crumpled and she started sobbing.

"Oh, Mom," Paige said, letting go of Brendan's hand and wrapping her arms around her mother's shaking shoulders.

They just stood there, both of them crying.

"How bad is it?" Paige whispered

"Bad," Denise said, pulling back. "It's pancreatic cancer."

Paige had a teacher in college who had died of pancreatic cancer. She knew that, on average, people who were diagnosed with it lived for less than a year.

"It's already spread to his other organs. They said four months is optimistic."

Nothing about this entire situation was optimistic, and hearing the word made Paige so angry she wanted to hit something. Four months wasn't good enough. Four months was a joke.

Paige wasn't prepared for this. She wasn't prepared for her father not being around for the rest of her life. He wouldn't get another birthday. Wouldn't get another Christmas. Her parents had celebrated their last wedding anniversary. The thought of her mother living out the rest of her life without her father made Paige physically ill.

"I need a minute," Paige said, pulling back from her mother. She turned to Brendan. "Bathroom?"

"Down there," he said, pointing down the hall.

Paige bolted, getting there just in time to empty her stomach of everything.

* * *

Somehow Paige calmed herself down enough to see her father. She walked into the dim room to find Trevor sitting up, a bandage over his head.

"Hey, Little Miss," he said weakly.

"Daddy," she whispered as she walked over and sat on the edge of the bed. He leaned forward, reaching for her, and they wrapped their arms around each other. Paige held onto her father for dear life. She didn't want to let him go, not ever. It wasn't long before she felt warm tears soak into the shoulder of her shirt; her own were streaming down her face. "Don't die. Please don't die."

"If only it were that easy," he said, pulling back to look at her. He gave her a sad, watery smile. "I love you, baby girl," he said, reaching for her face and running his thumb under one eye and then the other. "We still have a little time. And we'll make it count."

Paige nodded. Unable to say anything for fear she might lose it again.

* * *

While Paige went to talk to her dad, Brendan stayed out in the hallway and talked to Denise. She told him everything that Dr. Kendrick had told her and it didn't take long for Brendan to realize that Trevor hadn't told Denise when the real diagnosis had happened. Dr. Kendrick had explained everything to Denise like they'd just discovered the cancer.

So Trevor didn't want them to know that he'd been sick for months. Didn't want them to know that he and Brendan had known what was coming.

Brendan hadn't been prepared for this. But what the hell was he supposed to do? His father-in-law was dying, and he wasn't going to go against what Trevor wanted, so he just played along.

When Paige came out of her father's room, Brendan knew she was barely holding it together.

"You two should go home," Denise said, standing up and smoothing her hands along the side of her pants.

"Mom, we'll stay. It's no problem."

"No," Denise said, shaking her head. "I'm going to stay with your father. He should be released tomorrow. You need to get some rest, baby," she said, reaching up and patting Paige's cheek. "Go home and be with your husband. Grieve with your husband."

"But what about you?"

"I'm going to grieve with your father. We'll see you to-morrow."

"You'll call me if you need anything?" Paige asked.

"Promise," Denise said, kissing Paige on the forehead before she slipped back into the hospital room.

* * *

Paige did grieve that night, and every night after that. She'd curl into Brendan's side and cry herself to sleep, and he'd just hold her. Tell her how much he loved her. She didn't think she'd be able to get through the day if she didn't know that she had a safe place in Brendan's arms waiting for her.

He kept her going.

It didn't take long for things to get progressively worse with her father. Within weeks, he was so weak that it was a struggle for him to get out of bed. He slept for most of the day, only getting up when Paige and Brendan came over for dinner.

By the middle of August, Paige's dad was officially bedridden, attached to an IV and using an oxygen ma-chine to help him breathe. A hospital bed had been set up in the living room, and her mom slept on the couch next to her dad's bed every night. As the dose of his pain meds went progressively up, his lucid moments went progressively down. Denise was barely holding it together. Paige knew this because *she* was barely holding it together.

Paige spent most of her free time at her parents' house. She'd often sit by her father's bed and read him one of his favorite books; other times, she'd just talk to him. Brendan was there a lot too. Helping in every way he could. Doing everything that was asked of him, and about a thousand things that hadn't been.

Damn, did she love that man with every fiber of her being.

One morning Paige woke up sprawled across Brendan. She moved her hand to the center of his chest and rested her chin on it, looking up at his sleeping face.

The last month and a half hadn't been easy. She didn't know how she would've gotten through it without him. It shouldn't have surprised her that he knew exactly what she needed and when she needed it. He was her shoulder to cry on in a moment's notice. He knew when to give her space and exactly how much. She knew why he could practically read her mind. One reason was because he'd gone through this before with his mother. He knew what it was like to lose a parent to cancer. The other reason was because he knew her.

She'd been so incredibly wrong to think she'd ever been in love with anyone before Brendan. No one could compare to him on any level.

She watched him sleep. She studied the face of the man she loved more than anything. She needed him so badly it hurt. She slid her thigh between his legs and pressed her open mouth to his neck. He stirred beneath her, pressing into her even though he wasn't up yet. Well, not awake, at least.

She pulled her underwear off before she threw her leg over him and straddled him. She closed her mouth over his and knew the exact moment he was no longer asleep because his tongue started moving against hers and he groaned into her mouth. His hands were on her hips, holding onto her as she moved against him.

She pulled her T-shirt over her head, breaking their kiss for only a moment as the fabric passed between their mouths. She threw it over her shoulder and reached down, pulling him out of his boxers. When he was firmly inside of her, they both froze. He grabbed her face and pulled back, holding her head in his hands.

"Paige?" Brendan asked, studying her face.

She nodded and pressed her mouth to his, trying to show him what she wanted, because words weren't enough. She needed this, right now, no barriers. The kiss turned frenzied after a moment, both of them trying to consume the other. She moved over him as he thrust up inside of her, and when she came, he rolled her onto her back and started moving again. His hips bumped up against hers and she wrapped her legs around his waist. She wasn't sure how long they moved together, but at some point another overwhelming orgasm raked through her body. Brendan followed her over and collapsed onto her, breathing hard and shaking.

* * *

Everything had happened so fast. Brendan had woken up with Paige on top of him. One moment they'd been kissing, the next he'd been inside of her, absolutely nothing between them.

Nothing had ever felt like that before. Gravity had pulled him under and then he'd fallen to pieces. He was still lying on top of her, trying to come back down to earth, trying to piece himself together again. But it was impossible. She shattered him.

He couldn't have moved even if he'd wanted to, and right at that moment, he didn't want to move ever again. Paige's legs were still wrapped around his waist. Her hands were on the back of his neck, her fingers trailing through his hair. His face was pressed into her throat and every time he inhaled, he inhaled her.

"Are you okay?" Paige whispered.

He nodded. That was all he could do because he still couldn't remember how to speak. When his brain finally connected with his body again, Brendan got up on his forearms and looked down at her. He reached up and traced her hairline, pushing her hair behind her ear.

"That was…" He trailed off, shaking his head. He had no words.

"I know," she said and smiled, running her hands to the back of his head and pulling his mouth down to hers.

* * *

Paige had a lot of inspiration lately, most of it dark. She channeled it toward her work, and she assumed it worked because her pieces were selling like crazy. She'd actually cut back her hours at the funeral home, working only four days a week. Painting was one of the few ways she was able to escape for just a moment. Sometimes things would just build up to a peak and Paige needed something to think about besides her father and the constant pain he was in, because whenever she thought about it she couldn't breathe.

On her day off, Paige would paint from the time Brendan left in the morning straight through to when he came home at night. He'd started stocking the studio with water bottles and granola bars to make sure she ate something at some point during the day.

Paige had finished another painting for the funeral home, this one of the fishing piers in Mirabelle. She'd painted a dozen boats with dark gray storm clouds brewing in the background. Most of the paintings in the funeral home were old and falling apart, but some of the frames were beautiful antiques. Paige switched the new painting with the one that was in the frame, and it wasn't until the end of the day that she had time to hang it up.

The other painting might be old, but Mr. Adams hadn't wanted to get rid of it. It had been hanging up in the funeral home since he was little, so he wanted it put in the storage room. Problem was, the storage room was down the hall that Paige avoided like the plague. She headed over to Tara's desk and waited for her to get off the phone.

"We don't have any *situations*?" Paige asked, pointing to the door that led to the embalming rooms. Even though she'd worked there for over a year, she was still completely skeeved out by dead bodies and still insisted upon calling them *situations*. The idea of being in a room alone with one was still way too much for her to handle.

"No," Tara drawled. "Juris put Mr. Woods in the parlor this afternoon," she finished, giving Paige an amused little shake of her head. "How have you still not gotten over that little fear of yours?"

"A fear of dead bodies *isn't* little. And there is no reason for me to get over it. My job is done mainly up there,"
Paige said, pointing up the stairs. "And *they* are mainly
down here." She pointed to the floor.

"Mmm-hmm." Tara smiled as she answered the ringing phone.

Paige turned and walked to the door. She opened it and
eyed the empty space apprehensively.

No one is in there. No one is in there.

She took a deep breath and made her way down the
hallway, her heels tapping against the hardwood. The
storage closet was the last one at the end of the hall, so
she kept her gaze straight ahead of her, set on her destina-
tion. She put the painting away and shut the door behind
her, determined to make a quick escape.

Problem was, Paige didn't keep her focus on the end
of the hallway and as she passed the embalming room she
saw something large and green out of the corner of her
eye. Before she could stop herself she turned to find the
biggest and ugliest alligator she'd ever seen in her life.
Long black nails stuck out from its stubby legs and its
massive tail was sprawled out behind it. But it was when
Paige saw its black eyes staring at her that she started
screaming.

* * *

On days that both Brendan and Paige went over to her
parents' house, he dropped her off and picked her up from
work so they could head over together.

"She in her office?" Brendan asked as he stopped in
front of Tara's desk.

"No." Tara shook her head. "She had to go put something in storage. She's still completely freaked out to go by the embalming room. She thinks a dead body is going to jump out and grab her or something."

Brendan was cut off midlaugh when a blood-curdling scream made its way down the hall. For a second, everything in him froze as he tried to process the reason that Paige would sound so terrified. When his brain connected with his legs he bolted for the hallway only to have Paige slam into him at the doorway.

"Oh my God, oh my God, oh my God," she said, grabbing onto him for dear life.

"Paige, calm down," Brendan said, grabbing her shoulders and pulling her back. The fact that she was alive and breathing in his arms made him calm down enough to think. But his heart was still slamming inside of his chest. "What happened?"

"There," she said, looking at him horrified. "There is a—" She sucked in a shallow breath. "There is a—"

"What?" he asked.

"An alligator," she said, finding her words.

"A what?" Brendan couldn't help but laugh. He wasn't sure what he'd been imagining, but it sure as hell hadn't been an alligator.

"It isn't funny," she shouted at him, still hysterical. "There is a freaking al-li-ga-tor in there."

"Oh, I forgot about him," Tara said, from behind them.

"*Him?* That thing is the freaking creature from the black lagoon. What the hell is it doing here?"

"Someone dropped it off. Juris went to get his cousin to help him move it. It's too big for him to move on his own."

"*Big?* It's enormous. It's just sitting in the middle of the floor holding court. I thought it was still alive."

Brendan was now laughing so hard he had to hold his stomach.

"This isn't funny," Paige said, shoving him hard in the chest. "I thought it was going to kill me."

"Oh no, it's really funny. How in the hell could a live alligator get into the backroom of this building without anyone knowing? I mean, really, if you think about it, there would be claw marks on the floors, and it would have had to get through at least three doors."

"Stop looking at this logically. There is absolutely *nothing* logical about a dead alligator in a funeral home," she said, narrowing her eyes at him as her face got redder and redder.

The angrier she got, the funnier Brendan found it. He couldn't stop laughing.

"Stop it," she shouted and shoved him again. "Stop laughing at me."

"I'm not laughing at you," he said, wiping his eyes. "Okay, well maybe I am a little. God, Paige, when I heard you scream I thought you were dying. It probably cut ten years off my life," he said, pulling her into his chest.

"Well, it cut twenty off mine," she said against his throat. Her shoulders relaxed as she pressed into him. "I still can't believe you laughed at me," she said, pinching his pec hard.

"Ow." He flinched back and looked at her still-fuming face. "Okay, I shouldn't have laughed. But a dead alligator in a funeral home, come on, it's funny."

"Maybe a little." Her mouth quirked and then all of

a sudden she was laughing too. When she snorted Brendan lost it again. God, he'd missed her laugh, the way it warmed his heart and settled in his stomach.

"What is all this commotion about?"

Brendan turned to see Verna standing on the bottom step, her arms folded across her bony chest and her lips pursed.

"Juris needed to use the embalming room to store an alligator, and when Paige saw it she got scared," Tara explained.

"That man shouldn't be allowed to use this place to store those creatures. It's disgusting."

"It's really none of your business," Tara said.

"I'm going to report this to Mr. Adams," Verna said as her glasses slid down her nose.

"You go on ahead and do that," Tara said.

"I will. And while I'm at it, I'm going to report this ruckus that she's caused." Verna pointed at Paige. "Her and all of her troublesome ways. She's been a vexation ever since she stepped foot in this town."

A fresh dose of anger flared up in Brendan. They'd been laughing a second ago. For one glorious moment the world hadn't been a sad, dark place. It'd been bright again, and then Verna the Vulture had ruined it.

"Her name is Paige, and I'd appreciate it if you'd show some respect to my wife. And just so you know, the only vexation around here is *you*. So why don't you flap your wings and go bother someone else."

"Well, I never…you rude, disrespectful, ingrate," Verna fumed.

"I'm only respectful to people who deserve it, and *you* have never deserved my respect."

"Hmmph," she grumbled as she turned around and went back up the stairs.

"Bitter old hag," Brendan muttered under his breath.

When he turned back to Paige she was grinning at him, biting her bottom lip. "Defending my honor?"

"Always."

* * *

On Saturday, during the first week of September, Paige's father had a couple of hours of lucidity. Paige was in the living room with him when he grabbed her hand, his long fingers wrapping around hers.

"Little Miss," he whispered while he struggled to breathe. "I'm so proud of you."

Paige's heart flew up into her throat because she knew. She knew her father was about to say good-bye to her.

"You're painting and selling your art. I've…" He paused as he swallowed and licked his dry lips. "I've always thought that you were one of the most talented painters. And now you're living your dream. My beautiful, smart, talented little girl."

"Daddy," Paige said as her throat tightened.

"Sometimes life gives you challenges. When it does, all people can see is the difficult path in front of them and not the reward at the end. When you first came down here, I'd…I'd never seen you so sad. You weren't…" His breathing was becoming more and more labored. "You weren't happy and you had…hadn't been for a long time, long before you…you'd lost your job, and before Dylan. You weren't happy," he repeated.

Paige blinked hard and tears started streaming down her face.

"But you *are* happy now. And I got to witness one of the greatest things a father can witness. I...I got to watch my baby girl fall in love with a good man. A man who's worthy of you be-because he loves you and sees just how...how much you're...you're worth. I can die knowing that Brendan's going t-to take care of you and your mother, and that's a great comfort."

Trevor let go of Paige's hand and reached up to touch her cheek.

"I love you, Daddy," Paige said before she put her head down on his chest and started sobbing. He smelled like he always did, like laundry detergent and the soap he'd used as far back as she could remember.

His hand was on her head, stroking her hair for a couple of minutes before it stilled. Paige sat up and looked at her now-sleeping father. Her head was throbbing and she was struggling to breathe properly. She stood up and walked to the kitchen. Brendan was making lunch and he looked up as she walked through the doorway.

"Come here," he whispered, putting down the knife in his hand. She made her way into his arms and started sobbing again.

"He said good-bye," she said thickly. "He said good-bye."

Brendan didn't say anything. He just held her in that sure, calm way of his.

* * *

It happened four days later. Paige's cell phone rang at exactly 4:39 in the morning. Brendan watched her in their dark bedroom as a stillness came over her body.

Trevor was gone.

Denise had fallen asleep around eleven o'clock and sometime after that he'd died. Brendan could hear Denise's sobs from the other side of the phone. He reached up and touched Paige's shoulder, and she leaned into him for a second before she got out of bed. She switched on the light as she walked across the room.

"I'm getting dressed now, Mom. I'll be there soon. I love you," Paige said before she hit a button on her phone and placed it on the dresser.

Brendan got out of bed and walked up behind her as she riffled through a drawer. He placed his hands on her shoulders, but when she went to pull away he held on and turned her around.

"Brendan, I have to get over there," she said, staring over his shoulder.

"Look at me, Paige," he said, touching her chin and gently pushing it up.

Her eyes focused on his, and there was so much pain there that Brendan felt like he'd been punched in the stomach.

"Just don't push me away, okay. You're not in this alone. I'm right here."

"I know," she said and nodded, looking away before she disentangled herself from his arms and started getting dressed.

* * *

The next day, while Paige and Denise went down to the funeral home to start making arrangements, Brendan and Shep went and cleaned up the living room at Trevor and Denise's house.

Well, Denise's house now.

The hospital bed sat in the middle of the living room. All of the machines that Trevor had been hooked up to stood to the side of it. His slippers were on the floor, his sweater lay across the back of a chair, and his glasses sat on top of a book on the coffee table.

Neither Shep nor Brendan said anything as they moved the medical equipment out of the room and into Brendan's truck. Brendan grabbed an empty box from one of the closets and filled it with Trevor's stuff while Shep moved the room back around to normal.

Except there was no more normal. Trevor was dead.

He'd been a good husband to Denise and a good father to Paige. He'd been kind and generous, loving and self-less. He would've laid his life on the line for his family and he never would've abandoned them. He'd been a good man, one of the best that Brendan had ever met, and now he was gone.

It was bullshit.

It was bullshit that Brendan and Grace had worthless fathers who didn't give a damn about them. It was bullshit that Claire had died at the age of thirty-four. It was bullshit that she missed out on so much of Brendan and Grace's lives. She'd never seen them graduate high school. She'd never gotten to meet Paige and watch Brendan fall in love. She wasn't there when Brendan got married and she wouldn't be there when Grace did either. Neither Trevor nor Claire would ever get to meet their grandchildren. And it was all bull-shit.

Brendan grabbed a glass full of water on the coffee table and threw it against the wall. It smashed and water and glass spilled out over the hardwood floors.

"Feel better?" Shep asked from behind him.

"No," he said, staring at the wet patch on the wall.

"Good. I'm glad we discussed that. Now go clean it up."

* * *

The next couple of days were an out-of-body experience for Paige. She was going through the motions of everything. She had to, because if she let her brain and her emotions connect with her body she was going to fall into a black hole that she wouldn't be able to crawl out of. She couldn't let herself stop for a moment, which meant that at the end of the day she was so exhausted she would pass out before she had a chance to think.

Abby had flown down and she was helping Denise while Paige did everything she needed to do at the funeral home.

She was still working on the tribute two days before the funeral. It was long, way too long. She'd picked almost double the amount of pictures, but she couldn't eliminate any of them. She was flipping through the pictures on her screen when she came across one of her on her father's shoulders when she was about five years old. She had a cherry snow cone in one hand, her lips were bright red from the juice, and a stuffed elephant was clutched in her other fist. Paige was smiling at the camera while her father looked up at her with adoration in his eyes.

Paige lost it.

She wasn't sure how long she sat there sobbing, but at some point she felt hands on her shoulders and she looked up to find Brendan pulling her to her feet.

"We're going home," he said, grabbing her purse.

"I—I haven't finished," she said and sniffled. "I have to finish this."

"You can't finish this, Paige." He shook his head. "Shep and Grace are going to do it. I've also talked to Mr. Adams and you aren't working tomorrow."

"I have—"

"No," he said firmly. "You're running on empty. I know what you're doing. You think you can prevent yourself from feeling all of this pain. But you can't, baby. You can't."

He was right. She couldn't fight against it anymore. The pain was stronger than she was, so she let him take her home.

* * *

Paige would not be comforted. She didn't want to be touched or held. She didn't want to talk to anybody. At night, she curled up in a small ball on her side of the bed, as far away from Brendan as possible. The only time he'd seen her break down since Trevor had died was when she'd been working on the tribute, and the only reason he'd been there for that was because Tara had called him. Paige wouldn't let him in.

Brendan had no idea what to do. There was nothing he

could do, because the only thing Paige wanted was her father back.

On the day of the funeral, Brendan woke up alone. He went out into the kitchen to find Abby making coffee.

"Is Paige out here?" he asked.

"No," Abby said, shaking her head. "I haven't seen her all morning."

Sydney wasn't in the house either, so Brendan went outside and walked down to Paige's art studio. The sun had only just come up, so it hadn't had a chance to warm up yet. The door to the studio was open, and Sydney's head stuck out past the threshold. She opened her eyes and then closed them when she saw it was only Brendan.

He came up and leaned against the doorjamb. Paige had earbuds stuck in her ears, so she hadn't heard him walk up. She was sitting down in front of her easel, wearing one of his old shirts that was covered in paint. Her hair was piled up on top of her head, her neck completely bare. He wanted so badly to stick his face in her throat and inhale. To kiss her skin. To wrap his arms around her and just hold her.

But she didn't want that. Didn't want *him* at the moment. So instead he leaned back and watched her. Since Trevor died, it was one of the few times they'd been in a room together, just the two of them, and not been asleep.

He looked at the canvas in front of her. It was a black-and-white painting of a couple embracing, but the man was fading away. The woman's grasp on him was desperate. Both of their faces were filled with pain, longing, love.

It was beautiful.

Brendan watched Paige paint for a couple of minutes.

When she went to dip her brush again he leaned forward and pulled one of the buds out of her ear.

She jumped back, startled.

"Sorry," he said nervously.

When did he get nervous around his wife?

"What time is it?" she asked, putting down her brush and coming back to the moment. She'd most definitely been in a zone, and he wouldn't have pulled her out of it, but it was time to start getting ready for Trevor's funeral.

"Almost eight. How long have you been out here?"

"Since two," she said, rubbing her tired eyes.

"Two?" Brendan asked.

He was shocked he hadn't heard her get up. Hadn't known his wife wasn't in bed with him for almost six hours. But truth be told, she hadn't been with him at all the last week. He was so used to holding her at night, having his body pressed against hers. They'd never had space between them. They were always touching in at least some way or another. And now that space between them felt like miles. Miles he had no idea how to cross.

"I couldn't sleep," she said, standing up. Her shoulders were slumped and she looked exhausted. Defeated.

"Paige," Brendan said, taking a step toward her.

But she took a step back, holding up her hands. "Don't, Brendan. I just . . . I just can't," she said, shaking her head.

He stopped and nodded. "All right. We should get ready."

"I'll be up in a little. I just need to clean up first."

"Okay," Brendan said, turning around and heading up to the house alone.

* * *

Brendan stayed close to Paige, waiting in the wings to help her when she needed it. Needed him. But that never happened. She stood next to her mother, talking to all of the people who had come to the funeral. The building was packed with family and friends who had traveled to be there, and quite a few people from the town whom Trevor had managed to make an impact on. A lot of people wanted to offer their condolences and say good-bye to a very good man.

During the burial, Brendan reached for Paige's hand, and she let him hold it. He squeezed it and she lightly squeezed back before she laced her fingers through his. She didn't turn to him though. She just continued to look straight ahead all through Pastor Phillips's final words while they lowered the coffin into the ground.

Paige didn't cry. Didn't shed a tear. She just stared ahead blankly. Like it wasn't real. Like it was all a bad dream that she would wake up from.

Brendan knew the look, because he'd worn it himself when his mother had died. But this wasn't a bad dream; this was the reality, and sooner or later it was going to hit Paige like a bomb.

* * *

Paige sat in the empty viewing room, staring at the space in front of the pews. This was the last room her father had been in. That he'd ever be in again.

Well, that his body had been in.

He'd been gone for a week now. He'd just *left*. Left everyone and everything behind. Left his wife. Left his daughter. Paige knew that Trevor hadn't had a choice.

That if he had, he'd still be there sitting across from her at dinner, he'd still be looking up at her through his glasses as he read the paper, sitting on the couch and watching a game with Brendan, holding her mother's hand as they walked along together. He hadn't wanted to leave, but that fact was of absolutely no comfort to Paige.

She just wanted her father back. But that was never going to happen.

He was gone. Forever.

Someone came and sat down next to Paige. She didn't turn but she knew it was Brendan. Her hands were balled up in her lap, so he didn't reach out for her, which was good because if he touched her right now she didn't think she would survive it.

"Everyone's gone," he said softly. "Abby went with your mom and aunt. I told them we would meet them over at the house."

The house, her parents' house that would always feel empty without her father in it.

"All right," she said and nodded, still not looking at him. "Just give me a second. I need to get some stuff in my office." She stood up and walked past him, heading for the stairs.

When she got to her closed office door, there was a piece of paper attached to the wood. Paige pulled it off and read.

THE GRIM TRUTH

THE TRUTH WILL OUT

Rogue Whoreson isn't a stranger to the loss of a parent, or in his case, parents. His father, Dick Splits, abandoned him by choice, while his mother was forced to. Jeze Belle died of breast cancer almost thirteen years ago, so Mr. Whoreson is fully aware of the devastation that accompanies such a tragic death.

Brazen Interloper, Mr. Whoreson's new bride, is experiencing her own tragedy this week with the passing of her father. According to his obituary, Brazen's father was diagnosed with the fatal disease that killed him a little over two months ago . . . or was he?

A witness saw Brazen's father making regular visits to the oncology wing of the hospital starting in mid-April, two and a half months before his supposed diagnosis. And in May, Rogue Whoreson was seen accompanying the father to weekly doctor's appointments. It looks like somebody isn't telling the truth here, and Mr. Whoreson is the only one still alive to ask.

Why would this secret be kept? What else is going on? What other secrets are there? It seems a little early in Rogue and Brazen's marriage for lies, yet there appear to be many. It's sad, really, for Brazen. How can the woman not feel betrayed? How will Brazen deal with Rogue's deception?

* * *

Brendan stood on the front porch waiting for Paige. He leaned back against a wooden beam and closed his eyes. He was exhausted, but it wasn't even comparable to what he was sure Paige was going through. She looked like every single word was costing her, like she was going to fall apart at any moment. Brendan couldn't wait for the day to be over. It wasn't going to be easy, but each day after that day was time spent learning to adjust, learning to live in a world without Trevor in it. They just had to get through today.

The door opened a couple of minutes later and Brendan opened his eyes to find Paige standing there. He knew immediately that something was wrong.

"Paige, what's going on?" he asked, pushing off the beam and taking a step toward her.

"This," she said, walking up to him and slapping a piece of paper to his chest before she took a step back.

Brendan grabbed the paper and looked down at it. The blood drained from his face and everything in him stilled as he read. This wasn't happening. Could not be happening today.

Brendan had known he was going to have to tell Paige that he'd known about Trevor months beforehand, but the day of Trevor's funeral hadn't been the day he was going to drop that bomb. There really was no perfect time, but that day *definitely* hadn't been the day. He looked up at her unsure of what to say, unsure of where to even start.

"You knew," she said. "You knew my father was dying and you didn't tell me?"

"Yes," he said and nodded slowly. "I knew."

"How the fuck do you not tell me that, Brendan?" she yelled at him.

Shock rolled through his body and he took a step back from her. Paige had never talked to him that way before. He'd never heard her talk to anyone that way before.

"Paige, can we go somewhere and discuss this?" he asked.

"No," she said, shaking her head. "I'm not going any-where with you."

"I can explain."

"Really?" she asked skeptically. "You can explain why you lied to me?"

"I didn't lie."

"What the hell do you call it then?"

"I did what your dad asked me to do," he said.

"That isn't a good enough excuse," she said, shaking her head. "I had every right to know. My mother and I should've known. When was it? When did you find out?"

"A month before the wedding."

"Right," she said and nodded. "So you didn't tell me about my father because you were too selfish. Because you didn't want it to ruin something that involved you."

"You're joking, right? You honestly think that?" he asked incredulously.

"I have no idea what to think. You *lied* to me. You knew all that time and acted like nothing was wrong. Like my father's dying didn't affect you. Like it didn't mat-ter. You're not who I thought you were, Brendan. I don't know you at all."

Those words were a slap in his face. It took him a sec-ond to recover. "Paige, it killed me," he said, taking a step forward, his voice getting louder. "Every single day killed me. I hated that I couldn't tell you."

"Then what was stopping you?" she shouted at him.

"Your father's wishes," he shouted back.

"Just get away from me, Brendan. I don't even want to look at you."

He couldn't breathe. He actually thought he was going

to start choking. "What are you saying?" he asked, barely getting the words out.

"I'm saying I need to think about things. Think about us." She took a step back from him.

"Paige, you can't be serious," he said as his eyes welled up with tears that a moment later began to fall down his face.

"I am," she said as tears started to stream down her own cheeks.

"You promised you would never leave."

"And you promised you would never hurt me. Looks like we're both liars." She turned around and walked back through the door, leaving him alone on the porch.

Chapter Twenty-One

This Life Would Kill Me
If I Didn't Have You

Paige was numb. Cold. It was September in Florida and she was frozen.

She'd been staying with her mother for over two weeks. She hadn't seen Brendan at all. She'd stopped by the house to get some of her things, but she'd made sure to do so when he wasn't at home. She'd also been avoiding his calls.

Brendan had called three times, once the day after the funeral, once the second day, and once the third day. He'd left a message on the third day, and though Paige hadn't listened to it, she also hadn't deleted it. She couldn't bring herself to. Like if she did, she really was saying good-bye to everything they'd had, everything they could have.

She missed him so damn much it was physically painful. But she wasn't sure where that pain ended and the pain of him lying to her began. Like it was all one big ball of string, snarled and knotted, tangled up beyond recognition.

Paige thought about Brendan and her father constantly but she tried not to break down during the day. No, she left that for the night, when she was alone. She lay in bed crying for hours. And when she finally fell asleep, she slept restlessly, tossing and turning and searching for someone who wasn't there.

She'd started going back to work a week after the funeral, but it wasn't much of a distraction. Brendan had gotten her that job. She couldn't be there and not think of him. She couldn't be anywhere and not think of him.

She skipped the Thursday lunches with the girls at the café. There was absolutely no way she'd be able to see Brendan's sister, grandmother, and aunts. She couldn't face them. Couldn't handle seeing their disappointment. But she was disappointed too, and she had no idea what to do with that.

Thunderstorms had rolled into Mirabelle three days ago and they hadn't let up at all. The skies were covered in inky gray clouds that had been dumping rain. The gloom and doom were doing nothing to help Paige's mood, and she came home from work early one day to take a nap. Her lack of sleeping through the night had finally caught up to her and she was exhausted. She woke up around seven and when she walked in the kitchen she found her mother at the stove. The kettle was whistling and Denise pulled it off and poured hot water into a cup.

"You want some tea?" Denise asked.

"Please," Paige said, taking a seat at the table.

"I was going to put one of those many casseroles in the oven for dinner in a little bit. Sound good?"

"Yeah," she said and nodded.

Paige watched her mother as she moved around the

kitchen getting everything ready. She added sugar and just a little bit of milk to both mugs before she came to the table. Paige grabbed her mug and took a tentative sip. It was just hot enough. She took another few sips before she put it down and stared into it.

"So," Denise said after a moment. "What are you doing, Paige?"

"What?" she asked, looking up from her tea.

"What are you doing? You know I love you and that you will always be welcome in this house, always. But what are you doing with Brendan? With your husband? That boy loves you. Why are you running away from him?"

"He lied to me. He lied to you."

"Sweetie," Denise said, reaching over and putting her hand over Paige's. "He didn't lie. He did what your father asked. What else should he have done?"

"I don't know," Paige said, shaking her head. "But doesn't it make you angry? That they hid it for so long? That we lost those months?"

"What did we lose, Paige? Tell me, because I lost nothing. I didn't know your father was dying for those two months, but even if I had, there's nothing I would have done differently. Not a moment of it. My knowing or not knowing he was dying didn't change my love for him. So no, I'm not angry that I didn't know. I'm angry that I lost your father. And you're angry too, and you're taking it out on the last person you should be. Brendan didn't kill your father. Cancer did. Be angry at the cancer."

"I'm angry at myself," Paige whispered.

"Why?"

"Dad was dying while I was planning my wedding.

I was worried about colors, and flowers, and appetizers while he was dying."

"Oh, Paige," Denise said, shaking her head. "You can't look at it that way. Your father wanted your wedding day to be perfect. Not for him, but for you. He isn't the one who has to live with the memories. You are. And you can look back at that day and remember your father walking you down the aisle and giving you away to the love of your life. All we have now are those memories. That was your father's gift to you. Don't throw it away."

"What if I'm too late?" she asked desperately. "I was so upset when I saw that stupid article and I just lost it. I said horrible things to Brendan. And then I walked away from him, the one thing I promised I would never do, and I did it. I don't know if he could forgive me for that," Paige said, wiping at her face.

"Are you kidding me?" Denise asked incredulously. "You know he's come by here every single day."

"He has?" Paige asked, surprised.

"Yes. It's been when you're at work. Apparently, you told him you wanted space, so he was trying to give it to you. But he's come by, talked to me, asked how I was doing, dropped off food from his grandmother and sister. And he asks about you. Talks about you."

"What does he say?"

"That he misses you. That he loves you. That when you're ready to talk, he'll be there. He'll forgive you, Paige. You just have to ask. You just have to talk to him. You have to fix this. You know, the only regret I have when it comes to your father is that I didn't get more time. I cherished every second I spent with him. I loved him from the moment he came into my life, and I will continue to love him for the rest of mine. I know that if you walk away from that boy, you'll regret it, Paige. You'll regret it every single day for the rest of your life."

"I know," Paige said, and she promptly broke down.

Denise held Paige until the sobbing stopped. "Go fix this, Paige," Denise said, pulling back and holding her daughter's face in her hands. "Go get him back."

* * *

Paige went to her old room and sat down on the bed. She grabbed her phone and stared at it for a moment, her thumb hovering over the button to listen to Brendan's message. She pressed it and brought the phone to her ear.

"I'm sorry, baby, so damn sorry. It was just one of those impossible situations. I knew that no matter what, you were going to be hurt and that there would be absolutely nothing I could do to stop it. From almost the moment you came into my life, all I've wanted to do is protect you. Hurting you was the last thing I ever meant to do. I just didn't know what to do besides what your father wanted. I loved him too, Paige. He was my family. He was like a father to me," he said, strangled. "Being apart from you is killing me. It's ripping me up inside. I miss waking up next to you. I miss your smile and your laugh. I miss the feel of your hand in mine, the smell of your hair. I just miss you. I know you want space. Time to think about things. Work things out. But I don't need time. I don't need space. I just need you. I love you, Paige, and I'll always love you. So come back to me, baby, please just come back to me."

Paige listened to the message five times, crying the entire time. She put the phone down on the bed, laid her head in her hands, and promptly started sobbing again.

What the hell had she done? What had she been thinking? Time? Space? She was a freaking idiot.

She got up from the bed and went into the bathroom, gathering up all of her stuff. She reached under the sink to pull out her blow dryer and spotted an unopened box of tampons. She froze and just stared at it, a prickly feeling at the back of her neck.

Paige hadn't had her period this month. She was almost three weeks late.

"Oh my God," she said, feeling lightheaded. She turned and sat down on the closed toilet. "Oh my God."

She wasn't positive she was pregnant, but for someone who'd always had a consistent period, it was a distinct possibility. When the room stopped spinning she got up and finished gathering her stuff, throwing it all into bags, packing as fast as she could.

She had to get to Brendan.

* * *

Brendan was barely holding it together. He'd been apart from his wife for sixteen days and each day had been worse than the last. Time and space away from her was so damn painful he couldn't think straight. Sleeping in their bed without her was torture. That empty space next to him was a constant reminder of the hole in his life. Sydney wasn't dealing very well either. She'd lie by the door, waiting for Paige to come home. Waiting for her to come through a door that just wouldn't open.

Brendan had taken to leaving early in the morning, going to the shop before the sun came up, and then going home late. It wasn't that there was a lot of work to be done there or anything. He just couldn't sit in that empty house.

It was after seven o'clock when Shep walked into the office.

"You eaten yet?" he asked.

"Nope." Brendan shook his head.

"Then get your ass up and let's go," Shep said.

Brendan didn't argue. It didn't matter that he wasn't hungry; he knew how Shep worked. Shep would station himself in that office until Brendan followed. So he got in Shep's Mustang and they drove through the pouring rain.

Floppy Flounders had the best hush puppies on the Panhandle, and the second they stepped inside and the smell hit Brendan's nose, his stomach growled. Shep just smirked at him. The stupid ass thought he knew everything.

Before they were even settled at the table, Shep ordered a pitcher of beer.

"You need a drink?" Brendan asked.

"Nope, but you do," Shep said as he grabbed his menu and looked at it.

The waitress came back with the pitcher and they ordered their dinner. Shep made small talk and Brendan tried to give more than one-word answers. But it was pretty hard to do. All the while Shep kept filling up Brendan's glass, ordering two more pitchers. Brendan was pretty sure that Shep had had only two glasses of beer.

"This your plan to get me to talk?" Brendan asked. "Get me tanked?"

"Yup," Shep said as he poured them both another glass.

"Well, I don't want to talk about it."

"All right, then I'll talk. Go get her. Go stand on that porch until she comes out and talk to her," Shep said.

"She doesn't want to talk."

"Then make her."

"I can't," Brendan said a little too loudly. The beer was definitely taking effect.

"So you're just going to give up?" Shep asked, raising an eyebrow.

"You can't give up on a relationship that you're in by yourself. She already gave up. She already walked away."

"You feeling a little sorry for yourself?" Shep asked.

"No, I'm feeling a little drunk and it's all your damn fault."

"I'm sorry. Did I miss the part where I poured the beer down your throat?" Shep asked more than a little sarcastically.

"Fuck off," Brendan said angrily. "I don't need this bullshit from anyone, especially you."

"Especially me?" Shep asked slowly.

"When did you become the master on relationship advice? You're the guy who has a longer relationship with a toothbrush than with an actual woman."

Shep's eyes narrowed and he leaned across the table. "Brendan, you're my friend, and you're going through a tough time right now, not to mention you're a little under the influence at the moment, so I'm going to look past the fact that you're being a total prick when I'm just trying to help your sorry ass."

"I don't want your help," Brendan said, shaking his head.

"Then what do you want?" Shep asked.

"Paige. I want Paige. She's all I'll ever want. So it fits that I can't have her, doesn't it."

"Wow," Shep said, leaning back in his seat. "This pity party you got going for yourself is really something."

"Look, I love her. I love her more than I've ever loved anyone. But she walked away."

"So you've said. But that doesn't mean she won't come back," Shep tried to reason.

"I can't do it, all right? I can't be with someone who I'm constantly scared is going to leave me. We got married, something that was supposed to be for forever, but she left. She just left," Brendan said still a little too loud. But he could give a shit if people heard him. He just didn't care anymore.

"So that's it?" Shep asked. "It's done."

"I don't know. I don't know anything. I can't think straight," Brendan said, defeated. "Can we just go?" he asked.

"Sure," Shep said.

They paid for their meal and walked outside, smack into Chad Sharp and his two lackeys, Hoyt Reynolds and Judson Coker.

"Well, look who it is," Chad said and smirked. "Why aren't you with your wife, King? Oh, that's right, because she left you."

"Just walk away," Shep said to Brendan.

"But it looks like you replaced her," Chad said, looking at Shep. "I didn't know you played that way. So who's the bitch in the relationship?"

Nothing would have been more satisfying than punching the son of a bitch in the face, and it took everything in Brendan to walk away. He stepped around Chad and made his way down the steps to the parking lot, Shep at his side. The rain had let up for the moment, but the air was still thick and wet.

"It was never going to work out anyways, King," Chad continued. "It was just a matter of time. There was no way a girl like Paige was ever going to want a useless bastard like you. If your own father didn't want you, what makes you think a girl like that would? And I'm so glad I could do my part in breaking up the charade. I was the one who saw you at the hospital, King. I was the one that told Bethelda."

"Fuck," Shep said, coming to a stop at the same moment that Brendan did. "So close."

Brendan turned and launched himself at Chad, landing a punch square on his jaw.

* * *

Brendan's truck wasn't there. He wasn't home. It was almost nine o'clock and he wasn't there. The house was empty and dark, not a single light on.

Paige stared at the big empty house for a moment before she got out of her Jeep. Lightning flashed across the sky, and thunder boomed. The rain had stopped for a little while, but the storm that was coming was going to be bad. She grabbed her bags from the backseat and made her way up the steps carefully in the dark.

When she unlocked and opened the door, she stuck her hand in and flipped the switch. Sydney was standing there, and the moment that Paige was through the door, the dog launched herself at Paige. Sydney ran around

Paige in circles, her tail whipping her in the leg. Paige
dropped her stuff and got down on the ground.

"Hey, pretty girl," Paige sniffled as she wrapped her
arms around the dog. "Where's your daddy?" she asked
as she buried her face in the dog's fur.

Paige wasn't exactly sure why she was crying. There
was just something about the empty house that had set
her off. She was expecting to come back to find Brendan.
And how stupid was she? She'd walked out on him and
she'd expected him to just be sitting there waiting for her?

Sydney whined, moving so that she could give Paige a
big sloppy lick on the cheek.

"I missed you too," Paige said. "You want to go outside? Before the storm hits?"

Sydney pulled back and bolted for the back door. Paige
got up from the floor and followed Sydney, switching on
lights as she moved through the house. When she opened
the back door Sydney went down the back steps and
Paige stayed up on the deck. She had a flashback to the
first night that she'd stayed over, the first time she and
Brendan had made love.

He was everything to her. Had been for a very long time
and she'd almost let it all slip away, possibly had let it slip
away. What if he was done? What if she was too late?

Lightning flashed across the sky again and Sydney
came back up the steps. They went back inside together
and she looked around the empty house, desperate for
Brendan to get home.

Paige sat down on the couch, Sydney at her feet. She
turned on the TV but it was just noise in the background;
she couldn't pay attention. Where was he?

By ten she couldn't wait anymore. She picked up the

phone and called him. She held her breath as it rang, but it went to voicemail.

"Brendan, it's me. I'm at the house, and you're not here. Of course you already know that," she said stupidly. "I really need to talk to you. I don't want to tell you everything in a voicemail, but I'm sorry and I love you. Please come home."

He was probably out with Jax or Shep. Yeah, that's where he was. They were out getting a drink. He would come home when he was ready.

Paige eyed her bags, which were still by the front door. She'd stopped by the drugstore to buy a home pregnancy test, and this waiting was killing her. She'd planned to take it after she worked everything out with Brendan. But she couldn't wait any longer. She had to know. She grabbed the bag and went into the bathroom.

She ripped the box open and read the instructions. It said that the best time to take it was in the morning but Paige didn't care. She couldn't wait any longer. So she took the test and before she even flushed the toilet the little pink plus sign appeared.

Paige just stared at it, fear and excitement warring with each other, and the desperation in her to fix everything with Brendan brought her to her knees. She wasn't sure how long she sat on the bathroom floor sobbing, but Sydney came up behind her and pushed her cold snout into Paige's face.

Paige peeled herself up from the floor and undressed. She found one of Brendan's T-shirts on the back of the door and put it on before she crawled into bed. She would wait for him there, and when he finally came home, they would talk.

* * *

Brendan looked across the jail cell where Shep was sitting, his feet stretched out before him, leaning back against the wall with his eyes closed. Shep had a split lip, and his left eye already had a pretty dark bruise around it. Brendan had gotten away with a nice little gash across his right cheek and a patchwork of bruises across his ribs.

When Brendan had jumped on Chad, Judson and Hoyt had jumped on Brendan. Shep had of course gotten involved, throwing his own fists around and breaking Hoyt's nose. But while Shep was dealing with Hoyt, Judson and Chad were on Brendan. Judson was the biggest of the three men, just a little bit bigger than Brendan, and he'd held Brendan back so Chad could get in a few good hits, all of which he'd directed at Brendan's ribs.

They'd been going at each other for all of about three minutes before a county sheriff truck pulled into the lot, and it hadn't been Jax behind the wheel. All five of their asses had gotten hauled into the county jail. They'd been booked and were waiting to go up in front of a judge at eight o'clock that morning, which wasn't for another hour.

Brendan looked out past the bars at the blank wall in front of him. Really, it could have been much worse. Chad, Hoyt, and Judson had been put into a separate cell. Good thing too, because if Brendan had been locked in a room with them for ten hours he would have gotten into another fight.

Neither Brendan nor Shep had called anyone in their family. They'd called a lawyer though. Preston Matthews was one of Grace's best friends, and his father was a lawyer. In another couple of months they'd be able to call Preston himself, as he was in his last semester of law school. But Benjamin Matthews was just as much of a family friend and he'd come down at six that morning to start working things out.

"You still feeling sorry for yourself?" Shep asked.

Brendan turned back to him.

Shep's eyes were open and he looked just as tired and worn out as Brendan felt. Sleeping in a jail cell was not the most relaxing of experiences.

"Well, it doesn't really get all that much worse than this." Brendan indicated the room with his hands.

"You probably just jinxed us," Shep said, shaking his head. "A meteor is going to come crashing through any second."

"I'm sorry," Brendan said seriously. "You're here because of me."

"Come on. You think I would've let you get your ass kicked? I always got your back." Shep grinned, and then winced because of his lip.

"Thanks, man."

"You know Jax is going to kill us," Shep said.

"Oh God, I'm just praying we get out of here before he sees us."

"Me too. And what are you going to do when we get out? You've had almost ten hours to pull your head out of your ass. You still going to stop fighting for her?" Shep asked seriously.

"The thing is, I'll never stop fighting for her," Brendan said.

"So last night was just a pity party?"

"Maybe a small one."

"If this is the result of a small pity party, I don't want to be around when it's a big one."

"I don't either."

At that moment Baxter McCoy came up to their cell. Baxter was actually a pretty good friend. He played on the Stingrays with them during the county baseball season.

"I can't believe you two got arrested," Baxter said, shaking his head. "But man, looking at Chad's ugly face all banged up brings me so much joy I can't even tell you."

"What's going on?" Shep asked.

"Your lawyer wants to talk to you two. He might have worked something out."

* * *

Thunder shook the house, waking Paige up from a deep sleep. The light coming in the windows was weak and she couldn't tell what time it was. She sat up in bed and looked over at the clock. It was seven thirty in the morning.

Brendan hadn't come home.

Paige scrambled out of bed and grabbed her phone on the nightstand. No missed calls. A whole new kind of panic went through her.

Why hadn't he come home?

She tried calling him again but it didn't even ring; it just went directly to voicemail.

Why wasn't he answering his phone?

Paige's hands started to shake as she scrolled through her phone looking for another number.

"Paige?" Grace said. "Hey, sweetie. I've been worried about you."

"Grace," Paige said, barely holding back a sob. "I came home last night. I came back to Brendan, and he wasn't here. He didn't come home last night, and I—I don't know what to do," Paige said before she just broke down.

"Okay, Paige, it's okay. I'm at my apartment. I'll be there in five minutes and we'll go from there, okay. Try calling Shep. I'll call Jax."

"All-all right," Paige said before she hung up.

She called Shep's cell phone and it went directly to voicemail. She left a message and then called his house, but after a couple of rings the answering machine picked up. She left another message.

She changed into a pair of shorts, put on a bra, and grabbed a clean T-shirt from Brendan's drawer before she went into the living room to wait for Grace. Paige let Sydney out and dried her off when she came back in. A couple of minutes later the doorbell rang. Paige went to the door and let in a slightly damp Grace.

"Shep?" Grace asked.

"He didn't answer the phone."

"Jax doesn't know anything. He was working last night and just got off. He was meeting Bennett for breakfast to go over house plans, and Bennett hasn't heard from them either. They're going to drive around and look for them."

"Okay." Paige nodded as tears streamed down her face.

"Paige, I'm sure he's fine."

"Why didn't he come home?" she asked desperately. "I called him, told him I wanted to fix things, that I was sorry. And he didn't come home," she said before she just started bawling again.

"Sweetie," Grace said, bringing Paige into her arms, "if Brendan didn't come home last night, I'm sure there is a perfectly good reason. We'll find him and figure everything out. Come on, grab your stuff. Let's go down to the shop. I called but no one answered. Maybe he just fell asleep on the couch. He's slept there a couple of times in the past two weeks."

"He has?" Paige asked.

"It's been a little hard for him to be here without you."

"God, I messed up so bad," she said miserably.

"Paige, we're going to get this sorted out. Now go put your shoes on and let's go."

Paige did as Grace told her and five minutes later they were heading out the door. Lula Mae's SUV was parked next to Paige's Jeep.

"Where's your Bug?" Paige asked as they got inside.

"I brought the food to the Abercorn funeral last night, and my Bug wasn't big enough," Grace said as she put it in reverse and backed out.

The sky was almost black, and the rain wasn't heavy, just a steady drizzle. It was the thunder and lightning that was putting on the real show.

"Thank you for coming," Paige said softly when they got on the road. "I don't deserve it. Not after how I treated Brendan."

"Paige," Grace said, shaking her head, "we all make mistakes. Your father just died. You're allowed to get a little crazy. I did. When my mom died, I was a mess. And so was Brendan. He'll understand."

"But what if he doesn't?" Paige asked.

"He will," Grace said firmly. "It's been two weeks. It would take a lot more than that for him to give up."

"I hope so," Paige said, looking down into her lap.

Dear God, she hoped so.

All of a sudden the car jerked and Paige looked up just in time to see Grace swerve to avoid a massive limb that had fallen in the middle of the road. The tires started skidding on the slick pavement and they were sliding off the road. They slammed through a wooden guardrail and down to the river. They hit the water and something stopped the car with a jerk. The airbags deployed, throwing Paige back against the seat. Everything came to a standstill for just a second. There was just that one moment of shock before the panic set it.

"Grace," Paige said, looking over at the driver's seat.

Grace was cradling her left arm, clearly in a lot of pain. "I'm okay. It's just my arm," she said and gasped.

Paige looked down at her feet, and it was then that she noticed the car was filling up with water. She looked to see if they could get out on her side, but all she could see was a tangle of branches. They were probably the only thing holding the car, and they looked like they weren't holding them very well. One glance out of the windshield and Paige knew just how in trouble they were. The rain from the past few days had the current of Whiskey River running fast. Paige looked over at Grace's side and knew that Grace wasn't going to be able to push that door open. The water was slamming against her side of the car.

There was no way they were going to get out of this alone. Paige grabbed her purse that was next to her on the seat and searched for her cell phone. Her hand closed over it and she pulled it out.

No reception.

"This can't be happening," she said desperately.

The car shifted a little farther into the river and they both gasped.

"Try not to move," Paige said.

"What are we going to do?" Grace whispered, terrified as she looked out at the water in front of them.

"I have no idea," Paige said as she looked out at the water too. If the tree snapped, they were going to be pulled downriver and swallowed up. They wouldn't be able to get out in time.

Paige wrapped her arms around her stomach, where a little baby was already growing.

"I'm pregnant," she said to Grace.

Grace looked over at Paige, her eyes wide.

"I just needed to tell someone," Paige choked out. "In case we don't…" She trailed off.

"We're going to get out of this," Grace said seriously. She winced as she let go of her left arm, but she reached over and grabbed Paige's hand, holding it tightly. "You and Brendan are going to work things out and you're going to have that baby."

Paige nodded, tears streaming down her face. She reached up and wiped at them, and when she dropped her hand she saw Jax through Grace's window, waist deep in the water and struggling through the current to get to them.

* * *

Benjamin Matthews was an excellent lawyer. He worked everything out with Chad, Judson, and Hoyt's lawyer. It was true that Brendan had thrown the first punch against

Chad, starting the fight, so technically Chad would be able to press charges against Brendan. But Judson and Hoyt had tried to go after Brendan at the same time, and then Judson had held Brendan back so that Chad could get in some hits.

Yeah, that hadn't looked so good, and Brendan would be able to press some charges of his own. But the lawyers had worked it out with each other and Judge Mendelson. All five men were being released with little more than a slap on the wrist and a warning to stay far away from each other. Judge Mendelson said that he might be lenient this time, but that wouldn't be the case if they got into a fight again.

Baxter was getting off his shift so he said he'd give the guys a ride back to Floppy Flounders to get Shep's Mustang.

"You tell Jax?" Shep asked as they got into Baxter's truck.

"Nah, I figured it would be better for him to get that news when he was in sight of you."

"Great," Brendan said, but he couldn't help but smile. Jax was going to flip his shit.

Brendan leaned back and rested his head against the seat. He wanted to take a shower and go to sleep, but only one of those was going to be a reality. He wasn't going to sit idly by anymore and wait for Paige to figure things out. He was going to do what Shep had said, camp out wherever she was until she talked to him. He'd call her now, but his cell phone was dead.

Baxter's truck slowed and Brendan opened his eyes. There was a red truck pulled off to the side of the road with its flashers going. There were tire marks in the grass and part of the wooden guardrail had been smashed through.

"That's Jax's truck," Shep said from the front seat.

"I know," Baxter said, pulling up behind it.

All three men got out of the truck and hurried over as Bennett came running up the bank, soaking wet.

"It's Paige and Grace," he said as he ran to the truck.

Brendan bolted down the embankment. His grand-mother's SUV was in the river, the hood entirely sub-merged. It was up against a tree that was growing side-ways out of the ground and into the river. The tree wasn't thick at all. The current of the river was powerful and it was pushing against the car with an aggressive force. That tree wasn't going to last much longer, and the second it snapped that car was going to disappear.

It was a fear unlike any other that came over Brendan. His wife and his baby sister could both die before his eyes.

Jax was by the driver's-side window talking into it. Brendan waded into the river, and it was a struggle to not get swept away by it.

"Are they okay?" he asked coming up next to Jax.

Jax turned but before he could answer, Paige shouted, "Brendan!" Her face was sheer terror, and Grace looked like she was in agony.

"We're going to get you guys out. Okay?" he said, try-ing to reassure himself as much as them, because he had to get them out. Had to.

"Bennett went to get something to break the window and to see if there's any rope in the back of the truck."

"Okay," Brendan said and nodded, not taking his eyes off the women. "What's the plan?"

"We break the glass and get them out," Jax said.

The time it took for Bennett to get back down to them was pure agony. For Brendan, his life was flashing before his eyes. But Bennett was hauling ass down the hill less than a minute later and he was wading into the water next to him, handing Jax a Maglite.

"Turn away," he shouted into the car.

Both girls turned and a second later Jax smashed the bottom of the flashlight into the window. Glass poured out over Grace, and Jax continued to run the flashlight around the edge, breaking all of the little glass so that it wouldn't cut the girls when they pulled them out. Then he handed the light back to Bennett, who threw it to the shore. Brendan glanced back for just a second to see Baxter and Shep tying rope to the guardrail.

"All right, Grace, you're first," Jax said. "I'm going to pull you out. Paige, the second she's out I want you to move as carefully and as quickly as possible to this side of the truck. Brendan will help me guide Grace out, and then Brendan will pull Paige out and Bennett will help guide her. Do you understand?"

"Yes," they both said and nodded.

"Here," Shep shouted as he threw three separate strands of rope down to them. All three men tied the rope securely to their waists.

"Let's go," Jax said, reaching in and pulling Grace from the seat. Brendan grabbed her waist and lifted her, and when her legs cleared the window, Jax moved out of the way with Grace.

Branches snapped and cracked and the SUV moved, shifting farther into the river, but Paige didn't let it stop her. She moved over the center console, crouching in the seat and sticking her head out the window. Brendan grabbed her and pulled her to him. Her arms wrapped around his shoulders and he moved back, pulling her from the vehicle. Her legs came around him like a vise. Brendan took a few steps back and watched as the tree snapped and the SUV was swept downriver. He kept moving back to shore but he slipped, both he and Paige going under the water.

Brendan held on to her with everything he had. Praying that they'd make it out. He couldn't see. He couldn't breathe. All he knew was that Paige was in his arms, and for the moment they were both alive. And then their heads broke the surface of the water and they were both gasping for air.

The rope around Brendan's waist tightened and Bennett was next to him, pulling him to his feet. They struggled through the water, Paige saying something over and over again in his ear. And then they were being pulled onto the bank.

Brendan was on his side, and Paige was still wrapped around him. And it was then that he heard what she was saying.

"I love you. I love you. I love you," she sobbed into his neck.

"I love you too, baby," Brendan said, holding onto her as he broke down, crying harder than he'd ever cried in his life.

* * *

Paige pulled back from Brendan and looked into his face. They were still on the wet, muddy ground, rain pouring down all around them.

"I was looking for you," she whispered. "I came home last night, but you never came home. Where were you?"

"In jail."

"What?" she asked. That was the last thing she had expected.

"Shep and I got into a fight with Chad and a few of his friends."

"Why?"

"I've been going crazy without you," he said, reaching up and brushing back the wet hair that stuck to her face. "I just snapped."

"I shouldn't have left," she said, shaking her head. "I was stupid. You didn't do anything wrong. You did everything right and I punished you for it. I'm so sorry, Brendan. So, so sorry."

"Please don't ever leave me again." He brought his mouth to hers and hovered above her lips.

"Never," she said.

He kissed her, his tongue sliding into her mouth and finding hers. His mouth was hot and eager, and she welcomed the intensity. She'd missed him so damn much and his mouth on hers felt better than anything in the world. But she forced herself to pull back. She cupped his jaw in one of her hands and looked into his eyes.

"I'm pregnant," she whispered.

He stared at her, stunned. "What?"

"I'm pregnant, Brendan. We're going to have a baby."

Panic flooded his face. "We have to go to the hospital. We have to get you checked out. We have to make sure everything's okay," he said, sitting up and pulling her with him.

"Calm down. We'll get there."

"Paige," he pleaded.

"Brendan," she said, putting her hands on either side of his face. "Everything will be okay." She leaned forward and pressed her lips to his.

* * *

Brendan was going out of his mind. Paige needed to be on her way to the hospital now, and Grace…he had no idea what was going on with Grace.

Brendan pulled Paige to her feet and they walked over to where Grace and Jax were. Shep and Bennett were standing next to them, and Baxter was at his truck, presumably calling the accident in.

Grace and Jax were sitting on the ground, Grace leaning against Jax's chest crying. Jax just held her against him, whispering into her ear.

"Is she okay?" Brendan asked.

Jax looked up and nodded before he put a kiss to Grace's temple. "She will be."

"Pretty sure her shoulder's dislocated," Shep said.

When the ambulance got there, the paramedics came over, and when they tried to pull Grace away from Jax to set her arm, she clung onto him with her good hand.

"Just set it," he said to them.

One of them nodded, and as they got into place, Grace pressed her face into Jax's throat. They pushed her shoulder back and Grace screamed before she started sobbing, gasping for air.

"Just breathe, Grace. Just breathe. The worst is over. It's okay."

When she finally calmed down, they pulled her away

from Jax and loaded her into the back of the ambulance. It was when Grace was no longer in Jax's arms that Brendan saw it. Jax was shaking.

"You okay?" Brendan asked.

"I'm fine," he nodded, looking away.

"Jax?"

Jax looked back at Brendan; the full shock of the last twenty minutes had finally hit him. "We almost lost them," Jax whispered. "Bennett and I were right behind them on the road. We saw the car go off into the river. If we hadn't been there, this whole thing could have ended so differently."

"I know," Brendan said and nodded. "Damn, do I know."

* * *

Paige and Grace were going to be fine. Paige had a bruise across her chest and shoulders from the seat belt and both girls had sustained a few minor scrapes and bruises. Grace's arm was in a sling and it was going to take a couple of months for it to be completely healed. An OB/GYN came to do an ultrasound and make sure that the baby was okay. It was too soon to hear the heartbeat, but the doctor pointed to a tiny flutter on the screen and said, "This is your baby."

"He's so small," Brendan said, staring at the screen.

"He?" Paige asked.

"Or she," he said and smiled at her. He'd been holding one of her hands in both of his and he brought it to his mouth, kissing her knuckles. "We're going to have a baby," he said, looking back at the monitor, amazed.

They went home and Brendan had an overwhelming sense of relief at finally being back there with Paige. The second the door was closed he scooped her up in his arms and carried her into the bathroom. They undressed and got in the shower, washing off all of the river water and mud. They held each other as the hot water rained around them. Brendan's mouth was on hers, his hands all over her body, reassuring himself that she was there, that she was back in his arms and safe.

It wasn't until the water started to turn cold that they got out. Brendan wrapped Paige in a robe before he carried her into the bedroom. He put her down on her feet and sat on the edge of the bed. He pulled her between his thighs and opened the robe, gently running his hands over her still flat stomach.

"Brendan?" she whispered, putting her hands on his head.

He looked up at her, tears streaming down his face. "I almost lost you," he said, his voice cracking. "I almost lost everything." He shook his head.

He brought his mouth down to her stomach, placing soft kisses around her belly button. He straightened and pushed the robe off her shoulders before he pulled her back onto the bed. He settled her on top of him and looked up at her.

"I couldn't do it without you, you know," he said, brushing her hair back. "If I'd lost you, I would've never made it through." He rolled her beneath him, and she moved her legs so he could settle between her thighs. "I wouldn't have been able to survive without these arms of yours," he said, running his hands down her shoulders and all the way to her fingers. "Without these eyes," he said, looking at her. "Without these lips." He pressed his mouth to hers. "Without you," he said before he kissed every inch of her, loving her body with his mouth. He lingered at her stomach again, kissing her abdomen before he worked his way back up to her mouth. He kissed her as he slid inside of her and made love to her slowly, knowing just how lucky he was.

Epilogue

The End and the Beginning

They slowly started to adjust to life without Trevor. Denise had started coming to the Thursday-afternoon gossip fests at Café Lula. She also started working part time at the Atticus County Health Clinic. Brendan and Paige went to her house multiple times a week to have dinner. She was doing better, but it was still hard. It would always be hard without Trevor.

Paige and Brendan were having a little boy. Trevor Oliver King was due the end of May. When they found out the gender, Brendan painted the nursery a light blue so that Paige could paint a mural on the walls. She was painting sea turtles swimming through the ocean with a brilliant sunset over the water.

Brendan found a box of children's books that Claire had read to him and Grace. Paige and Brendan started a new routine every night. Paige would settle in with her back against the headboard, and Brendan would lie down by her stomach and read the baby a story.

One night, Brendan crawled in next to her without a book.

"No story tonight?" she asked, more than a little disappointed.

"No, there will be." He smiled, propping his head up on his arm. "This one just isn't in a book," he said as he slid his hand underneath Paige's T-shirt and rested it on top of her stomach. She loved the way he touched her belly. Loved the way his callused fingers would slowly move across her skin.

"Once upon a time, there lived a beautiful fair maiden," he said, looking up at her with twinkling eyes. "She'd been sent to this faraway land that she'd never been to before. She didn't like it very much either. It was filled with ogres and dragons, and while the ogres and dragons weren't necessarily dangerous, they were mean, especially to the fair maiden.

"Now, one day, as the fair maiden went on a journey, her carriage broke down on the side of the road. She was already having a bad day, as she'd dealt with the biggest and meanest dragon of the land."

"Hmm, this story is getting good," Paige said, reaching up and running her fingers through his hair. "This is where the white knight comes to her rescue."

"Shhh," Brendan said, trying to frown at her. He failed. "This is my story."

"Okay, I'll be quiet."

"So, as I was saying, her carriage broke down on the side of the road. And who should come along but her white knight on his faithful steed."

"You forgot to say how handsome the knight was, or that he had an incredible smile."

"Are you telling this story or am I?"

"You are," she said and grinned. "But it's vital to the story. You can't leave out his smile."

"And why is that?" he asked her, raising an eyebrow.

"Because that's when I started to fall for you," she answered simply.

Shannon Richard's sexy small-town
series continues!

Jax has been protecting his best
friend's kid sister, Grace, since they
were young. Now that they're all
grown up, they insist there's nothing
between them—until one night
changes everything...

See the next page for a preview of

Undeniable.

Prologue

The Princess

At six years old there were certain things Grace King didn't understand. She didn't understand where babies came from, how birds flew way up high in the sky, or where her father was. Grace had never met her dad, she'd never seen him, she didn't even know his name, and for some reason this fact fascinated many people in Mirabelle.

"What's a girl bastard?"

Grace looked up from the picture she was coloring to see Hoyt Reynolds and Judson Coker looming over the other side of the picnic table she was sitting at.

Every day after the bell rang, Grace would wait outside on the playground for her brother, Brendan, to come and get her and they'd walk home together. Today, Brendan was running a little late.

"I don't know," Judson said and smirked. "I think bastard works for boys and girls."

"Yeah," Hoyt said and shrugged. "Trash is trash."

Brendan was always telling Grace to ignore bullies, advice he had a problem following himself. Half the time she didn't even know what they were saying. Today was no different. She had no idea what a bastard was but she was pretty sure it wasn't anything nice.

Grace looked back down to her picture and started coloring the crown of the princess. She grabbed her pink crayon from the pile she'd dumped out on the table and just before she started coloring the dress, the picture disappeared out from under her hands.

"Hey," she protested, looking back up at the boys. "Give that back."

"No, I don't think I will," Judson said before he slowly started to rip the picture.

"Stop it," Grace said, swinging her legs over the bench and getting quickly to her feet. She ran to the other side of the table and stood in front of Judson. "Give it back to me."

"Make me," he said, holding the picture up high over her head as he ripped it cleanly in half.

Grace took a step forward and instead of jumping up and down like he wanted her to, she stomped down hard on his foot.

"You little bitch!" Judson screamed, hopping up and down on his foot.

Grace had one second of satisfaction before she found herself sprawled out on her back, the wind knocked out of her.

"Don't ever touch her again!"

Grace looked up just in time to see a tall, freckled, red-haired boy punch Hoyt in the face. It was Jax, one of Brendan's best friends, who had come to her rescue. And boy did Jax know what he was doing, because Hoyt fell back onto his butt hard.

"And if you ever call her that word again, you'll get a lot more than a punch in the face, you stupid little scumbag," Jax said as he put himself in between Grace and Judson. "Now get out of here."

"I'm going to tell my father about this," Hoyt said. This was a legitimate threat, as Hoyt's father was the principal.

"You do that," Jax said and shrugged.

Apparently the two eight-year-olds didn't have anything else to say and they didn't want to take their chances against a big, bad eleven-year-old because they scrambled away and ran around the side of the building and out of sight.

"You okay?" Jax asked, turning around to Grace.

It was then that Grace realized the back of her dress was covered in mud and that her palms were scraped and bleeding.

"No," she said and sniffed before she started to bawl.

"Oh, Grace," Jax said, grabbing her under her arms and pulling her to her feet. "Come here." He pulled her into his chest and rubbed her back. "It's okay, Gracie."

She looked up at him and bit her trembling lip. "They called me names," she said and hiccupped.

"They weren't true," he said, looking down at her.

"What's a bastard, Jax?"

Jax's hand stilled and his nose flared. "Nothing that you need to worry about," he said. "Grace, sometimes dads aren't all they're cracked up to be."

She nodded once before she buried her head back in his chest. By the time she'd cried herself out, Jax's shirt was covered in her tears. She took a step back from him and wiped her fingers underneath her eyes. Jax reached down and grabbed the two halves of her picture from the ground.

"We can tape this back together," he said, looking down at the paper. He studied it for a second before he looked back to her. "This is what you are, Grace. A princess. Don't let anyone tell you different. You understand?" he asked, lightly tugging on her blonde ponytail.

"Yes," she said and nodded.

"All right," he said, handing the papers back to her. "Get your stuff together and we'll go wait for Brendan."

"Where is he?" Grace asked as she gathered her crayons and put them back into the box.

"He got into trouble with Principal Reynolds again."

Grace looked up at Jax and frowned. She really didn't like the Reynolds family. Principal Reynolds wasn't any better than his son.

"No frowning, princess. Let's go," Jax said, holding out his hand for her.

Grace shoved her crayons and drawing into her bag. She grabbed Jax's outstretched hand and let him lead her away.

Chapter One

The Protector

The nightmares always felt so real. They started off the exact same way as the accident had. And then they morphed into something so much worse, something that haunted Jax even when he was awake.

As a deputy sheriff for the county, Jaxson Anderson was no stranger to being the first person to arrive at the scene of an accident. What he wasn't used to was being the first to an accident that involved two people he cared about. That day, it had been Grace and Paige King. Grace was the little sister of Brendan King, one of Jax's best friends. Paige was Brendan's wife.

It had happened six months ago. Violent storms had raged across Mirabelle for days, and the rains had flooded the river that ran through the town, making the current swift and deadly. By some miracle Jax had been driving right behind Paige and Grace. Jax and his friend Bennett Hart had watched as the SUV the girls were in swerved off the road, crashed through a barrier, and disappeared down to Whiskey River. The only thing that had stopped the car from being swept under the water was a tree that had been growing out of the bank. The tree was barely strong enough to hold the car back.

That day Jax had experienced a panic like no other. He'd gone into the river desperate to pull them out. And that was when the second miracle of the day had happened. Brendan, along with Nathanial Shepherd and Baxter McCoy, had shown up. It took the efforts of all five men to pull the girls out of the car before it was swept under the water. It had been just a matter of seconds of getting them out before the tree gave way.

Jax went over those moments, over and over and over again, replaying everything from what he'd said to what he'd done. The one thing he was absolutely sure about was that getting those girls out of that river alive was miracle number three.

But Jax's nightmares didn't play out like the miracle. No, in his nightmares he watched as Grace died.

When the accident had happened, they'd had to pull Grace out from the car before Paige. In the nightmare, it was Grace who was pulled out second. Paige was safe in Brendan's arms, and Jax would go to get Grace, but the tree would snap right before his hands touched hers. Jax would scream her name as the river dragged her away and she disappeared under the surface of the water.

Jax woke up, Grace's name still on his lips. He was breathing hard and drenched in sweat, the sheets sticking to his skin. He blinked in the dim light that was pushing its way through the window as he slowly began to realize that what he'd seen wasn't real. That it was just another nightmare. That Grace wasn't lost. She'd walked away from the accident with a dislocated shoulder and minor scrapes and bruises.

Jax lay there and when he got his breathing under control and his heart stopped pounding out of his chest, he turned to look at the alarm clock. It was ten after five in the morning. He didn't need to be up for another hour, but it was pointless for him to even attempt to go back to sleep. Whenever he had a nightmare about Grace, he was on edge until he saw her and knew that she was okay.

So instead, Jax threw back the sheets that were tangled around his legs and sat on the edge of the bed. He rubbed his face with his hands before he got up and padded into the bathroom. He brushed his teeth and then splashed his face with cold water. He looked up into the mirror as water dripped off the end of his long, freckled nose. The hollows under his eyes were tinged a light purple.

It was only Wednesday and it had already been a long week. Mirabelle had a whopping five thousand people in its six hundred square miles. The little beach town made up just over half of Atticus County's population, and boy did those five thousand sure know how to keep the sheriff's department busy.

Jax had to deal with a kid who'd stolen his mom's car to go joyriding with his girlfriend, two drunken high school bonfires, and four house calls for domestic disturbances, three of which had ended in arrests. He was also working on a string of robberies that had been going on in Mirabelle. There'd been five alone in the last three months, and they all looked to be connected. He was exhausted. For normal people that would mean sleep would come easier, but that wasn't the case for Jax. For Jax, deep sleep brought on his nightmares.

Jax had been having nightmares for as far back as he could remember, and at twenty-nine years old, that was a long time. It was hard not to have nightmares when you grew up in an environment that was less than friendly.

Haldon Anderson was one mean son of a bitch, and he took great pleasure in making his son feel like shit as often as possible. When Haldon wasn't in jail, he was out on a fishing boat making money to drown himself in a bottle of liquor and whatever pills he could get his hands on. And when Haldon got on one of his benders, there was absolutely nothing that was going to stop him. Whether Haldon used his fists or his words, he knew how to make a person bleed.

Haldon had laughed when Jax had joined the sheriff's department seven years ago. He'd thought it was one of the greatest jokes of his life.

"This is perfect," he'd said, wiping his fingers underneath his eyes. "My worthless son doing a thankless job. Working for justice, my ass. You're not going to do anything to make this world a better place. The only thing you could've possibly done to achieve that was to have never been born."

Yup, Haldon Anderson, father of the *fucking* year.

As a child, Jax couldn't understand why his mother let his father get away with all of the abuse. But Patricia Anderson wasn't a strong woman and her greatest weakness was Haldon. She hadn't protected her child like a mother should. Actually, she hadn't done anything that a mother should do.

Jax shook his head and pulled himself out of the past. That was the last thing he wanted to think about.

He pulled on a sweatshirt, a pair of gym shorts, and his

sneakers before he headed out into the chilly April morning. He stretched for a minute before he hit the pavement and attempted to run from his demons.

* * *

Grace King inhaled deeply as she pulled out a fresh batch of bananas Foster muffins. The rich smell filled her nose before it expanded her lungs. She smiled as she set them on the counter to cool. These muffins were going to sell out with the morning breakfast rush.

Grace didn't care if she was making cookies, pies, or cupcakes; she never got tired of it. One of her first memories was sitting in the kitchen at her grandparents' house while she watched her mother stir chocolate cake batter. Most of Grace's fondest memories of her mother were of the two of them baking together. Claire King had lost her battle to breast cancer almost fourteen years ago. But before she'd died, she'd passed on her love for baking to her daughter.

Grace had been working in her grandmother's café since she was eight years old. Now, at twenty-four, she helped her grandmother run Café Lula. The café was a small, brightly painted cottage out on Mirabelle Beach. The promise of freshly baked food kept customers from all over the town and county pouring in no matter the time of day or the season.

The day promised to be a busy one, as Grace had to fill up the dessert case with fresh goodies. She'd been experimenting with cupcake recipes the past couple of weeks. She'd wanted to make something amazing for her sister-in-law's baby shower. Grace had eaten dinner at Brendan and Paige's the night before, and she'd been the one in charge of dessert. For fear of disappointing a sassy pregnant woman, she'd brought her A-game and made two different types of cupcakes.

"I think my favorite is the blueberry lemonade," Paige had said as she'd rubbed her ever-growing belly. "But Trevor seems to like this red velvet cheesecake one. I think he's dancing in there."

Trevor Oliver King was supposed to be gracing the world with his presence around the middle of May. Grace couldn't wait to meet her nephew. Paige was just past her seventh month of pregnancy. She was one of those women who still looked beautiful even though she was growing another human being inside of her. If Grace didn't love her sister-in-law dearly, she would've been fifty shades of jealous. As it was, she was only about twenty shades.

But really, Grace couldn't be happier for her brother and her sister-in-law. Brendan was going to be an amazing father. Much better than his or Grace's had been.

Neither Brendan nor Grace had ever had their fathers in their lives. Brendan's dad had gotten their mother pregnant when she was seventeen. When he'd found out, he'd promptly split town and never looked back. But while Brendan at least knew who his father was, Grace had no idea who hers was. It was one of the great mysteries, and a constant source of gossip in Mirabelle.

There were many things in life that Grace was grateful for, her brother and Paige topping the list. They were a team and they worked together. They loved each other deeply. And Grace envied that stupid, dopey look they always got on their faces. She wanted that. And she knew exactly who she wanted it with. It just sucked for her that the man in question was stubborn and refused to see her as anything besides his best friend's little sister.

Grace took a deep breath and shook her head, bringing herself back to the muffins that she had to get out into the front of the café. There was no need to concern herself with frustrating men at the moment. So she loaded up a tray with an already cooled batch of muffins and went to load the display case before the eight o'clock rush of customers filled the café. But when she pushed her way through the door she found the frustrating man in question on the other side staring at her with her favorite pair of deep green eyes.

* * *

Jax's whole body relaxed when he saw Grace push through the door from the kitchen. The moment she saw him her blue eyes lit up and her cupid's-bow mouth split into a giant grin. She'd always looked at him that way. Like he was her favorite person in the whole world. God knew she was his.

"Hey ya, Deputy. Let me guess," she said as she put the tray down on the counter, "you came here for coffee?"

No. He'd come here to see her. He always came here to see her. But coffee was a legitimate enough excuse, especially since he had to pull a twelve-hour shift that day.

"Please," he said, drumming his long, freckled fingers on the counter.

"Did you eat breakfast?" she asked as she pulled a to-go cup off of the stack and started pumping coffee into it.

"I'm not hungry."

"Hmm." She looked over her shoulder at him and pursed her lips. "You know that isn't going to fly for a second. I got just the thing to go with this." She put the steaming cup and a lid down on the counter. "Go fix your coffee while I bag up your breakfast."

Grace turned around and pushed through the door to the kitchen as Jax grabbed his cup and went over to the end of the counter where the sugar and milk were.

Since Jax was four years old, the King women had been feeding him. Between them and Shep's mom, those were the only home-cooked meals he'd gotten after his grandmother had died. If it hadn't been for them, he would've gone to bed with an empty stomach more nights than most. Patricia Anderson wasn't much of a Susie Homemaker. Between her long hours working at the Piggly Wiggly and drinking herself into a stupor and getting high when Haldon was on parole, she sometimes forgot to stock the freezer with corndogs and mini pizzas for her son.

"Here you go."

Jax turned to find Grace by his side. She hadn't gotten the height gene like Brendan had. She was about five foot four and came in just under Jax's chin. Her petite stature and soft heart-shaped face inspired an overwhelming urge in him to protect her. She'd always inspired that feeling in him, ever since her mother had brought her home from the hospital all those years ago.

"They're bananas Foster muffins and they're fresh out of the oven," she said, holding out a bag.

"Thanks, Princess," he said, grabbing the bag and letting his fingers brush the back of her hand.

God, he loved the way her skin felt against his.

"Anytime, Jax," she said and smiled widely at him. A

second later she stepped into him and grabbed his fore-arms for balance as she stretched up on her toes and kissed his jaw.

It was something that Grace had done a thousand and one times before. She had no concept of personal bound-aries with him, and she was wide open with her affection. And just like always, when her lips brushed his skin he had the overwhelming desire to turn into her. To feel her lips against his. To grab her and hold her against himself while he explored her mouth with his.

But instead of following that impulse, he let her pull back from him.

"Eat those while they're hot," she said, pointing to the bag.

"I will," he promised.

"Do you need something for lunch? I can get you a sandwich."

"I'm good," he said, shaking his head.

"How late are you working tonight?" she asked, putting her hands on her hips and narrowing her eyes at him.

He couldn't help but grin at her attempt to intimidate him.

There was no doubt about the fact that Grace King was tough. She'd had to grow a thick skin over the years. Even though Jax, along with Brendan and Shep, had done ev-erything in his power to try and protect her, he couldn't be there to shield her from everything. So Grace had done everything to even up the score with whoever tried to put her down. She wasn't a shy little thing by any means, and she'd tell anybody what was up without a moment of hesitation.

"Until eight," he said.

"Twelve hours?" she asked, exasperated. "I'm getting you a sandwich," she said, turning on her heal and heading behind the counter.

"Grace, you don't have to do this."

"I know," she said, looking over her shoulder as she opened the display case. "But I'm going to anyways."

Jax watched as Grace filled a bag with two sandwiches, a bag of chips, a cup of fruit salad, and his favorite, a butterscotch cookie.

"This should last you till dinner."

Jax just shook his head at her as he pulled his wallet out to pay for everything.

"Oh, I don't think so," Grace said, shaking her head. "You are *not* paying."

Before Jax could respond, the bell above the door rang, signaling that someone else was in the café. He turned to see Lula Mae walk in the front door.

To the casual observer, Grace and Brendan's grandmother wouldn't strike a person as someone to be feared. She had a kind face and bright blue eyes that when paired with her ample stature and friendly disposition inspired a feeling of warmth and openness. But Lula Mae was fiercely loyal, and those blue eyes could go as cold as ice when someone hurt anyone who she loved. Lula Mae had declared Jax as one of hers over twenty-five years ago, and she'd marched down to his parents' house more than once to give them a piece of her mind.

Jax had spent more nights sleeping at the Kings' house than he could count. It was one of the few places he'd actually felt safe growing up. And even now, whenever he saw her or her husband, Oliver, he had that overwhelming feeling of being protected.

"Jaxson Lance Anderson," Lula Mae said, walking up to him, "what in the world is your wallet doing out? Your money is no good here."

"That's what I just told him."

Jax turned back to Grace, who was wearing a self-satisfied smile.

"Your granddaughter just gave me over thirty dollars' worth of food," he said, indicating the stuffed bag on the counter before he turned back to Lula Mae.

"I don't care," she said, shaking her head. "Now give me some sugar before you go and keep the people of Mirabelle safe."

"Yes, ma'am," Jax said, leaning down and giving Lula Mae a peck on the check.

"And the next time I see that wallet of yours make an appearance in this establishment, you are going to get a smack upside that head of yours. You understand me?"

"Yes, ma'am," Jax repeated.

"Good boy," she said and nodded, patting his cheek.

"Thanks again," he said, reaching for the bag of food and his coffee. "I'll see you two later."

"Bye, sugar," Lula Mae said as she rounded the counter and headed for the kitchen.

"See you later," Grace said, giving him another of her face-splitting grins.

Jax headed for the door, unable to stop his own smile from spreading across his face.

Grace stared at Jax's retreating form as he walked out of the café, and she appreciated every inch of it. He had a lean muscular body. His shoulders filled out the top of his forest-green deputy's shirt and his strong back tapered down to his waist. His shirt was tucked into the green pants that hung low from his narrow hips and covered his long, toned legs.

And oh dear God, did Jaxson Anderson have a nice ass.

Though her appreciation of said ass had only been going on for about ten years, the appreciation of Jaxson Anderson had been discovered a long time ago. He was the boy who saved her from bullies on the playground. The boy who gave her his ice cream cone when hers fell in the dirt. The boy who picked her up off of the ground when she skated into a tree. The boy who let her cry on his shoulder after her mom had died.

Yes, Brendan and Shep had done all of those things as well, but Jax was different. Jax was hers. She'd decided that eighteen years ago. She'd just been waiting for him to figure it out.

But the man was ridiculously slow on the uptake.

Grace had been in love with him since she was six years old. She loved his freckles and his reddish-brown hair. His hair was always long enough to where someone could run their fingers through it and rumple it just a little. Not that she'd ever rumpled Jax's hair, but a girl always had her fantasies, and getting Jax all tousled was most definitely one of Grace's.

Jax was always so in control and self-contained, and so damn serious. More often than not, that boy had a frown on his face, which was probably why every time Grace saw his dimpled smile it made her go all warm and giddy.

God, she loved his smile. She just wanted to kiss it, run

her lips down from his mouth, and trace his smooth, triangular jaw with her tongue.

Grace sighed wistfully as the door shut behind him and she turned to join her grandmother in the kitchen.

"You get your young man all fed and caffeinated?" Lula Mae asked as she pulled containers out of the refrigerator.

"I don't know about 'my young man' but I did get Jax something to soak up that coffee he came in for."

"Oh, sweetie," Lula Mae said, looking over her shoulder and shaking her head pityingly. "That boy did not come in here for coffee."

"Hmmm, well, he sure didn't ask for anything else," Grace said as she walked over to the stove and started plating the rest of her muffins.

"Just give it time."

"Time?" Grace spun around to look at her grandmother. "How much *time* does the man need? He's had years."

"Yes, well, he'll figure things out. Sooner than later, I think."

"I don't think so. To him, I'm just Brendan's little sister."

"There's no *just* about it," Lula Mae said, grabbing one last container before she closed the fridge and walked back to the counter where she'd piled everything else. "He doesn't have brotherly feelings for you, Gracie. I've never seen anyone fluster that boy the way you do."

"Oh, come on, Jaxson Anderson doesn't get flustered," Grace said, shaking her head.

"If you think that, then he isn't the only one who's blind."

"What's that supposed to mean?"

"You see, Gracie, you've never had the chance to observe him when you aren't around."

"And?" she prompted, gesturing with her hand for her grandmother to carry on.

"He changes when you're around. Smiles more."

"Really? 'Cause he still frowns a whole lot around me."

"Well, that's usually when some other boy is trying to get your attention and he's jealous."

"Jealous," Grace scoffed. "He doesn't get jealous."

"Oh, yes he does. Grace, you need to open your eyes. That boy has been fighting his feelings for you for years."

And with that, Lula Mae went about fixing her menu for the day, leaving Grace even more frustrated than she had been the minute before.

THE DISH

Where Authors Give You the Inside Scoop

From the desk of Marilyn Pappano

Dear Reader,

One of the pluses of writing the Tallgrass series was one I didn't anticipate until I was neck-deep in the process, but it's been a great one: unearthing old memories. Our Navy career was filled with laugh-out-loud moments, but there were also plenty of the laugh-or-you'll-cry moments, too. We did a lot of laughing. Most of our tears were reserved for later.

Like our very first move to South Carolina, when the movers lost our furniture for weeks, and the day after it was finally delivered, my husband got orders to Alabama. On our second move, the delivery guys perfected their truck-unloading routine: three boxes into the apartment, one box into the front of their truck. (Fortunately, Bob had perfected his watch-the-unloaders routine and recovered it all.)

For our first apartment move-out inspection, we had scrubbed ourselves to nubbins all through the night. The manager did the walk-through, commented on how impeccably clean everything was, and offered me the paperwork to sign. I signed it, turned around to hand it to her, and walked into the low-hanging chandelier where the dining table used to sit, breaking a bulb with my head. Silently she took back the papers, thumbed through to the deduction sheet, and charged us sixty cents for a new bulb.

There's something about being told my Oklahoma accent is funny by multi-generation Americans with accents so heavy that I just guessed at the context of our conversations. Or hearing our two-year-old Oklahoma-born son, home for Christmas, proudly singing, "Jaaan-gle baaaa-ulllz! Jaaan-gle baaaa-ulllz! Jaaan-gle *alllll* the waaay-uh!"

Bob and I still trade stories. *Remember when we did that self-move to San Diego and the brakes went out on the rental truck in 5:00 traffic in Memphis at the start of a holiday weekend? Remember that pumpkin pie on the first Thanksgiving we couldn't go home—the one I forgot to put the spices in? Remember dropping the kiddo off at the base day care while we got groceries and having to pay the grand sum of fifty cents two hours later? How about when you had to report to the commanding general for joint-service duty at Fort Gordon and we couldn't find your Dixie cup anywhere in the truck crammed with boxes—and at an Army post, no less, that didn't stock Navy uniforms?*

Sea life was great. We watched ships leaving and, months later, come home again. On one homecoming, the kiddo and I watched Daddy's ship run aground. We learned that all sailors look alike when they're dressed in the same uniform and seen from a distance. We spied submarines stealthing out of their bases and toured warships—American, British, French, Canadian—and even got to board one of our own nuclear subs for a private look around.

The Navy gave us a lot to remember and a lot to learn. (Example: all those birthdays and anniversaries

Bob missed didn't mean a thing. It was the fact that he came home that mattered.) I still have a few dried petals from the flowers given to me by the command each time Bob reenlisted, as well the ones I got when he retired. We have a flag, like the one each of the widows in Tallgrass received, and a display box of medals and ribbons, but filled with much happier memories.

I can't wait to see which old *remember when* the next book in this series brings us! I hope you love reading A MAN TO ON HOLD TO as much as I loved writing it.

Sincerely,

Marilyn Pappano

MarilynPappano.com
Twitter @MarilynPappano
Facebook.com/MarilynPappanoFanPage

♥ ♥ ♥ ♥ ♥ ♥ ♥ ♥ ♥ ♥ ♥ ♥ ♥ ♥ ♥

From the desk of Jaime Rush

Dear Reader,

Much has been written about angels. When I realized that angels would be part of my mythology and hidden world, I knew I needed to make mine different. I didn't want to use the religious mythos or pair them with demons. Many authors have done a fantastic job of this already.

In fact, I felt this way about my world in general. I started with the concept that a confluence of nature and the energy in the Bermuda Triangle had allowed gods and angels to take human form. They procreated with the humans living on the island and were eventually sent back to their plane of existence. But I didn't want to draw on Greek, Roman, or Atlantean mythology, so I made up my own pantheon of gods. I narrowed them down to three different types: Dragons, sorcerers, and angels. Their progeny continue to live in the area of the Triangle, tethered there by their need to be near their energy source.

My angels come from this pantheon, without the constraints of traditional religious roles. They were sent down to the island to police the wayward gods, but succumbed to human temptation. And their progeny pay the price. I'm afraid my angels' descendents, called Caidos, suffer terribly for their fathers' sins. This was not something I contrived; these concepts often just come to me as the truths of my stories.

Caidos are preternaturally beautiful, drawing the desire of those who see them. But desire, their own and others', causes them physical pain. As do the emotions of all but their own kind. They guard their secret, for their lives depend on it. To keep pain at bay, they isolate themselves from the world and shut down their sexuality. Which, of course, makes it all the more fun when they are thrown together with women they find attractive. Pleasure and pain is a fine line, and Kasabian treads it in a different way than other Caidos. Then again, he is different, harboring a dark secret that compounds his sense of isolation.

Perhaps it was slightly sadistic to pair him with a woman who holds the essence of the goddess of sensuality.

Kye is his greatest temptation, but she may also be his salvation. He needs to form a bond with the woman who can release his dark shadow. I don't make it easy on Kye, either. She must lose everything to find her soul. I love to dig deep into my characters' psyches and mine their darkest shadows. Only then can they come into the light.

And isn't that something we all can learn? To face our shadows so that we can walk in the light? That's what I love most about writing: that readers, too, can take the journey of self discovery, self love, right along with my characters. They face their demons and come out on the other end having survived.

We all have magic in our imaginations. Mine has always contained murder, mayhem, and romance. Feel free to wander through the madness of my mind any time. A good place to start is my website, www.jaimerush .com, or that of my romantic suspense alter ego, www .tinawainscott.com.

Jaime Rush

♥ ♥ ♥ ♥ ♥ ♥ ♥ ♥ ♥ ♥ ♥ ♥ ♥ ♥

From the desk of Kate Brady

Dear Reader,

People ask me all the time, "What do you like about writing romantic suspense?" It's a great question, and it always seems like sort of a copout to say, "Everything!" But it's true. Writing novels is the greatest job in the world. And romantic suspense, in particular, allows my favorite elements to exist in a single story: adventure, danger, thrills, chills, romance, and the gratifying knowledge that good will triumph over evil and love will win the day.

Weaving all those elements together is, for me, a labor of love. I love being able to work with something straight from my own mind, without having to footnote and document sources all the time. (In my other career—academia—they frown upon letting the voices in my head do the writing!) I love the flexibility of where and when I can indulge myself in a story—the deck, the kitchen island, the car, the beach, and any number of recliners are my favorite "offices." I love seeing the stories unfold, being surprised by the twists and turns they take, and ultimately coming across them in their finished forms on the bookstore shelves. I love hearing from readers and being privy to their take on the story line or a character. I love meeting other writers and hobnobbing with the huge network of readers and writers out there who still love romantic suspense.

And I *love* getting to know new characters. I don't create these people; they already exist when a story begins and it becomes my job to reveal them. I just go along for the ride as they play out their roles, and I'm repeatedly surprised and delighted by what they prove to be. And it never fails: I always fall in love.

Luke Mann, the hero in WHERE EVIL WAITS, was one of the most intriguing characters I have met and he turned out to be one of my all-time favorites. He first appeared in his brother's book, *Where Angels Rest*, so I knew his hometown, his upbringing, his parents, and his siblings. But Luke himself came to me shrouded in shadows. I couldn't wait to write his story; he was dark and fascinating and intense (not to mention gorgeous) and I knew from the start that his adventure would be a whirlwind ride. When I put him in an alley with his soon-to-be heroine, Kara Chandler—who shocked both Luke and me with a boldness I hadn't expected—I fell in love with both of them. From that point on, WHERE EVIL WAITS was off and running, as Luke and Kara tried to elude and capture a killer as twisted and dangerous as the barbed wire that was his trademark.

The time Luke and Kara spend together is brief, but jam-packed with action, heat, and, ultimately, affection. I hope you enjoy reading their story as much as I enjoyed writing it!

Happy Reading!

Kate Brady

♥ ♥ ♥ ♥ ♥ ♥ ♥ ♥ ♥ ♥ ♥ ♥ ♥ ♥

From the desk of Amanda Scott

Dear Reader,

The plot of THE WARRIOR'S BRIDE, set in the fourteenth-century Scottish Highlands near Loch Lomond, grew from a law pertaining to abduction that must have seemed logical to its ancient Celtic lawmakers.

I have little doubt that they intended that law to protect women.

However, I grew up in a family descended from a long line of lawyers, including my father, my grandfather, and two of the latter's great-grandfathers, one of whom was the first Supreme Court justice for the state of Arkansas (an arrangement made by his brother, the first senator from Missouri, who also named Arkansas—so just a little nepotism there). My brother is a judge. His son and one of our cousins are defense attorneys. So, as you might imagine, laws and the history of law have stirred many a dinner-table conversation throughout my life.

When I was young, I spent countless summer hours traveling with my paternal grandmother and grandfather in their car, listening to him tell stories as he drove. Once, when I pointed out brown cows on a hillside, he said, "Well, they're brown on this side, anyhow."

That was my first lesson in looking at both sides of any argument, and it has served me well in my profession. This is by no means the first time I've met a law that sowed the seeds for an entire book.

Women, as we all know, are unpredictable creatures who have often taken matters into their own hands in ways of which men—especially in olden times—have disapproved. Thanks to our unpredictability, many laws that men have made to "protect" us have had the opposite effect.

The heroine of THE WARRIOR'S BRIDE is the lady Muriella MacFarlan, whose father, Andrew, is the rightful chief of Clan Farlan. A traitorous cousin has usurped Andrew's chiefdom and murdered his sons, so Andrew means to win his chiefdom back by marrying his daughters to warriors from powerful clans, who will help him.

Muriella, however, intends *never* to marry. I based her character on Clotho, youngest of the three Fates and the one who is responsible for spinning the thread of life. So Murie is a spinner of threads, yarns...and stories.

Blessed with a flawless memory, Muriella aspires to be a *seanachie*, responsible for passing the tales of Highland folklore and history on to future generations. She has already developed a reputation for her storytelling and takes that responsibility seriously.

She seeks truth in her tales of historical events. However, in her personal life, Murie enjoys a more flexible notion of truth. She doesn't lie, exactly. She spins.

Enter blunt-spoken warrior Robert MacAulay, a man of honor with a clear sense of honor, duty, and truth. Rob also has a vision that, at least for the near future, does not include marriage. Nor does he approve of truth-spinning.

Consequently, sparks fly between the two of them even *before* Murie runs afoul of the crazy law. I think you will enjoy THE WARRIOR'S BRIDE.

Meantime, *Suas Alba!*

Sincerely,

Amanda Scott

www.amandascottauthor.com

♥ ♥ ♥ ♥ ♥ ♥ ♥ ♥ ♥ ♥ ♥ ♥ ♥ ♥ ♥ ♥

From the desk of Mimi Jean Pamfiloff

Dear People Pets—Oops, sorry—I meant, Dear Readers,

Ever wonder what's like to be God of the Sun, Ruler of the House of Gods, and the only deity against procreation with humans (an act against nature)?

Nah. Me neither. I want to know what it's like to be his girlfriend. After all, how many guys house the power of the sun inside their seven-foot frames? And that hair. Long thick ribbons of sun-streaked caramel. And those muscles. Not an ounce of fat to be found on that insanely ripped body. As for the…eh-hem, the *performance* part, well, I'd like to know all about that, too.

Actually, so would Penelope. Especially after spending the evening with him, sipping champagne in his hotel room, and then waking up buck naked. Yes. In his bed. And yes, he's naked, too. Yeah, she'd love to remember what happened. He wouldn't mind, either.

But it seems that the only one who might know anything is Cimil, Goddess of the Underworld, instigator of all things naughty, and she's nowhere to be found. I guess Kinich and Penelope will have to figure this out for themselves. So what will be the consequence of breaking these "rules" of nature Kinich fears so much? Perhaps the price will be Penelope's life. But perhaps, just maybe, the price will be his…

Happy Reading!

♥ ♥ ♥   ♥   ♥   ♥   ♥   ♥

From the desk of Shannon Richard

Dear Reader,

I knew how Brendan and Paige were going to meet from the very start. It was the first scene that played out in my mind. Paige was going to be having a very bad day on top of a very bad couple of months. Her Jeep breaks down in the middle of nowhere Florida, during a sweltering day, and she was to call someone for help. It's when she's at her lowest that she meets the love of her life; she just doesn't know it at the time. As for Brendan, he isn't expecting anyone like Paige to come along. Not now, not ever. But he knows pretty quickly that he has feelings for her, and that they're serious feelings.

Paige can be a little sassy, and Brendan can be a little cocky, so during their first encounter sparks are flying all over the place. Things start to get hot quickly, and it has very little to do with summer in the South (which is hot and miserable, I can tell you from over twenty years of experience). But at the end of the day, and no matter the confrontation, Brendan is Paige's white knight. He comes to her rescue in more ways than one.

The inspiration behind Brendan is a very laid-back Southern guy. He's easygoing (for the most part) and charming. He hasn't been one for long-term serious relationships, but when it comes to Paige he jumps right on in. There's just something about a guy who knows exactly what he wants, who meets the girl and doesn't hesitate. Yeah, it makes me swoon more than just a little. I hoped that readers would appreciate that aspect of him. The diving in headfirst and not looking back, and Brendan doesn't look back.

As for Paige, she's dealing with a lot and is more than a little scared about getting involved with another guy. Her wounds are too fresh and deep from her recent heartbreak. Brendan knows all about pain and suffering. Instead of turning his back on her, he steps up to the plate. He helps Paige heal, helps her get a job and friends, helps her find a place in the little town of Mirabelle. It just so happens that her place is right next to his.

So yes, Brendan is this big, tough, alpha man who comes to the rescue of the damsel in distress. But Paige isn't exactly a weak little thing. No, she's pretty strong herself. It's part of that strength that Brendan is so drawn to. He loves her passion and how fierce she is. But really, he just loves her.

I'm a fan of the happily ever after. Always have been, always will be. I love my characters; they're part of me. They might exist in black and white on the page, but to me they're real. At the end of the day, I just want them to be happy.

Cheers,

ShannonRichard.net
Twitter @Shan_Richard
Facebook.com/ShannonNRichard